LET A
SLEEPING
WITCH LIE

Let a Sleeping Witch Lie

Elizabeth Walter

Edited by Nick Freeman

SEREN

Seren is the book imprint of
Poetry Wales Press Ltd
Suite 6, 4 Derwen Road, Bridgend,
Wales, CF31 1LH

www.serenbooks.com
Follow us on social media @SerenBooks

© Elizabeth Walter 2024.
Introduction © Nick Freeman 2024.

The right of Elizabeth Walter to be identified as
the author of this work has been asserted in accordance
with the Copyright, Designs and Patents Act, 1988.

ISBN: 978-1-78172-779-9

A CIP record for this title is available from the British Library.

All rights reserved. No part of this publication may be reproduced,
stored in a retrieval system, or transmitted at any time or by any means,
electronic, mechanical, photocopying, recording or otherwise without
the prior permission of the copyright holder.

The publisher acknowledges the financial assistance of the
Books Council of Wales.

Printed by CMP UK Ltd.

This is a work of fiction. All of the characters, organisations,
and events portrayed in this novel are either products of the
author's imagination or are used fictitiously.

Contents

Introduction	9
THE SIN-EATER	19
TELLING THE BEES	47
DAVY JONES'S TALE	65
SNOWFALL	91
COME AND GET ME	127
THE DRUM	151
HUSHABYE, BABY	187
DEAD WOMAN	213
CHRISTMAS NIGHT	233
Glossary and Notes	251
Bibliography and Further Reading	254
The Author	255

Elizabeth Walter's stories date from the 1960s and 1970s. As such, they use language and demonstrate values, attitudes and social prejudices which were prevalent at the time but which some readers may find offensive. For authenticity's sake, the original text has been preserved in this collection.

INTRODUCTION

I

In the early 1960s, Elizabeth Walter was a young London-based novelist attempting to establish herself as a writer of literary fiction. Her first book, *The More Deceived*, had appeared in June 1960 to respectable reviews, with the *Sunday Times'* Storm Jameson admiring her 'skill and delicacy' in refusing to 'make a sentimental hash of a story about broken marriage.' Encouraged, she offered another astutely observed portrait of matrimony and its discontents, *The Nearest and Dearest*, in January 1963. At this point, Walter was treading a similar path to other women writers who were beginning to chronicle the moods and manners of the new decade, authors such as Margaret Drabble (whose first novel, *A Summer Bird-Cage* had appeared on New Year's Day 1963), but she was about to make a radical change of direction.

On 25 January 1963, the *Times Literary Supplement* reviewed *The Nearest and Dearest*, praising its astute observation and insightful psychological portraiture, and enjoying its occasionally acidic observations. The reviewer pronounced it, 'nicely made' and 'tremendously readable', but was more impressed by the ambition and originality of the book reviewed alongside it, Victoria Lucas's *The Bell Jar*. At this point, few were aware that Lucas was the pseudonym of the young American poet, Sylvia Plath, but Plath's suicide a fortnight later imbued *The Bell Jar* with a morbid glamour which has surrounded it ever since. Walter's novel, accomplished though it was, suddenly seemed a polite entertainment beside the horrors of Esther Greenwood's mental agony, a point underlined by the *Observer* two days later. 'Within its somewhat genteel limits,' said the reviewer, it is 'an honest and accurate book.' The faint praise continued:

> There is sharp observation, even an occasional offering of wan wit, but one can't help remarking a rather-too-well-bred, a

positively ladylike reluctance to turn the stone and have a really good look at the creepy-crawlies. The restraint is very English, the voice that of a good hostess. The floors are wholesome with the smell of antiseptic polish. One longs to tear up one of the boards.

The writer of these words was Anthony Burgess. The author of the recently published *A Clockwork Orange* was hardly the ideal reader of novels like *The Nearest and Dearest* but his patronising dismissal of the book now seems a watershed moment in Walter's literary career. She had already seen her new novel, in its admittedly dull grey and blue dust-jacket, eclipsed by a terrifying depiction of psychological torment, one clearly informed by traumatic personal experience. Now Burgess was sneering at her for the very things a more temperamentally attuned reviewer may have admired. Whether his review prompted her to grit her teeth and growl, 'I'll show him', her writing would take a very different course over the next decade. From the freezing winter of 1962-63, the coldest in London for over two hundred years, Walter would emerge with chilling stories which were distinct from anything she had published before, no longer 'very English,' and quite willing to turn stones, look at the creepy-crawlies, and, in that echo of Edgar Allan Poe's gothic masterpiece, 'The Tell-Tale Heart', to tear up the boards.

II

Elizabeth Margaret Walter was born in London in 1927, She grew up in Hereford, the ancient cathedral city which she would rename 'Carringford' in many of her stories. As a child she was a precocious reader but left-handed, something which the educational orthodoxies of the day did their best to 'correct'. One authority, J.W. Conway's *The Prevention and Correction of Left-Handedness in Children* (1935) even saw the 'sinistral condition' as a 'curse' which needed to be 'stamped out'! A common tactic was to tie the left hand behind the child's back and force her to use her right, but Walter was undaunted by such petty tyrannies and emerged from the ordeal as ambidextrous. As she was now able to write with both hands (a trick that became something of a party piece in later life), it is tempting to see the coercion to use her right hand as a metaphor for the fiction she would create in adulthood. In it, the 'normal' world, pragmatic, rational, and complacently materialistic, 'English' perhaps, is often undermined by 'Welsh' 'scientific impossibilities' and 'uncanny invitations.' If her first two novels depicted that approved English environment, the 'sinistral' would become her dominant mode in the years that followed. In her stories, everyday life is never quite as it seems: fairies live in suburban houses, gardeners talk to bees, retired civil servants seem to acquire magical powers, lifeboats are called out to rescue phantom ships. Rooting the supernatural in wholly believable settings and situations allowed Walter to emphasise the strangeness of its manifestations as ordinary people are drawn slowly into darkness and terror.

Walter had written short stories from childhood, graduating to supernatural fiction in her early teens. As a would-be author, it was unsurprising that she chose to study English language and literature, winning scholarships to London University's Bedford College. Based in Regent's Park, Bedford was a women-only establishment with formidable academic standards; Walter's contemporaries included the novelist, Jane Gardam, and the folklorist, Jacqueline Simpson. During her time there, she studied the Anglo-Scottish border ballads of the Middle Ages, and it was probably here that she encountered the story of Tam Lin which she reworked in 'Hushabye, Baby' (1971). Determined to remain in the literary world after graduation, she became a technical journalist, then worked for a firm of fine art booksellers where she honed her foreign language skills. Following this, she secured a position at Jonathan Cape, who published *The More Deceived*, and then, in 1961, moved to William Collins. Initially, she worked for George Hardinge, the editor whose obsession with whodunnits had propelled the Collins Crime Club, but when he moved to Macmillan in 1963, the Club became her fiefdom. She would remain its editor for thirty years until retiring in 1993, during which time she showed a keen eye for emerging talent, publishing the likes of Reginald Hill (of Dalziel and Pascoe fame) and Jonathan Gash (creator of Lovejoy). The Crime Writers' Association presented her with its prestigious Red Herring Award for services to the genre.

Editing crime fiction had a significant influence on Walter's writing. She began to combine the marital dissection and detailed character studies of her early novels with the taut plotting she encouraged from her Collins contributors and saw regularly in the work of the publisher's star author, the 'Queen of Crime' herself, Agatha Christie. 'I am a tiger where careless plotting is concerned!' she told readers of *Murder Ink*, a companion to mystery fiction, in 1977. Crime stories frequently depict unexpected disturbances of the social fabric, and several of Walter's early pieces share this trait—the missing person and murder investigation of 'Snowfall' (1965), the jealous husband hiring a private detective in 'The Drum' (1965)—but she added to it a distinctively macabre sensibility of her own and the mordant wit that had given piquancy to her novels. Her first collection, the punning *Snowfall and Other Chilling Events*, appeared in 1965, to be followed by *The Sin-Eater and Other Scientific Impossibilities* (1967), *Davy Jones's Tale and Other Supernatural Stories* (1971), *Come and Get Me and Other Uncanny Invitations* (1973) and finally, *Dead Woman and Other Haunting Experiences* (1975). All were published by Harvill, which signalled at once the distance between Walter's often quite lengthy tales and more throwaway genre fare. Unlike many of her peers, she did not write for the magazine market, preferring to craft her stories by her own rules rather than be subject to periodicals' constrictive word limits.

Collins Crime Club saw Walter editing an average of three books per month and managing a growing roster of writers. Her position was a demanding one and having breathing space away from the hectic London publishing world was vital. She had continued to visit her parents back in Hereford and now began to make the journey more frequently. 'For most of her life Mairi had travelled between South Wales and London,' she writes in 'Christmas Night' (1975). 'She knew the route backwards.' The appeal of the border country lay in part in its rural remoteness, its freedom from what the young fisherman calls in 'Davy Jones's Tale' (1971), 'the hemmed-in noisiness of city streets [...] the stench of humanity and exhaust gases'. She especially liked the Wye Valley, Elan Valley, the Pembrokeshire coast, and the villages around Hereford. 'Carringford is a county town not a hundred and fifty miles from London, but for all that, decidedly off the map,' says the narrator of 'The Sin-Eater' (1967), and this sense of being in unchartered territory runs through most of the stories in this collection. Walter found South Wales and the border country rich sources of inspiration, with nine of her thirty-one supernatural tales being set there. It was a place, she writes, in 'Dead Woman' (1975), where 'old ways die hard,' whether in a refusal to use the terminology of decimal coinage or in a lingering belief in the power of witchcraft and the evil eye.

In her article for *Murder Ink*, Walter confessed that 'I cannot write a crime novel. I tried once and gave up.' It was supernatural fiction where her true interests lay. 'The supernatural appeals to me,' she said, it is 'probably my Welsh heritage.' This belief shaped what might be termed 'Walter Country' which has Hereford at its centre, extending north to Shrewsbury and west into Pembrokeshire, but ignoring the larger Welsh towns and the industrial south—Davy Jones recoils from the prospect of leaving the coast for life in Swansea or Cardiff. When Walter was writing during the 1960s and 1970s, the first Severn Bridge had just opened (1966) and the M4 motorway had yet to advance west of Swindon, meaning that her drive from London was more time-consuming than it would be today. Wales was less easily accessible from south-east England, not yet heavily colonised by tourists and second-home owners.

III

Walter seems to have regarded rural Wales as a place where the supernatural was far more perceptible than in the big cities of Britain and the continent. She had little interest in an industrialised, modern Wales, but this was not because she wanted to portray the country as primitive, 'backward', or somehow 'unspoiled.' It was more that she recognised the imaginative possibilities encouraged by the contrast between rural South Wales and overcrowded, dirty London. Like Arthur Machen, another Welsh author educated in Hereford, she sensed the border country was a place where the veil between worlds was thinner, more permeable. This is very clear in her final story, 'Christmas Night,' when the policeman tells the narrator how he has heard the wild hunt riding through the night sky. 'Don't tell me you didn't hear,' he says, but the narrator can think only of 'the wind with its lupine howling, and the torn clouds racing like wolves across the moon.' 'We'll be glad to be getting back to London,' he says. 'Soon.'

But if Walter saw the border country as a darkly enchanted realm, she was unsentimental and often bleak about what was happening to Wales during the 1960s and 1970s. She was not an overtly political writer and did not speculate about successive governments' failure to invest in or defend Wales, but she repeatedly notes the country's remoteness, insularity, and its suffering gradual but nonetheless traumatic decline. The decaying farmhouse of the 'The Sin-Eater', the self-contained rural communities of 'Dead Woman' and 'Snowfall', the abandoned house and the lands drowned beneath the reservoirs in 'Come and Get Me' (1973) are all places being left behind by modernity and suspicious of the incomers associated with it, particularly the English. When Davy, the young fisherman, is told that the days of the small boats are numbered, he retorts, 'We may have unemployment in Milford Haven, but we still manage to get the catch away.' Such defiance cannot disguise the fact that 'The railways are threatening closure' and 'economic conditions are against you.' A few pages later, Davy mourns the loss of traditional crafts which have 'long languished' as the country gives itself over to the imperatives of tourism—the story comes from the same year as Shirley Toulson's coruscating satire, 'Playground of England'. The decline is longstanding. In 'Christmas Night,' the rerouting of traffic from a slate quarry ruins a Victorian publican's business. 'Come and Get Me' is set in deepest Powys, largely around an abandoned nineteenth-century house which is nine miles from Rhayader and overlooks the Elan Valley reservoirs, perhaps being inspired by a fusion of Cwm Elan House and Nantgwyllt House, which were submerged when the reservoirs were created in the early twentieth century. Those reservoirs were built to supply water to Birmingham and the industrial Midlands rather than to Wales and once again, there is a sense of the country's having been exploited and betrayed, one all the more powerful for its understatement. The wider context of the story subtly mirrors the domestic betrayals at its heart.

Walter knew the Elan Valley well. 'Settings to me are vitally important,' she wrote in her preface to *In the Mist* (1979). 'They give solidity, reality.' Her Welsh stories are filled with well-observed detail as they move between tradition and folklore ('Hushabye, Baby', 'Telling the Bees'), superstition and legend ('The Sin-Eater,' 'The Drum'), history ('Dead Woman,' 'Christmas Night', 'Davy Jones's Tale') and what was, for her original readers, the comparatively recent events of the Second World War ('Come and Get Me'). She was ambitious in mixing horror with more complex dramas of family and community, as can be seen in 'Davy Jones's Tale', which she said was 'one of the few stories I have written which I can still reread with pleasure,' and in 'Hushabye, Baby,' where Sarah Braithwaite's growing awareness that her child and husband are in danger becomes more convincing even as the police and social services question her sanity. Here, the brutally insensitive medical discourse of the time collides with older, folkloric beliefs and cannot conceive that the distressed mother may be right about fairies and changelings. Walter's talent for plot and characterisation is evident throughout, notably in 'Telling the Bees' (1975), a deft mixture of mysterious rural customs and the marital jealousy that had underpinned *The Nearest and Dearest*, twelve years earlier. The catty exchanges between Diana Lockett and her disapproving mother give the story an extra edge—here, as elsewhere in her work, there are some tart asides. 'Snowfall' combines the ghost story with a memorable portrait of village life in the remote Brecon Beacons. Like 'Christmas Night,' it pitches rural policemen against malign supernatural forces, again showcasing Walter's innovative fusion of criminal and familiar gothic motifs such as the stranded traveller. Modern readers however may be discomfited by its representation of the Caribbean and its people, its backstory of 'voodoo' and stolen relics, for though Walter handled her imperial theft plotline more subtly than some other contemporaneous works—the film, *Dr Terror's House of Horrors* (1965) springs to mind—her characters' choice of words only serves to underline the profound social changes which have taken place since the story's publication.

Reviews of Walter's novels had highlighted her literary flair and her skill in revivifying familiar situations. Storm Jameson had judged *The More Deceived* 'intelligent and perceptive work' and the *TLS* admired its 'intelligence and subtlety' along with its ability to 'cleverly blend' past and present. David Holloway of the *Daily Telegraph* judged *The Nearest and Dearest*, 'Very well written and quite superbly constructed,' a comment Collins used when advertising the book, though he had also pronounced it 'A woman's novel in the best sense of the word.' Such views signposted a road Walter chose not to take. She wrote no further novels until *A Season of Goodwill* (1986), a historical work set in 1907 which recalls the fiction of Isabel Colegate. Had she been able to assemble a crime novel, she might have used her psychological acuity to write the sort of mysteries associated with Ruth Rendell (who also wrote the occasional ghost story) or her dark alter ego, Barbara Vine, but she moved instead into translating French fiction and the compilation of books of seasonal and ritual customs, an interesting parallel to the events depicted in her stories. Figuratively speaking, Walter's right hand made possible a successful career as an editor and translator. It was her left which produced her brilliant supernatural tales.

IV

The reason why Walter abandoned novels for twenty years is unclear, but it may be that she realised her keen eye for marital discord (she herself never married though she did edit a book on wedding customs), her saturation in crime fiction, and what she saw as her Welsh fondness for the supernatural coalesced and became a natural development of her earlier work. 'I was born interested in the supernatural,' she wrote in the preface to *In the Mist*. 'It is the only explanation I can offer of why I have been convinced for as long as I can remember that there is a world beyond the usual limits of our consciousness—the world next door.' If she decided to pursue that interest because of the reception of *The Nearest and Dearest*, her change of direction was soon vindicated. Her first two collections sold reasonably well, and several stories were adapted for television and included in anthologies such as the *Pan Horror Stories* series and Herbert van Thal's *Ten Nights Awake* (1967). By the time *Davy Jones's Tale* appeared in November 1971—all Walter's books came out in November to catch the seasonal market for ghost stories—she was receiving respectful notices in the broadsheets. 'Miss Walter does not resort to horror for its own sake,' said Leonard Barras in the *Sunday Times*, praising an artistic restraint far removed from the 'good hostess' conjured by Burgess. 'Even without the uncanny element, these would be engaging stories.' His colleague, Oscar Turnill, called 'Hushabye, Baby' 'splendid' and compared it to T.F. Powys. The novelist, Robert Nye, was a particular admirer of Walter's work, hailing the title story of *Dead Woman* as, 'a real piece of buttonholing menace.' Barras went yet further, telling readers of the *Sunday Times* that 'there is no better writer in the field' because her stories 'grip quite independently of their supernatural element, delicious though that is.'

Dead Woman was certainly impressive, but it was to be Walter's last volume of original material. In 1977, Mike Ashley's *Who's Who in Horror and Fantasy Fiction* compared her to Roald Dahl and L.P. Hartley and claimed she was planning a sixth book, but her last word on the supernatural was to be *In the Mist and Other Uncanny Encounters*, a personal selection of her stories for the American market, published by genre specialists Arkham House in 1979. It included 'The Sin-Eater', 'Davy Jones's Tale' and 'Come and Get Me'. A brief authorial preface served only to tantalise readers who hoped for more strange tales. They were to be disappointed.

Walter's five collections appeared at a time when horror was becoming increasingly violent and sexually explicit both in print and on film. *Snowfall* was published in the same year as Roman Polanski's *Repulsion*. *Davy Jones's Tale* appeared in the same year as William Peter Blatty's international bestseller, *The Exorcist*, the film version of which overshadowed *Come and Get Me* two years later. 1974 saw the debuts of Stephen King in the United States and James Herbert in Britain, as well as the release of Tobe Hooper's *The Texas Chainsaw Massacre*. Walter had been praised by Dennis Wheatley for her skills in 'character-building and atmosphere' but Herbert was a very different kind of writer. His first bestseller, *The Rats*, was unflinchingly shocking, and for readers brought up on Wheatley's Satanic romps, viscerally disgusting. Its follow-up, *The Fog* (1975) went further still in its depiction of an English citizenry crazed by a chemical weapons leak. 'I won't publish anything that is explicitly sadistic,' Walter said of her editorial policy at Collins, but elsewhere, a wave of paperback imitators followed Herbert's lead, producing books that were a world away from the Crime Club, the Harvill Press, and the review pages of the *Sunday Times*. These authors were almost all male and, with the exception of King, usually had little desire to go beyond the horror genre. Walter however belonged to a generation of women writers who combined elegantly fashioned frissons with an underlying concern for female experience. From Marghanita Laski's *The Victorian Chaise Longue* (1953) and Elizabeth Jane Howard's contributions to *We are for the Dark* (1954), to the ghost stories of Elizabeth Taylor, Joan Aiken's idiosyncratic mixture of horror, fantasy, and fairy tale, and the weird imaginings of Daphne Du Maurier, notably *Not After Midnight* (1971), the collection containing 'Don't Look Now', distinctive styles of female-authored gothic fiction achieved critical and commercial success in Britain for twenty years. In the final quarter of the twentieth century though, these were often overshadowed first by the horror thrillers associated with Herbert and then by the horror-crime crossovers which emerged in the wake of Thomas Harris's *The Silence of the Lambs* (1988). Thankfully however, tastes and fashions change, and since Walter's death in 2006, there has been a renewed public appetite for the kind of skilfully constructed subtle stories she was writing sixty years ago. 'I hope to give my readers some chilling surprises,' she said. It is to be hoped that further recognition of her distinctive talent and her unique voice is not far away.

THE SIN-EATER

ALTHOUGH THE REFORMATION destroyed most of the roodlofts that formerly dignified English parish churches, one or two have survived in out-of-the-way places sufficiently inaccessible to discourage even Puritan zeal: remote Devon fastnesses, or villages and the remains of villages along the Welsh Border, before the real mountains start. One of the best preserved is at Penrhayader, well worth a visit for those who do not mind narrow roads, sharp bends, steep gradients, a trek through the mud of a farmyard, and an abrupt climb to the church. Clive Tomlinson was one who counted these deterrents an attraction. On an October day he arrived at the churchyard gate.

It is not necessary to observe that Clive was interested in old churches. No one came to Penrhayader who was not. It had been a village and was now something less than a hamlet, and what was left of it was half a mile away. In the fourteenth century it had no doubt clustered round the church mound; by the twentieth it had receded—perhaps symbolically. Only the farm, whose stonework looked as old as the church's, remained out of apathy.

Clive, surveying the scene from the churchyard, was not particularly concerned with the how or why. It was typical of his unquestioning, uncomplicated nature, as well-meaning as the printed verse in a Christmas card. Like the card, too, he was a symbol of goodwill towards all men. His life was one perpetual effort to be liked. This had naturally resulted in considerable unpopularity. His late-autumn holiday was being spent alone.

He had hired a small car and set out with no clear idea of where he was going, except that he was heading west. The roads were uncrowded in October; it seemed he could go where he would. Hotels had plenty of accommodation; the whole trip was so easy it was dull. Or perhaps he was bored by shortage of society. In this mood Clive came to Carringford.

Carringford is a county town not a hundred and fifty miles from London, but for all that, decidedly off the map. To the discerning this is its charm, and Clive was intermittently discerning. He surveyed it and decided to stop. The Red Lion was comfortable and quiet, its only other guest as solitary as himself and not disposed to hold long conversations, for he was an archivist at work in the Cathedral Muniment Room.

It was the archivist, Henry Robinson, who alerted Clive to the existence of Penrhayader church, for, finding that the young man was an architectural draughtsman, he mentioned the well-preserved rood-loft. No more was needed to send Clive off on a visit. He excelled at pencil sketches of architectural detail. Someday he intended to compile a book on *English Church Interiors in the Middle Ages*. Meanwhile he sketched diligently the unusual and the quaint.

Although it was October, the day was as warm as summer. Late bees were buzzing in the hedges, where blackberries glistened and sloes waited to sweeten in the frost. Clive had passed through cider orchards, skirted magnificent tree-clad hills, noted barns piled with hay for the winter and clamps of turnips, mangolds, and swedes. But as he approached the Welsh Border and its bleak hill-slopes terraced with sheep-runs, the farmer's lot by comparison was poor. When he had picked his way through the farm below the church at Penrhayader, no one had even come curiously to the door. No dog had barked, no cattle had lowed, all was silent; it seemed a house of the dead, especially since the windows were shut tight and curtained, as though the inhabitants were still in bed.

Yet though neglected, the farm was by no means abandoned. A few fowls scratched in the dirt; a pig could be smelt if not inspected; a cat squinted from the window-sill. Only the human inhabitants were missing, and they, perhaps, had merely withdrawn. As he passed, Clive could have sworn he saw a curtain twitch at a window, as though someone upstairs peered out.

Reflecting that country people were often shy of strangers, Clive strode energetically on his way. He was unimaginative and not inclined to introspection. What might have struck another as strange or sinister was to him without significance.

It was after two when he descended from the church mound. The rood-loft was the finest he had seen. A series of sketches reposed in his portfolio. He looked forward to showing them to Mr Robinson when he got in.

It was as he was picking his way through the farmyard, where the mud and filth and ooze were ankle-deep, that a voice behind him, waking and sepulchral, enunciated the word 'Afternoon.'

Clive turned. The door of the farmhouse had opened and an old wan stood blinking in the light, like some diurnally awakened creature of darkness, unable to understand why it is not night.

'Good afternoon,' Clive responded. His greeting lacked its usual warmth. He had taken quick stock of the farmer, and was not attracted by what he saw.

The old man seemed unaware of it. Clive reflected that country people could be very obtuse. Surely the old man did not suppose he wished to linger in conversation in this unsavoury spot?

The old man, however, appeared to have just that notion. 'Fine day,' he observed, not looking at the sky.

'Wonderful for October,' Clive returned. His voice was breathless as his foot slipped and he skidded in the mud.

The old man stood back and held the door open. 'Will you come in a bit?' he enquired.

'It's very good of you, but—no, thank you.' Clive felt increasingly the urge to get away.

''Twouldn't be for long,' the old man hastened to assure him. 'Just long enough to see my son.'

Clive had no desire to extend acquaintance to the next generation. 'I'm sorry,' he called. 'I can't wait.'

He made his way across the rest of the farmyard and began fumbling at the gate. It was a heavy five-barred one, fastened by the usual peg and chain. He had opened it easily enough, but now, encumbered by his portfolio and its contents, which he was afraid of dropping in the mud, he found the peg apparently jammed in its chain-link.

The old man watched him from the doorway, but made no move to help. He was short and stocky, with a paunch and a face at once sly and open—shrewd eyes and a toothless idiot mouth. He was dressed in a pair of stained and faded corduroy trousers maintained in place by a belt and a piece of string, and a shirt of indeterminate colour which revealed at the neck an edge of greyish vest. His coat was frayed at the cuffs, its buttons off or hanging, and like his cheeks, his jowls, and his paunch, its pockets sagged.

Clive struggled again with the gate-pin but could not shift it, although nothing held it that he could see. There was no help for it: he would have to climb over, for the old man obviously was not coming to his aid.

He placed one foot on the bottom bar, tucked his portfolio under his arm more securely, and prepared to swing astride, when the mud on his shoes made his foot slip, the portfolio jerked, and two of his best sketches fluttered down. With an exclamation of annoyance Clive turned to retrieve them, but the old man had got there first. He had seized the larger and nearer drawing, and was making off with it towards the house.

'Hi!' Clive called, 'where are you going?'

'"Twill dry off better in the house. And you can't put it away all muddy. You'd best come in, I reckon, and dry yourself.'

There was some sense in the suggestion. Clive reluctantly followed the old man. His shoes and trouser-bottoms were stiff with mud. Besides he wanted his drawing. If only the place were clean! He had already noted with horror the single tap in the farmyard, the absence of telephone wires, the suspect shack within easy reach of the back door, the cobwebs round the window-frames. The farmhouse, built of stone with a low-pitched slate roof, was unbelievably primitive. Its four small windows barely broke the wall's solid surface; they were not far removed from arrow-slits. Clive could imagine someone holding out in it as in a beleaguered fortress, and the picture did not comfort him. The combination of isolation, neglect, primitive conditions, and his own instinctive repugnance to entering the house or having anything to do with its inhabitants added up to something overwhelmingly grim.

He was unprepared for the heat of the living-room as they entered. Despite the warmth of the day, a fire glowed red in the grate. On top of it a black kettle sputtered. A gridiron leaned against the hearth. All cooking, Clive realised, was done on this fire or in the oven built into the wall beside it. There was no sink, though an enamel bowl stood on the table. Slops and scraps were presumably emptied outside. The ceiling was low and blackened by the smoke from the fire, from candles and a paraffin lamp. The floor was stone, uneven but not unswept, Clive noted. One wall showed patches of damp. In the corner a staircase rose steeply; from the room above came the sound of a shuffling tread. The old man went straight to the foot of the stairs and called softly, 'Mother!'

'What is it?' came a voice overhead.

'I've brought a young man to see Eddie.'

The voice came to the head of the stairs. 'Didn't I tell you someone would be coming? Have faith, Evan Preece, have faith.'

'Ay, you were right. You're always right, Becky. Tell me now, are you ready yet?'

'Not far off. Ask the gentleman to sit down a minute. He'll be glad to dry by the fire if his feet are wet.'

The old man turned to Clive apologetically, 'She'll not be long, but 'tis a woman's business, see. Sit you down until it's time to go up to Eddie.'

'I'm afraid,' Clive began, 'I can't stay.'

'You can stay long enough to see my son,' the old man insisted. ''Tis the only visitor he'll have. You were sent so that Eddie should lie easy and us have an answer to our prayers.'

In spite of himself, Clive found this solicitude for a sick son touching. Within their limits, they obviously gave him every care. And if one were bedridden in this outpost one might go from one year's end to the other without setting eyes on a fresh face. No wonder they were anxious for Eddie to have a visitor; it was an event they would talk about for weeks. It would be churlish to refuse this small act of kindness. Was not one enjoined to visit the sick?

He rescued his drawings from the old man, put them back in his portfolio, and was tying the tapes when a creaking from the corner made him look round; the old woman was coming down the stairs.

She was smaller, frailer, greyer than her husband, her back bowed in what was almost a hump. She wore a crossover print overall on top of her garments, black stockings and bedroom slippers on her feet. She had brown bluish-filmed eyes, moist with rheum or with crying, and she greeted Clive deferentially.

'Would you like to come up, sir?' she invited. 'It's all ready for you up there now.'

In the background the old man was hurrhing and hawking and trying to catch her eye.

'Did you put the wine out, Becky?' he asked at last in desperation.

The old woman nodded. 'With the plate on top of it like you said.'

The old man seemed satisfied. 'We'd best go up. Lead the way, Becky.' He closed in, bringing up the rear. Clive had no option but to pick his way up the steep, narrow staircase which opened directly into the upper room.

The curtains drawn across the small window shrouded everything in a curious daylight gloom, making the low room seem larger and mysterious, although it was ordinary enough. The floor sloped sharply that a chest of drawers near the window appeared to be tilted on edge, but except for a high-backed upright chair in the corner, most of the space was occupied by an old-fashioned brass-knobbed bed. On the bed a man of indeterminate age was lying, grey-haired but by no means old. His face was sunken, and the deep grooves from nose to chin had not yet smoothed out. His hands were folded and his eyes were closed.

It was so unexpected that Clive, who had never been in the presence of the dead until now, was tempted to turn and run, but the old people were standing as if on guard at the head of the steep stairs. There was nothing for it but to go on as he had begun. Besides, his instinct had been ridiculous. There was nothing to fear from the dead. The still figure—how wasted it was!—could not hurt him. He took a cautious step nearer the bed.

All the time one level of his mind was working frantically in search of something suitable to say. He was not even sure why he had been invited into the death-chamber, nor what response was expected or desired.

'I'm awfully sorry,' he said tritely. 'It must be very hard to lose a son.'

'Ay.' The old man nodded in agreement.

The old woman dabbed at her eyes. 'Cruel it is, and him not forty.' She added inconsequentially, 'He was our only one.'

The revelation of the dead man's age shook Clive considerably. He had taken him for fifty at least.

'Had he been ill long?' he asked, although he guessed the answer.

'About two year. Ever since they let him come home.'

Clive wondered if this meant that the dead man had been of unsound mind as well as consumptive. The parents struck him as being decidedly odd. They seemed to hover, waiting for something. He had obviously failed to find the right remark. Did the old woman expect compliments on her handiwork; 'How beautifully you have him laid out'; or the old man seek to have their family resemblance noted, for it was evident that they had been much alike?

His glance strayed towards the aperture in the wall near the bed-head where, quite obviously, there had once been a door. The old man followed his gaze and hastened to offer explanation.

'Couldn't bear to sleep in the back after what had happened, Eddie couldn't. Said he'd rather sleep in the mud of the yard outside.' His voice faltered; then he went on more strongly: 'So Mother and I had to let him have our room. ''Twas a bit awkward-like, but we'd have done more than that for Eddie. I took the door off its hinges because it squeaked. It opened inwards, you see; it were heavy for Mother to pull it; and we were afraid of waking Eddie with the noise.'

'He slept so lightly,' the old woman said in amplification. She turned away to wipe the tears from her eyes.

' "One shall be taken," ' Clive observed sententiously in what he hoped was an appropriate tone of voice.

To his consternation, this remark which he had thought quite suitable, appeared to upset the old woman very much. Her eyes filled with tears and her mouth trembled. It seemed that her whole body shook. Her husband laid a broken-nailed hand on her shoulder—a gesture of warning as much as of sympathy—but she shook it off and turned to face Clive in defiance, as though he had insulted her personally.

'Yes, one shall be taken,' she cried, 'and that the wrong 'un. My son didn't deserve to suffer as he did. I told 'em that, for the wench was nowt but a wanton and there's others to blame as well as him.'

'Becky, Becky—' the old man began in protest, but she turned on him. 'Hold your tongue, Evan Preece! Why should your own son suffer when there's another more guilty? You know right enough who I mean.'

'Ay, I know.' The old man sighed heavily. 'But 'tis the way of things, Becky, see. That other was—well, who he was,' he concluded.

'He's a—'

He raised his hand threateningly. 'Shut your mouth!' There was no mistaking his menace. He was suddenly the stronger of the two. The old woman cowered and mumbled, but was careful to keep her words indistinct.

'Now, sir—' the old man turned to Clive as if nothing had happened—'you must take a glass of wine with my son.'

For a moment Clive thought he had misheard him, but the old man was already moving to the foot of the bed, where, Clive now noticed, a small table covered with a clean white cloth was standing, and on it a jug and a plate. The plate, posed upon the jug, contained a small round drop-scone, something like a currantless Welsh cake, and no doubt cooked on the gridiron Clive had noticed in the living-room. The jug contained a blackish wine.

As Clive watched, the old man filled a wine-glass. There was only one glass and one plate. Refreshment was to be offered solely to the stranger. It was hardly a sociable meal. And partaken of in the presence of a corpse, too! Clive backed away and violently shook his head. 'No, really! Excuse me, but I couldn't. Not—not with your son lying there upon the bed.'

'But you *must* drink,' the old man exclaimed, 'else he'll never lie easy. You must eat and drink to save him from his sins.'

''Tis the last of my blackberry wine,' the old woman quaveringly insisted. 'I've been saving it for such a day as this.'

'Won't you—won't you join me, then?' Clive suggested.

As one, the old people shook their heads.

'Drink and eat,' the old man commanded, holding glass and plate outstretched across the corpse. 'And may all thy sins be forgiven thee,' he added.

The old woman's assent sounded like amen.

Clive sipped the wine and took a mouthful of the round cake. The wine was syrupy and very strong. The cake crumbled to a paste which he forced himself to swallow. It felt as though it were sticking to his tongue. His companions—two living and one dead—were still and silent. Only the old man's breathing sounded loud, and—to Clive—the movement of his own jaws and the constrictions of his throat as he swallowed, watched all the time by the old woman at the head of the stairs.

Clive had read about wakes and thought they sounded jolly in a macabre way, but this was like no wake he had ever known. It was more like some communion rite. Some mystic rapport between himself and the dead man. His sense of uneasiness increased. He could see no reason to refuse the refreshment offered; besides, he did not wish to offend, but he wished profoundly that he had not been prevailed on to accept it. As he gulped down the last of the wine and the round cake, his gorge rose until he feared he would vomit on the spot. It was as though his stomach itself was rejecting what it had been offered.

He turned to the old woman. 'I must go.'

Silently she stood aside to allow him passage; silently she followed him down the stairs; silently she watched as he gathered his portfolio together and turned towards the outer door. Then, suddenly, she was on her knees before him, catching at his hand, kissing it with her withered lips. 'Thank you for what you've done! A blessing on you for what you've lifted from the soul of my poor boy!'

'Becky!' Her husband's voice sounded angrily as he reached the foot of the stairs behind her. 'Let the gentleman alone and none of your carryings-on. 'Tis a miracle that he came, right enough, but we must let him go now—far away from us and our innocent son.'

'Yes, innocent!' The old woman's voice rose sharply in a strange, triumphant cry. Her husband opened the outer door and Clive passed through it.

Not one of them attempted a good-bye.

***

Unfortunately Mr Robinson was not in to dinner that evening, and Clive, his portfolio beside him, had to nurse his disappointment through three courses and prepare himself for an evening's solitude. He was therefore quite ready to be sociable when Barnabas Elms joined him in the lounge.

Barnabas Elms was well known in Carringford, though it could not be said he was well liked. He was a bachelor, a bore, and a busybody. Graver charges were hinted at, also beginning with a 'b'. He was present at many civic occasions in his capacity as a councillor, but was seldom welcome at any of these, partly because he had appointed himself a standing one-man watch committee to ensure that what he called 'decent people's feelings' were not outraged. It was Barnabas who rooted out 'dirty' books from the Public Library, returning them with the words objected to underlined. It was Barnabas who insisted that shop-window dummies should be discreetly veiled in dust-sheets in the intervals while their clothes were being changed. It was Barnabas who had objected to a nude by a well-known sculptor being erected in the Town Hall Square. Barnabas, in short, who upheld Carringford's reputation for being in the rear of progress and counted this a source of pride.

Having no friends, Barnabas was forced to fall back on the company of his relations, and he had rather few of those. But the wife of the proprietor of the Red Lion was his cousin, and he was in the habit of dropping in. If, as often happened, there were visitors, he would eagerly introduce himself. Since he was a member of the licensing committee, his visitations had to be endured.

Tonight it was Clive's misfortune to endure him. Even Clive found Barnabas difficult to like. He was about to give up trying and withdraw bedwards, when Mr Robinson arrived. Mr Robinson had had an excellent dinner with one of the canons in the Close. He had also deciphered a particularly illegible fourteenth-century document and his mood was such that he was prepared to be tolerant of anyone, even of Barnabas, whom he had already met and disliked. Not for a long time had Barnabas been welcomed with so much cordiality. He concluded that here at last was a sympathetic ear, and immediately launched into a denunciation of Carringford's latest offence against decency: the toleration of a coloured family on a council housing estate. Unfortunately—from Barnabas's point of view there had been no trouble.

'It's scandalous,' he complained, despairing of the folly of his fellow citizens. 'People will accept anything today. In ten years' time we shan't be able to recognise this city.'

'I wonder. Its citizens have some pretty permanent characteristics,' Mr Robinson observed. 'In the fourteenth century—or so I have been reading—they confiscated the property of those who traded or visited with the Jews.'

'Who's talking about the Jews?' Barnabas demanded.

Mr Robinson gave a long, exaggerated sigh.

Clive interposed, anxious to smooth things over: 'I went to Penrhayader today.'

Mr Robinson immediately looked interested.

'You pick the rummest places,' Barnabas objected. 'What's at Penrhayader, I'd like to know?'

'A rood-loft in the church.' Clive produced his sketches.

'What's a rood-loft?' Barnabas asked.

Clive did his best to explain, while Mr Robinson examined the drawings, and made gratifyingly appreciative noises, looking up at last to ask, 'What's the place like?'

Clive described it as best he could.

'I ask only because I've come across the name in old documents. In the seventeenth century the Puritans classified it as a hotbed of Popery.'

'I'm not surprised. It is a very remote village. Old customs have undoubtedly lingered on. I experienced an instance of that while I was there this morning.'

'I don't know about old customs,' Barnabas interrupted, 'but there've been some shocking goings-on there in recent times.'

Clive was determined not to be denied his story. 'As I was passing the farm by the church—it's very isolated,' he continued, 'an old man came out and insisted I go in to see his son.'

'What did his son want with you?' Barnabas demanded.

'Nothing. When I went in I found that he was dead.'

'Perhaps they mistook you for the doctor?' Mr Robinson suggested.

'No—' Clive shook his head—'they simply wanted me to go in and drink their son's health.'

'Drink his health!'

'That's what it seemed like. They insisted I must drink a glass of wine and eat a little cake, with this man laid out on the bed before me. It was all I could do to get it down.'

'You mean you had to eat and drink in the presence of the corpse?' Mr Robinson asked, his eyes staring.

'Yes, and very unnerving it was.'

'Could you describe what you ate? Did they say anything to you?'

'I had a glass of blackberry wine and a sort of small, flat, currantless Welsh cake.'

Mr Robinson exhaled very softly. 'The genuine articles, no less. And the people—what were they like? Did they give any explanation?'

'Not that I remember,' Clive said. 'They were very old, very frail, I should think illiterate—'

Mr Robinson nodded.

'They didn't eat or drink themselves,' Clive remembered, 'but they seemed terribly grateful that I did. The old man said something about making his son lie easy. I had to eat and drink to save him from his sins.'

Mr Robinson folded his hands in a reverent gesture. 'To think the practice still continues!' he exclaimed.

'What practice?' Clive asked, uneasy and bewildered.

'The custom of sin-eating for the dead. It is peculiar to the Welsh Border and is symbolised by the taking of bread and wine in the presence of the corpse.'

'And what was the point of it?'

'It was believed that the dead man's sins would be transferred to the account of whoever ate and drank in his presence, thus enabling him to sleep till Judgment Day, provided only that the bread and wine were handed across the body.'

Clive laughed nervously. 'I took on more than I knew. But why didn't the old people eat and drink to ensure the poor fellow slept easy? He was their son, after all.'

'Because the sin-eater must be a stranger, preferably someone who comes from far away, so that when he goes he will take the dead man's sins with him, away from the community in which he lived.'

'Like the Israelites driving forth the scapegoat.'

'Yes, the two ideas may very possibly be linked. What fascinates me is that sin-eating still survives. It was last recorded in the mid-nineteenth century.'

'My grandfather knew of it,' Barnabas said suddenly. 'I've heard him say he was asked to sin-eat for some man in an outlying village, but he knew what he was doing and refused.'

'Should I have refused?' Clive asked. 'They seemed so anxious.'

'Ah—' Barnabas paused dramatically—'anxious is just what those old folk would be.'

'Why they more than any others?'

Barnabas did not answer at first. Then: 'Their name's Preece, isn't it?'

'I believe it is,' Clive replied.

'And their son's name was Edward?'

Clive nodded.

'Then I wouldn't want to be in your shoes.'

'Why? Was Edward Preece particularly sinful?'

'He was a murderer,' Barnabas said.

***

A few days later Clive returned to London, having cut short his stay in Carringford. The sin-eating episode had upset him, although he could not quite say why. On the face of it, it seemed absurd to bother about some ancient pagan superstition surviving by a fluke from the past. Sin could not be transferred; it was against the Christian religion. It was also against common sense.

Nevertheless, the thought recurred to him constantly that he now had murder to his account. He was a murderer and no one knew it— a man who went unpunished and unhanged. Not that the original committer of the crime had been hanged either; he had merely been imprisoned for life, or more exactly for twelve years. 'Twelve years,' Barnabas Elms had exclaimed, 'that's all they gave him! Twelve years for murdering his wife!'

Clive was by now familiar with Preece's story, which Barnabas had needed no persuading to tell. It was evidently one which had made a deep impression upon him. He told it unexpectedly well.

Edward Preece had married his childhood sweetheart, a girl from a neighbouring farm. Elsie had been young and very pretty. Barnabas chronicled her charms. Unfortunately life with Edward and his bigoted parents had proved too narrow for the young wife's happiness. Twice in the first year she ran away and sought refuge with her own people, and twice she returned because of Edward's distress. For Edward loved Elsie to distraction; the world would have been too paltry to lay at her feet. 'He spoiled her,' Barnabas observed, with the subdued satisfaction of one who has successfully prophesied catastrophe. 'He made her feel there was nothing too good for her, so naturally she got to thinking she could do no wrong. And when she found a catch like Dick Roper was after her, she didn't bother to resist for long.'

Dick Roper was the only son of the local landowner, an arrogant, swaggering young dandy who had already caused his father trouble enough. Most of the trouble was over women—Barnabas gave details—for whom his appetite was vast. He had done his military service as a commando and then enrolled in an agricultural college, but he had been sent down because of some scandal, and his father was now keeping him on a tight rein, making him live at home, work hard at farming, and take his part in running the estate. Bored, sulky, and resentful, Dick met Elsie. When next he stopped to think, it was too late.

Barnabas had been loud in his condemnation of Elsie, but Mr Robinson enquired: 'Don't you think young Roper was more to blame? He seduced her, from what you've told us.'

'Mr Roper—Sir Richard I should say now—is a gentleman.'

'But he seduced the wife of one of his own—or his father's—tenants. I don't call that a gentlemanly act.'

'Boys will be boys,' Barnabas said with an attempt at lightness.

'And girls will be girls, no doubt. What happened? Did Elsie find she was pregnant?'

'What happened was that Edward Preece found out.'

'What did he do?' Clive asked, with apprehension.

'Ah, you may well ask that! It seems the husband was like they say—the last to know—and when he heard, he didn't believe it. He resolved to keep a watch, fooled Elsie into thinking he had gone ploughing, and then crept back towards the house. At the trial he claimed he saw a man cross the farmyard, but from that distance could not recognise who he was. Believing he would catch his wife red-handed, he burst in on her—and found her dead.'

'It doesn't sound very likely,' Clive objected.

'No. The jury threw it out. For Dick Roper testified that he arrived a quarter of an hour later to find Preece with his hands round Elsie's throat. She had been strangled—there were bruises—and Preece was a violent-tempered man. He had cause for anger—Roper admitted it.

What more natural than that he went a bit too far? It is easy to sin.' Barnabas sounded as if he had just discovered it.

Mr Robinson turned on him. 'Shouldn't that be a challenge, instead of being put forward as an excuse?'

Barnabas said, smiling smugly, 'It is not for us to judge.'

'And what became of Roper?' Mr Robinson enquired grimly.

'He went to Australia. He has a sheep farm in New South Wales. Doing well, too. He decided to stay on out there even after his father died.' Barnabas shook his head over this dereliction of duty.

'What about the old people?' Clive asked suddenly. 'Where were they while Elsie was being killed?'

'They were out. They claimed they knew nothing.'

'And the jury accepted that?'

Barnabas shrugged. 'Personally, I'm convinced the Preeces knew something. The old woman certainly did. She tried her best to pin the crime on Dick Roper. But she was too partisan—the judge directed the jury to disregard her.'

I can understand that, Clive thought. She'd count each breath Eddie drew, the hairs on his head would be numbered, if his heart so much as faltered she would know. He felt again her withered lips against his fingers, the senile trembling of her toothless jaws. She and her husband had continued to live on that farm where their daughter-in-law had been murdered, to sleep in the very room where she had died. 'The wench was nowt but a wanton,' Mrs Preece had protested. 'My son did not deserve to suffer when there was others as much to blame.'

As in some old ballad where emotions are not explicitly stated, her words were remarkable for what they did not say. Elsie had found life narrow and difficult with her in-laws. Twice in that first year of marriage she had rebelled and run away. It was easy to imagine the unforgiving resentment with which her return would be eyed. She had come back in response to Edward's pleadings, but the old people would sooner far that she had died.

And when she took up with Dick Roper—surely her mother-in-law would be the first to know. Was it she who had told Edward that his wife was no longer faithful, hoping thus to deal his love a deathblow?

There was no limit to the speculations one could indulge in. A thousand questions sprang to mind, destined one and all to remain unanswered. Clive wondered if their urgency would ever recede. For whether he liked it or not, he was now a part of this tragic situation: he bore the guilt though he had not done the deed.

***

This thought accompanied Clive back to London and was with him in daily life—in his work in the architect's office, in crowded tube-trains, in his bed at nights. He did not discuss his guilt for fear of ridicule. The whole story sounded far-fetched. Who had ever heard of sin-eating? And if he had, who would believe it? Clive assured himself repeatedly that nothing had been altered by his consumption of that tainted wine and bread. In vain. Now that he knew the significance of his actions he felt inextricably bound to the dead.

It was some such powerful but ill-formulated notion that led him to return to Carringford. The following autumn found him again at the Red Lion, where Barnabas Elms, who called by what he termed coincidence on Clive's first evening, inspected the young man with an air of mournful anticipation, like an undertaker visiting a sick friend.

'Returning to the scene of the crime?' he enquired archly.

'I don't know. I hadn't thought of it.'

Clive was astonished to hear himself lie so fluently. He had thought of nothing but Penrhayader all the way down. It was absurd, of course, and there would be no sequel to his longing—but he wanted to see the place again.

'The old folks are in the churchyard,' Barnabas informed him.

'Died last winter. There was no sin-eating for *them*. She went first and he followed. You'll be able to poke around the place in peace.'

'I have no intention of doing so,' Clive said unconvincingly.

Barnabas shook his head and solemnly closed one eye.

The next day brought a perfect autumn morning, laced with spiders' webs and mist and dew. Clive resolved to delay his visit to Penrhayader no longer, and after breakfast he set out. The drive passed without incident, and, off the main road, there was little traffic about. Within an hour he was turning down the lane leading to church and farmyard, so overgrown that it was almost lost. A robin singing cheerfully in the hedgerow fell silent as he approached. A blackberry trail, bent by the passage of some vehicle, freed itself and sprang back viciously. He noticed then that the hedges on either side of the lane were damaged, as though a visitor had only recently passed. Some other enthusiast to see the rood-loft in the church, perhaps, or a possible buyer for the farm.

Despite this, he almost failed to notice the car when he came upon it, so carefully was it concealed, backed out of sight into a gateway where the hedge was a profusion of blackberry and old man's beard. Clive wondered at the choice of parking place since there was open ground near the farm, but decided the driver must be unfamiliar with his surroundings and had stopped at the first suitable spot.

Clive had no wish to encounter the owner, but the farmyard looked empty enough. He had thought it desolate when he first visited it a year ago, but that was nothing to how it looked today. The peg-and-chain fastening on the gate had rusted. Once again he was obliged to climb. The mire underfoot had dried—from disuse rather than drought, he suspected—and it was possible now to see that the farmyard was paved with flags. But the chickens had vanished; the pig could no longer be smelt; and the door of the lean-to shack near the back porch swung open, revealing the earth-closet for what it was.

As Clive came round the side of the farmhouse, he received a further shock. The downstairs windows were broken and boarded; two planks nailed crosswise barred the door. It looked like a travesty of the plague sign; almost he expected to hear the cry, 'Bring out your dead!' Instead the silence was absolute; even the upland wind had dropped. The decay around him seemed that of centuries; he could not believe it was the work of a single year—of a twelvemonth, he thought, reckoning back to his last visit; a twelvemonth and a day.

The coincidence shook him for no logical reason. It was absurd to be affected by a ballad-monger's trite phrase. What if it was the length of time for which fairies were said to bewitch a man, the span between burial and first walking of the ghost? No one believed such nonsense in the twentieth century. He continued resolutely on his way.

It was as he was passing the far side of the house on his tour of inspection that something prompted Clive to look round. The single sash-window on this side was neither broken nor boarded, and a man was climbing out. The window was at ground-level and opened into a dairy. As Clive watched, the man dropped lightly to the ground. He was well-dressed, well-built, but rather stocky. His head was bowed to show dark hair thinning on the top but arranged carefully and expensively. Clive could not see his face.

As though aware of being scrutinised, the man looked up suddenly. Clive noted sun-tanned skin and brown eyes regarding him suspiciously, even while the man politely said, 'Good afternoon.'

Clive returned the greeting, adding, 'What are you doing here?'

'Having a look round.' The voice was twangy and unpleasing.

'Are you a prospective purchaser?'

The man laughed silently. 'Are you an agent?'

Clive disclaimed all agency connections with such conviction that t he intruder almost relaxed. He volunteered a little information: he had known the Preeces once, long ago.

'So did I,' Clive said automatically.

'But you're not from these parts.'

The stranger rapped it out so smartly that Clive was uncertain what to say. 'I'm a visitor here,' he offered.

'So am I.' The stranger seemed satisfied. Abruptly he switched to something else. 'This place has gone to rack and ruin. It's changed a lot since the last time I stood here.'

'When was that?' Clive asked with curiosity.

'Years ago.' The man seemed about to say more, but refrained. Instead he returned to the farm. 'I hear the old folks died only last winter. It must have been in a bad state long before then.'

'Oh, it was,' Clive assured him. 'When I saw it last year I thought no one lived here. But of course they were old and their son obviously hadn't been able to do much—'

The stranger interrupted him: 'Do you mean to say you knew Eddie Preece?'

Clive hesitated. Should he tell him? 'I didn't know him well,' he temporised.

'How long did you know him?' the stranger demanded.

'Not long.' Clive was carefully vague. He was beginning to resent the examination. What right had this intruder to question him?

The intruder, however, was unaware of Clive's resentment. Indeed, he seemed unaware of Clive. 'Then you didn't know him before,' he murmured.

Clive asked very deliberately: 'Do you mean before he murdered his wife?'

'So you know!' The stranger seemed almost relieved by this discovery, as though he could speak more freely now. Then an instant later: 'How do you know?' he asked quickly. 'You said you didn't come from these parts.'

'It's no secret,' Clive responded. 'I heard about it when I was down last year.'

'A bad business,' the stranger commented. 'Eddie Preece didn't deserve to suffer like that.'

There was so much sorrow in his voice that Clive was moved by it. This man must have known Preece well—a school friend, perhaps. They must be about the same age, he decided, trying to cast his mind back to the dead man lying on the bed.

'Why are you here?' he asked again.

'I thought it would be—interesting.' The man lingered over the word, as though it had some secret significance. 'I like to revisit old haunts.'

He smiled then, showing all his teeth in a shark's grin, and added: 'Though I should have preferred to be alone.'

Clive realised that he disliked this arrogant stranger. 'When I saw you, you seemed to be breaking in.'

'I was, but there's nothing worth the taking.'

'Are you telling me the furniture's still there?'

'It has to rot somewhere, and there's no point in taking it away—it might as well stay here. Since Eddie Preece died first, there's no heir.'

'Eddie Preece died a year ago yesterday.'

'So you know that too! You seem to be very well informed. But I assure you, I didn't come here to steal, if that's what you're thinking. I've touched nothing. Come in and see for yourself.'

With one hand the stranger thrust the sash-window upwards and stood back for Clive to go first. Once again, Clive felt himself outmanoeuvred. Who was this man to do the honours of the house?

He stood resolutely still. 'I'll take your word for it.'

'Don't do that.' The stranger's laugh had an unpleasant sound.

Clive turned on his heel.

'Stay!' the other man called after him. 'I can show you something interesting inside.'

Curiosity is a powerful human motive. In Clive it was particularly strong. He hesitated, and the stranger beckoned imperiously. 'It's quite safe, if that's what's worrying you, and I promise I shan't keep you long.'

Thoughts of hidden treasure or secret cupboards lured Clive, for what else could the house contain? Reluctantly he put one foot over the sill of the dairy window. As he did so, he was seized by a feeling of horror that he could neither combat nor satisfactorily explain.

The dairy was chill and vault-like. Its window darkened as the stranger clambered in. Instinctively Clive sought to put a distance between them. For some reason this man affected him unpleasantly.

The dairy opened into the kitchen, which was much as Clive remembered it, though hung with cobwebs now and made gloomy by the boarded windows. There were ashes still in the hearth. The place stank of mice and damp and mildew. Their footsteps rang loudly on the stone floor.

In the corner the staircase ascended, steep and narrow, to the room of death above. Clive led the way and the other followed. At the top he stood blocking the escape. Just so had the old couple stood, Clive remembered, and now they, like their son, were dead. There had been no sin-eating for them, Barnabas Elms had told him. He hoped they lay easy, even so.

It was as he stood in the middle of the room with his back to the window that he thought he heard the sound. A board creaked, as boards do in old houses, but there was something more besides. Without knowing exactly how he knew it, Clive became aware that there was someone in the room next door. It seemed impossible. He glanced at his companion to see if he had heard it. The man was standing rigid, a look of terror on his face. His eyes were fixed, the whites suddenly very prominent, on the open space where once had been the bedroom door.

Clive followed his gaze. At first he noticed nothing. From where he stood no one was visible. He was about to move to the head of the stairs to join the stranger, when his eye was caught by something on the floor. It lay, long and black, stretching out from the empty doorway, unnaturally elongated and—Clive could have sworn—unnaturally dark.

Though the light was not strong, the outline was unmistakable. It was the shadow of a man, unmoving, stark.

And not only of a man. The man had a companion, whom he was grasping, in fear or anger, by the throat. It was a woman—Clive could see her long hair streaming backwards, and—quite clearly—the outline of her breast. The shadows were as still as if of statues. Not even the woman's hair stirred. Apart from their elongation caused by the light's angle, no single detail was blurred.

Clive stood still for so long that he wondered if he too had become a statue—until he heard himself gasping for breath. Or was it the stranger who was gasping? Even across the room, Clive could see that his chest heaved. He was clutching the newel-post at the stairhead. From his colour and posture Clive judged he was about to faint. He glanced again at the shadows. They lay exactly as before. Whatever it was in the next room that cast them, he had to see what lay beyond that missing door.

In three quick strides Clive crossed to where the stranger was standing and gripped him firmly by the arm.

'It's all right. Take it easy. There are two of us. Whoever they are, they won't do us any harm.'

He was not certain of this; hence his insistence on equal numbers. His companion relaxed slightly as he spoke.

'Did you see them too? Then they *were* there. I thought I was dreaming. But now, thank heaven, they've gone.'

Clive looked and found the next-door room devoid of occupants, or at least that part of it which he could see. He looked at the floor, but the long black shadows had vanished.

'We must have been imagining things,' he said.

He knew in his heart that he had imagined nothing, but it was all he could think of to say. He hoped that the stranger would seize upon it. Between them, they would chase these shadows away. And Clive, at least, longed for such reassurance, for without it, what was it that had been in the room next door?

To his dismay, however, the stranger did not seize on his explanations. Instead he said: 'We imagined nothing. It was Eddie and Elsie in there. He was standing at the foot of the bed and he had his hands round her throat just like I saw them. Do you think I'll ever forget a sight like that?'

Clive said, without surprise, 'You're Richard Roper.'

The other nodded impatiently. 'Hadn't you guessed?'

Clive knew now that he had guessed; that he had known from the moment he saw him that this was the man responsible for Elsie Preece's death; and therefore the man responsible for the sin he, Clive, now carried.

'I thought you were in Australia,' he said.

'So I am—was—until a week ago. Then I decided to come home.'

'Why?'

'I don't know. It's only for a short visit. I flew in to London last night, hired a car, and drove straight down here. I wanted to see it *that* bad.' Roper snapped his fingers like a man clinching an argument. 'Funny how things get you, isn't it?'

He stood there, so sure of himself, so debonair and smiling, even though his face was still blanched with fear, that Clive felt himself choke with rage—an unfamiliar sensation, for his temper was normally cool.

Nevertheless, he managed to master it, and replied, 'You seem to have got more than you bargained for.'

'You're dead right,' Roper said.

'Did you see what you actually saw on that day when... when...'

'Exactly the same.' Roper indicated the stairs behind him. 'I came up there. The house was very still. As I crossed the yard, I had heard Elsie crying out and I was frightened. I had thought she was alone in the house.' He grinned suddenly. 'Everyone will have told you we were lovers. It was what lent lustre to the case. I used to wait till the Preeces were out and then go and see her. Sometimes we'd meet out, but it was difficult for her to get away.'

'But they were out that afternoon?'

'Yes, all of them. The old man had gone into town. The old woman was down in the village. Eddie had ploughing to do. I watched them all set off after midday dinner. Eddie was the last to leave. Elsie waved him off from the door—that was our signal. I knew then that the coast was clear for me.

'It takes about a quarter of an hour from the point where I was watching to get to the Preeces' house. As I crossed the yard, I told you I heard Elsie screaming. I wondered then if Eddie had come back. The screams stopped when I was halfway across the farmyard. There was a trail of mud over the kitchen floor. It looked as though Eddie had returned unexpectedly. I went upstairs two at a time. As I reached the head of the stairs, I turned and saw them. They were like statues, and Eddie had her by the throat. She was half-undressed, and her clothes were slipping off her shoulders. Her long dark hair had come loose and was hanging down. Her head was limp and lolling sideways. Eddie looked like a man in a trance. I don't believe he knew what he'd done to her—I told them that at the trial. I said, "My God, you've killed her!" and he looked at me and shook his head—slowly, like a bull that's bewildered. Then he let go of her and fell sobbing on the bed.'

Clive listened. The story had a horrible coherence. It also had the glibness of one told many times. He could picture Roper, a little drunk, talking to reporters and pub acquaintances. His dislike of the man increased. He also found him slightly sinister, in a well-dressed, snake-like way. Roper's eyes, small, bright, and unblinking, assessed his every reaction with an intentness that Clive found strange.

And yet not strange, for there was something wrong with the story, and Roper watched to see if this time his bluff would be called. But it never had been, and Eddie Preece had been convicted. Why after all these years should his confidence suddenly fail? Was it the apparition of the two figures that had shaken him, and the memories they conjured up? Or was it simply that he was out of practice? He could not have told his tale for many years.

Clive looked away from him towards the bedroom, empty and rotting like everything else in the house. From the stairhead he could see clearly where the two figures must have been standing, against the protruding foot of the bed. But in the old days… He turned to Roper.

'The door,' he said suddenly. 'The door.'

'What door?' Roper's voice was completely neutral.

'The door that's been taken down. It opened inwards—into the bedroom.' Clive pointed. 'You couldn't have seen them from here.'

'I don't know what you're talking about,' Roper said shortly. 'You can see for yourself: there's no door.'

'But there used to be. At the time of the—the murder. It was only recently the old people took it down. Mrs Preece mentioned it to me when I was here last autumn when Eddie was laid out dead in this room. They took the door down so that it would be easier for her to get to him if he should want anything in the night.'

'Very sensible. That door was a devil to open. The latch made such a clack.'

'And it screened much of the back room because it opened inwards. You couldn't have seen the foot of the bed.'

'Then I must have been further into the room.' Roper spoke easily, but his face had again gone white.

'It would make no difference,' Clive responded. 'You couldn't see them wherever you stood.'

'So?'

'So there's something wrong with your story. It can't have happened the way you describe.'

Roper's voice grew colder, more menacing. 'Are you trying to say that I lied?'

'Yes, I am. For your own good reasons.'

'What do you mean by that?'

'I mean—' Clive paused and swallowed—'that you have something ugly to hide.'

Roper laughed, and the sound was chilling. 'You've got a nerve, I must say. Are you by any chance accusing me of the murder?'

'Preece always maintained that it was you.'

'Preece was a bloody liar and a half-wit.'

'So I've heard. Invention wouldn't be such a man's strong point.'

'You forget—the jury decided he was lying.'

'Juries have made mistakes before now.'

'I don't know who you are,' Roper said with quiet fury, 'but by God I mean to find out. You'll retract that statement in public, unless you want to find yourself in court.'

'I may well find myself in court—as your accuser. It was you who murdered Elsie Preece.'

'Perhaps you'll be good enough to tell me how this crime was accomplished?'

'Quite easily. By manual pressure on the throat. You watched them all leave except Elsie, no doubt in the manner you describe. Then you stole in like a rat slinking into a corn-bin, and made your way up the stairs. Elsie was expecting you—she was half-undressed already, but what happened then I can't guess. Perhaps there was a quarrel and you lost your temper; perhaps she told you she was giving you up.

Perhaps, even, she was importunate and demanded money; or she may have tried blackmail—I don't know. Whatever the reason, you put an end to her, though, as you said of Preece, you may not have known what you did. But she was lying dead on the bed when you heard footsteps approaching. There was no escape, so you did the natural thing: you hid.'

'A very interesting reconstruction. Please go on with your detective story.'

'The intruder, of course, was Eddie Preece. Eddie had been suspicious of you for a long time—ever since his mother alerted him, in fact.'

'She always hated Elsie,' Roper muttered.

'This time Preece thought he'd catch you in the act. Instead, he found Elsie dead on the bed, half-naked. He caught her to him, just as you describe, and for a moment they stood just as we saw them—or their shadows. Then he flung himself on the bed and cried.'

'I congratulate you on your imagination. But you can't prove any of this.'

'Perhaps not—though I'm not sure that I agree with you on that point. I'm certainly going to have a damn good try.'

'Try if you like, but not all your depositions will bring Eddie back from the grave.'

'Apart from justice, I owe it to myself to clear him.' Clive did not feel he could explain quite why. But with every word Roper spoke, he felt the sensation of guilt slip from him. Eddie's sins were whiter than snow. And therefore his sin-eater had a lesser load to carry. For the first time in a year Clive felt himself light of heart. He almost laughed aloud as he announced: 'I'm going to have this case reopened. I shall go to London to see my lawyers for a start.'

'You won't, you know.' Roper spoke very softly. 'You're going to stay right here.'

There was so much menace in his tone that Clive was frightened, although he could see no reason for fear. Roper was stocky and well-muscled, but Clive was heavier. If he rushed Roper he could almost certainly get past him. He took a step forward.

Roper said harshly, 'That's enough.'

In spite of himself, Clive hesitated.

Roper said, 'It's as well for you if you did. I'm not a karate-trained ex-commando for nothing. You move, and I'll break your neck.'

Clive felt the sweat of fear on his body. It was unbelievable that this should happen to him—to be alone in an empty house with an uncaught murderer who was preparing to murder again.

He made a gesture of protest.

'Are you going to keep still?' Roper asked.

'What are you going to do?' Clive demanded. He could scarcely speak for the chattering of his teeth.

'See you silenced forever,' Roper replied brutally. 'You don't imagine you're going to walk out of here? I didn't ask you to come poking around in the first place. You've no one but yourself to blame.'

'You invited me in,' Clive said stupidly.

'Only because you'd seen the car in the lane. I couldn't afford to have it traced that I'd been here. From that moment it was inevitable that you should die.'

Clive squared his shoulders. There could be no rescue; no one even knew where he was. He reproached himself for not having told the proprietor of the Red Lion of his destination, or even Barnabas Elms. But it would have made no difference to his present situation. He resolved to put up a fight, and was mentally rehearsing his tactics when something moving on the floor caught his eye. It was a shadow, but not his own shadow. He was standing still as any stone, whereas this shadow was inching forwards, its menacing hands upraised like giant claws. It was advancing with terrible deliberation on Roper, and whatever cast the shadow was emerging from the open bedroom door.

Clive dared not turn his head to look behind him. There was a coldness, a dankness chill as the grave. It grew in intensity as the caster of the shadow came closer, yet no footfall sounded on the floor. So grotesque and distorted was the shadow that it was impossible to tell if its original were equally so, or whether a normal even if not living being cast it. Clive found he was afraid to know.

Instead he gazed straight ahead at Roper, who had gone deathly pale at the sight of what approached. He seemed unable to move, unable to stop staring with eyeballs that bulged from his head. It was almost as though someone were choking him. His mouth opened but he made no sound; his pale face was suffused darkly; he tottered as if about to fall.

Clive was now enveloped in coldness. There was an earthy smell, as of something long underground. And the shadow now reached all the way to the far wall and began to ascend it, blotting out that corner of the room, blotting out the staircase, blotting out Roper, who gave a dreadful gurgling scream...

Clive was never certain if the darkness was because he fainted, although he heard the thunder of Roper's fall as he bumped and clattered down the staircase. The noise seemed as though it would never end. He put his hands to his ears to try to deaden it, but the sound reverberated in his head. By contrast, the silence that followed was absolute; it had the vaultlike quality of a tomb. Roper neither stirred nor spoke when Clive called him. It came home to him that Roper was dead.

The room seemed suddenly brighter and warmer, the overwhelming shadow had gone. Fearfully Clive looked behind him; the back bedroom was as empty as the front. There was nothing that could cast a shadow; the sky outside was cloudless October blue. Roper must have lost his balance and fallen; no other explanation would do.

Even so, the accident might be difficult to account for; there were no witnesses—not, at least, whom he could call. Clive went downstairs and touched Roper's warm, limp body. He was lying face downwards in a heap. With an effort, Clive turned him over, and gasped as his heart missed a beat. Roper's face was set in a mask of pure terror. There were the marks of manual strangulation on his throat.

Clive straightened up very slowly. In one way it was a logical end. So it was that Eddie Preece's sin-eater was arrested, charged with murder, and in due course tried and condemned.

TELLING THE BEES

THE HIVES WERE on the south side of the orchard, where they got the maximum sun. Old Parry's habit of keeping bees, which in peacetime had seemed an amusing eccentricity in a gardener, had in wartime taken on a new significance. It helped out the sugar ration and the jam ration, and Old Parry, feudal to the last, insisted on regarding the hives as the property of 'the Master' (he could never remember to say 'Major', though that was now the Master's rank) and himself merely as the instrument of their survival. To him they were 'the Master's bees'.

Elizabeth Lockett, the Master's wife, accepted this attitude without question, as she accepted all the rights and privileges that marrying a Lockett implied: the long, low, half-timbered house that had been in the family for generations; the front pew in a church full of memorial tablets to past Locketts; the tenantry's respectful greetings; sick visiting; and the duty to provide an heir. It was in this last that she had failed so signally: one daughter, and nothing but miscarriages since. Now that she was pregnant again she was determined to take every precaution and present Henry with the son she knew he craved.

It was not surprising that five-year-old Diana Lockett regarded herself as a kind of second-best, an interim heiress, something to be going on with until the real heir came along. With her father away at the war and her mother occupied with her own state of body and mind to the exclusion of everything else, she had to get along as best she could. Luckily for her there was Old Parry. Between the child and the old man a friendship had sprung up, and though Elizabeth Lockett sometimes worried that her daughter would pick up the gardener's speech and accent, she was glad enough to have her taken off her hands.

All through the long, hot summer, Diana followed the old man around, carrying weeds to his bonfires, or fetching a lettuce for Cook.

She ate more raspberries than she gathered, but Old Parry obligingly gave her some of his, so that she still had a respectably filled punnet to show her mother. And of course there were the bees to visit every day.

'Darling, you'll get stung,' Elizabeth protested.

'Bees don't sting if you're not afraid.'

'That's a confidence trick.'

'What's a confidence trick?'

'Oh darling, never mind.'

Diana knew better than to try and get answers from her mother unless they were forthcoming the first time. Instead she asked Old Parry, who said, 'Well, missie, I don't rightly know. A confidence trick means acting as though a thing's so as folks'll believe it, but you can't do that with bees. They be the knowingest of little creatures and if you don't tell 'em the truth they'll be off. Swarm elsewhere they will if they're not told all the doings of the family. I mind telling 'em when you were born. And when your brothers wasn't I told 'em.'

'I haven't got any brothers,' Diana said.

'No, missie, that you haven't. But you should allus tell the bees when someone dies. It hurts their feelings, like, if no one tells them. And then, as I say, they ups and swarms elsewhere.'

'Suppose you forget?'

'The bees 'ud never forgive you. But I don't forget. I know when someone dies. When my wife went, it were sudden, like. She dropped down in the kitchen—stone dead. I were weeding the drive and it came to me all at once; Matilda's dead—just like that. And my boy Harry knew it too, for all they say he's simple-minded. I went and told the bees and then I went home and found him with her. If I hadn'ta told the bees they'da been off.'

Diana accepted the information in the way that children often accept startling statements: she stolidly pigeon-holed it away until a golden September afternoon in the orchard, when it came back to her vividly.

Her father had been home on leave in the meantime and had made much of her; she had always been a pet of his. She had not even cried when he had gone back because he had told her not to, and to take care of her mother, too. 'And perhaps next time I come you'll have a baby brother to show me. Wouldn't you like that?' he said. Diana said

'No' very distinctly, but he smothered it against his uniform. 'Of course you would,' he said. 'It would be company.' Then the taxi came to take him to the station and he was gone.

'I don't want company,' Diana told Old Parry later.

'No more you do, missie, but it 'ud be fine if the Master had a son. Your grandfather said when I were with him in the trenches in the last war that if anything happened to him there'd allus be the boy. And sure enough something did happen and your father had to carry on.'

'I should carry on if anything happened to my father.'

'Yes, missie, but you're a girl. Girls grow up and marry strangers. It ain't the same for the rest of us, you see.'

'I should make it the same, and anyway, nothing's going to happen to my father.'

'No, missie, God forbid. And now you can give me a hand with them currants as wants picking. Cook was saying we could do with a blackcurrant tart.'

Diana forgot about the conversation; there was always so much to do. The school holidays stretched invitingly before her. September was an infinity away. And when it came, it was warm and golden, with spider webs in the morning hung with dew, and dust at midday in the tracks by the cornfield, and a hint of chill in the air at night. The bees worked overtime, bringing in the last of their harvest; there was plenty of honey that year. Diana would sit for half an hour at a time in the orchard, watching the coming and going at the hive doors.

One afternoon she was lying on her stomach in the long grass, munching an apple that had dropped, when she saw Old Parry making his way across the orchard with a curious slouching step. He was normally as trim and erect as the young soldier who had long ago gone to that other war with Captain Lockett and come home to be gardener to his son. There was something unusual about him. Diana stopped munching to watch.

At the nearest hive he stooped as if to count the inmates, and his lips moved as though he were in church. Intrigued, Diana sat up but he did not see her. Instead he moved to the next hive. By wriggling through the grass, it was possible to get near enough to hear him. The child inched forward like a snake. As a rule Old Parry called her to watch when his bees required attention; she was familiar with the normal processes, but this was something new.

'Little brownie…' She could hear him very faintly, though she had never heard him use the old country name before. And then came a muttering she could not catch and the whole thing was repeated. She wriggled nearer, straining to hear.

'Little brownie…' This time she caught it quite clearly. 'Little brownie, thy master's dead.'

And then again, in gentle incantation: 'Little brownie, thy master's dead.'

'Thy master'. But the bees' master was her father! Surely her father was not dead. No one had told her mother. With a wild cry, Diana was on her feet, running with a fleetness that outmatched Old Parry back to the black-and-white house, back to the quiet drawing-room where her mother was resting, to the safe rebuttal of her mother's arms.

Fast as she was, the telegraph boy was faster. Diana, bursting through the front door, saw her mother white-faced in the hall leaning against the banisters, the telegram fluttering from her hand; saw Cook come rushing from the kitchen, summoned by the telegraph boy; and heard the great cry with which Elizabeth Lockett recognised that she was a widow before collapsing to the floor.

That night she gave birth to a son who lived barely long enough to be named after his father. Presumably nobody told the bees. At any rate, when Diana revisited the orchard a few days later, the hives were empty and the bees had gone.

***

Diana Lockett married twice, unsuccessfully and childlessly, before falling in love with Bernard Larch at the age of thirty-five. Bernard was some years younger than she was—she never said precisely how many—and an actor. He was not a very good actor, but he had played bit parts in the West End and Diana, like Bernard, was convinced that his talent was unrecognised rather than non-existent. He was not the kind of man anyone had expected Diana to choose for her third husband, the first two having been solid businessman types, but Bernard obligingly fell in love with Diana once her feelings had been made plain to him, and Diana proudly took him home to the old black-and-white house where Elizabeth still lived.

'I like that,' Bernard exclaimed as soon as he saw it, 'Yes, I like that very much.'

Something proprietary in his tone reminded Diana that if she married Bernard he might acquire some rights in the place. She said warningly: 'I don't suppose I'll ever live here. The upkeep must be pretty steep.'

'I wasn't thinking of it as a place to live in,' Barnard said.

'My mother lives here,' Diana said stiffly.

'But, darling, your mother's not on the stage.'

'No,' Diana agreed, and fell silent because she had always found the mother-daughter relationship one big act.

Elizabeth Lockett had never forgiven her daughter causing the death of her son. In vain she reminded herself, or allowed others to remind her, that Diana was five years old at the time. If the child had not come bursting in with that unnerving, almost supernatural foreknowledge that her beloved father was dead, the shock might have been less severe and disaster might have been averted. Elizabeth conveniently forgot that she already held the opened telegram in her hand.

The relationship between the two women was a cool one, tempered with positive spite. Elizabeth had played a part in the break-up of Diana's two marriages; Diana had driven her mother's only serious suitor off. She scarcely cared whether her mother approved of Bernard, but he had wanted to see her home so she had obliged. And fortunately Bernard turned the full battery of charm on his prospective mother-in-law. Elizabeth pronounced him the best of her sons-in-law to date.

It was typical of her to add 'to date'. Diana pretended to take no notice and pushed the wedding further forward still. It took place in London and Elizabeth was not invited. She said she did not mind, but the waste was a pity; she now knew by heart what to do.

***

The honeymoon was spent in the Bahamas since Diana could well afford to indulge her new husband's expensive tastes, and it would have been a time of blissful happiness for both of them, had not Diana nearly drowned.

She was a stylish though not a strong swimmer, and when she was caught in a cross-current in an unfrequented bay where the 'Danger' notice had failed to catch her eye, there was nothing she could do except scream for help as loudly as her lungs permitted, and hope that Bernard on the beach would hear. He might not have done had not someone in a boat providentially rounded the headland and hauled the exhausted Diana aboard. By the time Bernard realised what was happening and came cleaving through the water to the rescue, it would have been, as Diana and her saviour pointed out, too late.

The realisation of how nearly they had lost each other drew the newly-weds even closer, and soon a new bond was forged. They had not been home long when Diana was taken ill; she vomited constantly, and after trying various homely remedies, a doctor had to be called. He commiserated with her on her sickness and congratulated her on her pregnancy. Diana was thunderstruck. She had been told so often that it was highly unlikely she would ever conceive that she had given up hope and had even warned Bernard that he need not expect an heir. He had seemed quite content—so much so that she now feared to tell him the contrary. To her delight, his enthusiasm matched her own'

'Your others didn't have it in them,' he said proudly.

Diana was inclined to agree, except that she felt too ill to do more than press his hand feebly. Bernard seemed to understand. Indeed, no husband could have been more solicitous and attentive. He was constantly trying to tempt her appetite, bringing in titbits that he thought she might fancy and ready to produce hot drinks at all hours.

The doctor, as usual in such cases, was useless. He said it was something that had to be endured, that she ought to feel better after the third month, and that those mothers who had a hard time at the beginning often had the best of it at the end. But Diana did not feel better after the third month. Days of misery alternated with days when she began to hope the worst was over. It was Bernard who suggested she should go home.

'You might relax more,' he suggested, 'and the country air would do you good. And since I'm resting I'd be on hand to look after you. We'd be no bother to your mother at all.'

'She wouldn't want me,' Diana said dolefully.

'Why don't I ring her up and see? After all, you've never before looked like presenting her with a grandson. I've a hunch it might be a new beginning for you both.'

Bernard proved a better psychologist than Diana had expected. Her mother's welcome was surprisingly warm. And there was something about the black-and-white house basking peacefully in the richness of midsummer that made her feel like an exhausted mariner reaching port after a storm.

***

There had never been a summer of such profusion. Roses and clematis spilled over the garden walls; pinks tumbled on the flagged path that led to the front door, and lavender formed a blue hedge beyond. Hollyhocks stood sentinel in the borders and catmint sprawled at their feet. Everywhere that was not sunny was leafy. The early mornings were still loud with birdsong, and the noonday burdened with the buzz of bees.

Diana lay on a reclining chair in the garden and felt better. Bernard had been right to bring her home. Perhaps they might even live here some day and see their child grow up in this hallowed place. Generations of loving care must leave their mark on a house and perhaps it was now her turn to contribute. The idea was more pleasing than she had thought. If only Bernard could always be with her, instead of going off to London, as now, to audition for a new play that was being cast. Would he ever be happy away from town?

As if in answer to her thoughts, Elizabeth looked up from the small garment she was knitting—she was taking grandmotherhood seriously. 'When does Bernard get back?'

'Tomorrow, unless he telephones.'

'I like him.' Elizabeth said. 'He's better than your others. More considerate. He looks after you as if you were a queen.'

'Perhaps the others would have done if I'd made them fathers.'

'That's an unprofitable line of thought. He'll certainly be glad to see you better. He's only been gone three days and already you're getting quite a colour. It's wonderful what country air will do.'

It was true, Diana reflected. For the last few days she had felt better and there was a porcelain pink-and-whiteness in her cheeks that was most becoming. Perhaps this was what was meant by 'the quickening'. It was late, of course; her pregnancy was beginning to be noticeable; but better late than never, she supposed.

She said idly: 'The locals call Bernard "Miss Diana's husband". If he hears it, I hope he won't mind.'

'He could hardly expect village people to keep on learning the names of your mates,' Elizabeth said sweetly. 'They'll wait now to see if he's going to last.'

'Somehow I think he is,' Diana said, deciding to ignore this invitation to a catfight. 'I've never felt like this about anyone else.'

'I don't believe you have,' her mother agreed, surveying her, 'though goodness knows, you've waited long enough.'

'I don't feel thirty-six. I don't feel twenty. It's something to do with being here. When you've grown up in a place there's a tendency to regress to childhood. Everything here stays the same.'

'I don't,' Elizabeth said drily.

'Mummy, I know. I didn't mean that. But we have the same flowers growing in the borders, the same furniture, the same smell of polish and pot-pourri in the house; the same sounds—the stairs creaking, the grandfather clock ticking, the everlasting bumble of the bees. Why are there so many bees? I've never seen so many. I'm sure there are more than there were last year.'

'They're Harry Parry's bees,' Elizabeth said. 'I gave him permission to keep a few hives in the orchard, the way his father used to do.'

'Of course,' Diana said. 'I remember.' As if she would ever forget that soft country voice murmuring gently: 'Little brownie, thy master's dead.'

'Poor Harry's quite simple-minded,' Elizabeth was saying, 'but this seems to be something he can do. I should have felt churlish to say no when he came and asked me.'

'Are the hives in the same place?' Diana asked.

'Yes, on the south side. You must go and see them. Harry will be delighted if you do.'

'I'll go tomorrow,' Diana promised, feeling uneasy but unable to understand why.

But tomorrow Bernard returned, bursting with triumph at having secured a minor role in the new play. 'Rehearsals don't start till August and we open In September,' he informed Diana, 'so we'll be able to spend a little longer here.'

A cold hand clutched Diana's heart. She had not realised how much she had counted on spending the rest of her pregnancy in her old home. But when she cautiously suggested to Bernard that he should return to London without her, he showed such flattering reluctance that she was easily persuaded to give in. Nevertheless, the upset took its toll in the form of a violent return of the sickness. Even Elizabeth looked Worried: 'You ought to be over that by now. I'm going to ask Dr Grainger to have a look at you.'

Diana moaned. 'He won't do any good.'

She was partly right. Dr Grainger, who had known her since she was a child, was cheerful, talked to Elizabeth and Bernard about being highly-strung, and even more privately to Elizabeth about first pregnancies in older women; but he left some tablets which, temporarily at least, made her feel good—so good, in fact, that in the afternoon she took a stroll as far as the orchard to see Harry Parry's hives.

It was a warm afternoon. The heat and possibly the tablets made her feel drowsy. Or perhaps it was the droning of the bees. She sat down in the shade of a tree, her back against the gnarled bark's comforting roughness, and drifted in and out of sleep.

She did not know what sound awakened her, but she knew suddenly and with certainty that she was not alone. Peering round the apple tree's thick trunk, she saw Harry Parry shambling across the orchard towards her, looking oddly purposeful and no longer quite as half-witted as he was.

But he turned aside before he reached her. She realised he did not even know she was there. Instead, he went to the farthest hive, bent down and mumbled something. Diana felt herself go cold. It was like watching an old film played back slowly, except that now she could not wriggle forward to hear. She had to wait until he reached the last hive nearest her and strain every auditory nerve to catch his words.

'Little brownie…' This time she heard it quite clearly. 'Little brownie, Miss Diana's dead.' And then again, in gentle incantation: 'Little brownie, Miss Diana's dead.'

***

Diana's first instinct was to stand up and contradict him. She knew only too well she was not dead, and if simple-minded Harry Parry thought differently, there was nothing to be worried about. Her second instinct was to remember Old Parry speaking of his wife's death and saying: 'And my boy Harry knew it too.' Both the Parrys had had this strange awareness of the proximity of sudden death.

Diana sat quite still. She was not dying. She might not be in the best of health, but everyone insisted there was a perfectly normal explanation for what assailed her. Everyone was ready with comfort and encouragement. Even Dr Grainger had been deceived. Even Dr Grainger... Be careful, Diana warned herself. What are you saying? What do you really mean? And a little voice inside her answered unbidden: Bernard's trying to poison me.

She sat quite still and accepted what the little voice was saying. It was only putting into words the inchoate fear which had been gathering inside her since——since that day on honeymoon when she had nearly drowned. She had not seen the 'Danger' notice, so it was reasonable to assume that Bernard hadn't either. But it was Bernard who had suggested bathing there. And could he possibly not have heard her scream? Again Diana felt the salt water on her lips and in her nostrils and saw the land drawing steadily away, while Bernard sunned himself on the deserted beach unheeding and she gathered her remaining strength for one more try...

But afterwards, she reminded herself, he was so tender and loving. And back came the answer: He's an actor, isn't he? And not even a very good one, she admitted brutally. He's never going to be a star. For such a man, a woman with inherited wealth was an attractive proposition. She remembered his spontaneous exclamation when he saw the black-and-white house for the first time. Well might he like it, since it was evidence of what he might some day hope to inherit if he were left a childless widower.

And he had certainly expected to be childless. Diana herself had left him in no doubt of that. At the time his lack of disappointment had been endearing, but had it been quite natural? And what must he have felt when she had broken it to him that the doctors had been mistaken and that there would after all be an heir? Oh, he had seemed pleased enough and she had suspected nothing, but it meant he had no time to lose.

And he hadn't wasted any time. In all probability he had been at work already. Hadn't her sickness preceded her pregnancy? Frantically Diana thought back, but the vital dates escaped her—she had felt wretchedly ill for so long. But she was better when Bernard was not present, when he had no chance to doctor her food, slip something in those hot drinks he was for ever bringing or in those titbits chosen to disguise the taste. Yesterday's relapse had followed hard on his return from London. He must now be preparing a fatal dose, and Harry Parry, sensitive to the approach of the dark angel, had lost no time in telling the bees.

'Miss Diana's dead...' Diana stood up suddenly. At least she was going to fight back. But how, when everything seemed to play into Bernard's hands, when the advent of a child who was to rob him of his inheritance provided him with perfect cover for the effect of his graduated dose? There could not be many poisons that so well simulated a normal stomach upset, the kind of thing to which some pregnant women were prone. Diana ran through what she knew of poisons: cyanide, strychnine, mercury, paraquat... None of them fitted her symptoms. Whatever Bernard was using was slow to act and cumulative, building up in her system until in the end a comparatively small dose would suffice.

Arsenic. Suppose he was using arsenic? It was a dangerous poison, but not necessarily fatal in small doses. Hadn't Victorian women taken it in minute quantities for its beneficial effects on the complexion? And hadn't her own complexion improved? 'You're getting quite a colour'— her own mother had commented on it. Diana smiled grimly to herself. Elizabeth could hardly have suspected that it was because her daughter was being poisoned. What would she say when she knew?

For it was to her mother that she must turn in this emergency— Diana was sure of that. Whatever might have divided them, they would unite against a common enemy. She would need Elizabeth now.

And then she heard Bernard's voice calling. He had seen her, so it was no use to hide. Eagerly he came towards her, holding something in his outstretched hands.

'I've been into Shrewsbury,' he called cheerily. 'And guess what: I saw the most delicious chocolates. There was even a raspberry parfait, your favourite. Do try one, darling, I'm sure it would do you good.'

***

Elizabeth Lockett looked at her daughter coldly.

'Do you actually expect me to believe,' she said, 'that Bernard, the first decent man you've ever married, is trying to poison you?'

Diana nodded dumbly.

'Sometimes,' Elizabeth went on, 'I'm surprised somebody hasn't poisoned you already. I ought to have done it long ago. Or drowned you. Drowned at birth, that's what you ought to have been. Of all the wicked, criminal nonsense to come up with, this is extreme even for you.'

'It's not nonsense, Mummy. I've told you.'

'Sick fancies,' Elizabeth said. 'Let's hope they're just attributable to your condition, and not to something wrong in your head. Why on earth should Bernard want to kill you? I can think of plenty of reasons, but he seems to be in love. The more fool he, of course, but why now particularly?'

'He must kill me before the baby comes. Otherwise, there'd be someone else to inherit.'

'If that's what's worrying you, you can leave your money to me.'

'No good. He's my husband. He's entitled to fifty per cent however I will it—more if he can persuade me to remake my will.'

'Has he tried to?'

'No.'

'There you are, you see. There's no shred of evidence beyond the fact that you were nearly drowned through your own carelessness, and now you're pregnant—and the others never made you pregnant, did they?—your nerves and your age are making you feel unwell.'

'But it could be poison.'

'It could also be hysteria. Really, Diana, have you no control? Bernard won't take much more—poor boy, I can understand it. No man could put up with the way you're carrying on.'

'I was better while he was away,' Diana said obstinately.

'A temporary remission. You'll be better again.'

'Because I won't touch anything he could have poisoned.'

'Which means you insist on preparing all your own food. When you even refused those chocolates he'd brought you, I could have hit you. I ate one and was perfectly all right.'

'But you didn't have the raspberry parfait. That was the one he wanted me to have.'

'What happened to it?'

'I don't know. It isn't in the box any longer. I expect he threw it away.'

'More likely ate it. I never heard such nonsense. It's as if you're going mad.'

'I'm not mad. Mummy, won't you help me?'

'What do you want me to do?'

'Back me up when I tell Dr Grainger so that he'll take me seriously.'

'It would certainly be a good idea if you saw the doctor.'

'But I want him to make some tests. If there's arsenic in my body, he can detect it. Perhaps he could analyse some of the food as well.'

'You can ask him, but he'll more likely put you in a psychiatric clinic. I've heard of cases like this.'

'So you won't back me?'

'My dear girl, I'm convinced you're suffering from delusions. Unless arsenic softens the brain. In that case, I concede there's a very good chance you're being poisoned.' Elizabeth gave a little laugh.

'You'd be glad if I were dead,' Diana burst out bitterly. 'You've never loved me because I wasn't a boy. Now you've found yourself a surrogate son in Bernard. You and he are probably in league.'

This time Elizabeth laughed in good earnest and her daughter ran awkwardly from the room, intent on seeing Dr Grainger at all costs. Except that he was out on a call.

When she did see him later that evening, he was patient but unsympathetic—no doubt he had been forewarned. Or so Diana convinced herself as she answered his questions and poured out her own suspicious fears.

Dr Grainger listened and from time to time asked questions, which showed too clearly the way his mind was at work. He was obviously inclined to regard her as a hysterical schoolgirl, until she told him about telling the bees.

Diana had not meant to mention it to anyone, but inadvertently it slipped out. Dr Grainger seized on the incident as if it were something vital and insisted on hearing the whole story from A to Z.

When she had finished, he smiled with real kindness. 'There you are then. I think we have our answer there. When you were a very young child, a similar Incident was connected with losing your father. It was Coincidence, but you can't expect a five-year-old to know that. Now, quite by chance, you hear poor Harry Parry mumbling some nonsense to his bees and he happens to seize on your name—most probably because it's unfamiliar. At once your mind connects up with the past. Old Parry told the bees your father was dead, and behold, he was dead. Now Harry Parry tells them the same about you. He can't be wrong because his father wasn't. So you look around for reasons why you should die. Of course you've been having a rotten time of it— *hyperemesis gravidarum is* a beastly thing and I'm only sorry there isn't something we can do about it, although you'll find it'll ease of itself by and by. But for the moment it looms large in your thoughts, and what more natural than that you should create a connection between the two, making the natural unnatural and giving it an alien cause. In your subconscious your husband is to blame for your condition; many young wives feel like that; so you invent an external reason and claim that he's poisoning you.'

'He is poisoning me,' Diana insisted.

Dr Grainger smiled. 'Luckily we can prove you wrong. If you'll just allow me to do the necessary, we can have some tests made, and I'm sure an intelligent girl like you will abide by scientific results.'

'Very well,' Diana agreed. 'So long as you will.'

'Oh, I think so,' the doctor said, turning away to make his preparations. 'I think you can count upon that.'

***

Diana laid her hand on Bernard's and tried not to flinch. His hand closed warmly over hers. 'What is it, my love?'

'Nothing. Just something I suddenly thought of.'

'Your wish is my command.'

'That's why I hesitate to express it.'

'Is it so terrible? What do you want me to do? Jump in the lake? Kick the cat? Poison your mother?'

'No,' Diana said calmly. 'None of those.'

'Well, then?'

'I want some more of those chocolates.'

'But you wouldn't touch them. Elizabeth and I ate the lot.'

'I know, but I was sorry afterwards. I was an awful fool.'

'Yes, I admit I was disappointed. Never mind, pet. Next time I go to town I'll bring you the largest box I can carry and you can make a beast of yourself.'

'But you're not going to town again until August.'

'That's only a fortnight away.'

'It's ages when you fancy something. Couldn't you get me some today?'

'But it means going right into Shrewsbury. You can't get them in Aycester.'

'Would you mind *so* much?'

'Not if you want them. Tell you what: why don't you come with me?'

'No, darling. I might get car sick. I'd rather not, if you don't mind. You go, only drive carefully. And bring me back the biggest box you can find.'

Bernard departed with a minimum of grumbling. Mina watched him go, her hand upraised in farewell as he turned into the road from the driveway. She hoped he would remember her like that. She had promised to eat all the raspberry parfaits, so he would be able to doctor those. If he ever got as far as Shrewsbury... If he did not crash on Fourway Hill...

She went in to where her mother was sitting.

'Where's Bernard gone?' Elizabeth asked.

'To Shrewsbury, to get some more of those chocolates.'

'He spoils you,' Elizabeth said. 'Ah well, he's going to pay for it.'

Diana asked uneasily: 'What do you mean?'

'You'll lead him a dance, just as you led those others. He should have been firm with you from the start.'

Diana relaxed. Her mother obviously suspected nothing. She did not know her child was a murderer. She pressed her hand against her belly. 'I did it for you, my little one,' she said, but under her breath so that no one should hear her. 'I wasn't going to have you killed with me.'

She still marvelled how easy it was to destroy someone. Had Bernard found it easy too? You slipped a white powder in their food, or cut almost through the brake cable when no one was looking and then made sure they drove the car. Alone. And preferably down a steep hill where it could plunge hopelessly out of control. And then you sat and waited until they came and told you that you were a widow and your unborn child fatherless.

How long did it take to Fourway? Half an hour? Three-quarters? With a clear road and fast driving, the right-angled steep hill triangles of warning would be on him before he knew. And afterwards? In novels the car would catch fire and all that remained would be charred bones and metal, but things were less tidy in real life. Suppose it were possible to see that someone had tampered with the brake cable? Suppose Bernard were not killed outright? Worse still, suppose he recovered? She could not face committing murder again. Yet in this duel it was kill or be killed, and she had the child to consider. How long before they would come to tell her the news?

If only, in this respect, she were like Harry Parry and could sense the approach of death. He would know, but she could scarcely ask him. He was not too simple-minded to remember at some possibly inconvenient time. But he would tell his bees; he would not want to lose them and he would make sure they were the first to know. In the orchard she could hide and listen. What had twice happened in the past by accident could happen a third time by design.

Diana turned her steps towards the orchard and settled herself near the hives. The day was heavy, with a threat of thunder. She was sweating, not solely from the heat. The bees clustered in a thick, droning carpet about the doors of the hives; some came, some went; it was an ordered confusion, almost narcotic in effect.

Diana drowsed, and was so nearly asleep that she failed to see Harry Parry coming until he was almost at the hives. He had a shambling run very like his father's. For an instant Diana felt herself five years old. Then he leaned down and whispered something. What it was, she could not catch. But after waiting a few minutes with no appreciable alteration in the bees' comings and goings, he bent down and whispered it again.

Was there a change in the bees' humming, a rising note she had not heard before? Harry Parry moved steadily closer and Diana leaned forward to hear.

'Little brownie…' This time she caught it quite clearly. 'Little brownie, Miss Diana's husband's dead.'

And then again, in gentle incantation: 'Little brownie, Miss Diana's husband's dead.'

Diana stood up. She had triumphed. Bernard would never inherit now. She was safe at last, need no longer fear poisoning or drowning, or any other form of unnatural death. She wondered what Elizabeth would say, and had a sudden urge to be present when the news was broken, as though it was Elizabeth rather than she who had been bereaved. She took a step forward and gave a little cry of astonishment as something suddenly, sharply stung her arm.

It was a bee. But bees had never stung her. Angrily Diana brushed it aside. Bees only stung you if you were frightened. The creature was on the ground, and to show she was not frightened Diana stamped it underfoot. At once she felt a prick on her neck and another on her shoulders. She flailed her arms about. The bees were buzzing in a loud, angry way, such as she had never heard before. Simultaneously, two stung her face.

The sting on her arm was swelling with alarming rapidity. She might have an allergy. She must get back to the house and put something on, or perhaps phone Dr Grainger. Awkwardly she turned to run.

But the stings on her face were also swelling. It was already getting difficult to see. And behind her that sinister buzzing was getting louder. Above it, she heard Harry Parry's shout of warning: 'The bees, Miss Diana! Run!'

Blindly she blundered forward, but her arms were brown with bees. She put her hands to her face, but the bees crawled underneath them. She dared not open her mouth to scream. She heard Harry calling for help, heard Elizabeth come running but already she had sunk to her knees, her body tormented with thousands of red-hot pincers, the merciless stings of the bees.

'Merciful God!' Her mother's voice was frantic. 'She's dying. She's turning blue. For God's sake get Dr Grainger quickly. The bees have stung her to death.'

Whoever her mother was talking to must have raised some objection. Elizabeth's shrill voice rose. 'No, no, of course he's in.' And now her mother's hands were on her swollen, burning flesh in a vain attempt to give comfort. 'He telephoned not half an hour ago. He wanted my daughter to know that the tests were negative.' There was a buzzing note of bees in Diana's ears. It was becoming difficult to breathe but before she lost consciousness she heard her mother toying: 'There was no trace of arsenic in her or in her food.'

DAVY JONES'S TALE

THE GUIDING LIGHT, a barquentine of three hundred tons homeward bound from America, was shipwrecked off the coast of Pembrokeshire one hundred years ago, with the loss of all hands—for the lone survivor who was washed ashore next morning was raving and did not live more than a few weeks.

It is necessary that you should know this because without it nothing in this tale makes sense. There are those who say—though I am not of them—that it makes no sense even with it, but of that you must be the judge.

***

I was born David Matthew Jones in Porthfynnon, a village on the north coast of Pembrokeshire, in April 1945. My father, David Jones, had gone down with his ship when she was torpedoed a bare six months before. My mother used to say that the night he died he came back and stood within our cottage doorway, looking at her a long time and sadly shaking his head. But she was a woman, and fanciful. She died when I was eight.

Thereafter I was brought up by my uncle, Robert Jenkins, and his son Owen was like a brother to me, except that, two years older than I, he was tall and ruddy, whereas I am dark and slight. He could do everything in this world better than I could, except for swimming and making love. For the swimming, anyone in the village will tell you that Davy Jones is own brother to a fish. And for the love-making, I have Agnes's word on it, and that is good enough for me.

But in the time before Agnes, Owen and I were inseparable, and no sweetness in the love of woman can equal that in the companionship of men. What one did, the other did also. We fought often, and nearly always Owen beat me, but he would fight for me if need be. And as I grew older and better able to hold my own and no longer needed his protection, I fought his battles too, and he was glad of me.

But there were differences. When Owen left school he joined his father in his fishing-boat, but when I left school the master sent for me.

'Davy,' he said, 'you are down to leave us in the summer. What are you going to do?'

'Why, Mr Lloyd,' I said, 'I'm going in the boat with my uncle and Owen.'

'So you want to be a fisherman, hey?'

I spread my hands. 'My father was a fisherman. I was born to it, as you might say.'

'An honourable calling,' Mr Lloyd said. 'St Peter was a fisherman. But that's two thousand years ago. A more sophisticated age has more sophisticated opportunities. Have you never thought of staying on at school?'

'I'm sorry, sir, but I think school's a waste of time.'

He coloured a little. 'That sounds as if we've failed you.'

'No, no,' I said, 'you got me through the school-leaving exam.'

'But, Davy, there are other exams you could take, technical qualifications you could try for.'

'Will they teach me to handle a boat better than I do?'

'Probably not. But how much longer will your boat go on putting out? Economic conditions are against you. The small boat-owner's day is done.'

'We may have unemployment in Milford Haven, but we still manage to get the catch away.'

'But can you go on doing so? The railways are threatening closure. It's like the ports in the last century—too small to develop, not big enough to be economic as they were. There's no living to be made from the sea off Pembrokeshire.'

'A man can still drown in it, though.'

Mr Lloyd thought it an odd remark, and said so, but to me it was the most natural in the world. Too many of our secluded bays are ripped by cruel currents. When the wind's in the south-west, you can hear the surf far inland. For as long as I could remember, Uncle Robert, like his father and grandfather, had gone out with the lifeboat whenever there was a ship in distress. It happens surprisingly often in our Waters.

Now Owen too had joined the lifeboat's crew.

It was thinking of this that made me speak of drowning—that and the long row of graves in the churchyard, many being of anonymous sailors washed up along the coast around Porthfynnon, but the majority belonging to the crew of *The Guiding Light*.

I told Mr Lloyd so, but he saw little relevance in the fate of a vessel lost so many years before, and concentrated in trying to get me to go on with the schooling, which I was set against. It is hard now to say why, but it had something to do with independence. I wanted to rank with the men rather than the boys; to earn my own living even if it was not a fat one; above all, to be with Uncle Robert and Owen in their boat. These last two years I had wakened night after night and lain there biting my pillow to hear them creep downstairs in the dark and make ready to be off with the tide, while I, hours later, came down to Aunt Miriam scolding over breakfast and had to be away to school. Then, one afternoon, perhaps days later, I would return to find them feasting like heroes, the catch entrained and their oilskins and sea-boots hanging once again behind the door. It is small wonder that I wanted to be done with schooling. Only old Lloyd would have tried to get me to stay.

Mind you, once or twice since I have wondered if he was maybe less of a fool than I thought him, for it is right enough that the fishing has grown very bad. Several men in Porthfynnon have laid up their boats, and I knew—none better—that the living would never be a fat one, but we had luck and we managed to make ends meet. So I was the more surprised when one day Owen, while he was taking a turn at the wheel, with me beside him and Uncle Robert catching up on sleep below, announced in a voice that seemed to me to carry unnaturally far over the quiet-breathing, waters, 'Davy, I am going away.'

'Where to, then?' I asked, stupid.

'To Cardiff. Swansea, maybe. Where there's work and wages and a man isn't always scratching for a living.' He added softly: 'For I am sick of it here.'

If he had uttered blasphemy I could not have been more shaken. To exchange our world of wind and sky and water for the hemmed-in noisiness of city streets; to breathe the stench of humanity and exhaust gases rather than the gorse and seaweed on our salt-laden, gull-loud air—these were things so alien to me that I felt a shock of horror, for I had assumed that Owen felt the same.

Now he said matter-of-factly: 'You'll go on giving Dad a hand with the boat. It's a better living for two and she works easy. And quiet Mam when she starts fretting herself. It's not the end of the world I'm going to, and I'll come home and see you all from time to time.'

I nodded. I couldn't speak—it was as if Owen were dying. His next words made it worse: 'Oh, and Davy, take my place in the lifeboat—Dad'll like to have you along.'

Uncle Robert was coxswain now, and the *Margaret Freeling* was only less dear to him than his own boat. Although it was the motor mechanic's job to keep her at all times ready for launching, Uncle Robert went to check over her every week, and very often Owen or I went with him. I knew the lifeboat-station very well.

Although she is the Porthfynnon lifeboat, the *Margaret Freeling*'s launching station is more than a mile away, in a sheltered, westward-facing rocky inlet which is a natural harbour, with the lifeboat shed cliff-high and reached by a causeway, and the slipway a steep one-in-five gradient to the sea. There are not so many lifeboat-stations like Porthfynnon, and ours is less than a hundred years old, for the boat used to put out from Porthfynnon harbour itself until they discovered its limitations. But that was after the disaster of *The Guiding Light*.

I have mentioned *The Guiding Light* several times already, so I had best take time to explain what is so special for Porthfynnon about this disaster, and why it has such a bearing on my tale.

Off the Pembrokeshire coast are many isolated rocks and islands that have broken away from the land. Those which rise above the tide are now the haunt of breeding seabirds: eligugs—which is what we call guillemots—razorbills, shearwaters and puffins, and thousands upon thousands of gulls. But not all these rocks thrust up above the water; many are submerged even at low tide, yet near enough the surface to rip the plates of a ship's keel and hole her, and large enough to catch and hold her fast.

The Guiding Light was bound for Tenby—in 1870 Tenby was still an ocean-going port—but she was unlucky enough to run into an almighty storm, which blew her northwards and wrecked her on the Abbot and his Monks. This line of wicked rocks is less than a mile offshore just south of Porthfynnon. The Abbot is never quite submerged even at the highest tide, but his Monks are invisible even at neap tides; and in trying to avoid the Abbot, many a vessel has shipwrecked on his Monks. And *The Guiding Light*, though stoutly built, was a wooden vessel. In no time her planking was stove in, while great seas washed over her, sweeping her decks and pounding her to pieces. Within an hour her foremast had gone, snapped in two.

Fortunately it was still light and many people saw her. They raised the alarm and the lifeboat was pushed out. And then the horrid truth became apparent: the very winds and seas that had driven *The Guiding Light* on to the Monks and were battering her to pieces prevented the lifeboat from getting beyond the harbour mouth. And when she did so, by a superhuman effort, the men pulling at their oars until their sinews seemed about to break, the seas were so high that the coxswain, who was Uncle Robert's grandfather, my great-grandfather, realised he could never get near *The Guiding Light*. He ordered the lifeboat to put back to harbour. They would try again at first light. There were some who said he had given up too quickly, but it is not easy to see what else he could have done. He would only have added his crew to the bodies in the churchyard. Nevertheless, in Porthfynnon the argument about it sometimes still goes on.

I have heard Uncle Robert say that he remembers his grandfather explaining—he was everlastingly explaining—that at the time he thought the wreck would last the night. But for the next two hours the storm increased in violence, which would surely have put an end to the lifeboat. In the screaming wind, the rain and the darkness, *The Guiding Light* broke up.

No one will ever know exactly what happened. With the first grey light it was apparent she was no longer there. Only planks of timber showed dark for a moment on the sea's heaving surface. And then the bodies began to come in. The wind had veered, and though strong, it was no longer at gale force; it was driving straight on to the land, and as the tide came in inert human figures were visible, rolling over and over in the surf. The sea brought twenty of them ashore and left them at high-water in a bay that we call the Bay of Seals, because in spring the Atlantic Grey Seals use it as a nursery. Now it was a mortuary. Many of the bodies were mutilated by the rocks. One of them was a woman. She had a young child in her arms. Her eyes were still open as if in grief or horror, and nothing the village women could do would get them closed. She was thought to be the captain's wife, but no one knew for certain; in those days passenger lists were not kept. She was buried with the rest in a plain deal coffin in our little churchyard, which is sheltered and flower-bright and out of the sound of the sea.

One man, when they found him, was still breathing, though he lay unconscious for days, and when he recovered his wits were wanting, so he could give no one any help. Since he was not violent and no one came forward to claim him, he stayed in the village and two weaving women looked after him. From the orders he sometimes shouted, making passers-by start like jumping-jacks, he was thought to have been the first or second mate. But he did not long survive his companions. In the short days around Christmas he died. With him went the last trace of *The Guiding Light*, and the tragedy would soon have been forgotten had it not been for the re-siting of the lifeboat shed.

Men from London came down and held an enquiry, and looked at all the coast around, and made recommendations and went back to London, and in due course their decision was announced. Soon after the new lifeboat-station was begun a mile to the north of Porthfynnon, with a slipway that carries it beyond the line of the surf. Uncle Robert used to say it was a fine position and the wreck of *The Guiding Light* had done some good at least, but Aunt Miriam would shake her head and murmur that the poor souls who perished in her might not think so. Uncle Robert pretended not to hear.

They took Owen's going very well after the first announcement, but the cottage was not the same. Aunt Miriam was for ever watching for the postman, although Owen's letters were infrequent and never said much. He found a job in the docks in Cardiff, and came home once or twice, but when he did he was like a stranger. He talked of staying away indefinitely. Maybe it was this that lulled me, for I came to regard his absence as permanent. The boat was Uncle Robert's and mine, and I conveniently forgot about Owen, just as I forgot it was his place I had in the lifeboat's crew. So it fairly knocked me silly when, after three years, a letter came from him to say he was returning home for good and bringing with him the girl who would shortly be his bride. The night they were due, I drove into Haverfordwest to meet them and that is when I first saw Agnes. But that is another part of my tale.

***

I cannot say that Agnes was beautiful. If she had been, I should have been afraid of her and then none of this might have come about. It was sheeting with rain in Haverfordwest, and as I saw Owen come past the ticket-collector I thought of nothing but how good it was to see him again. I felt his hand in mine, strong and warm and vital, and heard the ring of his voice, and then he turned to the girl who stood silently beside him, and said, 'Agnes, this is my cousin, Davy Jones.'

I am not tall, so I did not have to look down on her; instead, her eyes were on a level with mine—grey eyes I thought them then, but later I learned better: Agnes's eyes were as many-hued and changing as the sea. Her voice too was low and murmuring, like waves that barely break on a summer's day. For the rest, I had an impression of rain glistening on a plastic mac and headscarf and running like tears down a round cheek.

Later, when I had a chance to see her in the cottage, I saw that everything about Agnes was round and full: her waist was too small, or her breasts and hips were too generous; her neck was too short, but the throat had the sweet firm whiteness of a nut. There are those who would have called her dumpy, and I cannot say that they would have been wrong; but even her detractors must have fallen silent at sight of the hair upon her head. Never have I seen such hair on a woman: she wore it piled high like a golden crown. When she let it down, as I discovered later, it rippled over her arms and shoulders as if she had undone a bale of silk.

I watched her all the time that first evening as though my life depended on it, and had not a word to say. I heard Owen's voice rise and fall as he talked about his plans and about the wedding, which was to be in Porthfynnon since Agnes was without near relatives, and for afterwards he would do up the old Davies cottage which was standing empty, and—'Davy, you'll be my best man?' I did not hear him, being too much occupied with looking at Agnes, and he had to say it again. I said yes without thinking, and there was much joking and laughter, and when I went to bed—early so as to be tactful—it seemed as if Agnes's laugh was still re-echoing in my head.

Never having been in love before, I was slow to recognise the symptoms, but next day and all the day after there was a restlessness in my blood like the urge to wander, except that I was centred on Agnes, and all journeys from the cottage, even so short a one as to the harbour, were bearable only because they would end in the joy of coming back to her.

Perhaps I use this simile of the wanderlust because I became aware after a few days that it was expected of me that I should go away. Owen had spent his years in the wilderness and was come home with a fine bride as his portion: now it was the turn of Davy, untried, unwedded, to leave home and be out of Owen's way. Not that anything was said, but when Owen talked about Cardiff, I felt Aunt Miriam looking at me; when we returned from a fishing trip and the proceeds were divided, it was as though Uncle Robert wanted still to divide by two and not by three. Only Owen himself showed no signs of resentment.

'Why did you come back?' I said to him one day.

His reply shook me. 'Because Agnes wanted it. She'd no love for the city and it was her suggestion we should come here. For myself, I liked it well enough away.'

My sister-in-law-to-be was good at the weaving, and she had some education and a brain. It was her intention to start up a weaving community in Porthfynnon, where the skill had long languished, like those throughout Wales which now cater to the tourist trade. With that and the fishing she and Owen would make a living. Some day, Owen mused, he might even have his own boat. Meanwhile the wedding was only two weeks off, the ring already bought and entrusted to my safe-keeping, and still I lacked the courage to make myself up and go.

I remember nothing at all of that wedding except that my new shoes were too tight, and I stood beside Owen shifting from one foot to the other as though I were the one impatient for the bride to arrive. When she did, I could not look at her, and strangely, I had the feeling that she could not look at me. But I did not drop the ring. The minister blessed it and Owen put it on his bride's finger, and I cursed it because it would lie for ever between my love and me.

***

After they returned from honeymoon, they moved into the old Davies cottage at the far end of the village and I saw little of Agnes—I supposed she was setting the cottage to rights. Aunt Miriam was often there keeping an eye on things—though she did not warm to Agnes—but Uncle Robert and I would not go uninvited. Owen often said, 'You must come and see us, Davy.' 'When Agnes is ready,' I would reply.

It was as though she were avoiding me. Often I would return from the fishing, clumping my way sea-booted up the street, in time to see Agnes slip out of our cottage and, not even pausing to turn and wave, set off almost at a run. And Aunt Miriam would say with grudging approval when questioned: 'Yes, Agnes was here. She saw you coming and went home to get the kettle on for Owen. She thinks the world of him.'

For Owen's sake I was glad, but Aunt Miriam's next words made me angry. 'And now I suppose it'll be your turn to go gallivanting off to Cardiff and bringing some street girl back.'

'How can you say such a thing of Agnes!'

'Ah, I've got eyes in my head.'

'And a vile tongue in your mouth.'

'Quick you are to defend her! Steer clear of her sort, Davy, when it comes time for you to go away.'

'I am not thinking of going away,' I told her.

'Oh.' She hid her disappointment. 'Well, you know what you're about, I dare say.'

I did not tell her that I had no idea, that I lived out each day and fell asleep at the end of it wondering what point there was in my life. Twice I almost went to the minister, but I could not bring myself to tell him I desired my cousin's wife. 'Whosoever looketh upon a woman to lust after her, that same hath committed adultery with her in his heart.' How often had I heard it thundered forth on Sunday. In Porthfynnon, despite all you see on the television; we took the Ten Commandments seriously.

When we were not at sea, with the three of us—Uncle Robert, myself and Owen—so close in the small boat that we could all but hear each other's thoughts, except that Owen could never have heard mine or he would have used his superior strength to throw me overboard, I took to going for long walks. Day after day I tramped along the cliff paths, past headlands blue with squill and pink with thrift; skirting clumps of sea-campion, heads bowed before the lightest breeze yet never breaking in a high wind, which lay among the rocks like drifts of springtime snow.

One day, when the air was warm with promise of summer and the short, flowered turf alive with bees, I walked rather farther than I meant to, and came to the Bay of Seals. I was walking into the wind, and on the close grass my footsteps were silent. I had an excellent view of the nursery: grey cows, almost indistinguishable until they moved from the smooth rocks on which they were lying; the white, brown-spotted baby seals with their round, wide-open, human-seeming eyes; and out to sea, the old bulls standing sentinel, their whiskered noses raised suspiciously.

I stood there for some time, listening to the grunting, snorting and barking, not very different from nurseries everywhere, until all at once the whole colony began slithering seawards, as though the rocks themselves were on the move. In a few seconds the Bay of Seals was empty, except for a crowd of round dark heads bobbing reproachfully offshore. I looked round to see what had startled them, and saw Agnes coming towards me over the turf.

Impulsively I held out my hands, and as impulsively she took them. For a moment we had no need of words. Nevertheless, I said, still holding her hands and guessing already at her answer: 'Agnes, what brings you here?'

'I needed air,' she said, as though Porthfynnon were a vacuum. 'And also'—she lowered her eyes—'I saw you come this way.'

My blood leapt but my brain stayed stagnant. 'I thought you were avoiding me.'

'I am. I have been.' She was laughing, crying. 'Oh Davy, are you never going to go away?'

It was as though the sun went in. 'Do you want me to?' I asked, still stupid.

'Don't you understand?' She broke from me. 'Davy, I am Owen's wife and it is you I should have married, and now it is all too late. I have made my bed and must lie on it. But if there is to be any peace for me in Owen's arms, it can only be when you are absent. Davy, for my sake— because I love you and I should not—I am asking you to go away.'

'Agnes—' I said. And tried again: 'Agnes—' And the words stuck in my throat.

She had turned from me, her shoulders shaking. When I touched her, she flinched as though my hand were red-hot iron. I drew her to me, but she kept her head down and I loosened her hair and rocked her as if she were a child against me, murmuring more to myself than to her that I had not known, had never known, had never even suspected…

'Don't!' she cried. 'You're making it worse. I didn't know either. You were so aloof. You looked at me as if I wasn't there. And now night after night you torture me because it's you I respond to when Owen takes me in his arms.'

'Is Owen no good, then?'

'I did not say that. But you would be better. I *know.*' She looked up at me, her face still tear-stained. 'There! Now I've shocked you—I can tell. I'm not the prim virgin you in Porthfynnon imagine. I told Owen—I don't cheat—and he was still ready to marry me, which is more than any of the others would have done.'

'Was that why you wanted to leave Cardiff—because of your past?' I said, thinking Aunt Miriam's suspicions were well justified.

'My past!' She laughed bitterly, then pulled free and said as if reciting a lesson: 'I am Mrs Owen Jenkins, a respectable village matron, and that is how I intend to stay. And then, before I was even wedded, the Devil sent you to tempt me. Is there to be no peace, no respite, from the everlasting temptations of the flesh?'

'Only by yielding to them,' I said, and it was not myself speaking. The Devil had entered into me too. I saw only the hunger in her eyes and I wanted her eyes to devour me, her body to enfold me, wanted to give myself to her because I was her master, as a strong swimmer gives himself to the sea.

The sun and the seals were our witness, and afterwards, as I lay face downwards in the grass, I thought how it was in this same Bay of Seals, face downwards, with the woman and child beside him, that they had found the captain of *The Guiding Light.* Through all my childhood I had heard that story: how he was a thickset, black-bearded man, in a dark blue coat with brass buttons that the sea had not yet tarnished, and with one blue eye, the other having been torn out by the rocks. And now it was my turn to lie prone in the Bay of Seals with a woman beside me, and at the thought a great shudder ran through me, so that Agnes asked 'What is it?' But she had never heard the tale, so I said it was the tail-end of ecstasy and rolled over on my back while her fingers traced patterns on my face, and for vanity I asked her, 'Am I better than Owen?' And at once I knew it was a mistake.

Her fingers slid off my face and she sat up slowly, gathering up her hair which lay over her shoulders like bright weed. 'Much, much better,' she said. 'And now, Davy, you have shown me that I am a weak and worthless woman, and for my sake you must go away.'

And because I am a godfearing man and knew that I had sinned in taking my cousin's wife, and because I knew there was no future for me with Agnes so long as Owen was alive, I went like Owen before me to Cardiff, and it was six months before Porthfynnon saw me again.

***

When I came back on a week's holiday it was October. Owen and Agnes came to supper the night that I arrived, and I noticed how Agnes's smooth face looked fuller under her piled-up hair. There was a new contentment about her and it maddened me, for I had expected to find her as lean and hungry-looking as Aunt Miriam said I was. Instead I was forced to recognise that 'Out of sight, out of mind' was as true as 'Absence makes the heart grow fonder', only the first was true of Agnes and the second, despite every distraction, even physical exhaustion, had become increasingly true of me.

Agnes was busy with the weaving, but I did not go to watch her at her loom because I did not trust myself to see unmoved those white hands moving the bright wools of the tapestry patterns, and her helpers and pupils might have observant eyes. So I sat and talked to Aunt Miriam, who was now full of praise for Agnes, went out a couple of times with Owen and Uncle Robert in the boat, and spent the rest of the time tramping the familiar cliff paths. I was on the cliffs south of Porthfynnon the day of the great storm.

The weather had been working up to something all week. There was an unnatural stillness in the air, broken on Thursday by little tremors of wind so faint they were barely discernible. By Friday morning it was blowing a good gale. None of the fishing-boats went out that day. Grey clouds scudded low over the sea, which heaved itself into long, powerful, sluggish-looking waves that surged ceaselessly shorewards and shattered against the cliffs in a tempest of thunder and spray.

By dinner-time the wind had reached Force 8 and was still rising. Aunt Miriam said I was crazy to go out, but something in me responded to the thrill of the storm and I went despite her. Two miles south of Porthfynnon, the grey clouds came down in rain. The rain was like big needles. I put my head down and turned for home when, above the scream of the wind and the drumming of the rain on my oilskins, I heard a tremendous crash. Instinctively I looked seawards. At first all was rain and spray in an early dusk, but then I made out the great swirl of white water about the Abbot, and at the edge of it a dark but unmistakable shape.

There was a ship on the Monks—a fair-sized vessel. More than that I could not make out, for she had no lights, fired no distress flares, and gave no sign of life. Fortunately for me, two other men glimpsed her also in the driving rain and the murk, and so they testified at the enquiry, or it would have gone badly for me. One of them was a van driver on the road from Fishguard to Porthfynnon; the other was the coastguard in his look-out, which is why I heard the double boom of the maroons to call out the lifeboat while I was still running and stumbling back to give the alarm. I was nearer to the lifeboat-station than to the village. Immediately I turned about, thinking I might help or at least watch the launching, with Uncle Robert and Owen among the crew.

When I reached the lifeboat-station, the first-comers were just arriving. Jack Davies, the motor-mechanic, was already in his oilskins and checking engines that he knew to be perfect. Frank Evans, the bowman, was pulling his kapok lifejacket over his head. At that moment a car stopped with a jerk and Uncle Robert and Owen fell out, followed by Mike Edwards, the second coxswain. When he saw me, Uncle Robert's face lit up.

'Davy! We're a hand short—you can come with us. Take Bob Hunter's oilskins there on that peg. He's had to go into Haverfordwest, and with weather like this I'd sooner have my full crew aboard. There'll be work for all of us tonight.'

In less time than it takes to tell, we had manned the lifeboat: eight yellow-oilskinned figures with life-jackets pulled over our heads. Someone pushed out the chocks and we held on tightly as the *Margaret Freeling* hurtled down her rollered slipway, gathering speed like a fairground switchback, until she hit the water in a shower of spray. Her engines came to life at once and sent her heading towards the storm and the open water outside the shelter of the bay.

Never have I seen a sea like it. The waves seemed housetop high, great sliding walls of water up which we climbed and climbed. Then for a few seconds the gale screamed and whistled across us, drenching everything in icy spray, before the boat plunged vertically as if down a lift-shaft and the steep, ever-steeper climb began again. Sometimes the boat leaned so far back on her beam ends it seemed she must capsize. Sometimes, before the top of the climb was reached, the wave itself toppled and broke. Cascades like Niagara thundered vertically down upon the *Margaret Freeling*, as though they meant to sink her there and then.

But our lifeboat was a stoutly built vessel, for all she was only 42 feet long. The *Margaret Freeling's* hull was buoyant as the English oak and Canadian pine she was made of; she was self-righting even if she did capsize. And a stouter-hearted crew never sailed her: I looked round at the faces grim under their sou-westers. Second coxswain Mike Edwards was at the wheel; I could see him peering ahead through his clear-screens while Uncle Robert checked the position of the wreck. Jack Davies and his brother Bryn, the motor-mechanics, were listening to their diesels, despite the scream of the wind and the thunder of the sea. Frank Evans, the bowman, never took his eyes from Uncle Robert's face, as though to anticipate every command relating to anchor, winch or line-throwing pistol. And Owen and I and Emrys Rees, the three deck-hands, leaned forward, sheltering as best we could.

At a command from Uncle Robert our searchlight shone out over the water, illumining the smooth cruel side of a great wave. Then, as we breasted it, I saw away to starboard a boiling and eddying of water in all directions, and a sharp black pinnacle of rock. I knew then that we had reached the Abbot and his Monks, and there in the midst of them loomed the dark mass of the wreck.

I noticed once again that there were no lights on board her.

Presumably her electricity had failed. Yet even so, there should have been handlamps to signal—if there was anyone left alive on board. But that was nonsense. A ship that size must carry a crew of twenty or thirty. They would not all have taken to the boats. It would be madness in such weather. Better to stay aboard and take their chance. When our signals remained unanswered, Uncle Robert tried the loud-hailer, but we were not near enough for his voice to carry, for still no answer came.

'No sense trying to get a line aboard her if there's no one to secure it,' Frank Evans said brusquely. He looked again at that wild water and added, 'Even if we could.'

It was in all our minds that the situation was impossible; we could do nothing except stand by and wait for the seas to abate and the dawn to dispel the darkness, but we said none of this aloud. It was in our minds also that once before the Porthfynnon lifeboat had had to abandon a wreck, and I know it was most of all in Uncle Robert's. He had his grandfather's dishonour to wipe out.

'We'll go round to windward of her and drop down on our anchor,' he ordered quietly. 'That should bring us under her bows.'

The manoeuvre sounded simple, but we knew as well as he did that it was both dangerous and difficult. To drop down on the anchor means to approach from the windward side, allowing the lifeboat to drift towards its objective on a cable attached to the dropped anchor and controlled by the boatswain at the winch. Frank Evans was already taking up position in the bows as the *Margaret Freeling* turned into the wind to make a sweep that would bring her round to windward of this lampless, silent vessel. Suddenly disaster struck.

We had only just begun scaling one of those walls of water when Frank Evans shouted. There was a note in his voice I had never heard before. We were in the trough of the wave and at an angle, and already the succeeding wave, a monster overtopping it, was beginning to curl and break. We were all on our feet, clinging to anything within reach, as the double wave crashed down upon us and the deck tilted sharply. I glimpsed Frank Evans, his mouth still open, step back and disappear as the sea swept his words away, and then I had no handhold, no deck beneath me, no air in my lungs, my chest was bursting, and for an instant I caught sight of the lifeboat's hull, white-painted below the waterline, and knew that we had capsized.

In that same instant I also filled my lungs, and with oxygen came calmness. It was useless to struggle in such a sea. All I could do was to give myself as utterly as I had once done to Agnes, as I had done a thousand times to this element, as—at the end when there is no more hope in him—a man may give himself to death.

The great surges bore me up. I snatched air when I could, and saw with horror that the waves were carrying me straight on to the Monks. I prayed then that I might drown before being dashed to pieces. I closed my eyes and tried to will myself to die. And at that moment one of the lesser waves picked me up quite gently and tossed me sprawling, spewing, gasping, on to the deck of the vessel whose crew we had come to save.

I clung, too shaken to realise it was wood I was clinging to, until coherent thought returned. I got to my knees. I was bruised, but nothing seemed broken, and for the moment I was in comparative safety on the wreck. At that moment a tremendous sea broke over her stern, I felt her shudder through all her length, heard a creaking and groaning, and realised how precarious my safety was.

I also realised that the decks were slippery with seaweed, that green hairlike wrack that is usually found on rocks. My hands touched wood where I should have expected metal. There was something very odd about this ship. I shouted, but there was no answer. Indeed, I scarcely heard my own voice. Gingerly I began to move forward and my feet tangled in knotted rope. I fell heavily and the rope was all about me, like rigging stretching away towards the listing side of the ship. Like the deck, it was weed-encrusted. I jerked sharply, and as a result of my puny efforts the once-stout manila broke. Rottenness and decay were everywhere. I was beginning to be frightened by now, not of death, not of drowning or of being dashed to pieces, but of something I could not name. The planking of the deck was so rotten that when I stamped a long sliver broke. Yet the seas breaking over the vessel had less effect than I did. I began to wish that another wave would sweep me off.

But curiosity and self-preservation both prompted me to enter a doorway which I now noticed on my right. Here at least I should be out of the wind and spray, for a steep wooden stair led downwards to the still intact forequarters of the ship. There was a faint light at the bottom of the stairway; it shuddered with every blow upon the hull, and I saw that the light came from an old-fashioned storm-lantern hung on a bracket. So the vessel had some crew after all.

The light showed me another doorway, through which a stronger light glowed. I knocked; then, thinking this might pass for one of the storm's noises, I called out: 'Is anybody there?'

Silence.

I could see that the cabin was furnished. Reassured, I stepped boldly inside—and stopped short, transfixed by the tableau before me. I see it in my mind's eye yet.

At the big table facing me a man was sitting, his head buried in his folded arms. He was black-haired and wore dark clothing. As my shadow fell across the lantern-light, he wonderingly raised his head. He had a square-cut black beard in a style no longer in fashion, and there were brass buttons on his double-breasted coat. One bright blue eye glared at me, the other was an empty socket. His face was nothing but a skull.

'Who are you?' His voice was deep and resonant.

I felt myself sweat with fear.

'Davy Jones from the *Margaret Freeling*, sir—the lifeboat—'

'The lifeboat, eh? One hundred years too late.'

Even before he said it, I knew him: the captain of *The Guiding Light*. Had I not heard of him through all my childhood, with his one blue eye, his square-cut black beard, and his coat whose brass buttons the sea had not yet tarnished? And now he was before me in his cabin, on board a ship which a century ago had been smashed to pieces, and he himself buried in our churchyard, out of the sound of the sea. But supposing that I was as dead as he was and that in death all men are equal, I answered him boldly: 'It's not rescue I'm bringing you, Captain. I'm the sole survivor. The *Margaret Freeling* capsized not half an hour ago.'

'The sole survivor,' he said. 'You hear that, Nancy? I promised you this when that lifeboat put back into port and abandoned us a hundred years ago.'

It was then that I noticed the woman sitting on the sofa under the porthole. She had her back to me, and her hair flowed down over her shoulders like Agnes's. Gold it was too, but there was a greenness about it as though it were tarnished with weed. When she turned her head, I saw that her eyes were wide and staring, but her face too was a skull.

'What's the use?' she said. 'Capsized or cowardly, so far as we're concerned it's all one. There's no help coming. We should have gone with the others.'

I asked the captain: 'Where are your crew?'

'They've abandoned ship,' he said. 'When the lifeboat turned back the first mate gave the order. They must all be drowned by now.'

'So there are only you two?'

'Three,' he corrected me.

I saw then that the woman had a child, in her arms.

'We shall wait for the end in this cabin,' he went on firmly, 'as we waited for it once before—the three of us and John Stallworthy, the second mate. He survived, you remember. You can have Stallworthy's place.'

He pointed to a seat at the table opposite the woman. She had bent her head to the child and her hair mercifully hid her face. I could not get out of my mind those staring eyes that the women of Porthfynnon had been unable to close.

The ship shuddered as another wave struck her. Seeing me flinch, the captain said grimly, 'We shan't have long to wait.'

'What happened?' I asked.

'What is happening now. The waves smashed her to pieces. After the lifeboat put back, we knew there was no more hope. We sat and listened to her breaking up. Nancy here was praying—' And above the child's head, I saw the woman's lips move.

'She might as well have saved her breath,' the captain went on. 'It was not God's will we died, but man's. When the coxswain of the lifeboat put back to port, he signed our death warrant.'

I said, 'He had to think of his own crew.'

'Yes, he saved his own skin and left Nancy and Hannah to perish.'

'He didn't know there was a woman and child on board.'

'Why so quick to defend him?'

'He was my great-grandfather,' I said.

The captain's one blue eye was fixed unwinkingly upon me. He went on: 'I said that I didn't pray, but I prayed that I might have vengeance on that lifeboat, if I had to wait a hundred years. And a hundred years I have waited. After this I can rest.'

I should have felt sorry for him if I had not thought of Uncle

Robert and Owen, and Frank Evans falling backwards, and the rest of the lifeboat's crew.

'If you're responsible for what happened to the lifeboat,' I said, 'may you burn in Hell for ever.'

His blue eye glared at me. 'Shut your mouth! You're going to live to tell the tale.'

'What do you mean?' I asked, for I still believed I was a ghost, as they were.

'When she breaks up,' he said, 'you're going to get ashore. John Stallworthy did and you're in Stallworthy's place. Besides, it's fitting: one man from *The Guiding Light* and one from the lifeboat. 'An eye for an eye'—isn't that how the Good Book has it?'

'Perhaps, but there is nothing good about this.'

'Well said, man. There is nothing good about drowning, nor about knowing that you're going to drown. Soon after the lifeboat turned back the main and mizzen masts went the way of the foremast, and shortly afterwards she broke her back. But this forequarter still held—she was stoutly built—and still the seas swept over us. Then there was a fearful crash and the storm-lantern went out. We could hear the water and soon we could feel it—it came pouring down that stairway and swirled about our knees. I took Nancy in my arms, and Hannah. We stayed on our feet as long as we could. Suddenly there were waves around us. I felt the wind. A balk of timber struck us. My grip relaxed, and after that they were gone.'

There was so much anguish in his voice that I shuddered in sympathy, but I hardened my heart and said:

'Captain—I don't know your name, but that does not matter—you have been dead a hundred years, but tonight you have risen from the churchyard where you were given Christian burial, and because of you seven men are newly dead. Seven men who never harmed you, whose only connection with you is that they are the crew of the present lifeboat. Do you intend to rise again in another hundred years and take fresh vengeance?'

'Not if all goes as it should tonight.'

'And if it doesn't?'

'If it doesn't, if any but you survive, I shall rise again down all the centuries so long as time shall endure.'

'Amen to that,' the woman said quietly, and turned her skull face towards me as she spoke. 'For the sake of my child, my husband, I have risen from the dead for vengeance. If it is not complete, I shall rise from the dead again.'

The child in her arms stirred, lifted her head, and I cried 'No!' with a loud voice because I could not bear to see those empty eye-sockets, those milk teeth… And at that moment the light went out.

There was a fearful crash and I could hear the sound of water. A moment later I felt it around my legs. The wind was on my face, the water was already waist-high. My feet went from under me and I was swimming in the open sea.

***

The gale was blowing itself out. I was aware of that even while I fought to keep my head above water. The sea heaved menacingly, but the waves were no longer house-high. Dawn was breaking, and I could hear the thunder of surf all along the coastline as the wind piled the long grey waves against the land. I gave myself to the sea and the sea took me upon her bosom and somehow I too was borne towards the shore. There was no sign of the wreck. The Abbot and his Monks were a swirling mass of white water, but it was empty. I saw no living thing except a cormorant.

It was while I was in this state of exhaustion, almost stupor, knowing that I could never keep afloat long enough to reach the land yet not greatly caring, that I heard the last sound I ever expected to hear. Across the waste of the waters, carried by the wind, long-drawn-out but unmistakable, came the sound of a human cry.

I trod water, struggling to look around me. To my right I made out a dark object among the waves. With the last of my strength I swam towards it. It was a piece of driftwood and clinging to it was a yellow-oilskinned figure with a lifejacket. As I too caught hold of the wood he raised his head for a moment. It was Owen.

I do not know how he had survived, but then I do not know how I survived either. Owen was pretty far gone, but already the sea seemed less hostile because there were two of us, and the land was coming nearer all the time. I could make out the indentations of the coastline, and I knew that if we could only be swept ashore in some sheltered bay there was a chance we might escape being dashed to pieces, and two at least of the crew of the *Margaret Freeling* would live to tell the tale.

Two of us! And one small piece of driftwood. And with that I heard again the captain's voice: 'If any but you survive, I shall rise again down all the centuries, so long as time shall endure.' Other lifeboats from Porthfynnon would be in peril, called out to phantom wrecks. Other women and children would be widowed, orphaned. And the woman's voice said in my ear: 'I have risen from the dead for vengeance. If it is not complete, I shall rise from the dead again.'

I looked at Owen. They had promised me I should be the sole survivor, and from the look of him that might well be so. Only an exceptional physique could have endured as long as he had, but it was obvious he could take very little more. With each lurching wave I expected to see his grip slacken, yet each time he managed to hang on. I thought of the captain of *The Guiding Light* and his threat, and I began to pray that Owen, my cousin whom I loved as a brother, might never come safe to shore; Owen who had married Agnes, my Agnes, who would never look at me so long as Owen was alive.

I do not know whether I unbalanced him or whether a wave did it for me, but suddenly one hand-hold had gone. He was kept afloat now only by the piece of driftwood under one armpit. I leaned over and he thought it was to grasp him—I saw the gratitude in his eyes. And then I pushed him in the chest and he went backwards all in one piece, as though he were stiff already, and he opened his eyes and smiled past me, not seeing me, and I heard him say 'Agnes'. Thereafter the sea filled his mouth.

So I came slowly to land, the sole survivor, not worried overmuch because it was promised me I should be, and because I should bring happiness to Agnes once her first sorrow was over, and Agnes was the only thing in the world for me. So, still clinging to my driftwood that had been Owen's, as some day I should cling to Owen's wife, I was washed up at last, quite gently, among the smooth grey boulders and the sand in the Bay of Seals.

***

That day was a day of mourning in Porthfynnon, but I knew none of it until the late afternoon, when I rose from my bed in the unaccustomedly silent house to which they had taken me and came stumbling down the stairs. There was a strange woman in Aunt Miriam's kitchen, a Mrs Bishop, who cried out at sight of me.

'Ah, Davy, you shouldn't be up. The doctor said you were to stay in bed and he'd call again this evening.'

'Damn the doctor,' I said. 'Where is everyone? Where's Aunt Miriam?'

Mrs Bishop put a hand to her mouth and stared at me as if I were raving. 'She's down on the shore with the rest.'

'And Agnes—Mrs Owen?'

'She'll be down there too.'

'Right, then, Mrs Bishop. I'll join them.'

'A cup of tea at least before you go.'

'Thank you, but it's time enough I've wasted already. How long have I been here?'

'They found you at first light this morning. Oh Davy, what happened, man?'

'The lifeboat capsized.'

'But about the wreck—the wreck that never existed? Jim Rhodes, the coastguard is almost beside himself. One minute he swears he saw it, and the next says he must be mad.'

'There was a wreck, Mrs Bishop. I saw it.'

The woman said fervently, 'Praise be!' and I wondered if she would be quite so loud in her praise if I told her about *The Guiding Light*.

'I must run and tell Jim Rhodes—' she was taking off her apron— 'he's had reporters round him all day like flies round a tray of offal at midsummer. There's no trace of the wreck, see.'

'She broke up.'

Mrs Bishop was hanging on my words, no doubt thinking of what the newspapermen would tip her, but she could give as well as get.

'There's two men coming down from London,' she volunteered. 'To hold an enquiry. Oh Davy, you'll have to give evidence.'

Dazed though I was, I realised that the truth would never be believed, so I said: 'There's nothing I can tell them. The ship broke up in the night.'

'But there's no one come ashore from her.' She meant dead bodies.

'They came ashore a hundred years ago,' I said, and I passed out of the house, leaving her staring after me as if my wits had gone.

The village street was deserted save for a dog lying unsleeping on a doorstep. He lifted his muzzle and whined as I went by. I was not the master he was waiting for. I saw then that it was Emrys Rees's dog. Everywhere blinds were drawn. The general-store-cum-post-office had its shutters up. Faintly the sound of hammering could be heard: Morgan the carpenter at work on seven coffins. There should have been an eighth for me.

When I reached the cliffs, it was as though the whole village was assembled. I saw that they had towed the lifeboat in and were now unloading something in yellow oilskins on a stretcher. I looked away and saw Aunt Miriam.

She was standing with a group of other women. I went up to her and spoke. She turned round as if a ghost had touched her.

'Davy! You ought to be in bed.'

'My place is here.' I told her. 'Have they—have they come ashore?'

'Robert has. Oh Davy, his face! The rocks had battered it.' She heard my silence and said in answer: 'Owen hasn't come in yet.'

I saw that the mother of the Davies boys was weeping. Emrys Rees's young wife looked old. Michael Edwards's father and brother were wading out towards the lifeboat, as if they knew who the canvas stretcher bore.

'And Agnes?' I asked Aunt Miriam. 'Where's Agnes?'

She pointed a little way apart. 'She neither speaks nor stirs. Unnatural it is. Go to her, Davy. Perhaps for you she will.'

Agnes was standing on a slight rise and looking seaward. She was like the figurehead of a ship. I approached her from behind and put my heart in my voice to say her name—'Agnes.'

She spun round, and the hope died in her eyes. 'Davy! You sounded just like Owen.'

I found there was nothing I could say. She had resumed her seaward gazing and was a thousand light-years away.

I said. 'I'm sorry, Agnes.'

I think she inclined her head.

I went on desperately, 'Don't weep, heart's treasure. I still love you.

I'd do anything to show how much.'

'Be quiet,' she said, not turning. 'This is no time to talk of love. Oh, you will tell me I began it, that day in the Bay of Seals. But I did not know what love was then—it is Owen who has taught me, and I feel I am in some way responsible for his death. Ridiculous you will say it is, but I know better. It is I who have brought him to this.'

I put from me the thought of Owen clinging to life and a piece of driftwood.

'You're talking wildly. Come away, Agnes. Come home.'

'Not without Owen.'

'But it's getting dark.'

'The darkness in my heart is greater.'

'We cannot stay here all night.'

'*You* need not stay,' she said indifferently. For an instant she turned her face to mine, and I saw her eyes, as grey now and still as the sea in winter. And a hundred thousand times as cold.

I wanted to tell her about the captain of *The Guiding Light*, and how, by enabling him to fulfil his revenge I had laid him to rest for ever, but instead my voice said for me: 'Owen spoke your name before he died.'

She wept then, and women came and surrounded her, and Aunt Miriam led her away. I heard one of the women say, 'High time too, and her in her condition,' and another answered, 'It'll be a comfort to her, the child.'

I knew then that I should never lie again with Agnes, that Owen's child would lie for ever between her and me. The realisation rushed over me like a black cloud of unknowing, and I fell unconscious where I stood.

***

There is little more to say. They held the funeral in the village church with six coffins only, for Owen never came ashore. I stood alone in my pew, and the whole village looked at me, wondering why I should be saved. Afterwards the six coffins were buried in the churchyard, and space left against the wall for Owen who had no grave. It was a generous space—I measured it. There was room for me as well, and so I told

Aunt Miriam, who said gently, 'We'll see,' as if talking to a child or a half-wit. Everyone talked that way to me.

The men from London came down and conducted their enquiry, but I was not called to give evidence. Instead they called Jim Rhodes the coastguard, and the man who had been driving a van on the road from Fishguard to Porthfynnon. The enquiry concluded that a tragic false alarm had called the lifeboat out, but added that though the two men had been mistaken, they had been mistaken in good faith, and that anyone glimpsing the Abbot and his Monks in certain storm conditions might think he made out the outlines of a wreck.

I talk to everyone I meet about the captain of *The Guiding Light*, but they do not believe a word of it. The doctor comes cheerily to see me and says he will soon have me out and about and back at the swimming and the fishing, but he talks a long time with Aunt Miriam and looks grave as he goes away. Agnes I never see, for she does not come near me, though I catch sight of her now and then, carrying her ripening belly proudly before her as she awaits the birth of Owen's son.

But it is all as if in a dream—a dream that will end shortly, somewhere around the time of the shortest day, when, like John Stallworthy one hundred years before me, I shall slip quietly out of life.

Aunt Miriam has promised that I shall lie beside the empty grave for Owen, in the lee of the churchyard wall, and I wait calmly for Death to gather the gleanings which he so unaccountably let fall.

Only when the wind blows from the south-west do I become restless, and walk down to the shore to watch the waves come in, in case they should be bringing Owen, who was like a brother to me. More than anything in this world I want to feel his hand in mine, strong and warm and vital, to hear the ring of his voice, but though I watch and wait the tides ebb and flow and never bring him, though their surges send a fever through my blood.

I know then that for those who are of the tribe of Cain there is no peace in this world. There is no peace anywhere for me, except the peace I shall find in our sheltered flower-bright churchyard, out of the sound of the sea.

SNOWFALL

THE SNOW HAD been threatening all morning. It began in earnest after lunch. Brian Bellamy, intent on reaching Swansea before nightfall, cursed the snow under his breath. It was bad enough that business should take him to Swansea in any weather; he did not love the town. That it should take him over the Brecon Beacons in a snowstorm added insult to injury.

He had had lunch in Brecon itself and had not enjoyed it. The food had partaken of the chill of the steel-grey air. So indifferent was the meal that he regretted his decision to halt for it; he would have done better to press on regardless, as was his wont. But Brian had a young man's healthy appetite and a young man's heedlessness of risk. He was confident that the twenty miles from Brecon to Merthyr Tydfil presented no dangers he could not afford to dismiss.

His car, a 1963 Triumph Herald, was owned and regularly serviced by the firm. He was accustomed to driving her in all weathers and road conditions. She had done the run to Swansea many times. All the same, he glanced anxiously at the sky as he left Brecon behind and began the long climb uphill. The road wound between high, grass-grown foothills; there was no possibility of a view.

Just as well, Brian reflected; it would have been depressing. The sky had an opaque, leaden look. The earth was rigid and frostbound by this unexpected cold spell in early March. Sparse snow had blown bouncing across the road's smooth surface and lay in a narrow line of white against the verge. Clumps of dead bracken also acted as windbreaks and had gathered round their roots a cotton-wool covering of snow.

When the snow began it fell suddenly, like a drop curtain. One minute the road stretched ahead clear and empty. The next the world had contracted to a cube of swirling greyness in which dark flakes swarmed, becoming lighter as they fell. Already the bonnet of the car was mantled; the wintry hill grass was catching and retaining the snow. The white line along the road verge had thickened perceptibly, was blurring, the wind being too weak to make headway against the all-enveloping snow.

Brian set both windscreen-wipers going and drove doggedly on towards the top of the hill and the open plateau of the Beacons, bleak and windswept even in summer, devoid of tree or shrub, except for the scant gorse and the bracken, which made patches according to the season of spring green, emerald and russet red. In summer the Beacons had their own beauty; in autumn they were best of all; even in spring, on a late, clear, twilight evening, the slopes could be majestic under a thinning lacework of snow.

But in winter! Brian shuddered. He had driven over them in winter only twice before. Snow was something new in his experience of them; he tried not to be frightened by the murk, which had the unnerving quality of any natural phenomenon magnified to an unaccustomed size. Already the road was thinly covered. Within the next two miles he had to slow down. The wheel-tracks behind him seemed to be obliterated while he looked at them. The car was crunching its way forward through freezing, new-fallen snow.

For the first time Brian allowed that he might have been foolish in attempting to complete his journey that afternoon. The absence of any other traffic worried him. He was as alone as the man in the moon. Despite his overcoat and the car heater, he shivered. From Brecon he reckoned he had covered a bare five miles; that left a further fifteen before he reached Merthyr Tydfil. If the snow didn't stop he'd never make it tonight.

Benighted on the Brecon Beacons in a snowstorm. Uneasy thoughts crept into Brian's mind. He had read of people fatally lost in these same mountains, whose isolation made them dangerous. Perhaps he might have done better to return to Birmingham or stay in Brecon, but neither alternative had appealed to him. 'Press on regardless' had always been Brian's motto; he wondered now if it was as insouciant as it seemed.

Brian was twenty-six, well-built and healthy, kind, unimaginative and not unduly bright. He was engaged to a young woman of similar disposition, and both were saving hard to buy a house. As a sales representative who earned commission, Brian was naturally out for all the business he could get. The prospect of a big order from Swansea had lured him; if he could land it, it would be quite a financial help. But his own was not the only firm in the running; hence his decision to drive down to Swansea without delay. The man on the the spot so often got the business; and this order, Brian promised himself, was not going to be one of those that got away.

All the same, despite his promise, he began to wonder if it would be—at least as regards his arrival in person on the scene. The Triumph's wheels were beginning to spin uselessly. The laboured activity of the windscreen-wipers was failing to clear the screen. There was no sign of the snowstorm abating. It looked as if it might continue to rage all night. He would be stranded alone, miles from anywhere. He dared not allow himself to think beyond negotiating the next bend.

The next bend, however, proved unexpectedly rewarding. A signpost reared gallows-like out of the snow, which had almost obscured the names painted upon it. Brian got out, the better to peer at it. The wind swooped upon him as he did so, snow dropping on his shoulders like a cloak. He brushed the arm of the signpost and read *Brecon 6 miles*. That meant he had a further fourteen miles to go. But he was not going to make it; that was obvious. He was not even going to be able to go back. There was nothing to be done but to pull into the roadside, switch off the engine, and hope the blizzard would be over before he froze to death.

The prospect was not appealing. Brian cursed himself for his folly in having set out. He should have taken the snow warning more seriously and not told himself that meteorologists were always an alarmist lot. Then he noticed that the signpost had another arm pointing at right angles behind it. He walked round and brushed off the snow. *Pant-glas 2 miles* he read in wonder. Well, two miles was not so far. A village meant human habitation: food and shelter, a bed for the night. He got back into his car and tried to turn down the almost obliterated side road which sloped sharply downhill to the right.

The wheels spun, the engine whined and nothing happened. The Triumph did not move a single inch. The choked windscreen-wipers were becoming increasingly sluggish. Small drifts were piling up ahead of the wheels. If he was to reach Pant-glas it would not be in the Triumph. Except as shelter, she was useless now. But in a blizzard like this shelter was not lightly to be abandoned. Brian hesitated whether to stay or to go.

There was a rug in the back. With that he might keep from freezing. On the other hand, the car might be buried feet deep. And the short March day, already curtailed by the snowstorm, would shortly give place to total night. Brian glanced at his watch and was startled. It showed only a little after three. It seemed years since he had pushed aside the remains of his lukewarm lunch in Brecon and set out so confidently. He would have preferred to stay in the car, out of reach of the wind and snowflakes, to close his eyes against this world of whirling white, but if he was to reach Pant-glas on foot he could not afford to linger. Reluctantly he made up his mind: he would go.

He wrapped the rug round his shoulders as protection, but soon discarded it. It impeded his arms as he slipped and staggered and stumbled, and his fingers were soon numb from clutching it. The coldness of the atmosphere seemed to him unnatural. On all sides the projecting blades of grass had disappeared. When he turned his head, he could no longer see the Triumph behind him; when he faced into the wind he was almost blinded by snowflakes blundering like May-bugs into his face. He had to blink rapidly and constantly to save his eyes from their their bruising, while the snowflakes lay on his forehead and cheeks unmelted, so cold was the icy air upon his skin.

The landscape was assuming that level, deceptive appearance characteristic of any terrain under snow. Some of the drifts he encountered were already knee-high. He had to lift each foot in turn and put it down. His progress was as uncertain as a paralytic's; before long his thigh muscles began to ache. But there was no shelter, nowhere to stop, no resting-place; only the white level snow stretching in front and the white level snow stretching behind, with his footsteps—dark stains on a tablecloth—bleached out by the ever-more-thickly-falling snow.

'Pant-glas two miles,' Brian repeated to himself at intervals. At the end of two miles all would be well. Two miles: a half hour's walk in normal conditions; say an hour's in view of the know. An hour's walk, and he had been walking how long already? He paused to peer at his watch. It showed just after three. But it had shown that when he left the car and began foot-slogging. Had it stopped? If so, how long ago? Perhaps it had already stopped when he first looked at it. He had no idea how long he had been picking his way through the snow.

Nor had he any idea if he was still on the road to Pant-glas. Underfoot everything looked the same. The snow crunched and squeaked as his feet depressed it, but gave no indication of what might lie below. Metalled road and rough grass were no longer distinguishable. Visibility of a few yards precluded any possibility of a view. The only thing definite in this alien world was that it was getting darker and that every step became more difficult.

About this time Brian felt the first intimations of panic. Things he had read recurred unpleasantly; men lost in deserts, walking endlessly in circles; Scott and his companions perishing miserably. In vain he reminded himself that this was not the Antarctic, that human beings and their houses could not be far away. Fear pressed down like a physical weight upon his shoulders. Without intending to, he began to run. The result was only to exhaust him still further without appreciably quickening his pace. The snow stuck to his shoes; his feet were as leaden as a diver's; he was being gradually imprisoned in a plaster-cast of snow.

Intelligence had given way to instinct. He ran now as animals run, not even pausing to see if his tracks made a straight line behind him, so frantic was he to go on. He knew that ahead of him lay only exhaustion, a final collapse in the snow, this year's 'Tragedy on the Brecon Beacons' in the papers; but he was incapable of rational thought. The white silence, the relentlessness of the snowflakes, muffled all his senses except for the consciousness of fear. He did not see the figure standing by the roadside. When a voice called out to him he did not hear.

It had to call a second time before he heard it, and then he believed for a moment he saw a ghost: some old man of the mountains lying in wait for him, to lure him on until he fell to rise no more.

'Not quite the night for a stroll,' the stranger greeted him. (The words reached Brian through a mist of snow and fear.) 'What in the world are you doing running loose on these mountains? There are easier ways than this to meet your death.'

'I misjudged the weather and the distance,' Brian said lamely. 'My car got stuck in the snow. Then I saw a signpost saying there was a village called Pant-glas in this direction. I was trying to make it, but I rather think I'm lost.'

'Pant-glas is a mile further on. I've just come from there.' (Never had words sounded sweeter in Brian's ears.) 'But you don't want to be out any longer than you need be in this blizzard. Better come in to my place. I live right here.'

He gestured through the darkness and the snowflakes. 'You can't see the house; it's at the bottom of the hill. But I can promise you a bed for the night and supper if you don't despise a bachelor's humble roof.'

Brian would not have despised any roof in the circumstances. He accepted with alacrity, mixed with murmurings about inconveniencing his host.

The stranger laughed. His laughter was loud and ringing. 'It's obvious that you don't know the ways of hill folk. We help one another round here. You can't do other when there are so few of you against the mountains. And the population's thinning every year.'

Brian thought to himself that this was hardly surprising. Who would choose to live in such a wilderness? Yet the stranger had an educated accent in which the Welsh intonation was hardly perceptible. 'I suppose you farm?' he hazarded politely.

'No.' The stranger shut his mouth and said no more. After a few yards he turned at right-angles, though Brian could see no indication of a path, and pointing to a darker part of the gathering darkness, announced: 'That's my house. Down there.'

Brian peered, but saw only an outline below them. There were no lights nor any sign of life. Then he remembered that his host had said he was a bachelor. He was not expected by housekeeper or wife. A little further and he could see the house quite clearly—a solid, stone-built, two-storeyed, slate-roofed affair, wedged securely into a dip in the hillside so that one gable-end was almost against the slope.

Brian would have been glad enough to see it had it been a hovel. He glanced around while his host was opening the door. There was no lessening in the snow's determined downfall. He wondered if he would ever have made Pant-glas. He would certainly never have noticed this house tucked against the hillside, merging already into the encroaching night, in which all outlines were blurred, rounded, softened by this endless covering of white.

He looked back with appreciation at what he was forsaking, and then gasped as though he had been struck a physical blow. So far as he could see into the darkness, there were only his own tracks visible in the snow.

***

Brian would have liked to run, but there was nowhere to run to. He would have liked to call out, but there was no one to hear. The snow seemed suddenly to be falling faster. Already his tracks were filling up. By morning there would be nothing to indicate that anyone had passed there, let alone two men with the footprints of only one. No one to whom he told the tale would ever believe it. That is, if he returned to tell the tale…

Brian toyed with the idea of making a break for it, of trying to cover the intervening mile between himself and Pant-glas. But something warned him that his trackless companion would prove fleet-footed, unimpeded by the clogging snow. Besides, he was cold, bewildered, hungry and exhausted. Never had four walls and a roof appeared more welcoming. When the stranger pushed open the heavy door, and the warmth and silence and safety of the house came out to greet him, he was half convinced he was imagining the whole thing.

In the hall ahead the stranger could be heard stamping. His feet had a solid, earthy, reassuring sound. Bits of snow broke loose from his boots and scattered on the front-door mat. He called to Brian: 'Aren't you coming in?'

Brian glanced back at the blizzard swirling behind him. Already his footprints were no more than smudges in the snow. Exhaustion might have made his eyes play tricks upon him. Could he be certain any longer of what he fancied he had seen? His host called out to him more sharply to hurry. Brian stepped into the house and closed the door.

It shut behind him with the heavy shock of wood on wood; with a clatter the latch fell into place. Dimly Brian made out the outline of heavy bolts at top and bottom as he stood stamping his feet and brushing and beating his coat.

'I'll go and light the lamps,' his host excused himself. 'Bolt the door, will you, while I go and get them. No electricity here.'

The fire, banked up, glowed comfortably but did not illuminate. Then a single candle quivered forth. By its light the stranger bent over the paraffin lamp on the table. Brian seized the Opportunity to look around. He was standing in the hallway with the stairs before him. To left and right opened two iron-latched doors. The one to the right was closed, but the one on the left was open and led into what was clearly a study-cum-living-room. Bookshelves climbed one wall from floor to ceiling, loaded with books, untidy piles of manuscripts, more books. An amorphous armchair, springs sagging, occupied pride of place. The room seemed to be cluttered with such a variety of objects that Brian felt as though he had wandered into a museum, where the staff had gone on strike leaving everything unlabelled. Then the big paraffin lamp bloomed softly, and there, confronting him at eye-level, was a skull.

Brian was too startled even to cry out in terror, while the skull showed all its teeth in a macabre grin. He had been frightened enough before he entered this charnel-house, as he now termed it. Blindly he turned to run.

'I'm so sorry,' said his host, coming quietly behind and putting a hand, unexpectedly heavy, on his shoulder. 'Did William frighten you?'

Brian looked at him, speechless.

'Naughty, naughty.' His host held up a reproving finger, not at him, but at the skull, which, perched on a bookshelf, appeared to be listening to him unmoved.

Brian looked round the room in search of the rest of headless William, but if there, it was not visible. He probably keeps the skeleton in a cupboard, Brian thought hysterically; in other circumstances he would have been pleased with this example of his wit.

'There's no need to be alarmed,' his host said kindly. 'William is at least one hundred years old. He was once the property of a Central African witch-doctor. He won't do you any harm.'

'Why have you got him?' Brian asked hoarsely.

'I brought him home with me as a souvenir. He was legitimately mine; he had been presented to me by his former owner as a token of affection and esteem.'

'What were you doing among Central African witch-doctors?'

'It's my job. I'm an anthropologist.'

Brian was not certain of the nature of this calling, but he knew it was respectable enough. There were anthropologists at universities. It was something to do with the study of savages.

'How interesting,' he said politely. Now that he knew, the room gave ample confirmation of this. Weird objects of obviously primitive origin abounded, including several idols, whose sex was crudely made clear. Brian looked away in some confusion; he was not sure he did not prefer the skull. To save himself embarrassment he concentrated on studying its owner, who merited attention in his own right.

Sturdy, thick-set, and muscularly well developed was Brian's first verdict on him. The anthropologist had nothing of the effete academic about him; he looked more like a rugby Blue. He was middle-aged and his thick hair was greying at the temples, above a face lined and seamed by exposure to tropic suns; yet the impression he gave was not one of health and natural vigour, but rather of a man who forced himself to go on. Beneath his tan he had a curious greyish pallor; his eyes, when not focused on an object, stared fixedly ahead; the white, which surrounded the iris in an unbroken circle, made it appear dilated and the whole eye starting from the head; and the head in turn was cocked in a perpetually listening attitude which had nothing to do with anything Brian said.

Perhaps because he was abstracted, the anthropologist's movements had an oddly jerky air. He obviously knew his way about the room's chaos and went from shelves to cupboards to writing-desk with perfect familiarity, yet he walked always in straight lines, keeping his eyes fixed before him, which made him appear like some magnificently functioning clockwork toy. Brian decided he must be slightly mental, as over-brilliant people so often were, although he was glad to note that the anthropologist was sufficiently in touch with reality to be busying himself with food and drink. He had produced a bottle of whisky barely started, and a selection of tins of spaghetti and baked beans. These he proceeded to heat in a pan on the open fire, as though unacquainted with any more modern means. While he worked, he said nothing. The silence grew oppressive. Brian cast round for something to say.

'How long have you been an anthropologist?'

The other answered drily, 'All my life. I ought perhaps to have introduced myself earlier. Iorwerth Rees is my name.'

Brian made himself known rather volubly to conceal the fact that the name Iorwerth Rees was familiar to him, although he could not have said where he had seen or heard it. Perpetual television and a popular daily impinged very little upon him, his concentration being reserved for the fortunes of Aston Villa and a paperback thriller or two.

But the whisky restored his confidence as well as his circulation. Before long he was trying another tack.

'You've certainly chosen an out-of-the-way spot to live in, Dr Rees. Don't you ever get lonely here?'

Rees did not answer directly, merely said as though it were an explanation, 'This was my mother's house.'

And hasn't been modernised in living memory, Brian thought, though he re-phrased it so that he actually said: 'I admire the way you cook on an open fire. It's jolly clever. I couldn't do half as well on a modern stove.'

'It's not usually so primitive,' Dr Rees said. 'I cook by Calor gas in the kitchen as a rule. But I've just returned here somewhat unexpectedly and it's a case of making do.'

'Have you been abroad?' Brian asked.

'Yes.'

'In Central Africa?'

Dr Rees's face contracted as if in pain. He pressed his hand to his side for a moment and half groaned, half grunted, 'My present location is the Caribbean.'

'Good show,' Brian said. 'That's where I'd like to be this minute. They don't have such a thing as snow out there.' He saw the Caribbean as it appears in travel brochures: palm-fringed beaches, bikinied girls and planter's punch. It was a paradise to which the key was golden, the ultimate symbol that one had 'got on.' Unless he won the pools he would never go there, but just to know the place existed spurred him on.

'There are more unpleasant things than snow in the Caribbean,' Dr Rees said, breaking in upon his dream. 'Poverty, ignorance, superstition, violence, weird rites, obscene practices—I'd rather be over here.'

He was leaning over the fire as he said it, intent on stirring the pan. Suddenly the quiet fire flared up with a hiss and a crackle, so nearly singeing his eyebrows that the Doctor, alarmed, drew back. Again a grimace of pain twisted his features, although Brian was sure he had escaped the flame. 'Yes, yes,' he cried. 'Leave me alone. I heard you. I have not forgotten why I came.'

He looked wildly round as if expecting to see some embodiment of the voice he all too clearly fancied had spoken. Brian had never seen an insane man at close quarters before. Dr Rees seemed harmless, but he could not help feeling nervous.

Suspecting that the Caribbean might be an exciting subject, he said: 'You must be glad to be home.'

'Home?' Dr Rees looked round vaguely. 'Oh yes. In a way I am. But my return isn't voluntary. They sent me. In the circumstances I didn't want to come.'

Brian had no idea what the circumstances might be that he referred to, but he could guess their outline well enough: sick leave or even compulsory retirement, made necessary by the Doctor's mental health.

'You're certainly in a good spot for rest and quiet,' he said soothingly. 'No doubt you'll feel yourself again before long.'

'Never.' The Doctor gave a bark of what might have been laughter. 'Besides, I ought to be starting back at once.'

'Not in this weather,' Brian said, humouring him. 'They'll have to get a snow-plough on the roads. Unless they're going to fetch you out by helicopter?'

The Doctor said, 'They'll fetch me out somehow.'

He emptied the contents of the saucepan into a chipped blue plate, which seemed to be the only one available; his house was not particularly well equipped, and though Brian supposed there must be a kitchen behind them, Dr Rees remained obstinately in the one room. Even tableware was not exactly abundant. Dr Rees handed over the fork with which he had been assiduously stirring the pan.

'You haven't left anything for yourself!' Brian protested.

'I'm not hungry,' Dr Rees explained. He reached for the bottle and poured a generous measure into Brian's glass.

Brian politely raised it in salutation. 'Your very good health,' he said.

Again that curious bark of laughter. Then the Doctor clapped a hand to his side. His face looked ghastly—or was it shadow? In the lamplight Brian could not decide. He noticed that the pain appeared to be on the left side. The Doctor's hand was clamped against his ribs, as though pressure could relieve the agony or stem the bleeding. Except that there was neither injury nor blood.

Brian put down his glass and started towards him, fearing a heart attack, but the anthropologist waved him back with such authority that, though bewildered he instinctively obeyed.

'Don't come near me,' Iorwerth Rees commanded. 'It wouldn't do. Not yet. Later we have work to do—I have not forgotten—but now you must eat and rest.'

Rest, Brian thought bitterly! A fine chance there was of that, cooped up with a madman who might peg out or go berserk on him at any moment, leaving him to face the enquiries that would result. That Dr Rees believed he heard voices was obvious; that 'I have not forgotten' was fairly shouted out. Equally indisputable was his physical condition: his staring eyeballs, his pallor, his jerky gait, to say nothing of the spasms that seized and shook him until the sweat ran down his face. He ought to have a doctor, Brian reflected, but how do we get one now? A telephone seemed unlikely in this remote hill cottage, and even if there were one, what use would a telephone be? A doctor could hardly be expected to go in for long-distance prescribing, and in all probability the lines were out of action because of snow. Perhaps the best thing would be to humour the anthropologist. With care, he could play him along. In the morning he could perhaps make the village and someone else would have to take this problem on.

Despite the uneasiness of his predicament Brian had a healthy appetite. He found no difficulty in disposing of the tinned food provided, and felt more optimistic as a result. After all, he had a roof over his head and shelter, a fire to warm him and the wherewithal to eat and drink. Compared to what he had feared might be his fate two hours earlier, he was better off than he had ever dared to hope. And what a story to tell when he got back to the office! Wouldn't this make his fiancée open her eyes! Why, he could dine out on this almost indefinitely—even if he was accused of telling lies.

He began to look around him with more curiosity. He might want to describe this room to others some day. Where did this spear beside him come from? And what was that clump of feathers surrounding an object like an egg? Dr Rees seemed neither gratified nor interested by his questions, though he answered them courteously enough. The spear was African, used for hunting a certain kind of buck, a sacred animal; the feathers were from a head-dress, also African, used during a fertility rite.

'Have you nothing from the Caribbean?' Brian queried.

'Oh, yes. You shall see it later on. I don't keep the Caribbean stuff in here; it's too precious. No one so far knows what I've brought home.'

'I'd very much like to see it,' Brian said politely.

Dr Rees gave him a curious look. 'You shall. Yes, all in good time. I promise.' The last words were shouted once again.

'I expect you find your work very interesting,' Brian continued, resolving to ignore this lapse.

'I find it very frightening,' Dr Rees said soberly. 'If I had known how frightening, I wouldn't have taken it up.'

Brian looked at him in mild astonishment. The man spoke normally enough. Even his eyes were less fixed, less staring. His body seemed almost relaxed. Perhaps his hallucinations were temporary only. Emboldened, Brian enquired: 'What is it you do?'

'I study magic and the black arts, as practised by primitive tribesmen and their witch-doctors. It was in Africa that I began the work. Then, two years ago—most regrettably—I allowed myself to be tempted farther afield. I accepted a research grant to go to the Caribbean and pursue my studies there. You know that the people of the West Indian islands came originally from Africa? They brought with them their old beliefs but acquired new ones also, from the Mexicans, Carib Indians, and so forth. The result is a distinctive culture in which the old and the new have fused to produce something infinitely darker and more evil, as well as more wickedly abused. Power over the physical body of an adversary has always been one of magic's aims. The credulity and superstition of the tribesmen have made this task easy in the past. What we know of modern psychology confirms it—if a man believes death imminent, he will die. Even you—' he shot out a finger at Brian—'will feel uneasiness if I tell you you will soon die.'

Scared as he was, Brian hastened to agree with him. 'You needn't tell me that. On the mountains just now in the blizzard, I thought my number was up. In fact, I'd just about given up hope when I met you.'

'Curious. You were already expecting to die?'

'Wouldn't you have been, stranded alone, miles from anywhere, and completely lost in the snow? If you hadn't come along, I'd have been a goner. I'm jolly grateful to you, you know.'

Dr Rees brushed the gratitude aside with impatience. 'You don't know what you say. How should you? You know nothing of power over the body—the body living or dead. Yes, my young friend, don't think death means physical dissolution. I have known a dead man rise and walk, and go among his family and his fellows without even occasioning talk because he seemed so natural, so lifelike, yet all the time subject to another's control. These things happen—oh, not here in the Welsh mountains, but on islands of swamp and jungle three thousand miles away. I am a scientist, not given to believing in marvels. If I had not seen, then like you, I should not believe. But I have seen evil in the flesh as well as in the spirit, felt its power in my own nerves and sinews, so that when I wanted to depart from this abhorrent spectacle, I could not—could not—leave.'

'Pretty unnerving,' Brian said feelingly. He shivered and drew closer to the fire, which glowed redly but had somehow lost its radiance, just as the lamp too gave out a lesser, duller light.

'Paraffin's giving out,' Dr Rees said in explanation, as if he had read his thoughts. 'Never mind, I've got some candles in the kitchen, and as I said, I ought to be starting back.'

Poor devil, Brian thought with a twinge of pity. It's not surprising he's odd. If I'd seen a quarter of what he says he has, I'd be stark raving bonkers by now. He had read something similar in a thriller about vampires and zombies, but that, though disturbing, was only between paper covers, whereas this had taken place in real life.

At that moment the lamp flared, smoked and guttered. Dr Rees got up to turn it out. The smell of paraffin was strong in the darkness. The silence was suddenly intense. The world outside was swathed in stifling whiteness. Through the curtains its reflection faintly gleamed, a sheen of innocence overlying evil; or so—for an instant—it seemed. Then Brian felt an icy cold assail him and from out of it he heard Dr Rees speak. The cold and the voice came from behind him, but he had heard no movement in the room. The hair at the back of his neck prickled— but of course the cold would cause that. Apprehensively he turned to look behind him. Again Dr Rees called out.

'The blizzard's stopped. Now we can get moving.'

He was standing in the open kitchen door. The kitchen opened out of the study, a fact which Brian had not realised before. The icy cold was no more than bitter air from the mountains blowing into the heated room. There was nothing supernatural about it. He was still this side of the tomb.

Beyond the door was an infinity of undulant whiteness, slashed with the blackness of shadows on the snow. The clouds were still thick; there was neither moon nor starlight. The cutting wind that had driven the snow had stopped. Instead there was a trance-like immobility about each tuft of snow on ledge or bracken frond or leaf-stalk: the sparkle and stillness of frost.

The air was so cold that it made breathing painful, yet Dr Rees was gulping it in as though he could never have enough of its sweetness.

Then he turned. 'It is time for us to begin.'

'Begin what?' Brian asked, bewildered.

'We have to get my Carib treasure out. Without your help I cannot move the beam to reach it. Get the shovel behind you and pass me the spade and we'll start digging. It won't take long to clear away the snow.'

He turned back, holding the candle, which cast a strange light on his face. His eyes were once more rigid and staring.

Brian objected: 'Surely your treasure can wait? At least until it's light, in the morning.'

'No,' Dr Rees cried. 'I have to get it now. Before midnight, they said when they sent me. Otherwise they'll torture me again. And I can't stand it, I tell you. I can't stand it! I'm getting it as fast as I can.'

Again he was speaking to an imagined invisible presence, and his face contracted as at the onset of pain. Suddenly he doubled up, gasping and clutching at his left side as though his heart were being torn out whole. This time Brian was in time to catch him and take the flaring candle from a hand which promptly fell on his shoulder, clawing, clutching, so that he lost his balance and both of them staggered back.

With a tinkle a window-pane fractured, pushed out by the handle of the spade over which they fell. The Doctor's breath came gasping and rattling. Brian feared he was about to die on him there and then. He looked down on the bowed head, the hand convulsively clutching, and noticed for the first time a scar running diagonally across the hand from wrist to knuckle and shaped like an arrow to the heart. It was an old scar, bluish and puckered, a brand, a distinguishing mark. A hand, Brian thought, that one could recognise in a thousand—if one had need to recognise a hand.

Slowly the hand relaxed upon his shoulder. With a groan Dr Rees straightened up. 'It's all right,' he addressed the air. 'I told you, I'm getting it. The time-limit you set is not yet up.'

'You're not getting anything tonight,' Brian assured him, 'unless it's your death of cold. With a heart like you've got, you ought to be bedridden. You certainly can't go out clearing snow.'

'I must. What do you know about it? My heart condition, as you call it, will not change. Such as I am, I shall be till my task is ended. I ask you to help me end it tonight.'

Brian hesitated. The anthropologist was already much recovered and stood grasping his spade in a decidedly businesslike way. If crossed, his mental state might deteriorate further. It was perhaps only prudent to agree.

'What do you want me to do?' he capitulated.

For answer, the anthropologist began to dig. He cleared the snow on either side of him like a snow-plough. Brian followed behind and shovelled it up. A pathway was quickly dug from the kitchen door to a lean-to shed against the side of the house some twelve feet distant. Brian looked in vain for Dr Rees's footprints, but the Doctor avoided treading in the snow. He dug straight before him with his clockwork movements, looking neither to right nor left.

At the door of the lean-to shed he halted. The sweat stood out on his brow, but Brian was astonished to find that he also was sweating profusely, despite the coldness of the air, and it was not altogether exertion that caused it: he had an unmistakable feeling of fear.

'Couldn't we go in now?' he suggested.

'Not yet, not when we are so near. You asked me if I had anything from the Caribbean. My Caribbean treasure is here.'

Dr Rees leaned forward and tapped the shed door. The structure, which was rotten, seemed to shake.

'The roof has collapsed,' he said in explanation. 'I need someone to help me move a beam.'

'Someone from the village would come,' Brian reasoned.

'But it has to be done tonight. Why else should I go out in a blizzard seeking assistance? And then you happened along. No, no, my friend, you are the instrument, the chosen. You shall see what no one in this country has ever seen.'

Brian was not at all sure that he coveted such distinction; he longed to escape the biting cold. Moreover, he was becoming increasingly nervous of the Doctor, who seemed now like someone possessed. His eyeballs gleamed in the darkness. He seemed to be taller and stronger than before. He might, Brian thought, become dangerous if thwarted, and he had no wish to fight a madman on his own.

With difficulty they got the shed door open. Inside there was at first nothing to be seen except a baulk of timber lying across the doorway and seemingly securely wedged. The Doctor tested it; Brian tested it; it did not give an inch; but when they put their united strength against it, they could feel it yield a bit.

The Doctor fetched a candle and a crowbar. By candle-light Brian could see further into the shed, whose roof hung in broken matchwood pieces, letting in the snow and the sky.

'It happened last winter,' Dr Rees said briefly, 'when the snow cascaded off the house.' He pointed to the overhanging slate roof above them, where the snow lay inches deep.

'Where's the treasure?' Brian asked, disappointed. He had been expecting he did not know what, but not this decrepitude and dereliction. Even a madman could not claim there was value in that.

'It's in the safe,' Dr Rees said, pointing and holding the candle so that Brian could see. Beyond the beam, in a space between it and the house-wall, he made out an iron safe, small and rusty but undoubtedly secure.

Dr Rees held out a key. 'If we could lever the beam, you could crawl underneath it. I say "you" because you're smaller than I am.'

Brian was not enthusiastic, but he consented. In for a penny, in for a pound, he told himself. He joined Dr Rees with the crowbar and they battled to lever the beam. At first it resisted; then slowly, with much creaking, it gave a fraction of an inch. Small bits of wood broke off around it, but there was no general threat to cave in. Sweating, panting, struggling, they raised it a few inches more.

'Now,' Dr Rees asked, 'can you crawl under?'

Brian bent down. He could just make it. 'Give me the safe-key,' he said.

'You'll have to take it from my pocket,' Dr Rees panted. 'I can't let go of the bar.' Indeed, his whole weight was thrown against the crowbar which was holding the weight of the beam.

Brian approached and put his hand in his pocket, then drew back with a cry. 'God, you're cold!' Despite his exertions, which caused the sweat to stand out on his forehead, the Doctor's body had no warmth. Brian wondered uneasily if the anthropologist might collapse while holding the crowbar, in which case he would find himself trapped, but he was not one to worry about the hypothetical. He took the key, ducked, and began to work his way under the beam.

The safe, when he reached it, opened stiffly. There was a lot of rust round the lock. The high-pitched squeak of its hinges and the Doctor's heavy breathing were the only sounds in the shed. Dimly Brian could make out an object, quite small and wrapped carefully in a cloth; otherwise the safe was empty.

'There isn't any treasure,' he said.

'What's that? There is. There must be!' The Doctor's voice was agonised now. 'No one could have got in and taken it. No one knows it's there except me. Is the safe completely empty?'

'There's something wrapped up in a cloth...'

'That's it! Bring it out. Bring it quickly.' The Doctor almost wept with relief. Brian began to back out very slowly, holding the object tight against his chest. It was very heavy, but he could tell nothing from the shape of it. He decided it must be a stone, wrapped up by the madman during one of the violent hallucinations to which he seemed increasingly prone.

'Careful now,' Dr Rees admonished. 'Don't drop it whatever you do. To show disrespect would be to ask for trouble.' His excitement by now was intense.

As Brian emerged and stood upright, he let go the crowbar. The beam subsided more awkwardly than before. But Dr Rees was indifferent to this. He took the object and reverently laid it down. The kitchen was only a few yards behind him, but he could not wait to get that far. Kneeling down, he began to undo the wrappings—there were several—talking to himself all the while.

'Ah, you monster, when I smuggled you through the Customs, I little realised what I did. I ought to have declared you as evil incarnate and let them impound you and lock you up. Would that have saved me, I wonder? No, they'd have been after me even then. O you god of the witch-doctors, of voodoo, cease troubling. You shall go back to them.'

He bowed his head as if in worship. Brian, fascinated, craned close. There, before him in the snow was a strange, chunky idol squatting on its haunches and made of solid gold. One eye was a ruby, one was emerald; the lips were drawn back to show the teeth; high cheekbones, broad flat nose, thick neck and shoulders, the creature was Negroid in every plane and line. About its waist a skirt of fine gold chains was fastened, barely concealing its sex, which was easily its most generously proportioned part.

Dr Rees moved aside to let him see. 'Look well,' he advised, 'for you'll never see this monster again. He is the sacred god of the witch-doctors, whom I managed to steal away.'

'Good for you,' Brian said automatically.

'No, it was bad for me. I should have chopped off my right hand before I touched it, before the white man's lust for gold tempted me. But enough of that. They want him back and they want me with him. We must be starting soon. But that is not all. I have to take an offering—something the voodoo men can regard as a prize. And they are impatient. I must be gone by midnight. So look your last on the god of the witch-doctors, whom no white man ever sees but what he dies.'

It took Brian an instant to assimilate the implication. Suddenly he swung round with a cry of fear. Behind him, Dr Rees, with upraised crowbar and face contorted, struggled to redirect his aim. He was too late. The heavy iron bar had started falling, gathering momentum from its own weight. Brian flung himself aside at the last minute, and it crashed with a resounding thud against the beam.

Breathless, Brian lay where he had fallen. He could not even think what to do next. He was alone with a madman bent on murder. The snow made it impossible even to run.

As he watched, Dr Rees, off-balance, struggled to regain his grip. The end of the crowbar had become wedged among the debris in the lean-to and resisted as he sought to draw it out. The fallen beam held it firmly. Dr Rees gave a great heave. With fanatical strength he strained, heaving and pushing. And suddenly there was movement in the shed. There was a grinding and a sliding and a cracking, a startled human cry. The outline of the shed changed and disintegrated at the point where Dr Rees had stood. Brian could not sort out the sounds till afterwards, but there was one which, though not loud, remained in his ear: a dull, hollow, sickening sound whose only comparison was ridiculously homely: as though a cricket bat had swiped a coconut.

When he ventured near to investigate, Dr Rees was lying face downwards in the snow under the ruins of the shed which had collapsed about him. He was unmistakably and horribly dead.

Brian stood there and began to tremble. He could not move from the spot. He remembered the dead anthropologist's words about the power of evil and how he could not—*could not*—leave. In the ruins he could see the idol, just out of reach of the Doctor's grasping hand, on which the arrow-headed scar showed faintly, still pointing towards the heart. The god of the witch-doctors had had his revenge, Brian was thinking, when the whole scene vanished with a sudden slithering crump under a mass of snow from the overhanging slate roof above the lean-to. Dr Rees and the god of the Caribbean witch-doctors were refrigerated and entombed.

***

Towards half past ten next morning Brian stumbled into Pant-glas. It had taken him over two hours to cover the mile distance, blinded by whiteness, lifting each leaden snow-clogged foot in turn. Sometimes the hard ground did not rise to meet him and he fell forward, arms flailing wildly, into a drift that might be five feet deep but lay hidden under the slopes and planes of snow.

On these occasions panic always seized him as he struggled and scrabbled to his feet. Always in his mind's eye he could see Iorwerth Rees's body in the ruins of the shed, and then—an instant later—submerged under the slate-roof's avalanche of snow. The wind caused as it passed had struck against him, blastlike, blowing a swirl of powdery snow into his mouth.

He had not even had time to cry out in horror at what had happened—at what had nearly happened—and the lucky escape he had had. But he could not hope for such salvation twice running; if he fell here, it was up to him to rise again.

Each time he rose, he rose a little wetter, more buffeted, more breathless than before. He did not know whether he followed the road or was on open moorland, but he travelled by the sun and kept his eyes ahead. So long as he stayed clear of the drifts the going was not impossible. None the less, when he saw Pant-glas in the valley below him, he could scarcely suppress a cheer.

Pant-glas was no more than a few houses huddled together: stone and slate, small-windowed, squat and grey as crouching toads. But this morning it presented an unaccustomed scene of activity, for every householder was out clearing away snow. Men who normally worked on local farms or travelled to Brecon were snowbound in their homes. Even the village schoolhouse had not opened that morning, and the children, muffled to the eyebrows in coats and scarves and berets, ran about like so many gnomes. As Brian came down the street it was the children who saw him and attracted their parents' attention with their eldritch cries, for they seemed to find the approach of a snow-covered figure irresistibly comic and did not trouble to conceal their mirth.

Some of the men came towards Brian. 'There's been a frightful accident,' he gasped.

They closed in around him, prepared to be accusing or sympathetic, according to the tale he had to tell, and he burst out that there was a man dead—under a beam—clutching an idol—and that then the snow had come and covered them up.

They looked at him, unconvinced. His wits seemed to be wandering. Someone asked: 'Been stranded all night in the snow?'

It had happened to other foolhardy motorists before him. When found they were often pretty far gone.

Brian sensed their thoughts, their incredulity. 'Yes. No. I mean not in the snow. In a house. He asked me in. I wouldn't have seen it otherwise; I should have lain down where I was and died. And now he's dead. He tried to kill me. But I swear I didn't kill him in self-defence. It was an accident; I know that. I saw it. Oh, God, I saw it. I'll see it all my life.'

'Where's Dai?' a voice asked, and other voices took it up and elaborated: 'Get Dai. Yes, Dai. Get Dai-the-police.'

Here it comes, Brian thought. They'll arrest me. I shall never be able to make them believe the truth. Their faces blurred suddenly and hands supported him. 'He's all in,' someone cried. 'Best get him into the warm.'

'Dai's house'd be the place,' someone else suggested.

There was a concerted movement of consent. Brian found himself being borne towards a doorway. A woman called out that she would make a cup of tea.

'I could use a drink,' Brian murmured, but the murmur seemed to pass unheeded in the shout: 'Here's Dai!'

Dai-the-police was a middle-aged, middle-sized Welshman, with serious, friendly brown eyes. He came forward almost diffidently to meet them, as though reluctant to be thrust into prominence.

'Good morning, sir.' His voice was soft and lilting. 'Would you like to step inside?'

The invitation was extended to Brian but others availed themselves of it as well. The front room, which was also Dai's office, filled up with an assortment of men. Towards Brian they showed the neutral curiosity that is characteristic of closed societies everywhere. He sensed their attitude and shrank away from it. Only Dai-the-police seemed to care in a personal way.

His wife, with one child and another expected, brought in a brown pot of tea. Brian did not see Dai-the-police lace it, but he felt its beneficial effect. His damp clothes seemed a shade less dank and sodden, and his teeth kept silence in his head. With the second cup he felt himself reviving. Dai-the-police seemed well aware of this. He had produced a pencil and an official-looking notebook and was sitting behind a desk which took up almost a quarter of the space in the room. The spectators had withdrawn to the hall and the doorway, where they clustered like a crowd offstage.

'Now, sir,' Dai said, endeavouring to sound impersonal, although his natural kindliness kept breaking in, 'will you please tell me your name and address, age and occupation, and then I think we can begin.'

Brian gave the required particulars and began his tale: the decision to leave Brecon, the snowstorm, the stranding and abandoning of the car; then the nightmare walk into the blizzard in an effort to reach Pant-glas, the encounter with the man who offered shelter, and—No, he would not mention the tracks in the snow, or rather their absence. He could already sense their doubt. For some reason they suspected his story, although God knew he had told them gospel truth. If he added anything fantastic they might conclude he was mental. They might not take action on anything he said.

'And this house now, where was it?' It was Dai-the-police, speaking softly but watching him with an alertness in his eyes.

'I don't know. By then I was lost, I tell you. It was a stone house with a porch and a window on each side...'

'There are a lot like that. It's the usual style up here in the mountains.'

'It belongs to an anthropologist.'

'Ah!' Light dawned as Brian had hoped it would at this definition. 'Would it be Dr Iorwerth Rees's place you mean?'

'That's it! That's what he said.' The name came back to Brian.

'It's likely enough, I suppose. With the place being shut up this long time a tramp might easily have moved in.'

'No, no,' Brian protested at Dai's obtuseness. 'It was Dr Rees himself who took me in.'

In the background there was a murmur of denial, of incredulity.

'It could not have been Dr Rees.'

'But it was. He introduced himself. I'm not lying.'

'No one is saying that you are. The man may have said that to allay your suspicions, but he was not Iorwerth Rees.'

'How do you know? He seemed very much at home there.'

Dai, weary with explaining, shook his head. 'Dr Rees is abroad, man. In the Caribbean. He has not been home this year past.'

'That's right,' Brian said. 'That's what he told me. He said he'd just got back last night.'

This time there was a babel of voices, excited, questioning, in which the words could be distinguished: 'Fetch Mrs Price.'

'If Dr Rees came back,' Dai reasoned patiently, 'he would have had to fetch his keys from Mrs Price. She keeps an eye on the place, like, in his absence. If he came home, she would be the first to know.'

Brian was not convinced of this assumption. The Doctor had not been anxious to make his presence known. Understandably, if he had returned for the foul deed of murder, designed to propitiate the purloined god. Or—a pleasanter explanation—his heart might have failed him. He was obviously suffering from disease. Angina, perhaps; Brian's medical knowledge was uncertain, but there was no doubting Dr Rees's distress. If he had reached his home in a final desperate effort (and the journey had not been made at his own wish), the last mile to the village might have proved beyond him. And it would have been easy for him to break in…

Mrs Price, however, flatly contradicted this reconstruction when she arrived flustered, breathless, and what she termed 'all of a do'. She was a stout woman, florid, with tight grey bobbing curls and glasses, and she looked at Brian with dislike.

'As if he'd come back to this country, and never a word of him for six months, without even letting me know! Why, he'd want food in, the place aired, the bed put ready—is it likely he'd do that himself? Never the handy one, Iorwerth wasn't. It's a wonder he hasn't been married before now, for if ever a man needed looking after… But there! He's always been away in foreign parts. Before he went away this last time (this was after his mother died; the cancer she had), he came to see me in the shop and said "Megan"—we were ever so friendly, see—"Megan," he said, "will you do something for me?" "If I can, you know I will," I said. "Megan, will you keep the keys of her house now she's gone and give an eye to it? I don't want it to rot now she's dead; and I'm off to the West Indies tomorrow and the Lord knows when I'll be back." "Don't you worry, Iorwerth my dear," I told him—I'd known him from a boy that high, you see—"I'll look after it as if it was my own place, and when you come back you'll always find the keys with me." '

'And he didn't come for them last night?' Dai-the-police persisted.

'Would I have kept it to myself if he had? Wouldn't I have been round telling you all the good news even in a blizzard; that Iorwerth Rees was home again, safe and sound?'

There was a murmur of assent from the spectators. Mrs Price dabbed freely at her eyes, pushing her glasses on to her forehead to do so, which gave her an air of comical surprise.

'But if he didn't have time to let you know he was coming?' Brian suggested.

She refused to consider this. 'If he'd been found again, it would be in all the papers, the same as it was when he was lost.'

She looked at Dai-the-police for confirmation. The policeman nodded his head.

'The man you saw cannot have been Dr Rees,' he told Brian. 'Dr Iorwerth Rees has disappeared.'

So that was why he knew the name, Brian remembered. There had been something in the papers a few months ago. 'Anthropologist missing on West Indian island'. At the time he had given it scant heed. Now the details came back to him a little. The man—he was sure the papers had described him as 'well-known'—had simply vanished on a visit to one of the smaller islands, and never a trace of him had been found. Of course, had he fallen into the sea, either dead or living, the sharks might have disposed of him. This was thought to be the likeliest explanation, although his death had not so far been presumed. An obstacle to this was the repeated reports of his presence in various out-of-the-way spots, where he had been seen sometimes by West Indians, sometimes by Europeans, but never close to: if they hailed him he would not stop. These glimpses did not prove anything, although dark rumours began to circulate. Dr Rees had been studying the cult of voodoo. There were those who talked about the power of the witch-doctors and hinted that the biter had been bit.

Brian felt a sudden shiver go through him that had nothing to do with wet clothes. The apparent absence of footprints came back to him strangely; he could almost believe he had met a ghost. Except that a ghost did not lift a heavy crowbar, nor die with his blood staining the snow…

'I still believe the dead man is Dr Rees,' he insisted.

Dai-the-police looked at him pityingly. 'If he'd been found, as Mrs Price says, it would have been in all the papers. His sister in Cardiff would have let us know.'

'But it's possible he could come back unknown?'

'It's possible. Could you describe him to us, do you think?'

'Middle-aged, greying hair, rather stocky; weather-beaten face and curiously staring eyes.'

There was a mutter of disagreement behind him. 'Iorwerth's eyes do not stare,' someone called out.

'And for the rest,' Dai pointed out, 'it is so general. It might have been any man of that type you saw.'

There was no mistaking their scepticism, their hostility.

'Wait,' Brian cried, 'there is more. Dr Rees,' he went on, 'has a heart ailment. I don't know what it is, but it's pretty bad. Bad enough, I should think, to cause him to be sent home from the Caribbean.'

They were silent this time. It was Dai-the-police who spoke.

'That settles it,' he said, relieved and decisive. 'It was not Dr Rees you saw. Iorwerth Rees is as sound as you or I, man. There is nothing the matter with his heart.'

'Perhaps it wasn't apparent,' Brian suggested.

'Some of us have known Iorwerth all his life. Besides, he is a baritone at the chapel.'

Mrs Price interpolated: 'Lovely voice he has.'

'Sings solo and all, see, at Easter and Christmas. Can a man do that and suffer from shortness of breath? Iorwerth holds his top notes with the best of 'em. No, sir, it wasn't Iorwerth Rees you saw.'

'And the scar?' Brian asked in desperation. 'How about the scar on his hand?'

He was conscious of a sudden tension all about him.

'What scar?' Dai-the-police asked. 'Which hand?'

'The left. On the back,' Brian said without hesitation. 'The scar is shaped like an arrow pointing towards the heart. It's an old scar. It looks blue and livid—'

He was interrupted by a sudden crash.

Mrs Price had staggered and almost fallen. Two of the men were struggling to hold her up. With some manipulation the best chair was pushed forward. All around confusion had broken out.

Mrs Price was moaning and rocking. 'Oh, Iorwerth my dear, why didn't you come? Did you think old Megan wouldn't know you anywhere the moment she saw your hand? I remember the day you did it as if it was yesterday. You put your hand through the cold frame in the garden. Your mam was that frightened and that upset! She thought you were going to die, and so did I for a moment, for your hand was all blood and slivers of glass. And afterwards, when it healed, it was like an arrow. There couldn't be a more distinctive mark.'

Someone gave her some tea from the brown teapot. Brian wondered if hers was also laced with rum. Whatever it was, it made her suddenly quiet. Around her the rest of the spectators clustered, struck dumb.

'We've all seen that scar,' Dai-the-police said very slowly. 'As Mrs Price says, there couldn't be a more distinguishing mark. Now, sir, let's have the rest of your story. You say Dr Rees is dead?'

Brian began his account of the night's happenings. They listened, drinking it in, investing him with the magic of the story-teller, the itinerant entertainer from inn to inn. The mention of treasure caused them to stir like trees when the wind blows through them; the mention of murder held them still, in the grip of frost; the final cataclysm of the collapsing shed and the snowfall set them muttering like a distant thunderstorm.

'How do we know it's true, what he's saying?'

With that question the storm approached.

'You can go there and see for yourselves,' Brian retorted.

'That wouldn't prove anything.'

'You will find him lying as I described him.'

'Very likely—seeing as you struck him down.'

'I didn't.' Brian's denial was spirited, but he felt his heart sink none the less. There were no witnesses, nothing that could be proven. How the devil had he got himself into such a mess?

'He's a deep one,' someone called. 'He wants watching.' (The remark was addressed to Dai.) 'Saw the treasure and stove in Iorwerth's head for it, and comes here to tell us all a lie.'

There was an angry growl of agreement, punctuated by a sniff from Mrs Price. The amateur detectives were having a field day, regardless of how they loaded the dice.

'Iorwerth would never have hurt a fly,' Mrs Price observed, still sniffing. 'To think he should end like this!' She rose suddenly and confronted Brian. 'You murderer!'

From the crowd behind there came a snakelike hiss.

'Telephone Scotland Yard!' a voice shouted, regardless of the fact that the wires were down.

Dai-the-police shook his head in bewildered remonstrance. 'We can't even get through to Brecon until they've cleared the road.'

'The snow-plough will be out this afternoon,' a young man pointed out cheerfully. (They were used to snow in Pant-glas; they had it every year.)

The remark seemed to goad Dai-the-police into action. He turned to Brian. 'We will investigate. You will take me to Dr Rees's house and show me his body and tell me again how all this came about. By that time they will have cleared the road with a snow-plough. We will drive into Brecon and tell them the story there.' After which it would be out of his hands, he reflected. He was surprised to find he did not greatly care.

***

After a bite to eat, he and Brian set off together, floundering their way through the snow. They were escorted by most of the men of the village, who were determined to see fair play. When they neared the house, which they reached by a shorter route than Brian had taken, passing the snow-plough on the way, the policeman ordered their escort to hold back. 'If there has been a murder,' he explained, 'there will be clues and we must not disturb them.' There was a murmur of admiration at this. Clearly they had bred a Sherlock Holmes among them. Dai-the-police went forward gamely. He was much encouraged by this.

They wandered down the path to the front door. The snow had completely obliterated previous tracks. It had even drifted against the door and now fell inwards as Dai-the-police turned the key and swung the heavy door back. The house by day looked grey and desolate; it had lost the cosy, welcoming air of last night. The wintry light through small windows fell coldly, illuminating the dead fire in the hearth and the empty, soot-stained, still slightly odorous paraffin table-lamp.

At sight of the skull, Dai-the-police started just as Brian had done. The spear, too, seemed to produce in him strange sensations, but all he said was: 'Dr Rees was a rum one all right.'

He examined the empty saucepan and the blue plate, but said nothing, and he looked at the discarded tins in the hearth. Very gingerly, wearing gloves, he lifted and sniffed the whisky glass. Brian felt a wild desire to laugh. Here he was, suspected of committing murder after nearly being murdered himself, compelled to stand by before they had even viewed the body and watch the village detective at work.

Dai-the-police, however, had method in his madness. Dr Rees was dead, he reasoned; he would not run away—particularly not with a beam and a load of snow on top of him. Where he was, there would he stay. Meanwhile, he would begin at the beginning and patiently go over the ground. He had heard the story; now he would reconstruct the action. In doing so, many useful clues might be found.

He led the way out to the kitchen, Brian following at his heels. Here the broken window claimed his attention, but he made no comment, merely noted it in his book. The kitchen door was fastened by a Yale lock, a fact which he again considered worthy of note. Outside were the cleared twelve feet to the wreck of the lean-to and the sinister avalanche of snow.

It lay jumbled like broken concrete in solid frozen slabs and peaks. There was nothing to indicate the horror that lay beneath it; it was a singularly innocent-looking grave. Brian wished it might stay undisturbed for ever, for surely the dead should be left to rest, but Dai-the-police, seizing the shovel, began to dig and commanded him to do the same.

Brian picked up the spade but he could not use it. A combination of fear and horror held him back. He did not want to see again that hideous idol, nor the anthropologist's mutilated head. Dai-the-police, however, unaware of what the snow was hiding, was working away with a will, making the snow fly like a human snow-plough as his shovel flew back and forth. Already the anthropologist's feet should have been uncovered. Brian watched for them to appear, when suddenly the shovel struck against the debris—something solid—with a jar that made him wince.

Dai-the-police excavated more carefully and uncovered the end of the beam. He probed the snow around it with his shovel, but it sank in easily everywhere. By rights it should have encountered resistance somewhere (Dr Rees had been a man of medium height), but so far there was no trace of him whatever. Once again Dai-the-police set to work.

He dug more slowly now. His pace was almost leisured. Gone was the furious haste of heretofore. Instead a small puzzled frown appeared between his eyebrows, which deepened as he penetrated further into the pile of wreckage and snow. Brian was frankly bewildered. The body should have been uncovered long before this. Yet it must be there, for the avalanche was undisturbed as when he left it, and who indeed would come to disinter? Even had Dr Rees not been dead by some miracle (and Brian was certain that he was), he could not have extricated himself from this cairn of stones, snow and rubble. Therefore his body must still be underneath.

Consequently, when Dai-the-police thrust his shovel into the remaining debris and announced 'There's no body under here,' Brian replied with conviction that there must be.

'There is not, man. See for yourself.' The policeman looked at Brian severely and added, 'It's a strange idea you have of a hoax.'

'There's no hoax.'

'There is no body. If you ask me, there never was. It's a fine tale you told, Mr Bellamy, but never a word of it was true.'

'Then why should I tell it? What have I to lie for?'

'That's what I'm going to find out.'

'But you've been in the house, you've seen the evidence that I was in there, the ashes of the fire, the empty glass and plate—'

'Oh, I don't deny that *you* were in the house,' Dai admitted. 'But there's no evidence that you were there with anyone else.'

'But I met Dr Rees in the snow. He invited me in, gave me supper—'

'There is no evidence of any of that. You found the house, but it must have been accidental, for last night Dr Rees was not in Pant-glas.'

'Was not known to be,' Brian corrected. Dai-the-police allowed the correction to pass.

'The doors are locked from inside,' he continued, 'therefore, you did not enter by the door, as you said. No, you broke a pane in the kitchen window, put your hand in and undid the catch.'

'I've told you how that pane got broken.'

'And a very fine story it was. When you told it, I believed it, I can tell you, because I thought you had murdered Dr Rees. But Dr Rees was not here living last evening and he is not here dead today. Only you were here. It was you who lit the fire Mrs Price keeps laid ready, and you found tinned food and got yourself something to eat. You had to heat it on the fire because there was no Calor gas for the kitchen; but you ate alone; there is only one glass and plate. There is no indication that Dr Rees or anyone else was with you.'

'Then why should I say that he was? Even if I had broken into the house in the way you imagine, last night's blizzard was surely sufficient excuse? I've no need to make up idle stories, and I swear to you this is anything but a hoax.'

The policeman showed signs of hesitation. Brian's sincerity carried considerable weight. He clearly believed he had had a companion, and there was that business of the scar on the hand... Dai-the-police had known Iorwerth Rees from childhood; he knew the shape and the colour of that scar. It was not a detail a stranger could have invented. And then, Iorwerth Rees had disappeared. For six months nothing had been heard of him. He might be alive, or—he might very possibly be dead. There are moments when the impossible becomes the probable... Dai-the-police shivered at such a thought.

Brian was still looking at him intently. Dai said: 'I take back what I said about a hoax.'

'You mean that you accept that Dr Rees was here with me?'

'Dr Rees—or Dr Rees's ghost.'

'Don't be a fool, man!' Brian shouted. (A Welsh accent was infectious, he found.) 'Whoever was here last night was no ghost but flesh and blood with a vengeance.' He added: 'Particularly blood.'

'So you may think, sir,' Dai-the-police countered. 'But I've heard a ghost can assume a very convincing shape, and though I've never believed in ghosts until this minute, it's likely you were mistaken in what you saw.'

'I was not mistaken. Can a ghost lift a crowbar? Can a ghost try to murder a living man? You seem to forget your Dr Rees is guilty of attempted murder. I can't be mistaken about *that.*'

'If he'd been living, there would be a body. It stands to reason, like.'

'Damn your reason if it makes me out a liar! I tell you I saw and heard him; I touched him, I felt his flesh.'

Cold flesh, Brian remembered with a shudder. He was cold even before he was dead. But that was perhaps not unusual with heart trouble. He wished suddenly that he were better read. There must be an explanation of this mystery which, if put forward, Dai-the-police could accept; some final proof that Dr Rees's physical body had been present, some trace that had not vanished with the rest.

Seizing the shovel which Dai the police had discarded, Brian began to dig furiously. There was only a small area from which the snow had not been shifted, and though he did not know what he expected to find, he was determined to prove the reality of the figure he had encountered. Forgotten now were his initial fear and horror. Now that the body he had dreaded to uncover had vanished, he was intent on proving its existence beyond all doubt.

The proof, when he found it, was unexpected. It was Dai-the-police who saw it first. As Brian flung a shovelful of snow-slabs to one side, he gave a cry of alarm. Brian stopped work on the instant, thinking some harm had befallen Dai-the-police, but the policeman, though white-faced, seemed uninjured. Instead, he was pointing to the pile of broken snow-blocks Brian had discarded. There was unmistakably blood upon the snow.

For an instant both gazed at it in horror. Then without a word spoken, they both began to dig, but carefully now, proceeding slowly, examining each spadeful of snow. As they progressed nearer to the fallen lean-to, to the point where the crushed head had lain, they uncovered further evidence. The snow seemed soaked in blood. But there was never a trace of a body, no broken flesh from which the blood had come. It was as though, tired of lying in the snow to await them, Iorwerth Rees had risen and gone back home. Or perhaps he had been summoned? Brian shuddered, remembering how he had cried out that he had to go. His departure, like his arrival, seemed not of his own volition—and had left no tracks in the snow.

Brian looked at Dai-the-police. 'Are you satisfied?' he demanded.

Dai shook a much bewildered head. 'This is like nothing I have ever heard or read of. How can I be satisfied? I cannot arrest you on a charge of murder without a body, not can I make any report as to how Iorwerth met his death. But I know that what has happened here is evil. I find myself anxious to get away.'

Brian too was aware of the brooding atmosphere that hung over the deserted house. It was something stronger than solitude and the mournfulness of disuse. Despite the brightness of the day, it was as though some noxious vapour had surrounded and pervaded the place. It was not so much the emanation of evil as an intimation that evil had passed this way, as the air may remain polluted by industrial effluents long after the recipient stream or river has diluted them and carried them away.

Dai-the-police looked at Brian in unspoken question and Brian looked back at him and gave his unspoken reply. Then they both turned, trying not to seem to hurry, and worked round to the front of the house. Their appearance was greeted with a cry from the watchers at a distance, one of whom was already half way down the slope. Dai-the-police recognised him and said briefly, 'It is Mr Evans from the shop.'

The shop was grocer-cum-ironmonger-cum-post-office, and sold newspapers, cigarettes and chocolate as well. It was also the power-house for village gossip since everyone met there perforce. Evans-the-shop was the best-informed man in the village, in touch with all that went on in Pant-glas and the world outside, for as newsagent and post-master he was linked to the world beyond the valley, and the village news was brought to his door. He was small and bald, garrulous and self-important. He was obviously a bringer of news.

'It is no use your looking for Iorwerth Rees, man,' he burst out at Dai-the-police as soon as he was near them. 'Iorwerth Rees is dead as a door nail.'

'Where?' Dai shot out a hand, gripping Evans-the-shop so firmly by the shoulder that the little man almost fell back. 'Where is he?' Dai demanded hoarsely. 'Where did you find him, then?'

'Let go, man. I did not find him. Take your bloody hands away from me. They found him on some island in the Caribbean. Been dead a long time, it says. You will see.'

He thrust a folded newspaper forward. 'The snow-plough on the upper road brought this.' The paper had been turned back to an inner page, whose heading—'Missing scientist found murdered'—straddled five of its eight-column width.

'See for yourself, man,' Evans-the-shop commanded. 'Iorwerth Rees was not here last night in Pant-glas. He cannot have been, for he was found buried on a Caribbean island with a knife thrust into his heart.'

Two men craned forward to read the paper, which was battered as though it had been many times passed from hand to hand. Its account, dated three days before, was what in essence Evans-the-shop had related: a farmer in a seldom visited part of his farm had noticed a disturbed patch of earth in a clearing; on investigation, it proved to be a grave. The occupant, a white man of about forty, had died from a knife wound in the heart. The facts had been reported to the police and the British Consul and the body was subsequently identified as that of Dr Iorwerth Rees, the well-known anthropologist, missing since August of last year. Dr Rees had disappeared while engaged in investigating ritual magic in some of the outlying islands. The item went on to give a brief resume of Dr Rees's previous career, mentioned that his home was near Brecon, and concluded: 'Police investigations are hampered by lack of evidence and the length of time which has elapsed. Informed sources said late last night that this might be a revenge killing by witch-doctors. Dr Rees is believed to have aroused their anger by witnessing some of their secret rites last year. It is thought that he may have removed a sacred idol or totem, although no indication of this has been found.'

'Of course it wasn't!' Brian cried in sudden enlightenment. 'It was here. That's what he came back to get. The god of the witch-doctors—he told me—whom no white man ever sees but what he dies. And he's taken it. He's gone back with it to the Caribbean. He kept telling me he was expected, he'd got to go…'

And as the others caught on to his meaning they left nothing but the tracks of three frightened men in the snow.

***

Dai-the-police decided against taking a statement. There was nothing that Brian could say. He had committed no crime and was not accused of any. Neither mentioned the blood on the snow. Dai told himself that it was a chemical reaction and Brian that his imagination had been playing tricks. This ignored the fact that Dai knew little chemistry and Brian was not imaginative, but each felt it was the best explanation he could offer. They parted with the mutual esteem of men who have shared a common demoralizing experience, and as soon as his car was freed and defrosted, Brian was on his way.

***

It was not until next morning, when he opened his copy of the *Western Examiner*, that Dai-the-police felt real fear run up his spine, for there in letters of suitably sensational dimensions was the single word: 'Outrage'. The news item went on to describe, in decreasing degrees of blackness, an outrage committed on the corpse of Dr Iorwerth

Rees, the well-known anthropologist, etc., whose body had been found three days before. 'During the night,' announced the *Western Examiner*, 'the mortuary was broken into and the dead man's head battered in. This atrocity is believed to have been committed by practitioners of voodoo, angry that their victim has been disinterred...'

Dai-the-police put the paper down. His hands were shaking. He felt as though he had had a narrow escape. Which is no doubt why he overlooked an insignificant item tucked away at the bottom of another page.

'Traffic on the recently cleared Brecon-Merthyr Tydfil road was held up for two hours last night when a Triumph Herald skidded outside Brecon and overturned, killing the occupant. His name was later given as Brian Bellamy, 26, salesman. His car had been stranded overnight in the snow, and he was returning to his home in Birmingham when the accident occurred. A police spokesman said later that there was no explanation; the car appeared to be functioning perfectly and the road was not icy at this point.'

COME AND GET ME

AFTER THE DEATH of General Derby, VC, in his eighty-sixth year the house was put up for sale. The General's wife had died some years earlier and his son in the war, so there was no one to inherit. Plas Aderyn was put on the market and found no takers. No one was entirely surprised.

The house (nineteenth-century) was large by any standards. In later years most of it had been shut off. It stood in ample wooded grounds and the woods were encroaching to a point where they threatened to engulf the house. The banks of rhododendrons bordering the drive had spilled over to create a tunnel of gloom; in places weeds smothered the gravel; everything was rank and overgrown. 'Needs a fortune spending on the grounds,' was the unanimous verdict. And that was before you got to the house.

'Commanding extensive views over the Elan Valley reservoirs,' said the estate agent's circular with perfect truth. The view from the front windows was probably the finest in all Radnorshire. Not for nothing did the overgrown drive wind uphill. Yet the same chance that had given Plas Aderyn its spectacular panorama had in a sense condemned it to death, for the village which had once served its needs and supplied its labour lay drowned at the bottom of the lake. The nearest centre—and that a small one—was now some miles away. The house stood in awesome isolation in a region not thickly populated at best.

So there was good reason for the place to stay on the market, despite a not-too-recent photograph in *Country Life* which gave prospective purchasers no idea of what was meant by 'nine miles from Rhayader' in terms of rural solitude. Soon even the estate agent virtually forgot the existence of Plas Aderyn. A winter gale blew his 'for sale' notice down. Unless you caught a glimpse of it from the other side of the valley, when it still looked singularly impressive, it might as well have sunk with its village beneath the lake.

It was precisely such a glimpse which brought Lieutenant Michael Hodges and three men to Plas Aderyn on a warm May afternoon. Army units were holding manoeuvres in the area whose object was a defence of the dams against an imaginary enemy driving northwards. Hodges, having caught sight of the house and learned in the village that it was empty, had secured permission to set up an observation post in the grounds, the only stipulation being that he should cause no damage. As his commanding officer reminded him, 'This isn't the real thing.'

Hodges was not an imaginative young man, despite the seriousness with which he played military games. Nevertheless, as his Army Land-Rover turned into the overgrown driveway, he felt a momentary unease. If this were for real, he thought, he would be proceeding with extreme caution, expecting an ambush or booby-trap at every turn. In fact it was more like jungle warfare than an exercise taking place in the Welsh hills. He was almost surprised that the only natives appeared to be birds and squirrels, so unused to man that they were unafraid. The whole wood resounded with birdsong. It was one of the loudest and most tuneful avian concerts that Hodges or any of the others had ever heard.

'You can see why they called it Plas Aderyn, can't you, sir?' said Corporal Miller as they stopped at the foot of the terrace in front of the house.

'No,' Hodges said, 'I can't. You tell me.'

'Plas Aderyn means place of the bird.'

'How'd you find that out?' asked one of the privates.

'A little bird told me,' Miller said with a wink. It was well known that the Corporal had been out with a local girl the previous evening, so the others did not press the point.

Meanwhile Lieutenant Hodges had quickly reconnoitred and decided to set up his observation post where the Land-Rover had stopped, and where a balustrade, still with a worn urn or two in position, marked the limit of once-cultivated ground. The terrace immediately below the house was slightly higher, but he had ascertained that the view was no better and, as he said, there was less chance of causing damage where they were. He did not specify what damage might result from their presence to a house whose ground-floor windows were already broken and boarded up. Instead, he concentrated on giving orders with unaccustomed officiousness, causing his men to glance at one another in surprise. They could not know that as he neared the house their officer had had an overwhelming desire to run away. If every window had been bristling with machine-guns, he could not have felt a greater reluctance to approach. That there was no reason for this fear had merely made it all the more terrifying. Lieutenant Hodges was not accustomed to nerves. Even now, safely back on the lower terrace, he was uneasy. He busied himself checking positions on a map.

It was Corporal Miller who put into words the anxiety Hodges was suppressing, though the Corporal's voice was cheerful enough as he said brightly, with the air of one intent on making an intelligent observation, 'Sir, d'you notice how the birds have stopped?'

Lieutenant Hodges made pretence of listening. So it wasn't his imagination after all. There really was a curious waiting stillness.

He said briskly, 'It's probably the time of day.'

No one was naturalist enough to contradict him. The two privates were already kneeling with field glasses clamped to their eyes, resting their elbows on the balustrade as they surveyed the road along the lake's farther side. It was as well, since they might otherwise have dropped the glasses when the silence was shattered by a laugh, a terrible, shrill ha-ha-ha that was human but maniac, and seemed to come from everywhere at once.

'It's all right, it's only a woodpecker,' Hodges said to the three white faces turned towards him, well knowing it to be a lie.

As if in mockery, the laugh came again, this time from behind them. They swung round as one man.

The house gazed vacantly back at them with a deceptively innocent air. Hodges was reminded of the childhood game of statues. Had it been creeping up on them while their backs were turned? Then he abused himself inwardly for a fool. What had got into him? Could a house move forward of its own free will? Even before the echoes of the laugh had finished bouncing back and forth across the valley, he was striving to get a grip on himself. The echoes, of course, explained the ubiquity of the laughter, but they did not imply more than one man. Some village simpleton, even perhaps a schoolboy, was playing tricks on them.

Drawing his revolver from its holster and wishing that for the manoeuvres they had not been issued only with blanks (not that he wanted to shoot anyone, but it would have been a source of confidence to know that he could), Hodges started to move towards the house, motioning the others to follow him. The distance seemed suddenly vast. His every nerve was tense as he waited for the next burst of laughter. Worse still, he had no idea what he was going to do next. Lead, he thought, I couldn't even lead men to their destruction, though I may be doing exactly that; for with every step he felt the old nameless horror: he did not want to go near the house.

It was Corporal Miller who saved him, by clutching his arm and pointing with a shaking hand, 'Look, sir, there's someone at the window. The place is inhabited. There must be some mistake.'

Hodges looked and saw he was pointing at a first-floor window directly above the front door. A white blur moved, vanished, reappeared. He ordered one of the privates to take a look through the glasses while the rest of them came to a halt.

'It's a man, sir,' the private reported, 'a young man with very dark hair. I can't see no more because of the angle and the window being so small. And he keeps ducking out of sight like he was in a Punch-and-Judy show. I don't think he wants to be seen.'

'He's probably trespassing, like us, and doesn't want to be prosecuted,' Hodges was saying when the maniac laugh rang out again. This time there was no mistaking its source: the man at the window was laughing his head off, except that no normal being ever laughed like that.

'He's escaped from some loony-bin,' Corporal Miller suggested. 'He's on the run and holed up here.'

It seemed the likeliest explanation. The little group halted uncertainly.

'We'll report it to the police,' Hodges said, trying not to let his relief sound evident. 'We don't want to get too near. You never know how it might affect a chap as far gone as he is. We don't want him throwing himself down.'

The man was leaning so far out that this seemed a distinct possibility.

'Careful!' Hodges shouted. 'You'll fall!'

The man looked directly at them for an instant, then waved his arms violently.

'Come and get me!' he shouted. 'Come and get me! I'm here. What are you waiting for?'

Suddenly, as though seized by unseen hands, he vanished. The window was nothing but an empty square. The silence was so intense it was as if he had been gagged in mid-sentence, or even mid-syllable.

The men looked at Hodges uneasily. 'Well, wha' d'you make of that, sir?' one of them asked.

Hodges said, 'I think he's an epileptic. He must have had a fit.'

'Perhaps he's got shut in there, sir,' Corporal Miller suggested. 'D'you think we ought to go and see?'

'Yes,' Hodges said, wishing Miller had not made the suggestion. He led the way forward resolutely.

The front door was locked, barred and padlocked, the windows on each side boarded up. The Lieutenant tested them, but everything was nailed securely. There was no obvious means of getting in. Nor was there sign that anyone had tried to. The dead years' mouldering leaves lay undisturbed, blown by past winds into piles along the terrace and rotted down by many seasons' rains.

'Place gives you the creeps, don't it?' someone said. Hodges did not contradict him, but merely ordered, 'Let's go round and try the back.'

The drive curved round the house to outhouses and stables, presenting the same spectacle of decay. A conservatory, mostly glassless, seemed to offer a means of entrance. Hodges climbed gingerly in. A bird flew out in alarm and in one corner there was a scuttling, but the door leading to the house was locked.

'Perhaps he shinned up a drain-pipe,' suggested one of the men who had not yet spoken. He put his hand on one to demonstrate. A rusted iron support clattered down, narrowly missing him, and the pipe leaned outwards from the wall of the house.

'I don't think so,' Hodges said quickly. 'Let's go back to the front and shout.'

They called loud and long, but there was no answer.

Miller suggested, 'Perhaps he's dead.'

'Dead long ago,' Hodges said before he could stop himself.

White faces looked at him. 'Cor, sir, d'you mean a ghost?'

'Of course not.' Hodges denied it quickly. 'Only I don't see how he got in. Unless he got on the roof and broke in that way.' He looked speculatively at the trees. There was no immediate overhang, no branch convenient to a window.

'Come on,' he said. 'One last shout, then we'll go.'

The echoes volleyed their voices to and fro across the valley, but the silence remained absolute. Nor was it broken as they returned to the Land-Rover, for no one had a word to say. In silence they piled in. In silence Corporal Miller started the engine, and in silence they drove away.

***

Lieutenant Hodges did not report the incident, he merely stated that Plas Aderyn had proved unsuitable as an observation post; but during the two days they remained stationed in the district he made some enquiries of his own. The general-store-cum-post-office proved the best source of information because he could go in there alone, whereas in the pub he risked making a fool of himself in front of his brother officers, which he naturally wished to avoid. The news that Hodges had seen a ghost, or even that he thought he had seen one, was not the kind he wanted to get around.

But if ghost it was, it was a recent one, he argued. There had been nothing unusual about the dress, nothing to suggest that the young man was not of their own time, even if not of their world. And Mr Thomas who kept the general store was very willing to tell the Lieutenant what he knew. Yes, it was seven or eight years or thereabouts since old General Derby had passed on, a fine gentleman he was, and his wife a real lady, he took her death very hardly, and such a pity about his son.

'What about his son?' Hodges asked, his ears pricking.

'He died, sir. During the war.'

'Tell me about it,' Hodges invited.

Mr Thomas did not hesitate, merely pausing to serve ice-cream to two small girls and some corn-plasters to a woman with bunions the size of eggs.

'Ever so good they are,' he assured Hodges. 'We sell a lot of them here. You want to keep some handy yourself, sir, for when you're marching. I first discovered them during the war.'

'Of course,' Hodges said, 'you were in it.'

'Three and a half years and for two of them I was overseas. Never came back on leave once in all that time, sir. Quite missed the old place, I did.'

'But you came back,' Hodges reminded him, 'which is more than young Derby did.'

'Oh, he wasn't killed in action. He was home on leave when it happened. Drowned he was. In the lake. Accident, they said. Missed his way in the darkness. But you hear so many tales.'

'What did you hear?' Hodges persisted.

'Well, sir, I was away, like, when it happened. But some said it was suicide.'

'Who did?'

'My dad did, for one. He gave him a lift up from the station—the railway was still operating then—and my dad had had to go down to fetch a delivery. He had the store then, you see. He saw Captain Derby get off the train as if he was sleep-walking and start up the road for home. He had no luggage, and he was in battledress. Looked as if he hadn't shaved for two days. It was a pouring wet July evening—must have been in 'forty-four—so my dad offered him a lift as far as the village and he was glad enough to accept. Not that he had a word to say for himself, just sat there like a sack of potatoes. We heard later he was on leave from Normandy, and my dad reckoned he was dead beat. He had to drop him in the village—there wasn't the petrol to go on, and it's another two miles to Plas Aderyn, but he must have made it all right. Two days later his father reported him missing. Said he couldn't settle and had gone out for a walk at night and never come back. He had the whole village searching, and they found where he'd gone down the bank into the lake. Of course it was hushed up a bit—no one wanted to hurt the old General, and it was bad enough the body never being found. But you can understand why there began to be rumours of suicide. Battle fatigue, I think they said it was. Some officers came down to see the General and it was all very hush-hush—but you know how these things get around. I only heard it from my dad, who had to give evidence at the inquest; he couldn't get over the way the Captain looked that night when he drove him up from the station. Talked about it to the end of his days, he did.'

'Didn't anyone else see Captain Derby while he was home on that last leave?'

'Only the people at Plas Aderyn.'

'Who was there besides the General and his wife?'

'The General's batman—Taylor, his name was. Oh, and old Olwen, of course. Servants were always hard to come by, with the place being so isolated. During the war they had to shut most of it up.'

'Are Taylor and old Olwen still alive?'

'Taylor I couldn't tell you. A few years later he came into money and moved away. Quite a large sum it was, though it was too bad it meant he left his old master. But I dare say the General could no longer afford his pay.'

'Why, were they poor?'

'The old man didn't leave anything except the house and some sticks of furniture. There was barely enough to pay the small legacy he left old Olwen.'

'Hardly a businessman.'

'No, he wasn't,' Mr Thomas said, glancing round his shop and reflecting that he was. 'They were well enough off when he came. He had his pension, mind, he wasn't starving, but everyone was very surprised. Didn't leave as much as I shall, I shouldn't wonder.' He smiled, self-satisfied.

'What about old Olwen, as you call her?' Hodges persisted.

'Olwen Roberts lives with her daughter now. But she is not good in the upper storey. You will not get anything out of her.'

'Is she very old?'

'Past eighty, but she is senile. Go and see for yourself, if you wish. Number two, Gwynfa Villas, just past the chapel. Mrs Hughes, her daughter is.'

***

When Hodges called on the pretext of being a distant relative of General Derby's, Mrs Hughes looked at him doubtfully.

'You're very welcome to come in, sir, but Mother's memory's not all it might be. I doubt she'll understand what you want.'

Old Olwen sat, a shapeless bundle, her jaws working ceaselessly. She did not look up when they entered, not even when her daughter said, 'Mother, there's a gentleman to see you.' Instead, Hodges found himself transfixed by the beady black eye of an African grey parrot on a perch beside her. He exclaimed aloud. 'You don't see many of those.'

'He belonged to the General,' Mrs Hughes explained proudly. 'We took him over when the old man died. Couldn't leave you to starve, could we, Polly? A wonderful talker he is, too.'

'Nuts,' said the parrot distinctly.

'Not again, you greedy bird.'

'Nuts. You're nuts,' the parrot insisted.

Mrs Hughes said proudly, 'Isn't he a clever boy?'

'They live to a great age, don't they?' Hodges said. 'Is this one old?' He congratulated himself on having avoided a gender, since there seemed some doubt about the parrot's sex.

'The vet says he's fifty,' Polly's owner answered.

'Did General Derby have him long?'

'Since just before the war, Mr Taylor once told me—the General's batman he was.'

'Taylor, where are my dress studs?' the parrot demanded in a completely different voice.

'That's the General,' Mrs Hughes whispered as if in the presence of genius. 'He imitates all of them—we know what they sounded like.'

'Who was the "nuts"?' Hodges asked, also in a whisper.

'That was Taylor.'

'Does he ever imitate General Derby's son?'

'No, because he hardly ever heard him. Captain Derby was away at the war, you see.'

'And does he imitate your mother?'

'Oh, yes. It makes me feel quite queer at times. It's her as she used to be. Sometimes I could swear she's recovered, but when I come in it's only Polly here.'

'It must be most peculiar,' Hodges agreed sympathetically. 'Rather like hearing a ghost.'

'Yes, there they are dead and gone and that parrot will say, "Thank you, Olwen, that will do nicely," just like Mrs Derby used to say. They were good people, very generous to Mother. It's a shame such a tragedy had to happen to them.'

'You mean their son's death?'

'Yes, dreadful to think of him lying at the bottom of the lake.'

'You won't fish him out of the lake,' old Olwen said suddenly. 'He was never in it.'

'Now, Mother, you know that's not true.'

The small shapeless bundle relapsed into silence. Mrs Hughes looked at the Lieutenant expressively.

'You see how it is,' she whispered.

'You're nuts,' the parrot said rudely.

Discomfited, Lieutenant Hodges took his leave.

***

A year later the unit was back in the Elan Valley for more manoeuvres, this time against an imaginary enemy striking southwards. No enemy would have done such a thing, but that merely added to the make-believe atmosphere. This was playing at soldiers on the grand scale. Plas Aderyn was still standing and still empty, but Lieutenant Hodges was relieved to find that he was posted at one of the lower lakes, to hold the road that ran like a dividing line between two levels, where the numbing thunder of the dam, unending, drove everything else out of mind.

So he was not best pleased when someone said to him in the mess that evening, 'Hear you saw a ghost up here last year.'

Of course he should have known the men would talk and the story get around, yet he was unprepared for it. 'I don't know about a ghost,' he said shortly. 'We encountered some village idiot hanging round an old house.'

He gave a brief account of the events at Plas Aderyn, saying nothing about the house being securely locked. 'He was getting excited,' he concluded, 'and I thought it best to come away before we frightened him. You never know what half-wits like that will do.'

'Nothing very ghostly about that,' the enquirer said in disappointment. 'I was expecting a headless lady at the least.'

'Where did all this take place?' a quiet voice demanded.

Hodges looked up to meet the gaze of Colonel Anstruther.

Several officers from other units had been invited to observe the manoeuvres. Anstruther was one of these. He was a legendary figure, his war service one long record of decorations and citations, and one of the youngest officers to achieve a full colonelcy. It seemed unlikely that his query was motivated by anything other than politeness.

'Plas Aderyn, sir,' Hodges said.

'Isn't that General Derby's old home?'

'I believe it is, sir.'

'And now you claim it's got a ghost?'

The grey eyes were amused and disbelieving.

'I don't claim anything,' Hodges said.

'Very wise. There are so many possible interpretations. The supernatural should always be our last resort.'

Hodges agreed with him, though in this case, where he had exhausted all natural explanations, the supernatural was all that remained. Fortunately for him, the talk turned to other channels, and it was only later, after the meal had been cleared away and the company had dispersed for the evening, that Anstruther sought him out.

The Colonel came to the point at once. 'Tell me what really happened at Plas Aderyn, Lieutenant,' he commanded, drawing up a chair. 'I'm sure there's more to it than you told us. Aha, I see from your face that I'm right.'

Nothing loath, the Lieutenant went over everything from the beginning. His superior listened without saying a word.

'What do you make of it, sir?' Hodges asked when the silence had prolonged itself into what felt like eternity. 'Do you believe in ghosts?'

'I don't know,' Colonel Anstruther said slowly, 'but if I did I could believe there'd be one here. I used to know the Derbys,' he added in explanation. 'That was why I was interested, of course.'

'Did you know their son, sir?'

The Colonel gave him a sharp glance. 'Very well. He and I were at Sandhurst together. Now tell me why you asked.'

'Only because I understand there was some question of suicide when he was drowned in the lake while on leave from Normandy, although I understand an open verdict was returned.'

'Jack Derby committed suicide all right.' The Colonel spoke with absolute conviction. 'It was the most sensible thing he could do. He was not on leave; he'd run away from the battlefield. For cowardice in the face of the enemy, he would have been court-martialled and shot.'

'Poor devil,' Hodges said involuntarily.

'Poor devil indeed. I don't believe Jack Derby was a coward. He'd kept up magnificently until then. It's just that when you're in an exposed position, with no hope of relief or reinforcement and being constantly pounded by the enemy's guns, most of us would walk out if we thought we could get away with it. The trouble was that Jack Derby did. What made it all the worse was that he was the son of a general, and a general who'd won the VC. General Derby wasn't equipped to understand what Jack had been through. It wouldn't surprise me if he hadn't suggested the lake.'

'But that would be murder!'

'No more so than putting a man against a wall and pumping lead into him. At least Jack avoided that disgrace, which would certainly have killed his father. But it can't have been an easy decision. On the whole I'm not surprised to hear he's a ghost.'

'The old woman who used to work there,' Hodges said hesitantly, 'maintains he's not in the lake.'

'What?'

'Yes, sir. Of course she's senile. I dare say she was getting confused.'

Colonel Anstruther showed a trace of excitement. 'Where is she? Is she still alive?'

'I don't know, sir. I saw her last year in the village. I can easily find out, if you like.'

'Do that,' the Colonel said. 'I'd like to see her. I'm going to lay Jack Derby's ghost. When a man's dead he has the right to sleep easy. And so have the rest of us.'

***

Old Olwen was still alive. She seemed the same in every detail when the two officers were ushered in, a hunched grey bundle sitting over a coal fire despite the warmth of May.

'Mother feels the cold,' Mrs Hughes explained unnecessarily. 'And of course poor Polly does too.'

The parrot, who had been dozing on his perch, opened his eyes at their coming. Grey, wrinkled, reptilian eyelids rolled up over his round black eyes.

'Good morning,' Colonel Anstruther said cheerily, approaching the old woman with a professional bedside air. 'You used to know some friends of mine, the Derbys. I thought you could tell me how they were.'

Silence.

'The Derbys at Plas Aderyn,' he prompted.

Old Olwen said suddenly, 'They're all dead.'

'Fancy that now!' Mrs Hughes exclaimed delightedly. 'Mother understood what you said.'

Anstruther shot her a warning glance. 'Do you remember Jack Derby?' he asked gently.

The old woman's eyes were blank. Behind her, the parrot clawed his way to one end of his perch, then the other.

'Excited he is,' Mrs Hughes informed them. 'Come, Polly, be a good boy.'

The parrot let out an ear-splitting screech that caused both officers to start nervously.

'Who's he imitating?' Hodges asked.

'No one, sir. That's just his parrot language.'

'Sounds pretty bad to me.'

'You blackmailing hound,' the parrot said distinctly, in what Hodges recognised as General Derby's voice.

Anstruther turned pale. 'My God! It's uncanny, I could have sworn the old boy was in this room.'

'He often says it, sir,' Mrs Hughes apologised. 'No matter who's here. Embarrassing it is.'

'You're nuts,' the parrot said.

'You're nuts,' old Olwen echoed.

Anstruther said, 'I should be if I had to live with that.'

'That's the General's batman, sir. Taylor,' Lieutenant Hodges explained.

'I know. I knew Taylor. But imagine the old General having to live with the fellow everlastingly saying that.'

Anstruther drew up a chair and took old Olwen's hand in his strong one. 'Tell me about the time Jack Derby died.'

The filmed moist eyes rested on his for a moment, then swiveled away, blank.

'It was summer, wasn't it?' Anstruther persisted. 'He came home unexpectedly on leave. He went out for a walk one night and didn't come back. They found where he'd fallen into the lake.'

Silence.

'Olwen, you may clear away.' Mrs Derby's gracious tones came clearly.

'Yes, madam,' Olwen said.

The Colonel tugged gently at her hand. 'You remember Jack Derby, don't you—Jack who was drowned in the lake?'

'He came back,' she said.

'Yes, I know. He took part in the Normandy landings and then he came back on leave. Tell me what happened, Olwen. I'm perfectly sure you know.'

'I used to take his meals. Up all those stairs. I was out of breath, I can tell you.'

Mrs. Hughes said, 'Fancy her remembering that!'

'You liked him, didn't you?'

'You blackmailing hound,' the parrot repeated.

Anstruther looked strained. 'Could we move him out?'

'It's your uniforms, sir,' Mrs Hughes said soothingly. 'They get him excited, see. He hasn't seen them for years.' She turned to Hodges. 'You were in civvies when you called last year.'

'Quite right. I was. But we can hardly do a quick-change. Should we come back again some other day?' This last was to Anstruther, who said quickly, 'Who's to say it wouldn't be exactly the same?'

'The same as before, sir, will do nicely,' the parrot said obsequiously. 'I wouldn't want anything to happen to Captain Jack.'

It gave another ear-splitting screech, and old Olwen said, 'It's none of our business, Taylor. I won't go along with you.'

'You're nuts.'

'Nuts in May,' Hodges said, joking. The non-sequiturs were getting him down. He did not feel the same desire as Anstruther to lay Jack Derby's ghost, for time had blurred the terror he had felt as he approached Plas Aderyn. If Jack Derby had yielded to the fear all men feel in the face of danger, he was neither sympathetic nor shocked. It had happened before he was born. In a sense he himself had run away from that laugh—

And suddenly the laugh was all around him, a terrible maniac sound, as the parrot reared up on its perch, wings flapping, while shriek after shriek came from its open beak.

'Come and get me, ha-ha-ha! Come and get me!'

In the sudden silence old Olwen said quite distinctly, 'That was Captain Jack.'

***

Colonel Anstruther recovered first. He put a hand on old Olwen's shoulder, almost visibly restraining himself from shaking her.

'What do you mean—that was Captain Jack?' he demanded. Hodges was surprised by the hoarseness of his voice.

The old woman shrank away from him. 'I heard him,' she said, and began to cry.

'Now you've upset her,' Mrs Hughes said reproachfully. It was impossible to tell whether she was accusing the Colonel or the bird. She pushed past and put her arms around her mother. 'There now, dear, it's all right.'

'Mrs Hughes,' Hodges interrupted urgently, 'do you ever let that bird out?'

'Let him out?' She stared at him stupidly.

'I mean, is he allowed to fly?'

'Oh, no. He mightn't come back, might he?'

'Could he—has he ever escaped?'

'No. We had a special chain put on him. But the General used to let him fly about the house.'

'Are you sure he didn't get out?' Lieutenant Hodges persisted. 'Just before I came to see you last year?'

If only that could be the explanation! But Mrs Hughes was already shaking her head. 'We take him outside sometimes in the summer, but we don't let him off his chain.'

'No good, Hodges. That would have been too easy an answer.' Colonel Anstruther looked suddenly tired. Old Olwen continued to whimper, and the parrot had become a bundle of ragged grey feathers hunched miserably in the middle of his perch. It was as though all three had been diminished by the bird's outburst and could never be the same again. Hodges felt the prickling of gooseflesh. He was unashamedly relieved when the Colonel stood up to go.

Outside, Anstruther hesitated.

'Where to now, sir?' Hodges asked.

'There's no need for you to come,' the Colonel said, 'but I'm going up to Plas Aderyn. I want to get to the bottom of this.'

Hodges's heart sank, but he said dutifully, 'I'll come with you.'

Anstruther looked at him keenly. 'I tell you, there's no need. Jack Derby was a good friend of mine. Besides, I've always felt guilty about him. It was my evidence that convicted him.'

'I didn't know it ever came to a court-martial, sir.'

'It didn't, but I was responsible for his arrest. Unfortunately, in the confusion he escaped—after all, it was a major battle—and made his way back here. It wasn't too difficult after D-Day; officers were to and fro across the Channel all the time. And by the time the military police got here to arrest him, he was lying at the bottom of the lake.'

'Mr Thomas in the general store mentioned something about some soldiers coming.'

'Well, now you know why they came. Naturally, the affair was hushed up in the circumstances. Jack was dead, and there was his father to think of. If it had got out, it would have sent the General round the bend. He was one of the old school: die at your post even if it's pointless, if that's what you've been ordered to do. To use your common sense was to besmirch your honour. I've often wondered if he knew.'

'About his son, you mean?'

'Yes. Did Jack tell him? It would have taken some guts if he did. Funny, when you think that Jack was accused of cowardice. Perhaps you understand now why I think the General may have suggested the lake.'

'I begin to, sir. The equivalent of presenting his son with a loaded pistol.'

'Exactly. Jack may have felt he had good reason to come back and haunt. So I'm going up to Plas Aderyn to see if I can help him.'

Hodges said, 'I'll come too.'

***

Nothing had changed at Plas Aderyn. It was quintessentially the same. The rhododendrons bordering the driveway might have been fractionally higher; there might have been another slate or two off the roof. One of the urns on the balustrade of the lower terrace had toppled over and lay spilling something more like dust than earth across the flags. As they parked the car a squirrel darted away, chattering shrilly, but no birdsong rang in the woods.

The old uneasiness settled upon Hodges like the weight of a heavy coat. He glanced at Colonel Anstruther, who was looking about him with frank curiosity.

'I expect it's changed since you saw it, sir.'

'I never did see it,' Anstruther answered. 'I wasn't in the habit of visiting Jack's home. It must have been a magnificent place once. Pity it had to go to rack and ruin. Let's go and take a look inside.'

Hodges followed, uncertain of how to account for his own reluctance and quite unable to tell Anstruther how he felt. The Colonel was striding boldly forward, as if he were an expected guest. His feet crunched confidently on the gravel. Overconfidently? Were his shoulders too square-set? Hodges dismissed such notions as part of his own disturbed imaginings. After all, he was keeping pace with the Colonel and not exactly hanging back.

By silent consent they ignored the main doorway under its portico and went round to the back of the house.

'Everything's locked, sir,' Hodges volunteered. 'I tried the doors and windows when I was here last year.'

'Then we'll just have to break in, shan't we?' Anstruther said testily. 'Most of the glass has gone in the larder window. Help me knock out the rest and see if you can squeeze through.'

The Lieutenant was much smaller and lighter than the Colonel; it was common sense that he should go first. Nevertheless, Hodges regretted his lack of bulk and inches. What might be waiting for him when he got inside?

Nothing was, of course, though he heard mice scamper and detected movement in the dust-swathed cobwebs where spiders lurked. He turned to Anstruther. 'I'll see if I can unbolt the kitchen door, sir. That would be the best way for you to come in.'

The bolts resisted him at first, and when he mastered them they squeaked resentment at their long deprivation of oil. He stepped out to join the Colonel, and as he did so the air was darkened by beating wings. Great black flapping wings that folded and settled about the body of an enormous carrion crow, who perched on an outhouse not half a dozen yards distant and said interrogatively, 'Caw?'

'Caw yourself!' Hodges answered in relieved reflex. The crow wouldn't do them any harm. And it was not unfitting that it should preside over what was literally 'the place of the bird.'

'Ugly brute, isn't he?' said the Colonel. 'Bet he's had his share of newborn lambs.'

Hodges looked at the cruel heavy beak distastefully. He had momentarily forgotten that, for all its name, the carrion crow did not always wait for death.

'Caw!' the bird said derisively.

'Perhaps, sir,' Hodges suggested, 'we'd better get inside.'

The Colonel led the way through the stone-flagged kitchen towards the hall. Hodges was surprised by the gloom. What with boarded-up or shuttered windows, encroaching trees, and dirt-encrusted panes, very little light entered Plas Aderyn and what there was was grey. There was no trace of the sunlight they had left outside; it was as though the sun had never shone in these high rooms with their elaborate plaster-work ceilings, although the house faced south-west. Nor was Hodges prepared for the smell, a decaying, musty odour that seemed to cling to everything.

'Dry rot here all right,' the Colonel observed.

As if in confirmation, his foot went through the tread of the bottom stair. The wood did not snap, it gave way almost with a sigh of protest, enveloping the Colonel's shoe in a cloud of feathery, spore-laden dust.

'Careful, Hodges,' the Colonel warned. 'Doesn't look as though these stairs will bear us. Keep well away from the centre of these treads.'

'Better let me go first, sir,' Hodges suggested. 'If it bears me, it ought to be all right for you.'

He led the way, keeping to the outside edge and walking gently as he gripped the banister-rail. Behind him he could hear the Colonel, who was breathing hard as if short of wind.

The first-floor landing, a replica of the hall beneath it, seemed to I have innumerable doors, all now standing open upon the rotting rooms within. Yet Hodges felt himself drawn as if by instinct to the right one—the room above the porch from which he had seen the figure wave. It was a square room, not as big as the master-bedrooms, with dressing-rooms that lay to either side of it. The glass in its sash-window was broken and rain and leaves had flooded in. The mess in the grate suggested that jackdaws had nested in the chimney, and a closer look revealed the body of a bird. Hodges felt the hairs on the back of his neck prickle. He had an overwhelming urge to get out. He glanced nervously behind him as though afraid the door might move suddenly upon its hinges and trap him forevermore. But no. It remained unbudging and wide open and Colonel Anstruther was attentively examining the door.

He looked up as Hodges turned towards him. 'The owners of this place didn't intend to be disturbed by nocturnal prowlers. Ever seen such a massive lock on a bedroom door?'

The lock would have done service for a strong-room. It was surprisingly strong, a kind of double mortice which shot two steel bolts into the jamb. The door would have given at the hinges before such a lock would burst.

Anstruther was looking about with interest. 'Odd that it's only on this one door.' He walked across to one of the master-bedrooms. 'The others have normal locks. They must have kept the family jewels in this room. Come on, let's see if they've left any there for us.'

Hodges could do nothing but follow the Colonel, but his every nerve cried 'Don't!' The square room had an inexplicable atmosphere of terror; all he wanted was to get out. It was as though the walls were closing in on him, the ceiling pressing down from above, the trees massing together outside the windows to prevent any escape by that means. While Anstruther stood still in the middle of the room and stared around him, he walked over to the window and gazed out. He could just glimpse the sunlit terrace like something in another world.

Anstruther joined him. 'Must have been lovely once. See what a good view you get of the driveway. No one could sneak up on you unawares. You can see the turn-in from the road and the stretch below the lower terrace. Gave you plenty of time to get the red carpet out.'

'You can see the lake too,' Hodges said involuntarily.

Anstruther nodded. 'So you can. That is, you could if the bars would let you.'

'Bars?'

'This window used to be barred.'

The Colonel ran his hand down the window-frame which clearly bore the marks of sockets which had once held bars in place.

Hodges shivered. 'It must have been like a prison, with that lock on the door as well.'

The distress which oppressed him, he realised, was very much like what a prisoner must feel: the caged hopelessness; the resentment of injustice; frustration and self-loathing; envy of all who had the freedom to come and go. He imagined himself sitting at the window, eyes fixed on the empty drive, for in its last years Plas Aderyn could have had few visitors; even a delivery van would have been an event. Then suddenly someone comes, strangers come, a chance of rescue; one leaped up and waved one's arms about: 'Here I am. Come and get me. Come and get me!'

'Steady on, old boy,' the Colonel said.

Hodges looked down at the restraining hand. Had he really waved his arms and shouted? Was it his own voice he had heard? Or was it the cry of madness or despair recreated by a parrot from the lips of a man long dead?

White-faced, he shook off Anstruther's hand. 'My God, sir, this room *was* a prison. It's where they used to keep Captain Jack.'

'Jack Derby? Who kept him? What's got into you? You know he was drowned in the lake.'

The Colonel's questions came like a hail of bullets, but Hodges was too excited to reply.

'Old Olwen said he didn't drown. She used to bring his meals up. And the parrot heard him often enough.'

Anstruther shook him. 'Will you kindly explain what you're talking about? You sound beside yourself.'

'No.' Hodges pointed to the door, where a line of bruised wood showed at shoulder-height. 'The poor devil must have beaten his hands to pulp with his hammering. And only his gaolers to hear.'

'And who were his gaolers?'

'Why, his parents, Taylor the batman, old Olwen.'

Anstruther looked shaken. 'I don't know what you mean.'

'Let's go outside, sir, if you don't mind.'

Anstruther led the way.

On the landing Lieutenant Hodges regained a little of his composure.

'I can't prove it,' he began, 'but Jack Derby's body was never recovered from the lake and old Olwen swore he wasn't in it. Yet he's never been seen again. So what happened to him when he came home accused of cowardice, with the military police hard on his heels? Obviously death was the neatest solution. But suppose Jack Derby wasn't willing to die? You mentioned that his father would have taken his disgrace hard and might have suggested the lake as an honourable alternative to court-martial. But what if Jack wouldn't agree? The disgrace would become public and the family name be sullied. Sooner than have that, I think his father locked him up.'

Anstruther said shakily, 'It's possible. General Derby was a determined and autocratic man. But what happened in the end? Where *is* Jack?' He glanced round—nervously, it seemed.

'I think he went mad,' Hodges said. 'You remember the parrot mimicking Taylor? "You're nuts," he kept saying, "You're nuts." Shut up here, year in, year out, seeing no one but those four, and with that insistent suggestion—if you weren't mad to start with, you'd probably end up that way.'

'It doesn't seem possible,' Anstruther said, 'that they should keep Jack here in secret for—what is it? Years, you say?'

'He was believed dead and there were only the four of them. Nobody came to the house. Or if they did, well, that window commands a good view of the driveway. Jack could be silenced while visitors were here.'

Hodges had a disturbing vision of that wildly waving figure swept from the window as if felled by a sudden blow. Mr Thomas had described the ex-batman as a big fellow... And no one had seen Jack's corpse.

For corpse there was, Hodges was convinced of it. Jack Derby was no longer alive. He could almost fix the date of his death if he knew when the ex-batman had departed...

He turned to Anstruther. 'I'll tell you something else.'

Anstruther looked at him in mute enquiry. He seemed suddenly to have shrunk.

'Taylor extorted money from the General as the price of his silence,' Hodges said. 'You heard what the General called him, over and over again: "you blackmailing hound." After Jack's death, Taylor quit with most of the General's fortune. We know he came into money and the General died nearly broke.'

'If he's still alive…'

'You could prove nothing. It would be a waste of time to try.'

There was a sheen of sweat on Anstruther's face. He said thickly, 'Let's get out of here.'

Hodges was only too eager to comply. Once again he led the way down the rotten staircase, the Colonel treading at his heels. The isolation, the emptiness, the silence, these were getting on his nerves. It was as if the atmosphere of unhappiness that clung to Plas Aderyn was seeping into his soul.

In the hall a single shaft of sunlight had found its way between the shutter-boards. It pointed like a finger up the staircase in the direction from which they had come.

The Colonel mopped his face. 'I don't know about you, Hodges, but I've had enough horrors for one day. I need time to think over what you've said, to get adjusted—'

And then above them they heard the laugh.

There was no mistaking it. Even though the Colonel had only heard it reproduced by the parrot, he knew it at once for what it was. But now it rang out immediately above them, from the empty room at the top of the stairs.

'Come and get me, ha-ha-ha! Come and get me!'

The maniac shrieks went on.

White-faced, Anstruther and Hodges stared at each other; then, with one accord turned for the door.

'Don't go. Come and get me, Anstruther. Why don't you? I'm up here.'

The Colonel stopped, transfixed. His eyes sought Hodges. Hodges had also stopped.

'There's someone there,' the Colonel whispered.

'There can't be,' Hodges said.

They both knew the room was empty. There was nowhere anyone could have hid. If in another room they would have heard him crossing the landing above them. But still the voice went on.

'Come up here, Anstruther. Come and get me.'

The Colonel took a step towards the stairs.

'Don't go, sir,' Hodges protested.

The Colonel seemed not to have heard.

'That's right,' the voice cried, as if its possessor could see them, 'since you should be here instead of me.'

The Colonel stopped again. His face was ashen. 'What do you mean?' he cried.

The voice seemed exultant at being answered. 'Don't tell me you've forgotten,' it called. 'How you turned tail and walked the other way in a battle and I went after you and brought you back. We could have hushed it up, I wouldn't have split on you, but you didn't trust me enough for that. You arranged things, staged some witnesses, and accused me of cowardice.'

'Why, you—'

'Liar, is it? All right, come and get me. Come and see what it's like up here, behind locked doors and barred windows where I spent the rest of my youth.'

'Jack, I didn't mean—'

'You meant me to be shot. A neat, quick ending, and no risk of my betraying you. When I escaped you were worried, until you heard I'd drowned myself. I wish now I had. My father suggested it, because he thought only of the family name. But I wouldn't agree. I didn't see why I should die when I was innocent. So he condemned me to a living death up here.'

'No! It's not true.' Anstruther's voice sounded strangled.

'It's as true as I stand here. Come and get me, Anstruther. Come and get me. I've waited for you long enough.'

Anstruther was clinging to the newel-post.

'It's no use,' the voice went on. 'All your honours and your medals can't save you. Your courage was founded on a lie. I know you tried to expiate, but while you expiated I rotted here. Was that right? Was that just? Was that honourable, Anstruther? Is that how an officer and a gentleman behaves? Come up and face me man to man, and see if you recognise me. After all these years I've changed.'

Like a man in a dream, Anstruther let go the newel-post, squared his shoulders, and faced the stairs.

'Sir!' Hodges called, not knowing what to say, what to make of these fantastic accusations.

Anstruther took no heed. As if on ceremonial parade, he mounted the staircase, head held high and hand where his sword hilt should have been. Hodges stood watching the stiff back, hearing the steady footsteps, until everything suddenly disappeared in a crash of splintered wood and dust.

He thought he heard Anstruther cry out, he thought he heard Captain Jack's laughter, but he was sure of nothing but the great hole which gaped halfway up the staircase where the rotten timbers had given way.

There was no sound now but a last patter of falling debris. With infinite caution Hodges approached and leaned over, clinging to the banisters, which still seemed firm enough.

Through the dust and the splintered timbers he saw Anstruther lying, his body unnaturally still. But there was something else, something lying beneath him; a glimpse of khaki; a scatter of buttons, tarnished gilt. As the dust subsided, whiteness gleamed. There were fingers. Forearms. Surely that was a skull, still with a lock of dark hair clinging to it. An officer's swagger-stick.

Hodges gazed, faint with horror, fighting against vertigo, to where in the cellars below Plas Aderyn the broken-necked body of Colonel Anstruther lay clasped in the skeleton arms of Captain Jack.

THE DRUM

THEY WERE FINISHING lunch in the Green Dragon when Cynthia Lawson looked at her husband in the way she always did when a request was important to her, and asked: 'Do you think we might visit the museum while we're here, Harry?'

'Why not?' Henry Lawson said indulgently. 'Since you want to and since we've plenty of time.'

Cynthia was in no doubt which of these justifications was the operative one. Seven years of marriage to a man twenty years her senior had taught her her place in his scheme of things. Henry Lawson had a wife in the same way that he had a place in the country and a flat in town, polo ponies, clubs, the discreetest of Bentleys and a connoisseur's taste in wines; his position required these things and he was able to provide them out of the ample funds left by his father and his aunts. This position, which was that of colonel of an exclusive regiment, also required that he should take a wife of the right social background, and although matrimony in itself held few attractions for him, that of doing his duty did. At the age of forty-two Colonel Henry Lawson, M.C, had put himself discreetly on the marriage-market and made overtures at house-parties and race-meetings to the mothers of several eligible young ladies, all of whom, seeing only the Colonel's annual income and elegant turn-out, regretted that they themselves were not widowed or twenty years younger, and resolved to forward his suit.

It was unfortunate—not least for the Colonel—that at this point he met Cynthia Lodge. Beyond a pretty face, a delightful figure and a sweet disposition, Cynthia had nothing to recommend her. Her parents were dead, and having some artistic talent, she earned her living as a window-dresser. It was while visiting an aunt who clutched at the fringes of society that she was introduced because politeness demanded it to

Colonel Lawson, who fell in love with her forthwith.

Falling in love was the one thing Henry had not bargained for. It upset all his plans. Cynthia's indifference to him was another. He was accustomed to consider himself a catch, and the ill-concealed eagerness of the matrons he had approached had strengthened him in that conviction. He redoubled his attentions, and Cynthia, wooed by Henry, urged by her aunt, and flattered by her friends into believing that Henry was her fate, accepted him. The wedding took place at St James's, Piccadilly, and the honeymoon was spent in the Bahamas.

It was not until they returned to London and Northamptonshire that it occurred to Henry that they had little in common except their name and address. Cynthia remained aloof and beautiful even in bed, and what was worse, she failed to produce an heir. Her beauty and taste, aided by Henry's money, ensured her photograph's frequent appearance in the glossier magazines, but while Henry was justifiably proud of his wife's ability to draw attention, he was much less pleased by its results. He was, in fact, exceedingly jealous of his treasure. The sight of Cynthia dancing with another man was more than he could bear, and while he was too sophisticated to resort to overt displays of his feelings, he let her know about them none the less. Cynthia remained as always—aloof and beautiful. It was the only consolation Henry had. Her indifference to the admiration she excited seemed to be total. Her husband at least fared no worse than anyone else.

Gradually the relationship established itself between them of extreme politeness and very little else. Cynthia accompanied her husband on all those occasions when it was seemly for a wife to be in evidence, and Henry lent her the support of his presence whenever he judged it was required. Despite the disparity in their ages, they were a handsome couple and socially they were much in demand. It was on their way back from a country house-party in Wales that they had stopped in Carringford for lunch, and the Green Dragon was the best hotel the town boasted. Even Henry had been pleased with the wine.

Perhaps it was the after-effects of this vintage—a 1957 Chateauneuf du Pape—that made him unusually accommodating towards his wife's suggestion that they visit the museum. Museums did not come within Henry Lawson's sphere of interest, which to many people would have seemed circumscribed. But Cynthia was looking exceptionally pretty; the week-end had gone off rather well; he was not in the mood to refuse a simple request that would make her happy and perhaps draw from her one of her rare but lovely smiles.

'What's in the museum of such particular interest?' he enquired as he tucked her small gloved hand under his arm.

'Nothing, Harry, really, except some china figures and I'd rather like to see them. That's all.'

'I suppose you'll be wanting me to buy them for your collection?'

'I doubt very much if the museum would sell.' She peered up at him from under her shadowy hat-brim. 'Besides, you think my collection is a waste of time.'

'Waste of money, rather,' he said kindly. 'But of course if it keeps you happy I don't mind.'

'You're very good to me,' she said as if she meant it, and turned into the entrance of the museum.

It was almost exactly three years ago that Cynthia Lawson had begun to collect eighteenth-century china figurines. The hobby had grown on her, to become a ruling passion. She frequented dealers and salerooms and junk- and antique-shops. Her husband was amused but not interested, although generous, regarding the hobby as ladylike and harmless enough. It never struck him as odd that a woman not yet thirty should choose to devote her life to china figurines. He followed her meekly past a startled-looking attendant and up the stairs labelled 'To the Museum'.

The stairs were flanked by an imperfectly reconstructed tessellated pavement—a foretaste of the glories that were to come. The museum proper was lined with stuffed birds in glass cases, all posed in disturbingly naturalistic stance. The rest of the cases contained a conglomeration of objects donated by local residents or their heirs. Old firearms gave place to a corn-dolly, a Victorian wedding-dress to local tiles. The windows, high up and operated by sash-cords, were tightly closed against the world outside. The atmosphere was timeless, faintly musty, and productive of awe in those who penetrated this tomb.

The Lawsons were the only visitors. It was not surprising that the attendant had given them a startled look. As a rule, no one came from one week's end to another, and those who did were quick to hurry away. The only exceptions were those like Cynthia Lawson who came expressly to see the china figurines. The fame of the collection, known as the Brightwell Gift, was widespread, and several of its items were unique. Visitors even came from America to see it, and often tried to persuade the museum to sell.

Cynthia picked her way through the ranks of sharp-angled glass cases to where a smaller room opened at the back. The doors into it were held open with giant wedges. A notice above the door announced the Brightwell Gift. Henry followed her more slowly, already bored with the visit. It was like Cynthia to have arranged their lunching in Carringford and engineered their visit to the museum. He felt obscurely resentful towards her, and this resentment was heightened by the absence of anywhere to sit. The trustees of the Carringford Museum had manifestly not reckoned with visitors unable to keep on their feet. A brisk walk round, a lingering, a returning—these were too evidently the moves one was expected to make. No concession was offered to peaceful contemplation, the trustees judging rightly that few objects warranted as much. Even the Brightwell Gift, though displayed with taste and to advantage, was designed to be inspected on foot. Henry, having walked all round its informatively labelled cases, was forced to retreat to the museum's main room, where at least he could pretend interest in a brace of flintlock pistols, a rusted pike, and other military mementoes of that kind.

Through the wedged-open door he could see Cynthia admiring. She had clearly forgotten both that he existed and was bored. Her concentration gave her the air of a sleep-walker as she moved very slowly from case to case of the display. If he could only put a glass case around Cynthia so that people would come and look their fill and turn away, he would be free for ever from the festering anxiety that his sleep-walker might someday awake—but to someone else. So long as she remained aloof and beautiful to all men, he forgave her for including him in their ranks; but let her show—just once—that she was human, and Henry trembled to think how he might react.

There had been a moment when he had feared the worst was about to happen. Three or four years ago there had been unmistakable signs. He preferred not to remember the episode, for after all the matter had ended well. At least it had if you could so describe a hushed-up scandal, a hasty resignation to save the regiment's good name. It was curious that Cynthia should have looked with favour on the one officer in the regiment who had almost brought disgrace upon them all. It was as though she had a nose for the unsound—the result, Henry feared, of her own unsatisfactory upbringing. Belonging to a so-called 'artistic' profession, involved to a degree in bohemian cafe-society, what chance had a girl like Cynthia to form standards, still less question their validity? Because he loved her, he—Henry—had forgiven her, particularly since she protested her innocence. Besides, he was convinced there had been no improper conduct; it was an indiscretion merely, a social lapse. Nevertheless, he had been shaken by his own reaction; he had not known how powerful his feelings were. The young officer's resignation shortly afterwards for other reasons had seemed to him Providence at work.

Henry was a firm believer in Providence, that is to say, in things going infallibly his way. 'The Lord helps those who help themselves' was one of his favourite sayings, and he certainly encouraged the Lord to be generous with his aid. It was in this spirit that he began his tour of inspection, and he caught sight of the drum with a sense of confidence not misplaced.

It was a small drum hung high on the wall with the drumsticks arranged above it, near the wedged-open doors that led to the second room. Its faded colours were not those of any regiment he recognised, and the style of its accoutrements proclaimed it an antique. It was the kind of drum a drummer-boy might have carried into action—a superior child's plaything for someone scarcely more than a child. Regimental as opposed to military matters were dear to Henry Lawson. With some difficulty (for he was slightly near-sighted) he stooped to read the label far below.

This told him that the drum had belonged to the 44th Regiment of Foot (barracks at Carringford), and had been carried in the Peninsular War and later in the Crimea, but upon the regiment's being merged with two others in 1861 to form the Royal Wiltshire Fusiliers, its colours had been solemnly hung up in Carringford Cathedral and the drum had found its way to the museum.

Henry Lawson was excited by this discovery in a particularly personal way. The Royal Wiltshires was his own regiment and the drum was therefore in a sense his drum. He knew all about the colours hanging threadbare and dusty in the Cathedral, but until this afternoon he had not known about the drum.

His first thought was to call Cynthia and tell her of his discovery. His second was that it would be pointless to do any such thing. Cynthia did not share his interest in the Regiment; she did not even understand it. To her, one unit in the British Army was very much like the next and all of them were dedicated to the same end of destruction. She was not an Army wife. It was Henry's weightiest condemnation of her; he could have forgiven her all the rest; but that she should look upon his beloved regiment as though it were another woman in his life—that Henry could never excuse. Moreover, it reminded him insistently of the essential unwisdom of his choice, for had he married a girl of the right social background, this unfortunate divergence would never have taken place. It was only the unexpected strength of his passions that had led him so sadly astray. There were moments when he almost hated Cynthia. Standing before the drum was one such. It was as much to spite his wife as to yield to some schoolboy compulsion to do it honour that Colonel Lawson stood rigidly to attention and saluted the regimental drum.

To his mingled amazement and horror, the drum began to beat.

The drumsticks suspended above it sprang suddenly into life. The drum's sound was excellent—the parchment must still have been taut—and the rhythm was crisp and distinct. It began very softly and rose in a quick crescendo, as though a child were beating it in terror and bravado before some irate adult rushed in and snatched the toy away. There was something insistent and desperate about its message, as though there was not much time, and at the same time it was ridiculously childish and conjured up visions of nursery tea. Rub-a-dubdub, rub-a-dub-dub, rub-a-dub, rub-a-dub, dub, dub, dub! With the last 'dub' the drumsticks struck the parchment as though they were determined to split it. And all at once the tattoo was over, the drumsticks back in their place, swaying slightly as if a breeze were blowing. The whole room was suddenly very still.

It was broken by a tattoo of a different nature—the tapping of Cynthia's high heels across the polished floor. She looked startled, but not frightened. 'Harry, what were you doing?' she asked.

'Nothing,' Henry Lawson said breathlessly. 'It was that drum. It started to beat.'

Cynthia followed the direction of his finger. 'That? But you couldn't play it hanging on the wall.'

'I didn't play it,' Henry answered grimly.

'Then who did?'

Her question was echoed by the attendant, who had come rushing in more startled than before, prepared to expostulate with the gentleman whose sense of humour was so misplaced. He looked disbelieving while Henry protested his innocence, remarking at the end, 'Well, sir, there's no one else.'

'That's exactly the point,' Henry said testily. His heart had begun to race uncomfortably and it was difficult to catch his breath. 'I was standing right here when it happened. There was no one else in the room.'

'Could it have been the wind?' Cynthia suggested. 'A sudden draught, perhaps?'

The attendant's eyes moved to the tightly closed windows. Henry had gone rather white. 'There's no natural explanation,' he said with difficulty. 'We're in the presence of a—a phenomenon, that's all. There's no need to be frightened, dearest.'

'I'm not afraid,' Cynthia said.

It was her husband, she thought, who seemed frightened. His brow was beaded with sweat. When he took her arm preparatory to leaving, it seemed as much for his reassurance as for her own.

The attendant still eyed them suspiciously. Henry essayed a tip. To his astonishment, the man drew back precipitately, as if he feared to be touched.

'I'll accept your word it wasn't you, sir, that climbed up and tampered with that drum. But if you ask me, these things don't happen without a purpose, though what that purpose is, I wouldn't know. All I do know is, you were standing here looking at it and it suddenly started to beat.' He turned aside and said very distinctly; 'I wouldn't want to be in your shoes.'

'Don't be a superstitious fool,' Henry told him, propelling Cynthia out. 'The incident has no significance whatever.' Not one of them believed what he said.

***

Henry did not refer to the incident again for some months, and when he did it was at the club. He had been joined at lunch by Syrett and Musgrave, and they were taking coffee in the lounge. Both men had held commissions in the Royal Wiltshires, which they had resigned to devote themselves to civilian life—Syrett as a partner in a firm of stockbrokers and Musgrave as a landowner and chairman of a local bench. Syrett was ebullient and cherubic, twice married and divorced by very pretty wives; Musgrave was angular and patrician, and an unmarried sister presided over his home. The three men had little in common except the Royal Wiltshires and regimental reminiscences had already loomed large in their talk. It was during an awkward lull in their conversation that Henry referred to the drum.

He began by asking if they knew of its existence. To his surprise, both did. Not that it was odd Musgrave should know of it; regimental history was a sideline of his; but that Syrett, who lived only for the present, should have heard of the 44th Regiment of Foot, still more of the drum their drummer-boys had carried—this was almost as unnatural as when the drum began to beat.

Henry looked enquiringly from one to the other of his companions. 'And I thought I had made a find!'

'Why should you think that?' Musgrave asked gently. 'The drum's existence is perfectly well known. It's mentioned in Bullingham-Jones's *Annals of the Royal Wiltshires*, as well as in one or two more popular accounts. Of course we haven't heard much about it lately.' He looked at Henry sharply over his coffee-cup with the look that had caused many a defendant to tremble in the dock. 'I hope you're not going to tell us,' he said equably, 'that the damn' drum started to beat?'

Some instinct caused Henry to keep silent. Smiling, he shook his head.

'Well, thank God for that,' Musgrave continued. 'We don't want to lose you.'

'Lose me? What are you talking about?'

It was Musgrave's turn to look surprised. 'The legend, you know,' he murmured. 'The drum always beats when the colonel is going to die.'

'Utter nonsense!' Henry said hotly. His heart had again started to race, although the doctor had assured him there was no cause for worry; a couple of tablets and he would be fine. He groped for the phial in his breast-pocket, aware of Musgrave's air of pained surprise. 'I mean,' he added hastily, 'that's an ignorant superstition.'

'But it happens to be a true one, all the same.'

Both men looked in astonishment at Syrett, who seemed the quintessence of imagination brought down to earth. He was no whit disconcerted by their expressions, in which politeness struggled with disbelief. On the contrary, he seemed to admit their right to be sceptical when he continued; 'My aunt heard it beat for Simmonds at Alamein.'

A German shell had cut short Simmonds's colonelcy, since when, Henry remembered, no colonel of the Wiltshires had died. He felt the sweat beginning to break out on his forehead, and hastily swallowed a tablet with his coffee.

'I think you'd better tell us the story, Syrett,' Musgrave pontificated from the bench. And no nonsense with it, either, his manner added. Stick to facts; the facts will speak for themselves.

Syrett, nothing loath, poured himself another cup of coffee. 'My aunt evacuated herself to Carringford,' he began. 'She feared her nerves "would not withstand an aerial bombardment", and her Pekinese's certainly wouldn't. Moreover, she had a large collection of very valuable china, and a house crammed full of antiques. She took a house in Carringford and migrated, and she was no sooner there than she was fretting to come back. She'd been born and bred in London and she loved it; in Carringford she had nothing to do. I suppose that was why she was alone in the museum one afternoon in October about a fortnight before Montgomery made his break-through. At any rate, the drum began to beat very quickly, although it hung too high for anyone to reach. My aunt insisted that it beat a definite rhythm which when I saw her later she was able to reproduce.'

With his fingers Syrett drummed out on the coffee-table the rub-a-dub-dub that Henry had already heard. Several club members looked round in protest at the disturbance. Henry swallowed a second tablet hastily.

'My aunt was familiar with the legend,' Syrett continued, 'and being superstitious, she believed it was true. When the news of El Alamein came through a week or two later, she told several people that Colonel Simmonds had been killed. Unfortunately it got to the War Office, who wanted to know how she knew the Wiltshires were there, and by what secret agency she knew their colonel had caught it before the casualty lists were even through. They sent someone down to see her about it, and my aunt told him all about the drum. Needless to say, the War Office didn't believe it; they kept an eye on her from then on.'

'What happened?' Musgrave asked eagerly. 'Did she convince them?'

'She had no time. She was killed by a flying-bomb while making a week-end visit to London.' Syrett paused. 'War Office or not, she certainly convinced me.'

'Why?' Musgrave demanded.

'Because she was not an imaginative woman. She could never have made that up.'

'But hallucinations…? Or possible natural explanations…?'

'She never had a hallucination in her life. As for natural explanations—well, there may be. But no one could find one at the time.'

'An interesting story,' Musgrave commented slowly.

Syrett smiled ruefully. 'An unlucky one for me. That damn' drum cost me an inheritance; I quarrelled with Aunt Minnie, you see. Don't forget, I was out in North Africa also. I was suspected of having opened my mouth too wide and given the old lady a bit too much information. I complained that she shouldn't have talked, and we had a row. She altered her will in a temper, and was killed before she could alter it back again. To teach me a lesson, she left all her priceless china to the local Carringford museum. They've got it there now in a special room named after her—the Brightwell Bequest, or something such.'

Syrett's smile, which had broadened to a grin, showed how little he really minded. He had already made more than the collection's worth. Nevertheless, as he rose to go a thought seemed to strike him. 'I wonder,' he said, 'why that damn' drum should beat and be so bloody selective into the bargain? Nothing less than the colonel of the regiment will do. There must be some incident or story behind it, only I'm always too lazy to find out.'

'I believe I can help you there,' Musgrave responded. 'The episode dates back to Napoleonic times. A drummer-boy was accused of some trifling misdemeanour and sentenced by the colonel to be flogged. The boy protested his innocence and offered to call witnesses to prove it;

the colonel refused to allow them to be called, and although several officers spoke up on behalf of the drummer, the flogging was duly carried out. The colonel presided at this entertainment, and he showed no mercy even then. As a result, the boy died a few days later, after promising that his drum would beat for joy every time a colonel was about to die. I had no idea the curse was indeed effective until you told us this story about your aunt.'

'Well, it didn't beat for old Lawson,' Syrett said jovially. 'He's all right. But watch out, Lawson, if you ever do hear it.' Syrett drummed the tattoo and was gone.

'A curious fellow,' Henry observed to Musgrave.

'Oh, I don't know. What makes you say that?'

'I mean you wouldn't think he was superstitious.'

'I don't think he is,' Musgrave said. 'He's related what to him are facts, not superstitions. The drum beats and Simmonds was killed at Alamein. It's only if you postulate a connection and then begin asking why there should be that you get into the realms of superstition; Syrett was careful not to do that.'

'But if I had heard that drum beat,' Henry persisted, 'would you think it was significant?'

'For myself, I should make sure all my affairs were in order.'

'You'd take it as seriously as that?'

'Just to be on the safe side,' Musgrave answered. 'Besides, it never hurts to be prepared, especially in these days of death on the roads, and death from smoking, and thrombosis and stomach-ulcers and the rest. We ought never to assume we are exceptions—"in the midst of life we are in death". That's why I think a man should have his affairs in order and his spiritual affairs above all.'

'You mean his conscience?' Henry hazarded. 'You can call it that if you like.'

Musgrave, Henry reflected, was not a comfortable companion. You asked for the bread of reassurance and he offered you a stone. Nevertheless, he was not seriously perturbed; his conscience was lighter than most men's—so light that he never troubled to have it weighed. What disquieted him was that Musgrave took a stupid superstition seriously and believed in the warning of the drum. Hitherto he had respected Musgrave as an upright honourable man whose love of justice found its social expression in his magisterial role; now he perceived that this passion for justice—quite apart from being (like any other passion) uncomfortable—was capable of creating in its victim a credulousness that had to be experienced to be believed. So long as the phenomenon of the drum could be interpreted as an act of retribution (Musgrave's justice), the magistrate was ready to believe in it. If he were pushed, he might even admit to satisfaction that his concept of justice extended beyond the grave.

Henry decided to push him, and said gently, 'If I had heard that drum beat, do you think I should inevitably die?'

'Not inevitably,' Musgrave said. 'Nothing's inevitable. But I think you should consider you'd been warned.'

'And how do you suggest I should react to the warning?'

'As I said. I'd put my conscience straight.'

'You think that might avert the disaster?'

'I don't know. I think it's worth a try. If it didn't, at least you'd be in a better state to meet it.'

'And what do you mean by "putting your conscience straight"?'

'Good God, man, I'm not the keeper of your conscience. That's something every man must decide for himself.'

'I don't think there's much on my conscience,' Henry said slowly, 'except the petty lapses of everyday—you know; impatience, irritability and so on.'

Musgrave nodded. 'I know.'

'As for big things,' Henry continued, 'I can't honestly think of much. I've not robbed or murdered or swindled. I'm not cruel so far as I know. My lies don't go beyond permissible degrees of greyness. I've done my duty. I've never knowingly been unjust.'

Musgrave, who was studying his finger-nails, interrupted. 'Some people might not agree with that last.'

Henry felt his face and throat flush a deep crimson. 'What are you getting at?'

'Don't you know?' Musgrave said evenly.

Henry decided to brazen it out. 'If you're referring to the business with young Randall,' he said, striving to sound dispassionate, 'I think we've been over it more than enough. You happen to disagree with my decision and you've a perfect right to do so. Equally I've a perfect right to stand by it. This is a free country after all.'

'The freedom to commit injustice is not included.'

'Who says it was injustice?' Henry cried. 'Damn it, Musgrave, Randall's financial position was hopeless. The fellow hadn't a penny to his name.'

'So because of a trifling debt at cards you ruined him.'

'I did nothing of the sort. I've no doubt he's done perfectly well since.'

'Did you ever learn what became of him?'

'I never tried to,' Henry said.

He would not willingly have heard the name Randall mentioned, still less have learned of its owner's whereabouts. James Randall, under pressure from his colonel, had resigned his commission in the Wiltshires. That was all Henry Lawson cared about. Of course there had been murmurs of injustice. Any decision except a unanimous one brought opposition in its train. And the decision to ask James Randall for his resignation had been anything but unanimous; indeed, Henry remembered with distaste, he had had almost to force it through, aided only by Major Williams, who always agreed with the most senior officer present and had become a major as a result. Technically, therefore, Henry and Williams had been able to ask for the lieutenant's resignation, just as, technically, they had grounds for doing so. An officer did not incur debts he could not discharge—even of fifty pounds; not even when the creditor—a fellow-lieutenant—was prepared to cancel the debt, which had been rashly incurred in the course of a game of poker. Henry still remembered the ingenuous way in which Lieutenant Randall had admitted that he was unable to pay. When Henry and Williams had requested his resignation, he had seemed thunderstruck.

The trouble was that he should never have been in the Wiltshires in the first place. He was only there because his father had been, but whereas the elder Randall was a fine officer whose death in action had been a loss to the Regiment, the son had—as Henry put it—'gone soft'. No doubt it was not to be wondered at; an only child brought up by a widowed mother; no doubt either that this helped to explain his attraction for women, all of whom responded in various degrees to his wistful, brown-eyed charm. Even Cynthia had responded, Henry remembered. And abruptly suppressed the thought. The flirtation—

no, not so much as a flirtation—had been so patently innocent that even Henry had been unable to find grounds for suspicion—a fact that had done nothing to dispose him favourably towards young Randall and had merely underlined the latter's offence. For it was an offence to win from Cynthia the kind of look her husband could not secure; to make her laugh with a wholehearted enjoyment Henry had never heard in her voice before. The fact that Randall saw her only in company and that nothing was ever said or hinted between them made it worse. It was as though his presence were enough to endow her with a radiance which, beautiful as she was, she did not normally possess. Of course Henry blamed himself for the situation. It was like calling to like—no doubt of that. A girl with the right background would not have wasted time on Randall, and if Randall had been the kind of officer the Wiltshires wanted, he would never have flirted with his colonel's wife. It was time he went, and Cynthia had shown no emotion—a fact which had pleased Henry very much. He had become (for the moment) more aware of her, more indulgent towards her, as if unconsciously he were trying to make up. When she first expressed an interest in china-collecting, he was eager to forward it by every financial means. He had been in this respect a generous husband, and Cynthia's contentment was his reward. Once Randall was removed, she recovered her usual composure, and Henry congratulated himself on a restoration of order all round.

It was all the more annoying, therefore, to be reminded that he was not universally admired, especially by Musgrave who had already left the regiment and consequently knew nothing at first hand. What the hell was he thinking of, Henry wondered, enquiring after young Randall like that; calling a perfectly straightforward action an injustice, and hinting that Henry was at fault? Did he expect him to go down on his knees to Randall and invite the puppy back?

'I am not aware of having committed any injustice,' Henry said coldly. 'I acted perfectly within my rights. Randall had debts and was unable to discharge them. In the circumstances there was nothing else I could do.'

'Evidently not—in the circumstances.'

'I'd like an explanation of that remark.'

'Very well,' Musgrave said, 'you shall have it. You acted, as you say, within your rights. But the fact remains that you chose to take action on a very technical point in order to get rid of Randall, whom you had strong personal reason to dislike.'

'I was hardly aware of the fellow,' Henry protested.

'You were aware that he was friendly with your wife.'

Henry managed a laugh which was not quite a true one. 'If you've nothing more against me than that…'

'You had nothing more against Randall,' Musgrave said mildly. 'It's only a suspicion, after all. However, if it doesn't trouble your conscience, there's nothing you need do. This whole discussion is hypothetical. It's not as if that drum had really begun to beat.'

***

Musgrave's words remained in the air long after he had departed; they even followed Henry Lawson home. He was not superstitious—no, of course not—but the day's disclosures certainly added up. First was the fact that the drum had undoubtedly beaten; both Cynthia and the museum attendant could vouch for that. Second was Musgrave's story, told without ulterior motive, of the prophetic nature of its act. Third was Syrett's unfortunate corroboration of an instance where its prophecy had proved true. Of course Syrett was not to know that the drum had beaten in his presence, but Henry found his corroboration tactless none the less. It was just like Syrett to thrust into what did not concern him—he had defended Randall, Henry recalled. By the same token, he might know the fellow's whereabouts. It might be well to sound him out some time.

Henry was not superstitious—of course not—but he was disturbed by what he had learned. He did not believe his death was imminent, but he could not rid himself of a feeling of unease. A further visit to his doctor did not dispel it, despite assurance that there was nothing physically wrong. But a man could have an accident or a thrombosis… It did no harm for a man to be prepared. He visited his lawyer and checked over the contents of his will very carefully, but there were no changes he wished to make. He had left everything to Cynthia, as was only proper. One did the decent thing, even in death. There remained the question of young Randall, and the injustice that Musgrave had alleged. While not conceding for an instant that there had been injustice, Henry was one who believed he could take a hint. If the time had now come for generosity, he was not going to be the one to hold back. It could do no harm to look up Randall, and perhaps—if he needed it—extend a helping hand. It could do no harm to let Musgrave know of it, either; from Musgrave the news would very quickly spread. It would also redound to the Colonel's credit when once it became known in the Mess. And if it redounded to his credit at a higher level—well, Henry Lawson would not be one to complain. He was not too sure that he believed in 'after death, the judgment', but as Musgrave said, it did no harm to be prepared. If he had at some unspecified date in the future to face a Being with Musgrave's magisterial eye, he would prefer to feel as confident as possible to meet it; and though death, he hastily assured himself, was not imminent, he was bound by his mortal nature, some day, to die.

The trouble was to trace young Randall. Syrett, as he might have guessed, turned out a broken reed.

'Don't know, old chap. Lost touch with him completely. It rather seemed as if that was what he wanted to do. Can't say I altogether blame him, although I was sorry he felt that way. Reminders of the regiment must be painful to him. Don't be surprised if he doesn't exactly rush to say hallo. In fact—' he looked at Henry with open curiosity—'unless you've some special reason for getting hold of him, take my advice and let him get clear away. After all, it's three years or more since all this happened. The dust has settled; let the dust remain.'

'I have no intention of disturbing it,' Henry said loftily. 'I was merely curious, I'm afraid.'

'Returning to the scene of the crime?' Syrett asked, laughing; although the laughter did not reach to the wrinkles round his eyes.

'Not at all,' Henry said, controlling himself with difficulty. 'Randall's name happened to crop up the other day and I was suddenly reminded of him.'

'Then I'd forget him again if I were you. I dare say his mother knows what's become of him, but I doubt very much if anyone else does.'

Henry did not pursue the matter. He was anxious not to seem to be seeking Randall, and besides, Syrett had already given him his next clue. Randall's mother's address was in the regimental records; she had been given as his next of kin. Henry had no difficulty in finding a pretext for it to be given him. She lived near Chislehurst.

Should he write, or telephone, or visit her? Henry could not decide. Whatever he did, he would have to have a good reason for doing it. Mrs Randall was not likely to be deceived. Nor were her feelings towards him likely to be friendly. The prospect of introducing himself did not appeal. In a mood of uncertainty, Henry resolved to drive down to Chislehurst. When in doubt, he would reconnoitre as a soldier should.

He ascertained from the telephone directory that Mrs Randall still lived there, and drove down to Chislehurst on a Thursday afternoon. Cynthia was attending an auction and would not be home till late. It was a golden day towards the end of August, with everything a little over-ripe; the apple harvest would be a good one; the first leaves were beginning to fall; dahlias blazed at him from every garden; the sunlight was yellow, sticky, dusty, without glare.

He found the house without difficulty and received a shock. A *For Sale* notice rose not quite vertically beside the entrance gates. *Sole agents Brownlow and Company,* Henry read. A spattering of bird-droppings along one side suggested the notice was not exactly new. Henry pushed open the gates and walked up a weedy, overgrown drive. The garden cried out for attention, but its form was recognisable still. There was lawn on two sides of the house surrounded with fruit-trees; Henry noticed that they had not been pruned. The flower-borders were colourful but contained few annuals; the vegetable garden had run wild. Everything pointed to neglect of the usual spring attentions; the house must have been empty since then. Henry peered through the windows, but there was no furniture. The house was empty as a ransacked treasure-tomb.

It must have been a pleasant house to grow up in. The thought came to him out of the blue. A boy could have fun in so large and diversified a garden, and the house itself was unexpected. Peering through the low casement-windows—so low it would have been easy to climb in and out—Henry saw pleasantly proportioned rooms in which the light was often filtered by the creeper which tangled over the panes. This year it had not been cut back as usual. It was like an overgrown head of hair—that of a boy whose mother no longer bothered. Abruptly Henry turned and strode away.

He found Brownlow and Company without any trouble. It was a double-fronted corner site. The young man inside was most anxious to be helpful, impressed no doubt by the Bentley parked outside. He recognised the house from Henry's description. It had only been on the market a few weeks. The owner had died and her son had instructed them to sell it. If Henry wished, he could let him have the keys.

'Died?' Henry said, a little sharply. 'Would it be Mrs Randall you mean?'

'That's right, sir. A pleasant lady. Died last spring, as a matter of fact.'

Before the pruning and the planting and the digging...

'I'm sorry to hear that,' Henry said. 'I used to know her son years ago, though I never met Mrs Randall herself.'

'She's greatly missed,' the young man hastened to assure him. 'She'd lived in that house for over twenty years. But of course Mr Randall doesn't feel like keeping it as a bachelor establishment, so he's asked us to put it up for sale.'

'He lived with his mother, then?' Henry queried.

'Oh no, sir. Mr Randall lives in town.'

'Could you tell me where I can get in touch with him?' Henry asked. 'I'd rather like to look him up again.'

'I'm sorry, sir,' the young man was apologetic—'but I'm afraid we don't have his address.'

'Don't have his address? But you must have! Suppose I made an offer for the house?'

The young man smiled slightly. 'It's all done through his solicitors— Messrs Belgrave and Knights of Lincoln's Inn. Mr Randall hasn't dealt with us direct in the matter. In fact, he hasn't been down here for years.'

Not surprising, Henry thought grimly. He must have been ashamed to show his face. But it was annoying that all trails ended in a dead end. The solicitors were not likely to be much help. He made a few more perfunctory enquiries about the property and was unable to get away without leaving his name. Driving home, he blamed himself for not giving a false one, but reflected that there was no reason why Randall should ever know.

Cynthia had returned from the auction before him, with a new china figure to her account. As always after such a purchase, she was good-humoured. Over dinner the conversation was brisk and light. Without intending to, Henry found himself steering it towards Randall, via items of regimental news, so that he hoped it sounded quite natural when he heard his own voice say: 'I wonder what became of that fellow Randall—the one we had to kick out?'

For a moment it seemed to him there was an utter stillness. Then Cynthia said: 'I've no idea. What makes you ask?' Her voice was still light, but her eyes had grown suddenly watchful.

Henry shrugged and reached to light her cigarette. 'Someone mentioned him the other day and it reminded me. I understand his mother recently died.'

'That must be a blow. He was very fond of his mother.' Cynthia spoke as impersonally as if Randall too were dead.

'Yes. Well, these things happen,' Henry said lamely. 'The rest of the world goes on.'

Cynthia still said nothing, and he continued; 'I wonder what became of him, all the same.'

'Why on earth should you wonder that?' Cynthia demanded, driven into reaction at last. 'I should have thought he was one of the last people you'd want to hear of. You were hard enough on him, God knows.'

'I did not share your partiality for him.'

'You made that very clear.'

'We're not going to quarrel over it,' Henry said pacifically. 'After all, what's past is past.'

Cynthia inhaled long and deeply before answering. 'Yes, Jimmy Randall's certainly part of the past.'

***

That was just the trouble, Henry told himself. Randall was so much part of the past that he had vanished into it. Now that he was wanted in the present, he could not be brought back. He was not exactly sure for what purpose he wanted Randall, but he knew it was becoming increasingly important that he be found. It was as though somewhere at the back of his brain he could hear the crisp, insistent rub-a-dub-dub of the drum in the museum beating for action and reminding him that he had not much time.

He was therefore not particularly surprised by his behaviour, even though part of him was shocked, when he turned into an unfamiliar doorway one morning and made for an office on the fourth floor. The notice downstairs, among a dozen others, announced the presence of a private enquiry agent's bureau. Henry had walked past it scores of times.

There were enquiry agents and enquiry agents, and he would have preferred one recommended by a friend. But one could not ask without making it obvious that one required such an agency, and this Henry was unwilling to do. He did not want gossip seeping through the regiment, and wrong constructions being put upon things. A man's private business was private. If he wanted to get in touch with Randall, it was his affair.

He had no difficulty in believing that the man who greeted him would be discretion personified. He was a unit detached from a crowd of identical units, all nameless, faceless and discreet. Medium height, medium colouring, medium age-group, a ready-made suit and a voice that was medium-bred. The man might have served as a model for a man-in-the-street advertisement. Henry almost smiled when he introduced himself as Smith.

Smith listened in silence to Henry's statement of his requirements, then reeled off a brief resume of the facts.

'I'm afraid I've not given you much to go on,' Henry apologised.

'Not to worry, Colonel Lawson. We've done wonders on less information than that. I suppose you wouldn't have a photograph of the gentleman? Exact identification always helps.'

'I believe there's one at home,' Henry said, remembering. 'I could arrange to bring it in.'

It was a snapshot taken at a polo match—Cynthia surrounded by a crowd in which Randall had come out rather well.

'It would be helpful if you could,' Smith was saying. 'Now let me get this clear. You just want to know where this gentleman is at present residing? No other evidence at all?'

'I don't want you to spy on him,' Henry protested. 'I just want to know where he lives.'

'Fair enough, Colonel Lawson,' Smith said smoothly. 'We'll let you know as soon as we find out.'

Privately he reflected that they were all the same, these proud ones, pretending not to care a damn; but they wanted their evidence just like the ones who were whining or indignant, and they all made the same use of it in the end. He had not built up his agency without learning that most men were contemptible in distress. It enabled him to treat the client as impersonally as the object of his enquiry, and Colonel Lawson was no exception to this. He was fairly certain of providing the information the Colonel wanted, but he liked to seem to earn his fee. He accordingly told Henry that it would be several weeks before he could expect to hear from him, and said goodbye as if he had a lot to do.

Henry had little expectation of hearing more from Mr Smith. In a way he was relieved, for he was half ashamed of having engaged his services. Admittedly he intended no harm towards Randall, but there was something despicable about employing a man to spy. He preferred to pretend that the incident had never happened and regard it as money down the drain.

Consequently he was surprised and not altogether cordial when Smith telephoned in due course. The call came through to the office, but it could not have been more discreet. Smith simply requested an appointment, as he had something of interest to disclose, and Henry, unable to avoid it, had perforce to make one there and then. He arranged to call at Smith's office; he would not have him coming to his own.

There was something sullying about Smith's presence, despite the neatness and cleanness of his dress. There was also a suppressed jubilation in his manner which Henry found distasteful in the extreme. He hitched his trousers with the hand which Smith would have shaken, and sat down without being asked.

Smith's india-rubber face underwent no change of expression. He merely stated in his nasal, slightly sing-song voice: 'The gentleman you were enquiring about, Mr James Arthur Lovejoy Randall, resides at 42 Paddington Gardens, off the Bayswater Road about five minutes from Notting Hill Gate.'

'Indeed?' Henry raised a well-groomed eyebrow. 'So he wasn't all that far away.'

'No, sir. Quite handy as it turned out.'

Something more seemed to be required of Henry. 'Has he lived there long?' he enquired.

'About a year,' Smith informed him proudly, as one who had done a thorough job.

'And what sort of establishment is it?'

'Well, sir, that's not entirely easy to say. Between ourselves—' Smith leaned forward confidentially—'it's what you might call very mixed. There's some very nice houses in Paddington Crescent and there's some that are let out like no. 42.'

'Randall has only a flat there?'

'No, sir. Mr Randall has a bedsitting-room.' Smith contrived to make this sound somehow more important, and hurried on as if to mitigate: 'The lady who owns the house is a not very successful artist, a divorcee, decidedly middle-aged. Most of her tenants are rather similar. A bit bohemian, you might say.'

'Randall isn't middle-aged,' Henry objected. Damn it, he was only Cynthia's age.

'No, sir. Mr Randall's the youngest,' Smith admitted. His face gave nothing away.

'Well, that all seems very satisfactory,' Henry conceded. 'What does Randall do for a living, do you know?'

'He's in business as an antique porcelain dealer.'

'Good God! Do you mean to say he's got a shop?'

'No, the business is carried on from Paddington Crescent. He buys on commission. Sometimes sells as well.'

'A sort of middleman in the porcelain business?'

'Exactly, Colonel. You've hit the nail on the head.'

Henry looked at Smith with a new appreciation. The fellow certainly knew his stuff. 'Considering that you didn't have much to go on,' he congratulated, 'you seem to have done pretty well.'

Smith accepted the tribute as a just one.

'How did you do it?' Henry went on. 'I mean, I didn't give you much except the photograph, and I don't suppose Randall's solicitors helped.'

Smith had grown to dislike Henry Lawson. He enjoyed his revenge very much.

'I followed my usual practice in such cases, sir. I started with the lady in the case.'

'The lady? I'm afraid I don't understand you.'

'Your good lady, sir. Mrs Cynthia Anne Lawson.'

Henry turned the colour of a petunia. 'If you mean what I think you mean, sir, I'd advise you to take care. Are you trying to tell me that my wife and James Randall are associating?'

Smith said: 'Of course they are.'

He was rewarded by Henry Lawson's expression, by the man's harsh breathing that seemed to come in gasps. Clients didn't always like being told as fact what they had previously only suspected, but it was rare for them to take it as badly as this. Almost he hoped that Colonel Lawson would lose control of himself and commit some violent and consequently embarrassing act, but with a tremendous effort the Colonel mastered his emotions.

'How do you know?' he asked.

'I have identified them together on no less than seven different occasions.'

'Are you certain you are not making a mistake?'

'We cannot afford mistaken identities in my profession, Colonel. I would swear to it in any court of law.'

'I can't believe it,' Henry said with perfect truthfulness. His brain was racing faster than his heart. Surely Cynthia had not found it so easy to deceive him, to make a mock of him and put horns upon his head? He would be the laughing-stock of the regiment if ever the story became known; and it would become known if he divorced her, which was the only dignified thing he could do. But Randall—Randall!—as co-respondent! That mother's boy with his devoted, doggy gaze. His hands caressing Cynthia's body and Cynthia's body responding to his touch. Henry was physically sickened by the prospect. The reaction from his fury left him pallid, weak and damp. He looked at Smith as if imploring him to deny it, and Smith looked back at him unblinkingly.

'I must emphasise,' he began, the sing-song twang of his voice more noticeable, 'that there is no evidence of any matrimonial offence. The meetings have all occurred in public places and no impropriety has been observed. It would be easy to show that Mrs Lawson and Mr Randall are acquaintances, but difficult to prove that they are anything more than that. I am obliged to tell you that my evidence, were it to be called for, would not furnish you with grounds for divorce.'

'I don't want a divorce,' Henry said thickly. 'I very much resent what you imply.'

He was afraid he might faint or be sick on the threadbare carpet. He saw Smith's face through a mist.

Smith was saying: 'I deeply regret, Colonel Lawson, any distress my investigation may have caused.'

'Distress!' Henry said. 'That's a fine word. Did you expect me to jump for joy?'

Smith continued to keep his eyes discreetly lowered. Clients seldom put on an act as good as this. He enjoyed thinking how Henry Lawson would suffer, touched in his pride which would be his tenderest spot. He could not have wished for his investigation to turn out better, for his evidence was no help while destroying Henry's peace of mind. When his client rose to go, he accompanied him, talking volubly all the time.

Henry heard not a word of Smith's discourse. He was concerned with only two things: maintaining a front against this enquiry agent's malicious implications, and confronting Randall man to man. He was not sure what he would say to Randall and even less sure of what he wanted Randall to say, but he had to know what was at the bottom of this nonsense, for some basis of fact it must have. Smith would not invent these meetings between Randall and Cynthia. No private eye, however evil, dare do that. Therefore he must know the extent of his wife's involvement—must know, indeed, if an emotional involvement did exist.

It did not occur to him to ask Cynthia. A wife was a possession, not an entity. Her fate would be decided between her husband and her lover, but she need not be consulted or approached. If the meetings were innocent, as Smith stated, Cynthia had nothing significant to hide. If they were as guilty as Smith implied and Henry concluded, she had forfeited the right to speak.

Henry took a taxi to Paddington Crescent, which was exactly as Smith had described. No. 42 was more in need of paint than the others, and none of its curtains matched. The woman who opened the door might have been the landlady or the charwoman, and Henry wasted no time in learning which. He asked decisively for Mr Randall, and was only half convinced of the truthfulness of the reply that he was out.

'Could you tell me when he will be back?' he enquired too casually.

'About seven, I should think. I really couldn't say.'

The woman eyed him with a curiosity which Henry less frankly returned. He longed to ask her all she knew about Randall, but forced himself to hold his tongue. How many times had Cynthia stood on this doorstep? Did this woman know her by sight? What would she say if he were to produce Cynthia's picture and ask her if his wife was now upstairs? Probably she would deny it and seek some way to warn the guilty ones—she would be agin the law and on the side of disorder, Henry felt. He therefore extracted a calling card with infinite circumspection and held that out to the landlady instead.

'Would you see that Mr Randall gets this as soon as he returns,' he instructed, 'and ask him to telephone me here.' He wrote on the back the phone number of his club, and added for good measure, 'I shall be there tonight till half-past ten.'

The woman took the card and her eyes flickered for an instant, as though she knew his name. Yet the face she presented to him was blank and unseeing, so that Henry asked sharply, 'Did you hear?'

'Yes, I heard,' the woman said slowly, placing the card on a table inside the hall. 'Mr Randall will see it when he comes in,' she added. She made as if to close the door. In the nick of time Henry put his foot in the opening. 'It's very urgent that he ring me,' he said.

Seeing the curiosity on the woman's face, he added to impress her: 'In fact, you might tell him it's a matter of life and death.'

***

Henry woke next morning abruptly, as though startled out of sleep by an alarm. He was in his own room and everything seemed normal, yet he had a sense of terrible disquiet. Something was wrong. He had a sense of impending doom for no reason. Then he realised that the drum was beating in the house.

His legs turned to water. He sat, half out of bed, unable to move in either direction while the sinister sound went on. There was no mistaking its dreadful insistence or the final frenzied crescendo, dub-dub-dub. Only now it was muted by distance, by closed doors and the well of the stairs. Or did it have a greater distance to travel—all the way from the Carringford museum? 'The drum always beats when the colonel is going to die,' Musgrave had told him. And now he recognised that it was a muffled drum.

The sweat ran down Henry Lawson's forehead and he felt too weak even to wipe it away. Great sobbing breaths shook him as he listened to the voice of the drum. Dub-a-dum-dum, dub-a-dum-dum, dub-a-dum, dub-a-dum, dum-dum-dum. The noise rolled and reverberated against his ear-drums. It must surely wake the house. Henry turned his eyes—the only part of him capable of movement—towards his watch on the bedside table: the hands showed quarter to seven. Surely the maid was up by now; why didn't she stop it? Unless—he pressed his palms to his ears in desperation—unless it were audible only to him?

But Cynthia had heard it last time; she had come running in from the next room. With a gigantic effort, Henry heaved himself upright and staggered the few steps to the door. He had to lean against the door-jamb for a moment, so great was his weakness and fear, but he overcame the weakness sufficiently to get as far as the door of Cynthia's room. It was a long time now since she had insisted on separate bedrooms. Henry cursed himself for giving in to her. If she had been by his side, as she should be, she could have told him at once if the beating of the drum was real. But she was not by his side. She had betrayed him with Randall. Fragments from yesterday came back into his mind: Smith; the abortive visit to Paddington Crescent; the evening spent waiting for a phone-call at his club. Randall had not telephoned; he had not had that much decency, or perhaps his landlady had torn up the card. Whatever the reason, there had been no word from him. At eleven o'clock Henry had given up waiting and gone home. Cynthia was out when he got there—gone to the theatre with friends, the maid had said. It was likely enough, but Henry's thoughts immediately flew to Randall. Was this the reason he had not telephoned? Half resentful, half relieved at Cynthia's absence, Henry had retired early to bed, and, though convinced he had a sleepless night before him, had been wakened only by the beating of the drum. It was strange that Cynthia had not heard it—that is, if Cynthia were there. He had not heard her come in last night, he remembered. A new fear assailed him at once. Suppose she had flitted with young Randall, leaving him a laughing-stock?

Henry opened her door brusquely, but quietly nevertheless. She was there; he could see her hair spread over the pillow; and she was pretending to be asleep. He knew she was pretending because, in the instant of opening the door, he had seen that her eyes were on him. He guessed their lids were trembling even now. She lay almost on her back, one arm flung out of the bed-clothes, and her face with its fluttering eyelids turned towards the open door. Even as he watched, she drew her knees up slowly and rolled over on her side with a sleepy, stifled yawn.

She had turned her back towards him. It was as pointed and deliberate as that. She knew he knew she was not sleeping, and she had chosen to make her feelings for him plain. She was always cool and unresponsive, but she had never refused him his due. Henry watched the too-even rise and fall of her shoulders a moment, and then, hating himself and her, withdrew.

The house seemed unnaturally silent. It took him a minute or two to realise that the muffled drum had ceased. The sounds he heard now were the ordinary household sounds of an early autumn morning: the chink of crockery being assembled in the kitchen, the thud of newspapers arriving in the hall. Slowly, clutching the banisters like an old man, Henry Lawson made his way downstairs. To go back to bed was unthinkable; equally, it was too early to get dressed. He needed something to distract his mind from Cynthia and the blow he felt he had just received: had his wife turned her back because she had had enough last night with Randall? Was this how she chose to show him he was deceived?

In the hall he met Jane, the middle-aged domestic, who was laying the table in the breakfast-room. She paused in astonishment as her employer came down the staircase, and seeing his face, asked solicitously if he was all right.

'Of course I'm all right,' Henry said sharply. 'I just couldn't sleep, that's all. Thought I might as well get up and look at the papers.'

Jane bewailed that the fire was not yet lit.

'It doesn't matter,' Henry said hastily. 'The electric fire will do.'

He looked at her a long minute as she stood there, feet apart and planted firmly on the hearth. Then: 'Jane,' he asked, almost coaxing, 'did you hear anything odd just now?'

'What sort of thing?' Jane asked guardedly, uncertain of what he wanted her to say.

'Well, like a muffled drum, for instance.'

Jane shook her head decidedly. 'I haven't heard anything like that, Colonel Lawson. You don't look well. Are you sure you feel all right?'

'Yes, thanks,' Henry said, sinking down in the nearest armchair and burying his face in his hands.

Jane looked at him in consternation. 'Shall I ask Mrs Lawson to come down?'

'No, no, no,' Henry exclaimed, his voice descending testily. 'Just go away, there's a good girl.'

He lay back expecting to die, and didn't; then thought that perhaps the drum had been a nightmare after all. Yesterday had been a day of considerable stress, he reminded himself, and he had slept very heavily indeed. The episode of the drum in the museum and Musgrave's explanation of its import had undoubtedly shaken him. Who knew what, in a moment of weakness, the subconscious might achieve? Even down to a repetition of the muffled drum-beats? It might all have happened in his mind. Neither Cynthia nor Jane had heard anything. He needed to pull himself together, that was all. If he didn't, he would never be able to deal with Randall, whom he would surely have to see some time today.

With a crackle, he opened the paper, annoyed to find his hands still shook. It made the type difficult to focus; even the headlines trembled before his eyes. Odd items of news detached themselves, presented legibly, and were gone: 'Actor Sued for Breach of Promise', 'Russia Warns the West', 'Three Die in New York Riot Area', '104 Today'. The great and small were jumbled up together in a kaleidoscope of trivial and important things. 'Man Falls on Line' was just another item, until a name in the fourth line of the paragraph caught his eye.

'Central Line trains were delayed for up to half an hour last night,' he read, 'when a man fell under an eastbound train at Notting Hill Gate station. The accident occurred during the peak period, and at one time Oxford Circus station was closed because of congestion. The dead man was later identified as James Arthur Lovejoy Randall (28), of 42 Paddington Crescent, W.2.'

Randall. Randall had escaped him. He had cheated him by dying as surely as he had cheated him in life. He would never now account for his meetings with Cynthia. Henry would never know if they represented guilt or innocence. Now there was only Cynthia who could tell him, and he would never mention it to her. He would humiliate himself by exposing his suspicions, which were very possibly unjust. She must last night have been to the theatre, for example, for Randall was dead by then. And was it accident or suicide—or was it something else that now he would never know? Henry paced up and down in uncontrollable agitation. He had his back to the door when Cynthia came in. To his surprise, she was fully dressed already (she usually breakfasted in a dressing-gown). She was wearing a tweed suit and walking shoes, as though for travel. She made no move to give him a morning kiss.

'You're going out,' Henry said in a voice of accusation.

'I trust I may do so if I choose?'

'I don't keep you prisoner,' Henry protested, coming towards her.

Cynthia side-stepped him neatly and sat down.

'You're early,' Henry said, again accusing. 'I don't think Jane's made the coffee yet.'

'I can wait.' Cynthia stretched out a hand for the paper. 'It's not as if I have a train to catch.'

'Going shopping?' Henry asked, hating himself for asking.

'No.'

'Or an auction sale?' He tried to make the sentences run on.

'I might. It depends on—other people. I don't have any settled plans.'

'But you'll be in for dinner, won't you?' Henry queried. 'You're not going out again?'

'Yes, I am,' Cynthia said, and added: 'You may as well know it, Harry. I'm never coming back.'

Henry wondered if the drum-beats could have affected his hearing. 'What do you mean—you're never coming back?'

'What I say, Harry. I'm leaving you. It's something I should have done long ago. You won't miss me. I've never been really necessary. If you accept that, it will be easier for us both.'

Henry listened in stupefaction. He could not believe that what he heard was true. If one of Cynthia's china figures had spoken, he could not have been more amazed. 'You know you're necessary,' he managed to stammer. 'I may not parade my feelings, but you matter very much.'

'No, Harry. Only as your most expensive possession. Another woman would suit you just as well.'

'I don't understand,' Henry said. 'How have I failed you? Haven't I given you every mortal thing you want?'

'You've been very generous, Harry, and I appreciate it—more, even, than I can ever let you know.'

'And what will you do now?' Henry demanded. 'You know you haven't a penny of your own.'

'You needn't remind me that I've been dependent on your bounty.'

'I'm sorry. But how will you live? Where will you go?'

Cynthia laughed. It was a sound both joyous and carefree. 'Only you would worry about things like that. It doesn't matter where I go—the world's my oyster. And so long as I live as I choose, that's all I want.'

'And I don't matter any longer,' Henry's voice was becoming harsher now. 'You've lived, as you put it, on my bounty, and now you're casting me aside. You make it plain that my feelings don't matter, but don't you realise I have a position to keep up? *You* have a position, Cynthia. You're the Colonel's lady, after all.'

'The Colonel's lady.' Cynthia was suddenly bitter. 'That's all I am. How well you put it, my dear. The Colonel's lady—a title. Not a woman. I've never been an individual to you at all. Perhaps that's why I've never borne you children. It might have made all the difference if I had. But our marriage has given me nothing except financial and social security. And now—you had to know this some time—there's someone else.'

'Randall.' Henry ground out the name involuntarily and had difficulty catching his breath.

Cynthia raised the eyes she had demurely lowered. 'So you know. Or was that simply a guess?'

'The enquiry agent told me you were seeing him.' Henry's legs had become so weak he had to sit down.

'An enquiry agent?' Cynthia's expression was scornful. 'I might have known you'd resort to one of those. Is he going to give the necessary evidence?'

'He told me the relationship was innocent.'

'Good for him.' Cynthia nodded in approval. 'So it was, until you made it something more.'

'I should be glad if you would explain,' Henry said thickly.

'Is it necessary? I should imagine you know the facts.'

They were sitting opposite each other at the breakfast-table, the newspaper still clenched in Henry's hand. Neither spoke while Jane came in with the coffee. Cynthia poured out and handed a cup to Henry. He took it and looked at her challengingly. 'Well?'

'When you forced Jimmy Randall to resign his commission—' Cynthia was sipping her coffee as she spoke—'I didn't care *that* much for him as a person, but like everyone else, I thought you'd been unjust.'

The snap of her fingers was like a whip-lash. Henry said: 'Not everybody thought I was unjust.'

'Major Williams didn't,' Cynthia admitted unconcernedly, 'but all the decent officers did. And they knew, too, why you had done it. Because Jimmy was fond of me. The fact that it was harmless and innocent didn't matter. Jimmy was too honourable for it to be anything more. And though I liked him, he didn't mean anything to me. I, fool that I was, was still in love with you.'

Again it was as though a whip descended on Henry's shoulders, and a burning, searing pain ran through his chest. Cynthia mistook his gasp for one of incredulity, and looked at him over the rim of her cup.

'Oh yes, Harry darling, I loved you. Did you think I'd have married you if I had not? For the first few years I was always hoping you would return it, but hope deferred... In the end my heart just got sick. If you'd been jealous of Jimmy because you loved me, I'd have been flattered. I think I'm woman enough for that. But it was only your sense of possession that was affronted. Your dignity. The position you had to keep up.

'Jimmy had very little money—no private income—and his widowed mother wasn't much better off. To help him, she sold a couple of china figures. I bought one. I felt I owed him that. Of course I didn't tell you where it came from. Your suspicions would only have grown worse. But I discovered Jimmy knew a lot about porcelain. To help him, I began to collect. Before long I was interested in collecting for its own sake—I assure you, I haven't been putting on an act—but I always used Jimmy as my dealer, and he soon began to build up a clientèle. He had a gift for it and he knew a lot about it. It was what he'd always wanted to do. He'd only joined the army to please his mother, who thought it was what his father would have wished.

'But if Jimmy was my dealer, he never was my lover. Your enquiry agent was perfectly accurate. I might never have realised how much I had come to love him, if you hadn't suddenly begun hounding him to death.'

This time, when the whip cracked, Henry was conscious only of agony within. He tried to restore himself with a sip of coffee, but his fingers refused to close about the cup. He sat hunched like some malevolent demon that a medieval builder had carved in stone and he looked at his wife with eyes in which hatred had begun to flicker. There was no emotion in her gaze.

'I don't know what made you remember Jimmy Randall,' she continued, 'or why you began behaving as you did, but it seemed suddenly that you were on Jimmy's tracks everywhere, and we began to be afraid. Not that we had anything to be ashamed of. Our relationship was still as innocent as the day. But you had already shown what you were like when you were jealous. Is it any wonder Jimmy was worried sick? He had lost his mother last winter—he was fond of her and she was the only relative he possessed. Then almost as soon as her home was put on the market, the estate agents told him a Colonel Lawson had been trying to get in touch. They said you made all sorts of enquiries and seemed very anxious to try and track him down. Next thing he knew, he ran into Syrett, who also mentioned the interest you had shown. When you mentioned Jimmy to me one night at dinner, I thought you were on to us at last. But it seems we were still a few steps ahead of you. Jimmy began to plan to go abroad.'

'And all this time you were his mistress?' Henry scarcely recognised his own voice.

'No, that only came much later. You'd be surprised how much later: yesterday afternoon. That was when I knew I had to go with him,' Cynthia continued, 'and that I must leave you and tell you why. You can do what you like about divorcing me, but you won't affect my decision either way.'

'I shan't divorce you,' Henry managed to utter. 'You won't be able to provide the evidence I need.'

'Don't worry, Harry. I'm not going to be ladylike about this. I'll make love with Jimmy in Trafalgar Square, if need be.'

'You will not make love with him anywhere,' Henry whispered. 'The dead are impotent.'

'What are you saying?'

Henry held out the paper. 'Your paramour, my dear, is dead. No doubt it was an excess of joy that killed him—joy at receiving favours so long deferred.'

He reached out to take the letters which Jane was discreetly bringing in. Cynthia, rigid and white-faced over the newspaper, did not even register the fact. He pushed his wife's two letters towards her, noting that—as usual—there were only bills for him. Would she insist on leaving him, he wondered. Already he was hoping she would not. This death, timely even if accidental, might be the saving of them yet. All marriages had their infidelities, crises. Theirs was not unique in that respect.

He was interrupted by a cry from Cynthia, a despairing, wailing 'Why?'

Henry shrugged. 'He has taken his secret with him.'

'You were not hounding him again?'

'I was not, Cynthia. I swear it.'

'Cross your heart and slit your throat if you lie?'

Henry made the requisite childish gestures but his wife did not even watch the performance. Her arms clasped about her body as though to comfort, she was rocking very gently to and fro. It was as if she were cradling herself or cradling Randall. Brokenly Henry could distinguish the repeated syllable 'Why?'

'There are some letters for you,' he informed her.

She took no notice, unheeding of all but grief.

'We were so happy,' she murmured to no one. 'So happy yesterday. Was it yesterday? I thought we should be happy for ever. Oh Jimmy darling, why did you die?'

'I'm sorry,' Henry said awkwardly. 'Though he was unbalanced. You admitted as much just now.'

'Whose fault was that?' Cynthia demanded. 'Tut you'll answer for it somehow.'

Henry took no notice of what she was saying, for very faintly once again he could hear the drum. Even as he listened, it grew louder. This time it seemed to be beating in his head. Cynthia gave no sign of having heard it, but he saw rather than heard her give a little cry and stretch out her hand half fearfully towards one of her letters, which lay looking blindly at the sky.

The handwriting was vaguely familiar, but Henry could think of nothing but the drum. This time it was not muffled; his body reverberated with its sound. He had such a sense of fear that it left him breathless. The sweat on his forehead gathered once again. It might be well if he took a couple of his tablets. He should have taken them long before. With fingers grown stiff he groped for his vest-pocket, where his phial of tablets lay. But his fingers encountered only the silken folds of his dressing-gown, while all the time the drum beat louder in his head. The tablets were upstairs in his bedroom. He would have to ask Jane to bring them down. But there was no bell, and it was too far to call to the kitchen, even if he had had the necessary strength of voice. He moved his stiff lips in a travesty of speaking, and Cynthia for the first time looked up.

Her face was ravaged already; even so her husband's altered appearance made her give a start. He could not tell whether she had spoken because all sound was drowned by the beating of the drum. Rub-a-dub-dub, rub-a-dub-dub. It was not one drum but a battalion. Through the din he heard himself give a gasp.

'My tablets are upstairs,' he said faintly.

Cynthia had obviously not heard. She pushed the letter across to him. The handwriting blurred before his eyes. Rub-a-dub, rub-a-dub, it was the beating of his own heart that he heard, thudding against his ribcage like a piston intent on forcing its way out. The realisation frightened him so much that he stopped breathing. Gasping, choking, struggling, he inhaled again in a long sighing ah-ah-aah, and for an instant all was clear down to the minutest detail of the inky, angular script.

Jimmy. The signature on the letter stood out so clearly that he could not believe what he saw. Jimmy Randall was dead. He had seen it in the papers. Did a man write letters from the grave?

He felt Cynthia's eyes upon him, eyes as cold and hard as a winter sea or sky. 'My tablets...' he struggled to tell her.

'Read it,' she commanded, sitting still.

It was a pathetic enough letter, full of trite phrases and pleas to forgive: 'Better for both of us this way... When I came in, I found that he had called. I can't stand any more of his hounding, and now he will really have cause. Don't blame me too much. He'd never let us be happy. What I'm going to do is for your sake.'

For your sake. Henry might have thought it ironic if Cynthia had not looked at him as she did, if the dreadful emptiness of his lungs were not killing him, if his heart, which had seized up, would only start again. He was cold all over; his skin felt clammy. He heard rather than felt himself draw another shuddering breath.

'My tablets...' he croaked again.

He wanted to explain that he had never hounded Randall, that he had simply wanted to rectify a mistake. An injustice, if you like—what did it matter? Something he ought never to have done. All men made mistakes sometimes. Women ought to realise that. What had he done to be thought worse than the next man? Why should his own wife hate him so? His eyes pleaded for her understanding, but she looked at him as if he were not there. It was how she had always looked at him. The thought caused him physical pain.

'For God's sake call the doctor,' he whispered.

She gave no sign of having heard.

'I think I'm dying,' he told her.

She replied: 'Yes, Harry, I think you are.'

Her voice, like her face, was wintry. She sat as motionless as a stone.

Henry got to his feet very slowly, and the ground rose up to meet him as he walked. It was gentle—much gentler than he had expected. He wondered if the rails had seemed gentle to Randall too. Did one have a chance to ask these things—later? Was he going to meet Randall after all? Randall. And they would neither of them have Cynthia. But—there was blood or bile in his throat—some fellow would. He remembered suddenly that he had left her all his fortune. Young, beautiful and wealthy, she would surely marry again. Someone else would possess her, touch her. Perhaps not one, but many other men. The pain was so great that he lost consciousness, his body twitching. After a moment he breathed out again and died.

From the table Cynthia watched his dissolution. There was no expression on her face. When she was quite sure that he was dead and the doctor could safely be summoned, she picked up the telephone.

HUSHABYE, BABY

WHEN THE BABY was about six months old, it began to be whispered that the Braithwaites' first child wasn't normal. At first the whispers were only within the family. The elder Mrs Braithwaite described him as 'a bit poorly'. Sarah Braithwaite's brother said 'a bit puny' was more like it, and added from the eminence of his six foot three that it was obvious the boy took after Bob's side. His wife murmured that you couldn't beat breast-feeding and neither of her two had ever been fed on milk powder out of tins. And Bob's young sister Stella said the baby was an ugly little brat, wasn't he, and she hoped hers wouldn't look like that.

Sarah Braithwaite held her head high and continued to push the pram down a long, dark tunnel of misery which felt as though it led to the pit of hell. In fact, it led eventually to the children's department of the local hospital, where the nurses and the pædiatrician himself were always unfailingly kind. On the day the pædiatrician told Sarah that tests showed that her child was irremediably retarded, his kindness seemed to touch new heights.

But it didn't touch Sarah. She stared at him uncomprehending. 'He *can't* be! Why, except for a bit of difficulty in feeding, he was perfectly normal until six weeks ago.'

It was not an unusual reaction. The pædiatrician said gently, 'He only seemed normal, you know. Not all defects show at birth. You can't measure the intelligence of a newborn baby: he hasn't begun to use it yet. Unless the motor centres of the brain are affected, it takes time for retardation to show.'

'My child isn't retarded. Something happened to him. Our own doctor never noticed anything wrong. Nor did the health visitor, nor the people at the clinic. He was gaining weight steadily. He had two teeth and he laughed whenever he saw me. Then suddenly he went like this.'

She looked down at the wizened, yellowish infant and her eyes began to fill with tears.

'It was after lunch on a Tuesday. I'd fed him and changed him, and as it was a fine day I left him in his pram in the front garden while I went upstairs to change—we were going to my mother-in-law's for tea. When I came down he wasn't asleep; he just stared at me as if he hated me. He's been like this ever since.'

The pædiatrician reflected that the admission of abnormality in one's own child was always harrowing, but the admission was usually slow, the result of a growing fear that refused to be smothered; Mrs Braithwaite made drama out of it. But then, Mrs Braithwaite was a dramatic woman, the kind who saw herself as an archetypal figure crooning 'Hushabye, Baby' as she rocked an infant at her breast. The best thing she could do would be to have another baby quickly, and he proceeded to tell her so. Like most women in her situation, she rejected the suggestion out of hand.

'I want to know what's wrong with this one first. How do I know I mightn't have another the same?'

Patiently the pædiatrician explained that the defect was not hereditary and no stigma whatever was attached. To his astonishment, Mrs Braithwaite rose to her feet while he was still in mid-oration, clutching her child to her breast.

'Thank you very much, Doctor, but I see now exactly what happened. While I was upstairs, someone stole my baby and left another child in his place. I'm sorry I ever troubled you with this business. I realise now that I ought to have gone straight to the police.'

***

The police were sceptical when Sarah arrived at the station, still with the baby in her arms. They asked her why she hadn't reported the incident earlier. What proof had she of her allegations? What did she expect them to do, anyway?

'Surely you can do *something!* My baby's been stolen.'

'We can take the particulars, of course.'

'But can't you make enquiries, find out if any defective child is missing, or has made a sudden, complete recovery?'

'What makes you think the other party lives locally?'

'I don't know. I just have a feeling she does.'

The sergeant on duty made an entry in the day-book which it was as well Sarah could not see.

'Perhaps the neighbours might remember seeing someone suspicious,' she continued. 'You could ask them, couldn't you?'

The sergeant, who was old enough to be her father, leaned forward confidentially.

'You don't want the neighbours dragged into this, with police all over the place asking questions. You take my advice, miss—beg your pardon—madam: go home and forget the whole thing.'

Sarah half-lifted the baby. 'How can I forget about *this?*'

'I mean this baby-swapping nonsense,' the sergeant said firmly. 'Things like that don't happen—we'd know, if anyone would. Babies taken from their prams, yes; but it's either kidnap or some poor woman who hasn't got a baby of her own. People don't switch kids, not even defective ones. You're letting your imagination run away with you.'

For all his firmness, his voice was not unfriendly. After all, it must be a dreadful shock to be told that your child, your first-born, was abnormal. Mrs Braithwaite couldn't be blamed for being emotionally disturbed.

***

He was less inclined to think so when Sarah reappeared two weeks later, still with the baby in tow. This time she was confident, breathless with excitement.

'Officer, you must come. I've found my child.'

The sergeant pulled the day-book towards him.

'Well, now, you'd better tell me about this.'

'It was in Woolworth's. I turned round and there he was. In a funny old pram not half as comfortable as our pram, being pushed by a woman who was barely five feet high. He seemed very well cared for, but he knew me, I'm certain. He gave me the loveliest smile.'

'When was this, Mrs Braithwaite?'

'On Monday. Three days ago.'

'You've taken your time about telling us, haven't you?'

'I had to find out where the woman lives.'

'Where does she live?'

'In Denbigh Road, No. 42, I made a note of it. Oh, Officer, let's go and get Paul back.'

'Just a minute, Mrs Braithwaite. Can you prove any of this?'

'I can recognise my own son when I see him.'

'Could your husband?'

'I should hope so,' Sarah said. Privately she had doubts. Bob had taken very little notice of the baby, apart from bathing him once or twice. She hoped he would recognise Paul, but she wasn't certain.

'Have you told your husband of this theory of yours?' the sergeant asked.

'Yes!' She said no more.

'I take it he doesn't believe in it?'

'He admitted the woman's baby was like Paul.'

'He's seen it, then?'

'Yes. He drove me to Denbigh Road, and the baby was in that funny old pram in the front garden. Bob got out and went to have a look.'

'But his identification wasn't positive?'

'I told you: he said it was like Paul.'

' "Like" isn't sufficient, Mrs Braithwaite. I'm sure you're speaking the truth when you say this woman's child reminded you of your son before h... before h... before his condition was diagnosed,' he concluded with a flourish. 'But the police can't act on that. If it was a straightforward baby-snatching we might be able to take action on what you've told us, but you've got your own baby, you see.'

'Not my own.'

'It's going to be difficult to prove that.'

'Aren't there blood tests, paternity tests?'

'We can't compel independent parties to undergo them.' 'But you can make enquiries about her, about where she got this baby?'

'Oh yes,' the sergeant said grudgingly. 'We can do that.'

***

The enquiries proved negative. The sergeant himself called on Bob Braithwaite at his office to tell him, because he felt he needed a man's support in this. Bob Braithwaite was a young accountant who was beginning to have a harassed air.

'I've told Sarah she's talking nonsense,' he confided to the sergeant. 'The doctor at the hospital says it's the shock. He says in cases like these it's a very natural reaction to try to blame someone else, and nothing's easier than to claim it's not our baby. Sarah actually believes it, you know.'

'Yes,' the sergeant said, remembering the intensity in her eyes, 'I know she does. But there's nothing in it. We've had the other lady checked. She's a Mrs Forest, a widow, so she says, when she came here, but the baby's definitely hers. She gave birth to a normal, healthy boy, though rather small, in the County Hospital the same day your wife had Paul in Uplands Nursing Home. Everything's in order, she bought the house outright and seems well provided for—no need to draw on national assistance or anything like that.'

'Of course,' Bob said, 'it doesn't necessarily mean she didn't switch the babies.'

'There's nothing suspicious anywhere.'

'Except in my wife's mind?'

'Well, Mr Braithwaite—exactly.'

'Poor Sarah. She's going to take this hard.'

'Convinced, is she?'

'Unshakably. It's awkward. You see, Mrs Forest's baby really does look like Paul. He's certainly not a bit like his mother.'

'What's Mrs Forest like?'

Bob hesitated. 'A tiny woman. Bones like a sparrow's, and bright brown eyes, very small. Ugly, really—but she can make you think she isn't. It's something in the way she looks at you.'

'You've spoken to her, then?'

'I admired the baby.' Bob coloured a bit, and went on: 'I'd gone on my own—Sarah doesn't know about it—because I wanted to see for myself. I'd been with Sarah, of course, but somehow her conviction affected me. I wanted an unprejudiced view.'

'Quite right,' the sergeant said, nodding in approval.

'Glad you think so. I wasn't sure. Anyway, while I was looking at the baby, who was gurgling in his pram in the front garden, the woman—Mrs Forest—came out. Naturally I felt a bit of a fool, I had to say something, and admiring the baby was the easiest.'

'Did she seem fond of it?'

'Like any other mother. As a matter of fact she told me her husband was dead. I should think it's a bit lonely for her, in a strange town with only an infant for company, but she doesn't seem sorry for herself.'

The sergeant rose to go. 'Well, Mr Braithwaite, there's nothing more I can do. We've looked into the matter officially and we're quite satisfied your wife's mistaken.'

He grinned suddenly.

'Over to you.'

***

A few days later the sergeant had an opportunity to judge the remarkable Mrs Forest for himself. She called at the police station, all alarm and indignation, to complain that Sarah Braithwaite was watching the house.

'She's always around, Officer, with that pathetic infant of hers. I'm sure she's up to no good. Twice I've found her bending over my Michael—the second time when he was in the back garden and she'd had to come through the side door. She said she heard him crying and thought something was the matter, but I'm his mother, I ought to know. She looks at him so hungrily I'm afraid she'll try to harm him, out of jealousy because hers isn't normal. Is there anything the police can do?'

The sergeant murmured something indistinct, and Mrs Forest went on quickly:

'I know it must seem rather drastic to come rushing to the police like this. If my husband were alive I'd ask him to have a word man to man with that woman's husband, but I don't know what to do, being on my own.'

She was so small that only her head and shoulders showed above the counter. The sergeant noticed that her brown eyes were clear as glass. 'Like empty beer-bottles,' he said to his wife later. He had the illusion that he could look in and see her thoughts.

'Well, now, Mrs Forest, don't you worry,' he reassured her. 'I'm sure no harm is meant to you or your child. Leave it to me and I'll have a word with the people concerned. As it happens, I know them.'

The brown eyes glowed with gratitude.

'Thank you so much, Officer. It *is* good of you.'

Only after she had gone did he notice she was wearing scent. It was a haunting, spicy fragrance, so delicate that he thought he was imagining it, but instead of fading, it seemed to grow stronger and carry with it the unmistakable breath of summer woods.

'I can see what young Braithwaite meant about her being able to make you think she's beautiful,' he confided to his wife later on, 'although I thought she was a mousy little thing when she came in.'

His wife did not encourage him to talk about other women. She asked practically: 'What are you going to do?'

'Have a quiet word with young Braithwaite, poor devil, and tell him to keep that wife of his on a leash, unless he wants to see her committed to a mental home. She'll end up having to be put away, if they don't watch out.'

***

As a result of the 'word with young Braithwaite', Sarah's mother received a pressing invitation from her son-in-law to come and stay. Mrs Spencer was a widow and was her own mistress, as she was fond of telling people. She accepted with alacrity.

Her coming was a not unmixed blessing, for while she kept Sarah company during the day, helped with the chores and the difficult feeding of the baby, and made sure her daughter did not go again to Denbigh Road, she also made no secret of the fact that she considered Bob's genes responsible for the baby's condition, and medical opinion notwithstanding, she persisted in this view. She had never in her life allowed facts to cloud her judgment, and she didn't propose to start now.

Between her and her son-in-law a state of armed neutrality existed. Both hoped for trouble, but neither wished to appear in the wrong. They were excessively polite to each other, and this made conversation of any kind beyond remarks on the weather and please-pass-the-bread-and-butter difficult. Even with TV, the evenings began to seem long. Bob Braithwaite took increasingly to working at the office in the evenings—a fact which Mrs Spencer did not fail to note.

'Seeing as it's his child, poor little mite, you'd think he'd be around a bit more,' she said.

'Oh, Mother, don't keep on so. I don't believe it's his or mine.'

Sarah had grown thin and pale. Her eyes glittered too brightly. The tranquillisers prescribed by the doctor had little or no effect, since Sarah mostly refused to take them, complaining that they made her feel doped.

'Why don't you go and have a nice lie-down?' her mother suggested.

'No!' Sarah shook her head vigorously. 'That woman might come back—I don't trust her.'

'Well, on your own showing she couldn't do much more harm than she has done.'

'Oh, Mother, don't you understand? *She's got Paul.*'

'Yes, dear, I know you say so. Bob said she seemed very fond of him.'

'But he's my child! Do you think I can rest easy knowing another woman's got him? I tell you I haven't slept for weeks.'

'You look like it,' Mrs Spencer said, 'but, darling, you know it's nonsense. Mrs Forest's little boy is her own.'

'Then why is he so like Bob?'

'There could be a very natural explanation.'

'Mother! You can't mean that!'

'When you've known men as long as I have,' Mrs Spencer observed sententiously, 'you'll know that the best of 'em are like the worst. And I seem to remember Bob didn't keep you much company the second year of your marriage.'

'He had a lot of work to do.'

'So he said. There's many a man been kept late at the office when he was in no hurry to go home.'

'He gave it up as soon as we realised I was expecting.'

'You mean as soon as he realised he'd put you both in the family way.'

'In any case, Mrs Forest wasn't living here then.'

'Where was she living?'

Sarah hesitated. 'I don't know.'

'I'll bet your husband does.'

'I'll ask him. But if he does, it wouldn't prove anything.'

'It would prove a whole lot more if he didn't know.'

Bob Braithwaite, however, knew exactly where Ann Forest had been living: in a village some four miles away.

Mrs Spencer sniffed. 'Easy of access and not near enough to foul his own doorstep.'

'For God's sake, Mother, shut up!'

'I know when to do that, I hope.' Mrs Spencer was all offended dignity. She departed towards her room, but came back to add: 'You ask that husband of yours how often he's been to see that woman and her baby. Not that he'll tell you the truth.'

In this Mrs Spencer was mistaken. When asked, Bob inwardly cursed the innocent police sergeant for lack of discretion, but told Sarah the truth at once.

'I never went to visit her, but I did go on my own one day to look at the baby, and she came out and caught me. I had to think of something to say.'

'Why didn't you tell me about it?'

'I thought you'd think I was doubting you.'

'Doubting me! Of course you do. You've never believed me.'

'I've never said her baby wasn't like Paul.'

'And why is he like Paul? Did they have the same father?'

'Sweetheart, you're not yourself.'

'Yes, I am. My trouble is I'm not Ann Forest.'

'Has she been here, filling you with lies?'

'Why should you think she has? Is there something she could tell me?'

'There's something I can tell you: stop being a bloody fool.'

'So that I don't upset your apple-cart, is that it? Why not try telling me where you've been these last few nights?'

'I've been working late at the office.'

'Prove it.'

'Why the hell should I? I'm telling you the truth.'

'Do you swear you haven't been near Ann Forest?'

'Of course I swear it. On a stack of Bibles, if need be. Look, sweetheart, do you think I don't care about our baby? It's quite as bad for me as it is for you.'

'Yes, I know, but—'

'Come and sit down. What put this into your head about Ann Forest?'

'Her baby's so like you.'
'Babies look like the oddest people.'
'But you like her, don't you? I can tell.'
'I think it's tough for her on her own.'
'Do you believe she's a widow?'
'Does it matter what I believe?'
'Yes!'
'Then—no. I think he probably didn't marry her.'
'You know it, don't you?'
'Darling, don't start again.'
'I'm not starting again. I'm just continuing.'
'In other words, you're spoiling for a fight?'
'I just want to know where I stand. It's her or me, Bob.'
'Why, you damned little bitch—!'
'I thought that would make you mad.'
'Mad! It's you who are mad. You're out of your mind, Sarah. I've been afraid of something like this.'
'That's right, call me mad, it's very convenient. You'll be able to have me put away and then you can spend every night with your whore, and I hope you enjoy it!'
Bob struck her across the face.
'Shut your filthy mouth! We'll talk about this tomorrow, when you've had a chance to calm down. For tonight, you can get on with it by yourself or ask that precious mother of yours to help you. I'll bet you anything you like she's at the bottom of all this.'
'Where are you going?' Sarah asked dully.
'What's it matter to you?'
'You're going to that woman.' It was a statement not a question.
'Oh, for God's sake!'
Bob seized his coat and banged out.

***

He had no intention of going to see Ann Forest, but he could not face the bawdy joviality of the pub, and the cinema with its anonymous, amorous darkness would remind him of Sarah too poignantly. There was nothing for it but to walk the streets, but a chill wind was blowing and there was a cold small rain on the wind. For the last night of April the weather was unusually wintry. He turned up his coat collar and strode on.

It must have been by chance that he found himself in Denbigh Road, but chance was all-powerful. He paused to look at No. 42. All was in darkness save for one downstairs window whose curtains gave the light a greenish hue. He leaned on the gate, thinking of the petite Mrs Forest and her baby, and of Sarah's claim that the children had been switched. He paid little attention to tonight's hysteria, not only because he knew the accusations were untrue, but because the doctor had warned him that Sarah was over-strung, her taut nerves ripe for snapping. He would do his best to comfort her when he returned, but not while she sat bolt upright and tense in the living-room; bed was a better place for comforting.

At that moment the front door of No. 42 opened and a long beam of light streamed down the path, outlining him as he leaned on the gate gazing housewards. At the other end of the beam, silhouetted in the lighted doorway, the tiny figure of Mrs Forest appeared.

He saw her hand go to her mouth. Don't scream, he willed her. His will must have had some effect, for she stayed silent as he started up the path towards her, cursing himself as he went.

'I'm sorry to have disturbed you,' he called out to her, 'though I wanted to do just that. I've been meaning to come on behalf of my wife and myself to apologise…'

She recognised him.

'Mr Braithwaite! Won't you come in?'

In the hall he stood looking down at her. She was wearing a short tunic and tights. With her boyish, elfin figure, she could have modelled for Peter Pan.

Her small brown eyes gazed up at him and glittered. 'I was just thinking of you,' she said.

He coughed, embarrassed. 'We do seem to have difficulty in getting away from each other, but I felt I ought to call and explain…'

'Then why not do so in the sitting-room?' She put up a tiny, clawlike hand. She seemed scarcely higher than the door-knob. He felt a hulking, clumsy brute.

The sitting-room was in shades of green. There was very little furniture, but curtains, carpet, walls and paintwork were all in toning shades—not the bluish-greens of underwater, but the clearer greens of summer woods. The hearth, where a bright fire burned, was the colour of a dead oak-leaf. A branch of bursting horse-chestnut was stuck in a vase above. There were no ornaments on the walls except a dim mirror in need of re-silvering in a curiously carved wooden frame. The room was small, but as he looked at it, it seemed to elongate, stretching out like a forest ride.

He glanced down at Mrs Forest. She had seated herself cross-legged on a pouffe. He wondered uneasily if she was some crank who practised yoga. She pointed to the only armchair.

'Please sit down.'

Her voice was very soft, but commanding. Obediently he did as he was told.

'You wanted to see me?'

Bob felt himself increasingly at a loss. He blundered into explanations, but Mrs Forest peremptorily cut him short.

'I understand. Your wife is emotionally disturbed after the shock of finding that she has a defective baby. In her case I dare say I should be the same.'

'I'm sure you wouldn't,' Bob said, and meant it.

She waved a dismissive, airy hand.

'Why have you come tonight, when it is cold and raining? Have you quarrelled with your wife?' she asked.

Bob felt himself bridle. 'I don't feel obliged to answer such a question.'

'Of course not, since I can tell already that you have. Don't be so stuffy,' she went on, seeing him flush with anger. 'I'm not going to ask anything more. Tell me instead how you like your coffee and I'll put on a record to amuse you while I'm out of the room. Then you can tell me how long you've lived in this town, and what it's like, and what you do for a living, and we shall have so much to talk about the evening will soon be gone.'

She was as good as her word. The time passed very quickly. Only one small incident disturbed the harmony. As he took his leave he noticed in the hall that the newel-post at the bottom of the stairs was lacking a head. The wooden head lay on the stairs beside it.

He said, smiling, 'Don't tell me a little thing like you knocked that off?'

'Oh no,' she said, 'the moving men did it.'

'But my dear girl, that's months ago!'

'Before Michael was born'

'But it only needs a couple of nails. Look here, have you got a hammer?'

'Yes, but I can't touch it, it's iron.'

'What on earth—!'

'Don't ask me why, I can manage everything in this house, including the hardware, so long as it isn't made of iron.'

'Then give me the hammer. And a couple of nails, if you've got them.'

She pointed to the cupboard under the stairs. 'They're in there.'

After fumbling in the dim light he found them and backed out triumphantly.

Ann Forest seemed to shrink away from him, to become physically even smaller. Her face had a greenish tinge. As he drove the nails home with two or three firm blows that made her shudder, Bob wondered if she was going to faint.

'There!' He stood back to admire his handiwork. 'That's better than having it lying on the stairs.'

'Yes. Thank you very much. But please put that hammer away now.'

Bob glanced at her. She was really scared.

When he backed out of the cupboard under the stairs minus hammer, a little of her colour had come back.

'So silly,' she murmured, 'to let a little thing like that affect you.'

'It must make things awkward around the house.'

'I manage.'

'You need a man to manage a few things for you.'

She looked up at him. 'You can say that again.'

'If you like,' he offered, 'I'll call round and lend a hand occasionally. Sarah says I'm rather good'

'Your wife won't mind?'

'Now why on earth should she?' He knew that was not the answer, and hurried on: 'I've just about done all the jobs at home that needed doing, and the baby doesn't leave Sarah much time. Especially as her mother's staying with us at present.'

Mrs Forest said: 'I'd be glad for you to call again.'

It was only when he got outside that he realised he still had her scent in his nostrils, that faint whiff of moss and violets and leafmould all in one.

He returned home whistling the Overture to *A Midsummer Night's Dream*, and, so Sarah angrily said, waked the baby. He never even recognised that it was the music Ann Forest had left on.

***

Bob could never remember when he and Ann Forest became lovers. To make love to her seemed so natural an extension of the pleasure he took in her company that it had none of the watershed significance of his first furtive matings with Sarah. Ann was a part of himself, and he entered upon a long tunnel of enchantment whose end he did not want to foresee. That it must have an end, he knew, but so long as Sarah remained unsuspecting, bowed over the puny infant's cradle, crooning 'Hushabye, Baby' incongruously, oblivious of or openly accusing him, he felt himself in some way liberated from her. He did not matter to her, and she had lost whatever hold she had had on him.

She never again mentioned Ann Forest. Bob thought it curious sometimes that Sarah's suspicions should have been premonitory rather than actual, but he was only too thankful that this was the case. Mrs Spencer's on the other hand seemed to grow darker as the evenings lengthened.

'I suppose you'll be working late again tonight,' she challenged him.

'I suppose I will,' Bob retorted.

'About time you got some help, if you ask me.'

'I can manage perfectly, thank you, Mother.'

'Yes, three's a crowd. So they say.'

'I'm sorry, I must go.'

'Anyone'd think you had an appointment.'

'I have—with a pile of work.'

'A piece of work, that's more like it. Just you watch out, my lad. That's all.'

Bob turned and left her. She was getting meddlesome. He'd been warned at work about this. Mothers-in-law who came to stay for lengthy periods almost always ended by trying to boss the show. It became increasingly a relief to return to the green sitting-room of Ann Forest, and to the deeper green bedroom above.

So no one would have been more surprised than Bob if he could have seen his mistress, on the afternoon of Midsummer Eve, push open the gate of his home, park her rickety old pram with the sleeping Michael next to Paul's in the front garden, and, raising a thin brown hand to her eyes, which were on the level with the letter-box, give a resounding rat-tat at the door.

Sarah opened it. When she saw Mrs Forest her face darkened.

'What do you want?' she asked.

'To see you.'

'Sorry, I'm not on exhibition.'

'You can be invisible, so long as we talk.'

'Are you going to give me back my baby?'

'That depends,' Ann Forest said.

'So you admit you stole him?'

'I admit nothing. Must we go on talking here?'

'Yes,' Sarah said. 'I don't want you crossing my threshold. You've done harm enough as it is.'

'Then I can't do more. Or can I?'

Sarah laughed harshly. 'You'd better not try.'

'That sounds suspiciously like a challenge.'

'Take it how you like. Only go away—or give me back my child.'

'How do you know that isn't what I came to do?'

Sarah was taken aback. 'You're joking.'

Ann Forest said, 'I never make jokes.'

'Then you *do* admit it! Why, you wicked woman, I'll have the police on you.'

'You have no witnesses. Your mother's out—I made sure of that, I watched her going. And I am not concerned with the police.'

'Then what are you concerned with?'

'That's my business. Look, surely we can go inside?'

Sarah grudgingly led the way. In her modern sitting-room Ann Forest looked strangely out of place. She was wearing a short green dress and her legs were bare and suntanned. Her hands too were slim and brown. She looked like an old, wise child, not mature enough to be a mother, yet with something about her that was ageless and of all time.

Without invitation, she squatted cross-legged on the hearthrug. Sarah, standing over her, felt clumsy and huge. She sank down awkwardly on a stool. It was as if her tiny guest had the advantage. She said belligerently:

'Why do you insist on pushing in where you know you're not welcome?'

'I don't know any such thing. By the time you've heard my proposition, you may be thanking your God I called upon you. Don't you want to hear what it is?'

Sarah was silent.

'Sarah, do you love your baby?'

The words were so soft Sarah thought she had not really heard them.

'Do you want him back, rosy and smiling and normal? Exactly as he used to be?'

Sarah made a strangled sound. Mrs Forest took it for assent.

'Very well, but on one condition.'

Sarah looked up, haggard-eyed.

'One condition which it will be dangerous to break: my child for your husband. Well, Sarah, is it a deal?'

'What do you mean? You hardly know my husband.'

Mrs Forest smiled. 'That's what you think.'

'You mean—my mother's right? It's you he goes to?'

The visitor bowed her head.

'No!' Sarah stood up. 'I won't give him up. Why should I? You took my baby; now you want to take my husband as well!'

'Not as well,' Mrs Forest corrected her. 'Instead of. I didn't mean it to work out like this. I wanted a child—any child the right age—yours, as it happened. I've always been content with that before.'

'Before! Then this isn't your first child-stealing?'

'I only take one every seven years.'

'But—but how old are you?' Sarah said stupidly.

'As old as my tongue and a little older than my teeth.'

The answer given to children seemed suddenly sinister.

'I don't understand,' Sarah said.

'There's no reason why you should. It doesn't matter. What matters is whether you're prepared to agree to the deal.'

'No.'

'Think, Sarah: do you love your husband?'

Sarah said, 'Of course I do.'

'There's no "of course" about it. Instead of standing by you in your sorrow, he's unfaithful. Do you suppose that I shall be the last?'

Sarah said nothing.

'Well, if you won't answer that, tell me: do you love your baby?'

Sarah found her voice. 'You know I do.'

'And you would like to see him strong and healthy and normal?'

'Oh *yes!*'

'Then why not give him this second chance in life?'

Sarah stood up. 'What must I do?'

'You must make me a solemn promise, repeating the words after me, whereby you renounce all rights in your husband, and give him body and soul to me.'

'I can't do that. I've never owned his soul.'

'It's only a formula.'

'What will happen to Bob?'

'He will come away with me—far away, where you will never see us. You can even divorce him, if you wish.'

'And my baby?'

'He will be given back to you. Come and see how beautiful he is. I have kept him well. I wanted him in perfect condition.'

'You sound as if you are going to make a meal of him.'

'Don't be melodramatic.' Mrs Forest walked lightly across the room to face Sarah. 'Well, Sarah Braithwaite, is it a deal?'

'What if I say no?'

'You will wear out your youth with an idiot child and an unfaithful husband. Frankly, I can't see why you hesitate.'

Sarah couldn't see it either; she only knew that she did.

'What do you want Bob for?' she asked curiously.

'Didn't you want him once?'

How long ago that seemed! Yet to be without him, to bring up Paul on her own, to find herself in fact in Ann Forest's position—that too she did not want.

Something did not ring true about this offer. Whichever way you looked at it, she was being robbed. Why should she be forced to choose between husband and child, she demanded.

Mrs Forest said impatiently, 'Because every woman is basically either mother or wife.'

'Which are you?'

The little woman pirouetted. 'I'm an enchantress. It doesn't really count.'

At that moment the baby began to cry in the garden, a lusty, bawling sound, straight from the lungs of a healthy infant. Sarah ran to the window and looked out. It was a sound her heart had ached for, very different from the wizened infant's puling cry. And at that moment the baby looked up and saw her. He stopped roaring, and a slow smile spread over his face. It went on widening and deepening until he had at least three double chins and his eyes were glinting, happy slits above chubby cheeks still tear-stained. It was a smile for her and it melted Sarah's heart. Whatever happened, she had to have that baby, had to feel her arms encircle warm, firm flesh, had to count ten fingers, ten toes on hands and feet that were pink and supple, instead of being scaly like claws.

She turned to confront Ann Forest. 'Very well, I accept your terms: my husband in exchange for your baby. What must I do?'

Ann Forest gave a small sigh of relief, and said matter-of-factly: 'Nothing. Leave all the rest to me.'

***

'You know, Mrs Braithwaite, you're a very lucky woman,' the pædiatrician said. He looked up, smiling, from his examination of the baby. 'Your son's normal again in every way.'

I know, sang Sarah's heart; her lips merely murmured, 'Are you certain?'

'As certain as I can be. I've never before come across spontaneous remission in the case of a retarded infant, but there's a first time for everything.'

'How do you explain it?' Sarah asked out of curiosity, knowing that the truth would never be believed.

The pædiatrician spread his hands. 'I don't. Perhaps some temporary malformation of a gland which rights itself before irreversible damage is done. Perhaps the removal of some minor blockage. Perhaps—oh, anything. I've never known another case like it and I hardly dare hope to again.'

'It seems too good to be true,' Sarah admitted, clutching Paul to her, feeling his firm body respond, and putting from her, she hoped, for ever, the memory of Ann Forest's malevolent, yellow-faced child.

It had been, as Ann had promised, easy. She had simply repeated some words—strange words whose import she understood only vaguely—while standing with her hand upraised. When she had finished, Ann Forest said with odd intensity:

'This is like no oath you've ever sworn before. You have made a pact that is not with heaven, nor hell, nor yet with this world. See to it that you keep your word.'

Then she had gone outside and deftly switched the babies, going down the path with the defective in her rickety pram. Except that the child's wizened face now bore a look of sharpness and his brown eyes glinted with a kind of unholy glee.

'You and your husband should get down on your knees and be thankful,' the pædiatrician said to Sarah. He was a devout and godfearing man.

'I do.' Sarah was careful not to mention her husband, but the pædiatrician was too busy mentally drafting the paper he would present at the next annual Child Health Congress to worry about a little thing like that.

Not even Sarah worried about it, to begin with. She had accepted Mrs Forest's terms wholeheartedly. 'My child in exchange for your husband' had seemed to her at the time a good bargain. It was only later that the doubts came creeping in.

Her mother had returned home, and night after night Sarah was alone with the baby, while Bob kept up the fiction that he was working late. Once the child was asleep there was time to speculate on what the father might be doing. In imagination Sarah accompanied him to Denbigh Road.

Outwardly their life went on much as usual. Bob Braithwaite did not change dramatically. A clean, tidy, well-dressed husk went through the motions of living, paid bills, ate meals, spoke when spoken to and lay down at nights by Sarah, but in every real sense, he was elsewhere.

Bob did not even notice the relics of his former life around him. Everything that was not Ann Forest had become a dream. He would have left Sarah outright and gone to live with her, but whenever he suggested it, she said, 'Wait.' She was vague when he tried to pin her down about the future, promising that 'In the autumn we will go away.' When he demanded where, she became evasive: 'Somewhere you have never been before.' She seemed to have no relatives and no friends; at least he never met any. About her child's father she was reticent. 'These things happen,' was all she would say before changing the subject. Bob was more than ever convinced that some brute had abandoned her.

He was therefore agreeably surprised to be invited to a Hallowe'en dance, along with some friends of hers. She added that it was to be fancy dress 'from the neck upwards'. The infatuated Bob made a special journey to the nearest large town, where he visited a theatrical costumier's and hired an ass's head for the occasion at very considerable expense. He returned home with it and Sarah saw it.

'What are you doing with that?'

'I'm going to a Hallowe'en party. Fancy dress from the neck up.'

'Bottom,' Sarah said bitterly. 'How appropriate. I suppose you're going with *her*.'

'That's right. Any objections?'

She looked at him. 'Bob, must you go?'

'I don't have to, but I want to. What difference does it make to you? You've got the child, that's all you care about.'

'Did that woman tell you that?'

'I've got eyes in my head, haven't I? You make it pretty obvious.'

'But you're my husband, Bob. Paul's father.'

'You've wakened up to that rather late.'

'If I've neglected you, I'm sorry. It's because I was so worried over Paul.'

'That's right. So worried you even accused me of having fathered Ann Forest's child, if you remember.'

'I didn't know what I said.'

'The irony of it is that at that time I'd done no more than speak to Ann in her front garden.'

'I dare say you've made up for it since.'

'You're dead right I have. It's no good, Sarah, we're finished.'

'Only because she's cast a spell on you.'

'If she has, I hope it doesn't wear off in a hurry. I've never been so happy in my life.'

'Come back, and I'll see if I can make you even happier.'

'No good, my dear. I'm another woman's man.'

'But there's something so odd about her, and about her horrible baby. Something almost evil, wouldn't you say?'

'No I wouldn't. But I suppose it's too much to expect you to admit that she's attractive.'

'Yes, she *is* attractive—I can see it. But attractive in a dangerous way.'

Bob laughed. 'The spice of danger. It's what she ought to call that scent of hers. I've never known a fragrance so exciting, haunting.'

'Bob, stop it, and come back to me.'

Bob looked at his wife as if she had suddenly started speaking Arabic. Then he said: 'Not on your life. You'll have to come and get me if you want me. But I frankly don't advise you to try.'

***

Bob's challenge and Ann Forest's warning weighed on Sarah for days. Why should she sit back and allow this diminutive woman to rob her of her husband? Her resolution hardened as Hallowe'en approached. On that night, at the dance, her husband would be introduced to Ann Forest's friends. Hitherto the liaison had not been public. His lawful wife had been able to hold her head high. Therefore on that night she would challenge him before them. If he intended to desert her, then at least his desertion should be made plain. Where her pride was involved, Sarah lacked neither courage nor cunning. It was a simple matter to discover where the dance was being held and to work out the route by which her husband would be returning with his mistress. She would wait at the first crossroads, before the party split up. The dance was due to end at midnight. By half past eleven, Sarah was in her place.

It was a bright moonlight night. Every star in heaven had come out to wink and twinkle as if in mirth. The road stretched empty before and behind her. The grass verges sparkled with the first frost. From the hotel where the dance was in progress the throb of the band came faintly. Along the other three arms of the crossroads street lamps and houses began, but this one, heading towards open country, was unlighted and the hotel in a slight hollow was the only house.

Muffled in a thick coat with a hood and fur boots, Sarah waited patiently. She had left her mother at home with Paul, though without telling her where she was going, much to Mrs Spencer's annoyance. She had merely warned her that she would be home very late. The time passed slowly. Sarah glanced repeatedly at her watch, thinking it must be wrong. Then, very faintly on the crisp, still air, she heard the chimes of the city hall clock striking midnight. A few minutes later a tremendous din broke out.

Laughing, shouting, singing, the revellers surged from the ballroom towards their waiting cars. Several of them were to say later they noticed a hooded figure near the crossroads, but now they wasted no time on Sarah, nor she on them. One or two even thought the grey, hooded form pressed against the hedgerow was one of themselves trying to give the others a fright. Bob Braithwaite was one of those who thought so, until the figure stepped forward and caught his arm.

Bob and his party were the last to emerge from the hotel. They lived near and several of them were walking. The advance party had already linked arms across the road and were singing and swaying, a little tipsy, as they jostled to get in step for the walk home. Behind them came a second group, chattering and laughing, several still wearing on their heads their fancy dress. Sarah saw a witch, a devil, a horned goat and a pumpkin, this last a grinning mask. The smallest figure in the company was Titania, with a crown that looked as if it were made of cobwebs hung with dew, strange, slanting eyebrows and a greenish tint to her skin. The natural face beneath was almost unrecognisable, so skilful was the disguise, but Sarah, looking with what seemed to her preternatural vision, perceived that Titania had Ann Forest's eyes.

Bob walked alone, a little behind the others, the last of the third company to pass. The ass's head completely concealed his features, but Sarah recognised his shoulders and his walk. When she caught his arm and the animal mask turned towards her, she wondered fleetingly what expression was on his face, but his sudden stiffening, his attempt to draw away from her told her what she most feared to know.

'What do you want?' he asked roughly.

'Bob, come home with me.'

'For God's sake Sarah, must we have a scene like this in public?'

'Paul needs you and so do I.'

'Then you'll have to go on needing me. I've finished with you, Sarah. Can't you get that into your head?'

'Please, Bob.'

'No!'

'Bob, it's your wife who's asking.'

Bob swore with sudden savagery and tried to pull away. Sarah, unexpectedly strong, would not let go. She had managed to get both arms round him in a clumsy hug that looked almost like affection. They swayed back and forth across the road in a kind of staggering dance. Neither of them had cried out, and their shadows were long in the moonlight. Their breath made a halo of steam in the midnight air. The rest of the revellers had gone ahead when one, chancing to look back, let out a shrill cry: 'Hey! Our Bob's making off.'

There was a pattering of feet, one lighter and swifter than all the others, but Sarah was aware only of the cloth beneath her hands becoming smooth, becoming cool, of the ass's head changing shape, rearing high above her into an elongated downward-running crest. The skin she now clutched was clammy, she could see a tail trailing on the ground, there was webbing between the fingers. She was clasping not a man but a giant newt.

Sarah held on despite the sick, unnatural horror. Newts, she reminded herself, weren't poisonous. And as if in answer to her thought, she felt the clammy skin becoming dry, felt the contraction of powerful muscles, almost lost her hold as the arms seemed suddenly to disappear. She was clasping a monster she could get no grip on, who twisted and turned all ways, seemingly without end or beginning. A slight hissing sound above her made her look upwards. She was clasping not a giant newt but a giant snake.

Sarah held on, although snakes were her pet aversion. She had had nightmares after visiting the reptile house at the zoo. The snake's coils writhed and folded about her. Since she felt no venom, she assumed it must be a crusher. Her arms strained in a weird gymnastic, striving to hold on, yet hold the horror off.

She was gasping, sweating with exertion, encumbered by her winter coat, when she realised that it was not only her heat that was responsible, but the snake's blood was getting warm. Beneath her hands the skin was changing its texture, it was growing short, close fur, she could feel the bone structure underneath. Cloven hoofs sounded on the roadway, stepped on her own booted feet. The animal kicked and plunged, she felt hot breath on her face, saw a wild, rolling eye looking up at her, and realised she was holding not a giant snake but a deer.

It was a doe; there were no horns, thank goodness, but it leapt with the speed and strength of a gazelle, almost breaking her hold as it endeavoured to plunge for the open country. Sarah gritted her teeth and held on.

She was not afraid of the deer, as she had been of the serpent, but she found it no easier to hold. The heat of the beast's body was excess-ive, although its kicking grew fainter and it seemed physically to contract. It was becoming hard and smooth and burning. It was not a doe at all. But by now Sarah was conscious of nothing but the pain searing into her palms and fingers, and a curious smell—was it her own roasting flesh? She could see quite clearly the dull glow of the red-hot metal she was clasping. She was holding not a doe but a red-hot iron bar.

The agony in her hands was so great that she tried to let go and couldn't. The searing metal had stuck to her flesh. She almost expected her bones to melt and the iron to burn its way through them. She wondered dimly if she would ever be able to use her hands again. But even in this state they had not lost all feeling. The glowing metal was cooling, cooling, growing soft, growing larger, taking on again the characteristics of living flesh. And this time its touch was familiar even while it fought her like a man possessed. For that indeed was what the thing in her arms was becoming. She was holding not a red-hot iron bar but a naked man.

Sarah looked up. The man's legs were kicking out wildly, his arms flailing like a threshing-machine out of control. He had Bob's features, but the face was suffused, the eyes glared with the light of unreason. Flecks of foam formed on his lips and ran unheeded down his jaws.

If madmen do indeed have the strength of ten, I'm lost, Sarah thought as the man's arm broke free and was raised to strike her a great buffet. She closed her eyes against the blow she knew must come. There was a kind of explosion in her head, but she clung the more tightly to the flesh beneath her fingers, willing it to be calm, be still. As the man's struggles slackened and died away, she became aware that she was sobbing. It was her own gasping breath she heard on the frosty air. There was no other sound. All the revellers had vanished as if they had never existed. From the grass verge the ass's head of Bottom grinned at her mockingly.

Ann Forest, still with Titania's head on her slim shoulders, stood beside her.

'Well, Sarah Braithwaite, are you satisfied with your night's work? I warned you not to break our contract, but of course you had to know best.'

'I want my husband.'

'You had exchanged him for my baby.'

'No, the baby was mine. You stole him and left your hateful brat as a replacement. But why? Why persecute us so?'

Ann Forest shrugged. 'Nothing personal. It was the tithe that had to be paid.'

'What tithe?'

'Every seven years we owe a human soul to Hell. It's not much really, for the continuance of our elfin world.'

'And for that you stole my baby?'

'It's usually the easiest way. Fewer and fewer adults believe in us. In that they make a mistake. But of course a full-grown soul is better. I was quite willing to do a deal when I saw you were prepared to trade child for husband. You've even despatched him for us, I see.'

'What!'

'Oh yes, my dear. Take a look at him. Your Bob is very, very dead. You strangled him in your jealous rage when you caught us together. Everyone knows you've been unhinged since the baby's birth. I tried everything in my power to make you let go of him, but you were determined to hold on. No, don't fly at me. You can't touch me. Mortals have tried before now. Hark! There's a siren. A police car will be coming. Some of my company will have dialled 999 before they disappeared. What will you try and make the police believe, I wonder, poor mad creature that you are?'

Sarah had ceased listening long since. The last words she heard were 'very, very dead'. She knelt down and turned Bob over. It was obvious that Ann Forest was right.

Bob's mouth was open, his tongue protruding. There were purple bruises on his throat. His face was an ugly, mottled colour. His head lolled helplessly.

Perhaps it was the head, seeming suddenly too big for the body, that made Sarah think of a child. Awkwardly, clumsily she gathered her husband into her arms. Stooping over him, cradling his head on her breast, she began to sing 'Hushabye, Baby' in a voice suddenly cracked and out of tune.

That was how the police found her, crouched over her husband like some wild beast at bay. Neither then nor at the inquest (she was found unfit to plead) did she say anything coherent. She was still singing 'Hushabye, Baby' when they finally led her away.

DEAD WOMAN

THE HILL WAS called Dead Woman. There was no possible doubt of that, for the words stood out clearly even amid the hachurings on the map. The map was dated 1770, and was expensive but something of a find. It would look well hanging on the wall in my bungalow, which lay in the shadow of the hill.

The hill was low and thickly wooded and extended like a protective arm along the road which was also the village, for the houses straddled its length. My bungalow, somewhat isolated and standing well back in a large garden, was the last one if you started counting from the church, and beside it a path struck up into the woods on the slopes of Dead Woman. Even before I had finished buying the map which so named it, I found myself calling it that.

I hadn't been searching for a map when I entered the print shop. It would have been difficult to say what I was searching for, except that I had an urge to buy old things for the bungalow to make it look less new. All my life I had wanted to build my own house, but now that I had at last achieved it, I was uncertain about the result. The bungalow, which had been designed to blend with the landscape at the insistence of the local planners, seemed to me to stick out like a sore thumb.

I told myself that this was only because I had left it rather late in life to go in for new things; one does not normally start building when one is about to retire. But when Mr Slade's piece of land came on the market, it seemed that it was meant. An unsuspected sentimental streak had made me crave to return to the land of my fathers—the England on the borders of Wales, and as retirement approached I began looking for a suitable property, only to find them rarer than I had thought. Then I learned, almost by accident in the estate agent's, that there was a building plot coming up for sale in one of the prettiest villages. I bought it, paid far too much for it, and the project was under way.

It all took a very long time, but I had started early. By the time I retired from the administrative Civil Service in which I had worked all my life, the bungalow was ready and waiting. I said goodbye to London and moved in. Perhaps I was too rash, too insouciant; with hindsight it is easy to say I was, but I had known and loved the Welsh Border since childhood. It never occurred to me that I might not fit. After all, my ancestors had come from villages between Usk and Ludlow for seven generations. I had the Welsh lilt in my voice. In a district still thick with Welsh proper names and place names, Jane Davies would soon be indistinguishable from the rest.

After a year I had to recognise ruefully that I was paying for my sentimental streak. Everyone was polite but no one was friendly. I remained totally unabsorbed. Perhaps it was my fault in some ways— I was too intellectual in my tastes, used words with which the local people weren't familiar, or indulged in irony which they failed to recognise except as an alien element in my speech. Of course I made a few friends, but they tended to be people from outlying big houses, which made the villagers think I was a snob. And perhaps I was. Perhaps it would never have been possible for me to settle there, even without the happenings I am about to relate.

It began with Dead Woman—of that I am certain. I naturally wondered about the old name for 'the hill', as everyone local now called it, but I had not expected to arouse such hostility by a casual enquiry made in the crowded village shop. When I asked if anyone happened to know the origin of the name, there was a bristling silence. Then Mrs Francis, the proprietress, declared: 'Folks used to have all sorts of queer names for things in the old days, Miss Davies, but "the hill's" always been good enough for me.'

Mr Baxter, churchwarden and retired butcher, overweight and florid of face, told me no good ever came of enquiring into what was best left forgotten, and seemed to feel he had made a profound remark.

'So you'd dismiss all history,' I couldn't help saying.

'I'm dismissing nothing, ma'm, but Dead Woman's not a name that's used any longer. Round here we call it "the hill".'

Mr Baxter and Mrs Francis were well established. There were memorial tablets to their forebears in the church dating back to the 1590s. They exemplified the local tendency to stay put. Their ancestors must certainly have called the hill Dead Woman. What in the world was there to conceal? Yet other customers in the shop were muttering their agreement: better to keep calling it 'the hill'.

***

The next incident was so trivial it must seem ridiculous in the telling. It was at the spring flower show, where I had entered a small floral arrangement which was awarded second prize. I must say in all honesty that it deserved to do better and several people told me so, for though the first prize-winner's blooms were beautiful, she offered nothing but an overfull vase containing something of everything, as different as possible from my spare oriental scheme. Nevertheless, knowing that a newcomer would not be a popular winner when Mrs Probert won the flower arranging every year, except when Mrs Lane-Turner won it, I endeavoured to take it in good part and admired her plump vaseful extravagantly. She seemed genuinely pleased at my praise.

'I must say I like a bit of colour,' she expounded. 'Those daffs now—they show up a treat. And that red tulip and the forget-me-nots and wallflowers, they make a lovely show. My husband likes flowers so you can see 'em—he says you can't have too much of a good thing, just as a man 'ud rather have a woman with some flesh on her than try to put his arms round a stick.'

She said it with a warm chuckle, but someone must have nudged her, for she broke off, looking confused. I suppose the remark was considered unfortunate in view of the fact that I have never married, my best friends couldn't call me anything but skinny, and my floral arrangement incorporated a twig.

I can't say I was bothered by Mrs Probert's *faux pas*. I made some vague, amiable reply and moved away, and it was not until some little time later that I became aware of a commotion at the floral arrangements end of the marquee. I made my way there to see what had happened. Mrs Probert, sobbing noisily, was surrounded by sympathetic friends. Her prize-winning arrangement had overbalanced, and broken vase, crushed blooms and first prize-winner's ticket lay in a sodden heap on the ground. I doubt very much if anyone had touched it. The vase had a narrow base and that clumsy mass of flowers was more than enough to topple it, but I naturally commiserated.

To my surprise, the women surrounding Mrs Probert drew back and looked at me with hostile eyes, while Mrs Probert herself held up a meaty hand like a policeman's as though to ward me off.

'It's all your doing,' she exclaimed. 'Don't come near me.'

'Mrs Probert, I was at the other end of the marquee.'

She took no notice. 'If you hadn't looked at 'em it would never have happened.'

Still sobbing, she was led solicitously away.

I took no notice because the accusation was too ridiculous. No one could have seen me near the flowers, whereas plenty of people had seen me at the far end of the tent where a competition for the best chocolate sponge was being judged. I was demonstrably innocent. Of course I had known a moment's chagrin when Mrs Probert's inferior exhibit had won, but to suggest I had deliberately wrecked it was not only untrue, it showed a lack of understanding of my character which made me feel afresh how alien I was.

The next incident was also trivial, though this time I admit I was provoked. My next-door neighbour had a pear tree which overhung my hedge and shaded what would otherwise be a sunny corner of the garden. I asked him to cut it back. Admittedly the blossom was beautiful, but the blossom time is short and the subsequent leaves very thick, and in any case the tree was so neglected that it had reverted almost to a wild state. When one or two hints had no effect on Mr Humphries, I wrote him a little note. There was no reply, so I wrote him a second letter. That produced results all right. One afternoon when I was gardening Old Man Humphries came to a gap in the hedge and proceeded to tell me what he thought of me. I listened to the tirade and replied that speaking his mind was his privilege, but I rather thought it was my right to have my garden's share of the benefits of earth and air undiminished by someone else's carelessly pruned tree.

'That tree is not carelessly pruned,' Mr Humphries ranted.

'You're right,' I said, 'it isn't pruned at all. And the pears you get from it are small, hard, green things unfit even for stewing. Why don't you chop it down?'

Old Man Humphries came up close to the hedge, bent down and shouted through it: 'That tree was there in my father's day and it ain't being cut down for you, Miss High-and-Mighty Davies.'

'Blast you and your tree,' I said in anger.

A month later both of them were dead.

About Mr Humphries's death there was nothing mysterious: he had a fatal but not unexpected stroke. But the pear tree began shedding shrivelled leaves—on to my garden, of course—and was bare before midsummer. I was as puzzled by it as anyone else.

So puzzled was I that I asked friends in my old Ministry to put me in touch with an agricultural research station which specialised in pomology. Was it an old tree, these young experts asked me grandly, and when I said yes, and in need of pruning and general attention, they said old trees quite often died like that. 'It's like old people,' they explained rather tactlessly. 'Some of them seem to live out their allotted span and then they curl up and die for no apparent reason. It's nature's means of getting them out of the way.'

It was after this that I began to notice a change in the villagers' attitude towards me. When I went into the village shop the conversation died down and I fancied they edged away from me. No one said good morning any more. They didn't refuse to answer if I addressed them, but they did so warily. Small children were grasped firmly, dogs called to heel as their owners passed me. In church I was usually alone in a pew. I was disturbed and irritated, a little perplexed at what I had done to upset the locals, but I was not seriously alarmed.

Then came the incident of Barbara Harris's dog, and that was different. For one thing, Barbara was my friend. A widow, a little lonely, a great gardener and golfer, she had seemed as glad of my company as I was of hers. The only snag was the dog, Rollo, a cocker spaniel, a breed I particularly detest since I find them both treacherous and fawning. (I am a cat lover myself.) Rollo, of course, knew that I disliked him in that infallible way dogs do, and made it no secret that he returned the feeling. He always growled at me. Barbara dismissed it—'He's never bitten anyone'—but I was not so sure. Since I valued my friendship with Barbara, I resolved to see to it that at least Rollo had no excuse.

One afternoon I had gone down to the shop, which was also the post office, for some stamps I badly needed. Two or three women were waiting in a queue and Mrs Francis was serving them slowly. She was never anything but slow. I took my place at the back, prepared to wait, but to my surprise, when she had finished serving one woman, she called out 'What can I get you, Miss Davies?'

I said pointedly, 'These ladies were first.'

'They won't mind waiting,' Mrs Francis announced, uncontradicted. 'Did you want a postal order, like last time?'

'No, I want some stamps,' I said, enumerating the values. Mrs Francis busied herself. The other women drew aside so far as the shop's small space allowed it. The one who had been served made no move to go.

'Nice day,' I said.

There was a perceptible pause before anyone would admit it, but at last one of the women spoke.

'Gather you don't like Mrs Carrington's lilac, Miss Davies.'

'I love lilac,' I said truthfully. 'What's the matter with Mrs Carrington's?'

'We was hoping you might know.'

'Is there something wrong with it? I'm not a gardening expert. Ask Mrs Harris,' I said as the shop door pinged and Barbara came in. She greeted everyone generally and me in particular.

'What is it you were wanting to know?'

'We were discussing Mrs Carrington's lilac.'

'Yes, I noticed it as I came by. Such a shame. It seems to be blighted. It's shrivelling and shedding its leaves.'

'Just like Mr Humphries's pear tree,' said one of the women.

Mrs Francis raised her head. 'That'll be one pound seven shillings. One pound thirty-five pence to you, Miss Davies,' she said.

Old ways die hard on the Welsh Border, where 50p is still referred to as 'a ten bob bit'. I had once or twice corrected Mrs Francis, and she was getting her own back now. The other customers, who were discussing Mrs Carrington's lilac with Barbara, broke off long enough to smile. And at this moment of confusion and irritation, I discovered I had left my purse in the car.

With a muttered apology for keeping everyone waiting, I made hurriedly for the door. And at once there was a yelp of pain from Rollo, in the way as usual, because I trod on his paw. In a reflex of fear he turned and bit me, or rather he seized the hem of my coat, and I heard the fabric tear as I tried to pull it from him, and exclaimed irritatedly, 'Damn that dog!'

Barbara grabbed hold of Rollo's collar. 'Naughty boy! Has he done any damage, Jane?' Out of the corner of my eye I could see her patting the spaniel.

'Only to my coat,' I said frostily. 'Not to me.'

'It's because you moved quickly and trod on him,' Barbara continued. 'Spaniels are nervous dogs. But Rollo says if you'll come and have tea with him and his mum on Wednesday, he'll try to make amends.'

I accepted with pleasure—I enjoyed Barbara's company—and thought the incident at an end. But on Monday I had to go to London for a couple of days and I did not return until Tuesday evening. It was to the news that Rollo was dead.

'Went straight in front of a car,' they told me at the station. 'Mrs Harris is rare cut up.'

I could imagine it, for even I had to admit that Rollo was normally an obedient creature.

'What on earth made him do a thing like that?'

'Dunno, miss. I dare say *you* do, though. He was trotting; along as peaceful as you please when it seemed an if something got into him and he suddenly made a dive across the road. The motorist warn't to blame. That dog pretty well committed suicide. Something drove him to it, as you might say.'

'The likeliest explanation is that something stung him.'

The station-master/ticket-collector/porter looked at me curiously. As soon as I got home I rang Barbara.

'Barbara—it's Jane.'

'Jane. Oh yes.'

'Barbara, I'm so sorry. About Rollo. I've only just got back and heard.'

'Thank you.'

'You must feel dreadful.'

'Yes.'

'Poor Rollo, he was so well-trained. What could have made him do it?'

'I'm afraid he didn't leave a note.'

'Barbie, instead of my coming to you tomorrow, why don't you come to me?'

'Sorry, Jane, I couldn't. And I'd rather you didn't come here.'

'But it's the worst thing you can do—shut yourself up and refuse to see anyone.'

'I'm not alone. My cousin has come to stay.'

'Then why don't you both come over?'

'No, Jane, thank you. I may as well tell you: I don't want to see you again.'

'What's the matter? What have I done?'

Barbara said in a low voice, 'I think you know.'

'I don't. I've been in London for the past two days,' I protested.

In the same low voice Barbara went on: 'I didn't believe it at first when the villagers said you ill-wished things, but you ill-wished darling Rollo, and he's dead.'

'Ill-wished? What are you talking about? I don't know what you mean.'

'Anything you don't like you put a curse on: Mrs Probert's winning flower arrangement, Mr Humphries and his tree, Mrs Carrington's lilac, and now my poor darling dog.'

'I never cursed anything in my life.' As I spoke, I was uneasily aware of saying 'Damn that dog!' but that was only an expression of annoyance. No one would take it seriously.

Barbara, however, did. She said with icy coldness, 'I'll leave you to your conscience, Jane,' and hung up quietly and decisively. I realised I had lost a friend.

I had done more than that. I had made enemies. I became aware that people were avoiding me. When I went out, the village street mysteriously emptied. Those who could not escape an encounter crossed to the other side of the road. They were afflicted with deafness, and did not hear my greetings; with blindness, and did not see me nod. Small children were called indoors, and received a clip for less than instant obedience. I might have been a leper approaching with a bell.

Of course there were exceptions, chiefly among the children, of whom the boldest were hostile but unafraid. They followed me whispering and calling, 'Miss! Miss, are you going to ill-wish us?' If I turned round they instantly scattered and ran. Once a small stone flew past me. I was in time to see who threw it: Tommy Jones. I might have known. The scruffiest, cheekiest urchin in the village and our local policeman's only son.

Tommy had no fear of me. He was eleven, possibly twelve, freckled and intensely inquisitive. If I were working in my garden, he would lean on the gate and ask, 'What are you planting, miss?' I had caught him stealing apples and threatened to tell his mother. He dared me to: 'Yah! G'won!' I knew he went birds-nesting and suspected him of taking more than the traditional 'one egg only'. I was pretty sure he had broken a pane of glass in the lean-to outside my scullery. Yet for all that, I liked the boy. He was completely without malice, frank and open, his eyes as clear and bright as a summer sky. Even now, though he would not come near me, he hung around my house to see what was going on.

But Tommy was alone in this veiled friendliness. When I was told in the shop that they would no longer be able to deliver my weekly order, I decided things had gone far enough. After all, I had done nothing. The incidents Barbara mentioned were pure coincidence. Every bit of bad luck was being laid on my doorstep, including Mrs Carrington's lilac which I had never even seen. Surely someone could explain how the idea had started. I called at the vicarage.

The vicar, whom I did not know well, was polite but distant. Had he always seemed so remote? I came to the point at once by asking: 'Are you aware that the locals think I have the evil eye?'

He did not deny it, but offered some platitude about education being often less effective than the educationists supposed.

'I wouldn't call Barbara Harris uneducated,' I retorted, 'and she thinks I caused Rollo's death.'

'The dog has been everything to Mrs Harris since she was widowed.'

'I know, but she was also my friend. I admit I didn't much care for that spaniel, but why should she think I'd destroy it? It simply doesn't make sense.'

'She was upset and perhaps not uninfluenced by—well, ignorant gossip. You're an outsider, Miss Davies, you see. It takes quite a time to get accepted in this village. I've been here six years, and I'm by no means certain that my parishioners have accepted *me*.'

He smiled as he said it, but the smile was uneasy. I sensed he wanted me to go.

'Do you believe I ill-wish people?' I asked him.

He said firmly, 'I'm sure you don't.'

'Then how did this idea become current?'

'As you may have noticed, round here old ways die hard.'

'Calling fifty pence a ten bob bit,' I said bitterly, 'is a long way from the evil eye.'

'I think you may have inadvertently stirred things up yourself with your enquiries about Dead Woman.'

'What's the hill got to do with it?'

'Only that the woman who was hanged there in the seventeenth century was reputed to be a witch.'

'Is that why the hill was called Dead Woman?'

'Probably.'

'But when I asked no one even knew the reason for its name.'

'Perhaps not, but folk memories are surprisingly long. They remember that the name has evil associations. After all, a lynching—even in the seventeenth century—is a pretty shameful thing.'

'A lynching!'

'Oh yes, it was the villagers who killed her. I'll show you her grave if you like.'

He led the way to the remotest corner of the churchyard.

'You see? Only just within consecrated ground.'

'Why was she killed?'

'She was alleged to ill-wish people. Women miscarried, cattle dropped their calves, crops withered. Eventually a child died and the villagers considered her responsible. They took the law into their own hands. She was seized and taken to the top of the hill behind your cottage, and I'm afraid they hanged her there.'

'And no one was ever brought to justice for the murder?'

'It proved impossible to find who did the deed. The villagers, as you may have noticed, are very clannish. No one could be found to talk, though there were dark hints about a man named Baxter, our church-warden's ancestor. But after three hundred years the story is almost forgotten. I learned of it only by chance. Then you come along and start asking questions about Dead Woman, and in some way the qualities of the original victim, Jennet Paris, are transferred to you—perhaps because you live where she lived.'

'I do?'

'Yes, the record of her death in the parish register makes that abundantly clear. Afterwards the villagers dismantled her cottage, "leaving no stock nor stone standing", as the contemporary records say. The land was eventually bought by a Thomas Slade, who I've no doubt is the ancestor of our Mr Slade in the village. And *he* sold it to a certain Jane Davies. As we know.'

'So until I built the bungalow no one had lived there since Jennet?'

'So it would seem,' the vicar said.

'And you think some association of the place with witchcraft lingers on in the village?'

'It is not impossible.'

'So what do I do? Jennet Paris was probably innocent. So am I, but how do I convince people of that? They won't even speak to me any longer.'

'None of them?'

'One or two of the children. Tommy Jones particularly.'

'Yes, Tommy doesn't scare easily. Couldn't you make a start with him? If you win one of them over, the rest will soon come. And the parents will follow the children. I'll do whatever I can. We can't expect miracles but we ought to be able to achieve your rehabilitation.' He smiled suddenly, winningly. 'At least it's worth trying, isn't it?'

I felt more cheerful as I came away.

***

It wasn't easy, but I persevered with Tommy, who continued to hang around, largely I am sure because I had the lure of the forbidden. He said as much when I invited him in.

'My mam says I'm riot to talk to you, Miss Davies.'

'Really? Why does she say that?'

'"Cos you'll ill-wish me.'

'Why should I ill-wish you?'

'"Cos—'cos you will. Like Mrs Harris's dog.'

'I didn't ill-wish poor Rollo.'

'My mam heard you do it in the shop.'

'Nonsense, Tommy, your mother was mistaken. Now, are you

coming in or not? I'm going to have my tea and you're welcome to join me. There are chocolate biscuits,' I added casually.

'I don't mind,' Tommy said, doing me a favour. He followed me into the house.

In a village an incident can have no witnesses, but everyone knows of it just the same. It went from one end of the village to the other that Tommy Jones had been to tea with me.

It was a week before he came again, and then he did not approach the front gate. He called to me through the hedge bordering the lane— the lane that became the track that led up on top of Dead Woman.

'Hallo, Tommy. Where have you been?' I said, trying to hide my pleasure in seeing him.

'My mam kept me indoors.'

'Haven't you been well?' I asked, thinking the child looked paler than usual.

'I'm all right. She said I shouldn't have come here.'

'It did you no harm, did it?' I said sharply.

'Yes, it did. My dad belted me.'

My anger rose against the Joneses. Against my will, I suggested Tommy should go home.

'Okay. I'm just going.' He added thoughtfully, 'Those biscuits were all right.'

'There are some more if you like to come in for them.' I added hastily, 'You can have some to take away.'

I could not believe biscuits taken from a packet put out by a well-known manufacturer could lead to a poisoning charge, even in the unlikely event of Tommy's parents discovering the donor. He accepted and gave me his widest grin, then shifted from one foot to the other like a parody of a bashful suitor. I guessed he had something more to say.

'Can I come again?' he blurted at last, red with embarrassment.

'So far as I'm concerned, you can come all you want. But I don't promise there'll always be chocolate biscuits.'

'That's all right,' he said magnanimously. 'I like plain ones too.' And was off through the gap in the hedge by the lane before I had realised he was going. I could have wept with relief. It was working, just as the vicar had predicted. Where one child came, others would soon follow, and parents could not indefinitely ignore their children's friend.

He paid me two or three more surreptitious visits, but it did not work out like that. He seemed listless, and I noticed that he played less often with the other children, though he had always been the ringleader.

'What's the matter, Tommy?' I asked him.

'Nothing. Mam keeps on at me.'

'About your coming here?'

'Naw. I don't tell her. Dad 'ud give me another belting.'

'Then what does she keep on about?'

'I dunno. She's taking me to the doctor.'

'You're probably growing too fast.'

'I'm not growing,' he said indignantly. 'I'm thinner. Look, Miss Davies, you can count my ribs.'

He hauled up his T-shirt to reveal ribs like a washing-board.

I said as much.

'What's a washing-board?' he demanded.

I found myself trying to explain, but he cut me short. 'I think I'd better be going.'

'There's no need,' I said quickly, anxious that he should not desert me. 'You can stay a bit longer if you like.'

'I'd better be going,' he repeated.

'No, Tommy,' I begged. 'Please stay.'

He turned to leave. I put a hand on his shoulder to restrain him, but he twisted away from me like an eel, stumbled and clutched at an occasional table. The table tilted and there was a shattering crash.

The vase that lay in shards on the floor was one of my favourites. More than that, it was valuable. And having been brought back from China by my great-uncle, it had acquired the status of a family piece. The anger I felt at its destruction was my anger, but the words that issued from my mouth were not my words, and from a long way off I heard myself cursing Tommy. The child gazed at me in terror, then turned and took to his heels.

I sat down. I was shaken, but I could explain the incident to my satisfaction. I had momentarily lost control. I naturally prize possessions, and as with many people who live alone, my house was a substitute for the husband and children who ought perhaps to have filled it, and the loss of something cherished since childhood had proved too much for me. When I next saw Tommy I would apologise—publicly, if need be. It would be good for my arrogant image; it might even be good for me. Tommy had a generous heart, and I was sure he did not dislike me. His visits would be resumed and in his small, grubby hands would lie my salvation.

I saw with a pang that he had left his chocolate biscuits behind.

When a fortnight passed and I hadn't seen him even in the village, I rang the vicar.

'What's happened to Tommy Jones?'

'Nothing's happened to him,' he said edgily. 'We're awaiting the results of the tests.'

'What tests? What are you talking about?'

'Didn't you know the boy was ill? The doctor wasn't satisfied so he sent him to hospital for a check-up. They're keeping him in while they do tests.'

'Tests for what?'

'They suspect a blood condition.'

I was suddenly out of breath.

'Do you mean leukaemia?'

'Well, it hasn't been mentioned…'

I couldn't take any more. I rang off.

What had happened to me that my curses, even when lightly uttered, were coming home to roost in no uncertain fashion? Was I really afflicted with the evil eye? Until now I had taken none of it seriously, thinking it coincidence, misunderstanding, village gossip—something quite unconnected with me. Now it began to seem that anyone who crossed me was in some way marked down by Fate. I remembered reading somewhere that certain persons had the ability, acquired or inborn, of projecting their hate in physical terms. Had I? Was this what was happening to me? Or was it something to do with Jennet Paris, whose house had stood on the spot where mine was standing, and who had given her name to the hill that lay behind? I thought of the vicar's words: 'women miscarried, cattle dropped their calves, crops withered'—all because Jennet looked at them. It had been so easy to suppose he was speaking in terms of seventeenth-century superstition, but what if it were happening today?

I said Jennet's name aloud, very softly, and something creaked in reply. Was it the house we had in common? Did she resent my taking over her ground, my raking up a past that was best left buried? In that case, the simplest solution might be to go away. But… 'You let yourself be driven out by a ghost?' I could hear the voices, scornful, amused, incredulous, of my former colleagues in the Ministry. 'Poor old Jane,' they would say, 'she went downhill fast once she retired. It often happens. Became a bit disturbed, you know.' No one was going to say that of Jane Davies if I could help it, but it might be a good idea to take a holiday.

***

It was the most sensible decision I could have made. Two months of visiting friends and travelling on the Continent restored me to a healthier frame of mind. No untoward accidents befell any of those I mixed with. My friends laughed at the idea of my having the evil eye. I began to laugh at it myself, it seemed so ridiculous. I had been a fool to listen to tales about Jennet Paris. She had died—been lynched, I remembered—more than three centuries ago.

In this mood I returned to the village. It was a Saturday afternoon when I arrived, lugging a suitcase because there had been no one on duty at the little station; my car, of course, was laid up. It was a hot, still August day with a brassy sky and a hint of thunder. My cottage, as I approached, gave me a shock. Town-bird that I was, I had not realised what two months' neglect would do to the garden; it was riotously overgrown. Tall nettles, even brambles, gave it an unclaimed, uncultivated air. I was surprised to find the door opened when I turned my latchkey; I half expected to find everything bolted and barred.

I went round opening windows. The place had an unused smell. Had it not been my home I should have said there was something alien about it, as though I were an intruder there. Ignoring it, I switched on the fridge and decided to go down to the village for a few essential supplies. As I came out of the house a voice shouted from the lane. I turned exultantly towards the gap in the hedge. Tommy! But it was an unknown child who jeered at me and took to his heels when I went towards him. From a safe distance he looked back and shouted, 'Witch!'

So it had not died down. My heart sank and on leaden feet I went towards the village, bracing myself at every step. I saw no one, and most of the houses had blinds down or curtains drawn as protection against the heavy, unnatural heat. The shop was empty, but the bell pinged as I entered and Mrs Francis bustled in from the back. Her face changed, became hostile when she saw me.

She said, 'What are you doing here?'

'I've come to buy half a pound of butter, half a dozen eggs, a pint of milk, a small white loaf—' I began sweetly.

'Not from this shop you won't.'

'—and some back bacon if you have it,' I went on, ignoring the interruption.

For a few seconds neither of us spoke.

'Mrs Francis, what's the matter?' I said at last to break the tension.

'I'm not serving you.'

'But why? What have I done? In any case, you're obliged by law to serve me.'

'Tell that to PC Jones.'

Tommy's father!

I said quickly, 'How is Tommy?'

Mrs Francis looked at me stonily. 'As if you didn't know!'

'I don't. I've been away two months. I only came back on the 2.20.'

'That's right. Come back to gloat, you have.'

Mrs Francis was backing away from me, keeping the counter between us, feeling with one hand for the door that led out of the shop. The other hand was raised in a curious two-fingered gesture which seemed familiar, though I connected it with Italy. Suddenly my brain registered the last time I had seen it. In Naples. It was the universal sign to ward off the evil eye.

The shop door pinged again behind me and I set up the long, hot street. But now it seemed that baleful faces glared at me from every window. The news of my return had spread. As I passed each house it seemed as though its occupants issued from it to stand in the middle of the road, gazing after me but making no move to follow or molest me. There was the waiting stillness of thunder about them too.

It was the longest walk I have ever taken. I was too proud or too frightened to look round. At any moment I expected a stone to hit me, and jeers and catcalls to break out. Instead—nothing. Only a low growl of thunder—or was it a mutter from the crowd? I reached my front door and shut and locked it behind me. When I sat down I was shaking like a leaf.

My peace was short-lived. I had not been sitting there fifteen minutes trying to think what to do when the telephone shrilled. I answered it, expecting obscenities or heavy breathing. Instead I heard the vicar's voice.

'Miss Davies? Thank God you answered. Look, lock your doors and your windows at once.'

'Why? What's the matter?'

'Don't argue—just do as I say. I'll phone the police. With any luck they'll be here before there's too much damage. Why the hell did you have to come back today?'

I was too shaken to heed his unclerical language. 'What's special about today?'

'You mean you don't know? Then I'm sorry to have to tell you that Tommy Jones died last night.'

'Oh no!'

'Yes. It's tragic, but at least it was mercifully quick. Now lock yourself in like I told you, unless you want to be assaulted as a witch.'

'Surely people don't believe—'

'My good woman, look out of your window. I'd fetch you by car if I could, but you're at the other end of the village and in the mood they're in at present, they'd never let me through. Lock your doors, hide yourself where they can't see you. Remember the police will be here soon.'

He rang off and I did indeed look out of my bay-window. What I saw turned the day cold, darkened the sun.

The men and women of the village were advancing up the road. Some had sticks, some garden forks, some pitchforks. They chanted savagely as they came. At that distance it was like hounds baying, a bloodcurdling, unearthly sound, but as they approached I could distinguish rhythm; a little nearer and I heard the words.

'We want the witch,' they chanted. 'Bring out the witch.'

They wanted me! They wanted me dragged out and… Panic overtook me. I should never be safe indoors. One blow would shatter the lock, and though the bolts might hold, the door was weak on its hinges. It would be only a matter of moments before they broke it down.

I had one chance. If I escaped through the back door and through the gap in the hedge I could be in the lane that led to the track over Dead Woman before they knew I had gone. I ran out, but the overgrown garden impeded me. Someone caught a glimpse my dress. There was a cry—'There she goes!'—and like an advancing army, the whole mob broke into a kind of shambling run.

I had a start because the garden provided a short cut, whereas they had to go round by the road. Nevertheless, I soon heard the advance guard on the track behind me. There was no way I could shake them off. I might have dodged one pursuer, but there were at least twenty, and as the track zigzagged upwards, some of the bolder spirits attempted to cut across. They failed, but each time my lead was shortened. It was increasingly difficult to draw breath. I staggered, almost fell. Soon my legs would no longer support me. Still fighting for air, I darted a quick glance back.

Two young men, both lithe and active, whose names I did not even know, were in the forefront and gaining rapidly. Mr Baxter panted close behind. I could see his bulging eyes and the gleam of sweat on his forehead. Even in this weather he wore a tweed sports coat. He waddled rather than ran, but it was an effective waddle. I had not dreamed he could move so fast. As I watched, he raised his fist and shook it, and I heard him cry hoarsely, 'Hang the witch!'

Just so had the villagers, led by Baxter's ancestor, pursued Jennet Paris. She must have run up this very track when some of the mighty oaks were saplings, and brushed her skirts as she passed. Her heart must have thudded as mine was thudding, her breath come in the same short, painful gasps. She must have felt every emotion I was feeling. Was I, like her, to meet my death on this hill that had once been called Dead Woman? To flee in fear and find no escape at last?

I ran on. This could not be happening in the twentieth century, when men could walk on the moon. Suddenly I should wake up, or hear the reassuring wail of police-car sirens. How long would they take to arrive? Ten minutes? Fifteen? Or longer? The vicar had said he would phone at once. If I could hide or fend off the mob a little longer, I might perhaps stand a chance.

The path emerged suddenly into a clearing. We had reached the top of the hill. Through the trees I had a glimpse of fields and farmsteads strangely lurid against an ink-black sky. There was another growl of thunder, and an answering growl from the mob. Then I staggered and this time fell heavily. When I got to my feet, it was to face a solid wall of hate.

The path to my bungalow was blocked by a posse of lowering villagers. There was no other way out that I could see, for the whole of one side of the clearing was filled by a massive oak whose branches overspread it, and for the rest I was surrounded by thick undergrowth, young saplings, dense bushes, cutting me off on every side. Even so, I noticed that none of the villagers dared approach me, except Baxter who had stepped forward and stood, belly heaving, only a few feet away. I looked at him, unbelieving. There was a thin coil of rope over his arm. Did these people really mean to hang me out of hand as three hundred years ago their ancestors had hanged Jennet Paris? These could not be the people I knew. Their faces were closed and hostile, their eyes blank like those of the blind. They were no longer human because to them I was no longer human. I was a quarry and they were in at the kill.

Baxter edged forward. I could see a dribble of saliva coming from the corner of his slack mouth. His face was suffused, but the thread-veins on his cheeks were still apparent. He ran his tongue over his lips. It was so horrible that I could not believe no one shared my revulsion, but as my eyes went from face to face I saw only reflections of his eagerness and excitement as my neighbours savoured my death.

My neighbours? No, my judges. The same people who had hanged Jennet Paris on this hill—Jennet, who was almost certainly as innocent as I was, and had taken her revenge through me. So far I had been her tool; now, in desperation, I was her accomplice. If I was to be hanged, I might as well be hanged as a witch. If she had evil powers, I craved them. If I had them already, I wanted them intensified. I concentrated all my being on calling her—Jennet! Jennet! Jennet! And suddenly I was not alone.

Jennet was beside me, with me, in me. I could feel her power in my limbs, her breath in my lungs, her gaze looking out through my eyes at our tormentors, Baxter the chief of them. She stiffened my spine and concentrated our wills into one narrow channel which found its outlet through my lips. It was Jennet who spoke with my voice and loathed with my loathing and commanded Baxter to drop dead.

The darkness deepened to blackness. There was a crack of thunder overhead. Someone screamed. The heavens unzipped. There was a blaze of brightness and I was thrown violently to the ground. In the instant before I lost consciousness I thought I saw the oak tree split, saw Baxter's prone body twist and blacken, heard the white hissing of the rain. Then the wail of police-car sirens rose in urgent crescendo as the worst thunderstorm in living memory broke.

***

After the inquest, which of course went off quite smoothly since those who stand under oak trees in thunderstorms quite naturally put themselves at risk, I put the bungalow up for sale in the shadow of the hill that had so nearly known a second Dead Woman, and left the village never to return. Never again would I call on Jennet Paris. I devoutly hoped I would never again have need, but I should feel easier away from the Welsh Border and my ex-neighbours' shamefaced guilt.

'Don't think too hardly of us,' the vicar pleaded. 'After all, Providence intervened.'

'Bully for Providence, if that's what it was,' I said tartly.

He laughed. 'You're feeling better, Jane.'

'No,' I said (he had come to see me off at the station), 'I'm leaving Jennet to keep an eye on you. She knows how to look after her own.'

'You think she's still around?'

'I don't know. Maybe you'll find out if you try another lynching. But take my advice and let a sleeping witch lie.'

He didn't say anything, but I could see it was not because he didn't want to. I hastily said goodbye. And as the train pulled out I had my last glimpse of the thickly wooded bulk of Dead Woman—Dead Woman who would never die.

CHRISTMAS NIGHT

'ON CHRISTMAS NIGHT all Christians sing.' I don't know about that, but we were certainly singing, Mairi and I, as we came over the top of the Callow and saw the lights of Carringford five miles away in the valley below us. Clear roads, clear skies, and a hundred and forty miles still to London. The beauty of the night almost made up for having to leave Mairi's family in South Wales and drive back so that I could open in a new play on Boxing Night.

'We haven't seen another car since we left St Devereux,' Mairi said.
'That's because only rogues, vagabonds and actors are about.'
'And only actors drive cars.'
'I don't know. Some of the biggest rogues I know drive Rolls-Royces.'
'We've still a way to go before we're in that class,' Mairi said, and I could feel her dimpling in the darkness, 'but at least we'll be seeing your name up in lights in the West End tomorrow night.'

And at that moment the car gave a sudden lurch and began to bump rhythmically, and I said, 'That's our offside rear tyre gone,' and got out to look at it. And of course it was.

Now I know every car carries a spare wheel and is required to do so by law and all the rest of it, but the fact is I didn't have one. I know I ought to have had and I'm not making excuses, but I'd left it to have a new tyre fitted and in the rush of rehearsals and last-minute hitches, I hadn't had time to pick it up.

So there we were on top of the Callow, with no lights nearer than those of Carringford and a car we couldn't drive.

Mairi got out and stood beside me.
'What now, John?'
'We'll have to hire a car in Carringford.'
'But everything closes at half past five even on weekdays.'

'Not, presumably, the hotels. I'm not having you hanging about on a Welsh hillside. You'll get pneumonia again.'

She'd had it two years ago and nearly died of it, and I wasn't taking any chances.

'We'll lock the car and start walking,' I said, trying to sound masterful.

She looked down at her feet. 'In these shoes?'

I'm familiar with the usual gripes about women's footwear, but I happen to like to see a girl in high heels and Mairi knows it. She hadn't packed anything beyond the delicate sandals she was wearing and a pair of fluffy bedroom mules. After all, for a thirty-six-hour trip home why bother, when we had all the family Christmas presents to take? Nevertheless, I must have sounded a bit ruffled as I suggested she should stay in the car.

'I'll get a taxi or hire a car—there must be something, even at Christmas—and come back and pick you up.'

'No, John, I don't want to stay here.' Her voice had a hysterical note.

'The only alternative is to walk.'

'No, it isn't. There's an inn, I think. I'm almost certain.'

'An inn in this benighted spot? Where?'

'Down there.' She pointed to what appeared to be a cart track.

'There'll be nothing down there but a gate into a field.'

'There's an inn,' she said with an odd certainty. 'I don't know how I know it, but I do.'

I reflected that it must be a childhood memory. For much of her life Mairi had travelled between South Wales and London, first in her father's car, then in her own, now in mine. She knew the route backwards and I relied on her for navigation. If she said there was an inn, there probably was.

'Come on,' I said, taking her arm and reaching for the powerful torch we always carry. 'What are we waiting for?'

We didn't need the torch. I have never seen moonlight like it, and all from one small, high, brilliant globe. The furrows in the field, the twigs in the hedges, everything was rimed with frost. What was not black was silver. The stiff grass crunched under our feet. And we had not gone a hundred yards before the track curved and on our left was a two-storeyed, slate-roofed building.

'There,' Mairi said a little breathlessly. 'I told you there was an inn.'

As we drew nearer we could see a sign swinging gently, but the place appeared to be closed.

'You forgot about Welsh licensing hours,' I told her.

'We've been in England for the last fifteen miles.'

I bowed to her superior knowledge. It was not yet ten o'clock. But when I tried the inn door, it was unyielding. I lifted my hand to knock.

'John—don't!'

'What's the matter?' Mairi was clutching my arm.

'I don't like this place. Let's go away from here—quickly.'

'I must say I've seen more prepossessing inns. But it's Hobson's choice, I'm afraid, love. We'll only stay long enough to use their phone.'

'I don't think there's anyone at home.'

'There's a light in that window.' I pointed to one of the downstairs rooms which appeared to be shuttered on the inside. 'It beats me how they make the place pay.'

'Perhaps they don't.'

'Then how do they keep going?'

'They may have other ways…'

My knocking drowned the rest of her sentence. It seemed to reverberate through the house. Then, somewhere within, a door opened and footsteps shuffled down the hall.

'Someone's coming,' I said, but Mairi was looking at the sign, not listening.

'John, d'you see what this inn is called?'

I glanced up, but the inn sign was in shadow.

'It's called the Hanged Man,' Mairi went on. 'Isn't it horrible? It must be the most offputting inn sign anywhere.'

At that moment there was a dull creaking and moonlight fell upon the sign as it swung. There was indeed a crude representation of a gibbet from which a body hung. As the sign moved it was as though it was the gibbet creaking, swaying out of darkness into light. It was eerily lifelike, except that that is not the word for a dead body. I too was suddenly afraid of what might lie behind the inn's inhospitable door.

The landlord, when he appeared, did nothing to reassure me. He was squat and scowling and none too clean. I apologised for disturbing him if he was not open, and asked if I might use the phone.

'There's no phone here.'

The absence of telephone wires endorsed his statement. I felt he thought I was a fool.

'Perhaps we could at least come in and have a drink if you're open.'

He grudgingly held the door.

Inside it was all wainscot and low ceilings. The room on the right was the bar, stone-flagged, with a sullen fire smouldering in the open hearth and a couple of oak settles drawn up at right angles. It was unwelcoming to say the least. We were the only customers. The shuttered window was bare. Above the bar a paraffin lamp cast the only illumination and fought an unequal fight against the shadows.

I ordered a beer and Mairi a gin and tonic, though what she got was a gin and ginger ale. The landlord claimed he was out of tonic.

'Ah,' I said, 'you've had a busy night.'

He missed the irony, and once again I felt myself a fool in his eyes. To recover, I said: 'You're very much off the beaten track. Do you get many customers?'

'There's always them as remembers the way,' he answered. His eyes were on Mairi as he spoke.

I didn't altogether care for the way he looked at her, but I had to keep in with him.

'Since you've no phone,' I said, 'and our car's broken down and we've no means of getting in to Carringford, do you think you could put us up for the night?'

'Ah,' he said noncommittally.

'Unless you know of anywhere else?'

'Nothing nearer than the Tram Inn at Garton.'

I turned to Mairi. 'Where's that?'

'At the end of the old tramway that used to run over the hills from South Wales. They used it for hauling slate at one time. Garton's a good three miles.'

'We might as well stay here, then.'

'If mine host will give us a bed.'

'Landlord, can you put us up?' I asked again with some asperity.

He did not answer directly. 'Long time since anyone stayed here.'

'That means it's damp and there are bedbugs,' Mairi said under her breath.

'But you can stay if you want,' the landlord continued. 'I'd best go and see about a bed.'

We heard the stairs creak as he ascended, and then a floorboard groaned overhead. Evidently he was single-handed. I wondered he wasn't melancholy mad. When I said so, Mairi gave a hysterical giggle. 'Perhaps he is. Oh John, I hate this place. It's so primitive. Do you suppose there's a bathroom? I thought licensed premises had to conform to a certain standard, but I've never seen anything like this.'

'It's probably so out of the way the inspectors missed it. You'd never expect to find an inn here. Except of course that you did.'

She shivered. 'I just knew it was here. I don't understand it. I must have come some time with Dad.'

'The place mightn't look so bad in daylight.'

'No, but it would feel as bad. Don't you notice it, John—how cold it is, and evil?'

'You're being fanciful,' I said.

I never knew an actor who wasn't superstitious, but Mairi had us all beat. No doubt it was her Celtic blood, but her extraordinary sensitivity amounted at times to ESP. At other times it amounted to nothing and I called her fanciful. I hoped this was one of those times as I poked the smoky fire, which merely became smokier, and teased her about her premonitions and dreams.

No circumstances would cause me to describe the return of our landlord as welcome, though this time he was trying to smile. I couldn't honestly say it improved his appearance, but at least it showed goodwill.

'Well, sir and madam, we're all ready for you,' he said, rubbing his hands as though he had a treat in store. 'And how about a glass of mulled wine as a nightcap? It would warm the cockles of your heart.'

I looked enquiringly at Mairi. It seemed to me the landlord did the same, but his eyes rested on the diamond pendant she was wearing, which caught the light as she moved. It had cost a lot and some people said I was crazy, but a combination of a big West End part, our fifth wedding anniversary and Christmas had caused me to give my natural extravagance free rein. If a man can't buy his wife jewellery occasionally, what's the good of having a wife, and money and prospects and one foot on the ladder, and all the rest of it? I counted the money well spent, but I didn't care for the way mine host was eyeing the pendant. I was about to refuse his offer of mulled wine when he said ingratiatingly: 'On the house.'

Perhaps a refusal would seem churlish. It would certainly help Mairi to get warm. I thanked him and he produced it at once. It must have been mulling in the kitchen and for the moment was too hot to touch. Mine host also produced a large candle in an old-fashioned candlestick and prepared to light the way upstairs. Clasping our mugs, we followed him like children up to the room above the bar.

There was a washstand in the corner and nothing else except a high old-fashioned double bed covered with a white honeycomb quilt which looked spotless, with one corner invitingly turned down. There was a bolster and a positive mountain of pillows and three steps to help you climb into bed. As we watched, our host set the candle down upon a small night-table we had not noticed and withdrew two flannel-wrapped hot bricks from the bed. He stood there holding them like weights and bowed slightly.

'I hope you sleep well, sir and madam, and I wish you a very good night.'

The door latched behind him. Mairi, who had been examining the bed, exclaimed, 'John, feathers! It's a real old-fashioned feather bed.'

'They don't exactly go in for all mod. cons. at the Hanged Man,' I observed ruefully, surveying the washstand and wondering if the morning would produce hot water for a shave.

Mairi was already nestling among the feathers and sipping her mulled wine. Without more ado I joined her, after flinging back the shutters so that the moonlight flooded in. The room was as bright as day, and with this mock daylight the inn seemed to have become alive. Not only could I hear the groaning sigh as the sign of the Hanged Man moved uneasily below our window, but there were all sorts of creaks and cracks from boards inside the house. When an owl hooted, seemingly in the chimney, I jumped almost out of my skin. I drank a little of the wine but it had grown tepid and I did not care for the taste. Mairi was asleep already, snuggled deep in the feather bed. Gradually I let its warmth suffuse me and felt myself relax. I was drowning in feathers, sinking deeper, ever deeper. The last thing I remembered was the scent of lavender from the sheets.

CHRISTMAS NIGHT

***

I don't know what wakened me, but my eyes went at once to the door latch. It was still in exactly the same place. Reassured, I let my gaze rove round the room and to the window. The moon had gone but the stars were large and clear. And then, as my eyes went back to the door, I felt my scalp prickle. The latch had risen an inch silently, and as I watched it moved again.

I looked at Mairi sleeping peacefully and slid my hand under the pillow at her head. The pendant was there, where I had told her to put it. I had no doubt he had come for that. For who else could the visitor be but our ungenial landlord who thought he saw an easy way of compensating for lost trade? While I was wondering whether to shout for nonexistent help or walk boldly forward and face him, the door itself began to move.

I glanced at my watch. It was two o'clock in the morning, the time when all the vital forces run low. No less a general than Napoleon had praised the possessors of two o'clock courage, but I was not numbered in their ranks. The panic that gripped me was far worse than first-night nerves, and it came to me uncomfortably that last-night nerves might be a better term. Did the landlord intend violence in any case, or would he resort to it only if challenged? Was I actor enough to call his bluff?

The door had now opened about a foot. At any moment I expected to see the landlord's head peer round. And then, faint but drawing steadily nearer, came one of the commonest of twentieth-century sounds. Someone in the early hours of Boxing Day morning was driving a car down the track that led to the Hanged Man.

I don't know whether I or our sinister landlord was the more startled, but on our respective sides of the door, we froze. Then, as the car drew up outside the Inn, our latch fell gently into place, and an instant later there was a thunderous knocking downstairs as the car-driver demanded admittance. Very quietly I slipped out of bed.

The car was a yellow Austin, and the registration number began KCJ. The rest was in shadow and I couldn't see it, and all I could see of the driver was the balding top of his head. As I watched, the inn door evidently opened and a shaft of light streamed forth. I had time enough to glimpse our landlord and to note that he was still fully

239

dressed. I could not catch a word of the conversation, but the balding man came inside and I heard him with the landlord in the bar-room just below us as I crept back to bed and dozed the rest of the night.

***

When next I woke it was seven-thirty, though not a soul was astir. In little more than twelve hours I was due to open in the West End of London. I could not linger here.

I shook Mairi gently by the shoulder. 'Wake up, we've got to go.'

She looked at me blankly 'There are no horses…'

Obviously she was still in the land of dreams.

'Quite right, sweetheart. We're going to walk,' I said lightly. 'And since the landlord isn't up, I'm not waiting for him. Get your clothes on and let's go.'

To be honest, I was only too anxious to avoid the landlord. I did not know what I might say. Of course I could prove nothing and he would say I had imagined the door opening, yet if that car had not come I was convinced we should have been robbed, perhaps murdered. I led the way downstairs.

The stairs creaked and groaned and we made no attempt to be quiet. Despite this, no one came. I left the landlord what I hoped was fair recompense on the bar counter, and we stepped out into the frosty air. The yellow Austin was still parked underneath the inn sign, only now it glistened with frost.

'So we weren't the only visitors,' Mairi said, surprise showing.

'You were asleep when he came.'

Briefly I described the nocturnal arrival, though without mentioning the incident of the door.

'I suppose the poor fellow was lost,' Mairi said as we stumbled along the cart track. 'Otherwise he'd never have left the road.'

'Either that or he remembered the place, as you did.'

'I didn't remember it.'

'But you were positive it was there.'

'That's different.'

I did not bother to ask why because at that moment a car came along the road. I hailed it and explained our plight. In no time we had a lift into Carringford and I was rousing a grumpy garage proprietor and telling him the tale of our flat tyre. Even so, it was ten before we were on the road to London and I drove fast all the way. Thereafter I was caught up in the excitement of an opening, and knew nothing about the murder till next day.

***

Mairi brought me breakfast in bed next morning, and the papers. I knew from her eyes that the notices were good. We turned to them eagerly, strewing papers all over the bedroom. Several singled me out by name. We hugged ourselves and each other in the small, safe, egotistical world of success. The usual gloomy headlines meant nothing. It was some time before we turned to the front page.

Even then, it was while I was on the telephone, accepting congratulations with a falsely practised air, that a small item datelined Carringford caught my attention and then held me riveted.

It described how the body of the seasonably-named Mr Noel Hutchins, aged 42, had been discovered savagely battered in a field five miles from Carringford. Near him his car had been found abandoned. It was in perfect working order and there was no indication why it had been left. Mr Hutchins, a bachelor, had been driving home alone from a late-night party, but there was no excess alcohol in his blood. Why had he stopped and where had he been murdered? Who had driven his car off the road? One theory was that he had given a lift to his killer, but as he was known to have had little money with him, it was impossible to say if he had been robbed. Police were anxious to contact anyone who might have seen his yellow Austin, registration number KCJ 7333, on the 26th between the hours of 1 a.m. and 11 a.m., at which time the body had been found.

I pushed the paper across to Mairi, mouthed 'He was at the Hanged Man,' and strove to terminate my telephone conversation which had reached its end some time ago.

As I put the receiver down, Mairi looked up at me. 'His car was certainly there at seven-thirty when we left.'

'Yes, but where was he? What happened to him after his two o'clock arrival?'

'Oh John, you don't think...'

'I don't know what to think, but I don't trust that landlord. He was trying to get into our room. I'll swear he was after your pendant, only the arrival of Mr Hutchins disturbed him. We owe the poor fellow a lot.'

'I don't know what you're talking about.'

'No, sweetheart, you were asleep.'

Briefly I told her what had happened.

'Yes,' she said thoughtfully, 'it fits. That wine was drugged. I suspected it. I don't usually sleep heavily like that.'

'And I hardly touched mine,' I said, remembering, 'which is why I was instantly awake. There may be some innocent explanation, but mine host had better give it to the police.'

The inspector who came in answer to my telephone call to the local police station was accompanied by a sergeant who took down everything I said. He made no comment and indeed seemed to know no more about the case than he could have read in the papers, but he promised to be in touch. The upshot was that the next day, after the matinee, I was told an Inspector Reece would like to see me and was waiting in my dressing-room. I was tired and resentful of this intrusion. In the worst of moods I went along.

Inspector Reece was a small man with an accent like Mairi's father's. It is one I find difficult not to catch. Before long it sounded as if I were rehearsing Fluellen, and I was mortally afraid Inspector Reece would take offence. But he didn't; he merely took me through my statement at a brisk pace, asking an occasional question, and then tapping his pencil and looking thoughtful.

'What did you say the inn was called, sir?' he said at last, after a pause.

'The Hanged Man.'

'Funny name, isn't it? You would not expect many customers with a name like that.'

'There weren't many. My wife and I saw no one but the landlord.'

'Ah yes. The landlord. Could you describe him, sir?'

'Squat, thickset, unprepossessing.'

'Too vague, sir, I'm afraid. His name now, did you hear it mentioned?'

'No.'

'You're very sure of that.'

'He didn't tell us his name and there was no one else to do so. We never saw another soul.'

'Except Mr Hutchins,' the inspector reminded me. 'You say he arrived very late.'

'Around two o'clock in the morning. I know because I looked at my watch.'

'You were awake, then?'

'Yes. You know how it is—strange beds.'

'But your wife—she was not awake?'

'No, she'd had a nightcap. Some mulled wine that sent her off.'

'Mulled wine, now. There can't be many inns where that is offered.'

'I told you, we think it was drugged.'

'Yes, well, it might be an effective vehicle, but strangely old-fashioned.'

'The Hanged Man *was* old-fashioned. I'd call it primitive.'

'So you did. The very word.' The inspector glanced at my statement. 'Now, sir, where was the Hanged Man?' He leaned forward with peculiar intensity as he asked me, as though my answer mattered a lot.

'Well, we'd come over the Callow—'

'How far over?' he interrupted.

'I don't think I could say. Over the brow, to a point where we could see Carringford. But we hadn't come very far down.'

The inspector repeated my shaky location. I said sharply: 'I expect my wife would know. She's been travelling that road since she was a schoolgirl. It was she who found the Hanged Man.'

'We shall certainly ask her,' Inspector Reece said drily. 'Your own directions are a little imprecise. And the truth is, there's no inn at the spot you mention, neither the Hanged Man nor anything else.'

I looked at him in astonishment. 'But we spent the night there.'

'Yes, sir. So you say.'

'Well, there's no other inn we could have mistaken it for, is there? Not with a name like that.'

'The nearest inn is the Tram Inn at Garton.'

'It certainly wasn't the Tram. The landlord mentioned it and my wife knew it. She said it was three miles away.'

'Yes, it's about that from the spot you're describing.'

'And we didn't spend the night at the Tram.'

'No, sir. We've already checked.'

Suddenly I was angry. 'You think we're not telling the truth.'

'It's true enough that your car developed a flat tyre on the Carringford side of the Callow. The garage proprietor confirms that.'

'You *have* been doing your homework.'

'It's our duty to find out facts,' he said stiffly, slightly emphasizing the last word. 'And you and your wife are the only people to have admitted seeing Mr Hutchins and his car between the early hours of Boxing Day morning when he left his friends' party and eleven o'clock when his body was found. Now, sir, why exactly did you come forward?'

I said equally stiffly, 'It is every citizen's duty to help the police.'

'True enough, but some people place a pretty liberal interpretation upon it. Enjoy the notoriety, you might say.'

'I assure you I've no need to seek more limelight.'

'No, sir, they tell me you've made a hit. Nevertheless, I shall have to ask you and your wife as good citizens to tear yourself away from the capital and come back to Carringford. On the spot and by daylight you will perhaps be better able to identify the place where you spent Christmas night.'

'But the play——'

'I'm aware of your commitments,' he said smoothly, 'but you don't work a seven-day week. I'll be on my way now to see your wife and leave you to rest before your next performance.'

He stood up and I deliberately hesitated before doing likewise.

'About Carringford,' he said, 'would Sunday suit?'

***

Everything was different. Grey, low skies, air dank and moisture-laden, Carringford invisible in a miasma of river mist. When we got out of the car at the point the inspector indicated, I accepted his word that this was where we had parked on the Callow, but I might have been a thousand miles away.

The inspector was accompanied by a sergeant and a constable. The constable never said a word the whole time. The sergeant was a local man, and as he led the way confidently towards the cart track I had the feeling that he knew the terrain better than his superior. He gave me a sympathetic look.

The inspector paused at the beginning of the cart track. 'Now, sir,' he said, 'where's your inn?'

'Down here,' Mairi said with sudden confidence. 'I remember.'

It was she who led the way.

After about a quarter of a mile the track curved gently. Just beyond the bend a small piece of ground had been fenced off and covered with a tarpaulin.

'Where we found Hutchins's car,' the inspector said.

'It was parked outside the inn when we saw it.'

'Then someone drove it here.'

'They didn't,' Mairi said softly, in a little-girl-lost sort of voice. 'This is where the Hanged Man was.'

On either side of the track ploughed fields stretched emptily.

'You're being fanciful,' I said gently.

'I am not. The inn was here.'

'Then they did a quick job of demolition,' the inspector said.

I had been accused once of seeking the publicity which association with a murder case can give. I did not care for the thought that we should soon be accused of frivolous time-wasting, or even of obstructing the police.

'I was surprised myself that there should be an inn down a cart track,' I told the inspector, 'but my wife was positive. And there certainly was an inn. A two-storeyed, slate-roofed building like dozens I've seen round here. It was primitive; no phone or electricity, and lit by candles and lamps, but it existed as true as I stand here. They even put hot bricks in our bed.'

'There *was* an inn round about here once, sir,' the sergeant said hesitantly. 'I've heard my grandfather speak of it, but it was pulled down a hundred years ago.'

'What was it called?'

'I don't know, sir, but it wasn't the Hanged Man, that's for sure.'

'But why have an inn on a cart track in open country?' I asked him.

He smiled. 'It must seem funny now, but you see this wasn't always a cart track. It's all that's left of the old tramway to South Wales.'

'With the Tram Inn at the bottom,' Mairi said, understanding dawning.

'That's right, ma'm, but this was a convenient stopping place. The beginning of the downhill run or the end of the first climb, depending on which way you were going. It must have done good business once. But of course, after they closed the tramway the inn was stuck in the midst of nowhere and there wasn't the trade any more. They hung on for a time because there was talk of using the old tramway as the route for a new road over the Callow, but in the end'—he gestured—'the new road went elsewhere.'

I looked at the muddy, rutted track and thought how once its rails had gleamed darkly on drizzle-dull days like this, or shone silver in the Christmas moonlight, or glinted in the midday sun. And now—this. The earth reclaimed her own with a vengeance, nature triumphing over man's short primacy just as she was asserting herself over what had been railway lines in my boyhood and were now fast becoming sunken lanes.

Inspector Reece brought us back to the present. 'I fail to see,' he said, 'how a building pulled down a hundred years ago can have been mysteriously resurrected to enable a murder to take place.'

'I don't either, sir,' the sergeant said, 'but there was an inn here once, so the lady's not being entirely'—he glanced at me—'fanciful.'

A sudden chill breeze started blowing.

Mairi had gone very white.

'I told you there was an atmosphere of evil about the place, John.'

'Yes, love, I know you did. My wife,' I explained to the inspector, 'is exceedingly sensitive to atmosphere. If a murder was being committed in the vicinity—and we must suppose that it was—it is not surprising that she picked up some reverberations.'

'Indeed?' the inspector said. 'The jury may be interested to hear it, but they won't be convinced, I'm afraid.'

Any more than I am, we could hear him adding.

He said abruptly, 'We'd better go back. But I'd be obliged if you could stay on until tomorrow, in case something else comes up.'

Or in case you decide to tell the truth and stop fooling, his unspoken thought said loudly.

We drove thoughtfully and rather slowly back into Carringford.

***

That night neither Mairi nor I slept well, despite the fact that the Red Lion at Carringford is a first-class hotel. It was a wild night, for the breeze we had noticed that morning had become a high wind by sunset, hunting down clouds against a livid sky. All night it blew gustily through the streets, setting doors banging and dustbin lids clattering, and rising sometimes to a long, mournful howl that sounded strangely like a wolf. It dashed scuds of raindrops against the window, and then, when we looked out, parted the racing clouds to show us a high and pallid moon.

Yet the tumult was within me rather than without. What had become of the Hanged Man? How could an inn whose every physical impression was remarkably vivid, vanish so utterly? I had that indeterminate aggressive feeling of one who has been in some way tricked. And as a result the police suspected me of being a vulgar seeker after notoriety—and perhaps of something worse. Did they think Mairi and I were in some way concerned in Noel Hutchins's murder? True, we had no motive, but neither had anyone else. It seemed a completely purposeless crime. He must have given a lift to a madman. God alone knew what went wandering about the roads of the Welsh Border after dark.

We were finishing a late breakfast when we were told that Sergeant Price was waiting to see us. I asked them to bring him in. He sat down shyly and accepted coffee. We waited for him to begin.

He looked from one to the other of us, and a smile spread over his face. 'The inspector asked me to tell you, sir, that for the moment he doesn't need to see either of you again.'

'You mean we can start back to London after breakfast instead of waiting till after lunch?'

'If you so wish, sir, though there's one or two things in Carringford worth seeing.'

'I dare say, but we've had enough of the place.' I remembered too late that he was a local. 'In other circumstances, perhaps.'

'Are you any nearer to catching the murderer?' Mairi asked to distract attention.

'Not really.' He smiled a slow, secretive smile. 'Perhaps we're never going to catch him.'

'What makes you say that?' I asked.

'Hunch. Oh, I know policemen aren't supposed to have hunches.'

He mimicked the inspector. ' "The jury might be interested, but they won't believe you, I'm afraid." But I've found out a bit more about the Hanged Man, if you'd care to hear it.'

I spoke for both of us. 'Of course we would.'

'The inn was pulled down, like I told you, about a hundred years ago. It was already derelict and local folk said it was haunted.'

'I'm not surprised,' Mairi said, 'with a name like the Hanged Man.'

'Oh, that wasn't its name when it was an inn. The inn was called the Peacock. It acquired the other name afterwards, first as a nickname and then some joker hung up a sign. Not surprising, perhaps, since the last landlord was hanged for murder.'

'How do you know all this?' I asked.

'Local history's always been an interest of mine. Industrial archaeology, really—like the route of the old tramway or of the canal that used to link us with Gloucester, but the local history bit comes in. I'd heard of the inn in connection with the tramway, and also some things my grandfather knew, so I looked in the library first thing as soon as it opened. They've an interesting local collection in there.'

'And what about this landlord?'

'Well, it seems that his name was Prosser—Prosser of the Peacock—and so long as the tramway was open he did quite a bit of trade, with the men coming over with full trucks but returning with empties, but when the tramway closed he fell on hard times. It wasn't the same for the Tram Inn down at the bottom, because that's in Garton and on the road, but the Peacock was high and dry on the hillside and no one any longer went by. Prosser hung on for a year or two in hopes that the new road over the Callow would bring him business, but when they drove it through it was half a mile to the west. Soon after that, in desperation, Prosser committed his first murder.'

Mairi and I spoke in unison. 'His first!'

'Oh yes, sir, he did several. Anyone staying overnight at the inn who looked to have a bit of money about him was likely to end his journey there. The place was so isolated that no one ever heard anything, and Prosser used to turn the horses loose so his victims couldn't get away.'

I looked at Mairi oddly. 'You said something about there being no horses when first I woke you up.'

'Did I? I don't remember.'

'I thought you were dreaming, of course.'

'So I was. I had nightmares all night. I told you the place was evil. What happened to Prosser in the end?'

The sergeant cleared his throat. 'He committed one murder too many. A young lady, the last of 'em was. But she was rich and had influential connections who raised a hue and cry.'

'And she was found?'

'Her and the others. But it was for her murder Prosser was hanged.'

I thought of the drugged wine, the lifting latch, and the way the landlord had eyed Mairi's pendant, and a shiver went down my spine.

'I don't know what it has to do with the murder of Hutchins,' I said to the sergeant, 'but I think there's something you should know.'

And I filled in some details I had omitted in my statement to the inspector.

'What d'you make of it?' I asked at the end.

He met my gaze squarely. 'I reckon Hutchins did you a good turn by coming, but it's not a matter for the police.'

'But why did he come there?'

'Why did you, sir?'

'You know that. Our car broke down. And my wife must have had a faint recollection of some story about the inn.'

'Perhaps the same went for Mr Hutchins.'

I heard the landlord's voice: 'There's always them as remembers the way.'

'You don't think his murder will be solved, do you?' I challenged the sergeant.

He shrugged. 'That's for the inspector to say. But I know what I think, and I'll warrant you do too, sir. I'd best be getting on my way.'

As we escorted him to the door, Mairi said, 'It's dreadful to think of that horrible inn resurrecting at Christmas.'

'That's when they say round here the graves do gape.'

'Oh no,' I said, dredging up lines from *Hamlet*, 'at that season "no spirit dare walk abroad".'

'Very comforting,' the sergeant observed drily, 'but we say the twelve nights of Christmas are the most haunted of the year. That's when the Wild Hunt rides—Cwn Annwn, the Welsh call it. It was out last night by the sound of it. Don't tell me you didn't hear.'

I thought of the wind with its mournful, lupine howling, and the torn clouds racing like wolves across the moon. I had heard of the ghostly huntsman and his pack, but I had not thought of them in this connection.

I looked significantly from Mairi to the sergeant. 'We'll be glad to be getting back to London. Soon.'

***

So far as I know, the killer of poor Noel Hutchins is still unapprehended. A verdict of wilful murder was returned against a person or persons unknown. But the story had one curious and unexpected addendum, which came about in this way.

I sent Sergeant Price and his wife two front stall tickets and invited them backstage after the show.

They were as excited as children when they joined Mairi and me and one or two other members of the cast for drinks in my dressing-room, and made no secret of the fact.

At one point in the socializing I became aware that Sergeant Price was trying to draw me aside. 'Got something here you might like to see,' he said portentously, producing a wallet as thick as a small book.

From it he extracted a photograph of a drawing. The original's in the library,' he said. 'It's Prosser's last victim. I came across it when I was delving into him a bit more deeply and had this taken special. I thought you'd be interested.'

It was a drawing of a girl in the costume of the eighteen-forties or fifties: poke bonnet, and sloping shoulders beneath a shawl; the kind of thing you see in Christmas cards and Dickens illustrations and say, 'How pretty.' But in this case that wasn't all.

The room swam and I sat down weakly. Beneath the bonnet's brim frilled with lace, dark eyes looked out at me, a soft round chin and a dimple. I was looking at Mairi's face.

Glossary and Notes

THE SIN-EATER

The custom of sin-eating is recorded in John Aubrey's *Remaines of Gentilisme and Judaisme* (1680): 'In the County of Hereford was an old Custome at Funeralls to hire poor people, who were to take upon them all the sinnes of the party deceased.' Walter seems to have mixed this tradition with one from East Anglia, where unsuspecting people are tricked into eating food that has been laid with a corpse and acquiring its sins. The blackberry wine and drop-scone suggest a variant of the bread and wine of holy communion.

Here, as elsewhere in her work, Walter renames Hereford 'Carringford.'

Penrhayader: seemingly fictitious but strikingly Welsh compared with the names of the villages surrounding Hereford.

TELLING THE BEES

Black-and-White timbered buildings are very familiar sites across Shropshire and Herefordshire.

Throughout the story, Walter mixes actual places (Shrewsbury) with inventions of her own. 'Aycester' may be Albrighton or Atcham.

The tradition of telling bees bad news is widespread across rural England and the Welsh borders, as is the idea that they must be spoken to softly. There are numerous local variations of the practice.

DAVY JONES'S TALE

Porthfynnon: Probably based on Porthgain on the north coast of Pembrokeshire, which has a harbour very like the one described here. References to actual towns in the region—Tenby, Milford Haven, Haverfordwest, and Fishguard—add to the verisimilitude of the story. In *In the Mist*, Walter remarks that she was inspired to write story after being 'haunted' by reading about a nineteenth-century lifeboat station that had to be moved after wind and tides prevented its crew rowing out to a shipwreck.

SNOWFALL

The terrible weather in this story is clearly inspired by the ferocious winter of 1962-63. With an average temperature of -2.1 degrees Celsius, January 1963 remains the coldest month on record in the UK; heavy snow arrived in Wales on 29 December 1962 with drifts as deep as twenty feet bringing down powerlines and cutting off rural districts. The freeze lasted well into the spring of 1963.

'Pant-glas': literally 'Blue Valley.' This village is Walter's invention, though there is a Pantglas in Powys and a Pant Glas in Gwynd. Even today there are few houses between Brecon and Merthyr Tydfil, making Brian's decision to drive through the blizzard in a Triumph Herald all the more foolhardy.

COME AND GET ME

'Plas Aderyn': literally, 'the place of the bird.' In *In the Mist*, Walter says the story derived from a friend telling her 'She had once visited a derelict house in North Wales and been so overcome by an atmosphere of evil emanating from it that she took to her heels, pursued by mocking laughter.' She added that 'since I do not know North Wales, I transferred it to the Elan Valley in South Wales, which I do know well.' The parrot in the story is a conflation of another friend's budgerigar (which spoke in the voice of its deceased owner) and a malign parrot which bit Walter when she was a girl. 'I have always owed him a nip in return,' she wrote.

'Gwynfa Villas': Ironically, 'Gwynfa' is the Welsh word for 'paradise'.

THE DRUM

Although most of this tale takes place in London, its eerie opening is set in Carringford. It is clear that Walter is describing Hereford, as the town has a cathedral, and its best hotel is the Green Dragon (still the case today). The museum has been updated since Walter's visits, but it is still immediately recognisable from her account of it.

The tradition of the drum beating as a portent of death is an adaptation of the belief that Sir Francis Drake's drum in Buckland Abbey sounds when England is in danger and needs Drake to defend her.

HUSHABYE, BABY

Walter probably encountered the medieval ballad of Tam Lin when she was a student. It has many variants. In the most familiar, Janet and Tam are lovers, but Tam is stolen away by the Queen of the Fairies who pays a tithe of human souls to hell. Only by clinging fast to Tam as the Queen changes him into a succession of dangerous animals is Janet able to save her lover and have their child.

The ballad was a popular choice for singers in folk clubs during the late 1960s. It appeared on Fairport Convention's *Liege and Lief* LP (1969) and was the basis of the film, *Tam Lin* (also known as *The Devil's Widow*), released in 1971.

Walter's characters use the harsh medical language of the day in describing the baby, something which only intensifies his mother's desperate isolation.

DEAD WOMAN

Set in an unnamed village on the Wales-England border, this slice of folk horror may have autobiographical elements in its depiction of the villagers' reaction to the English outsider (even if Janet Davies' name strongly suggests her Welsh roots). The finale is strikingly similar to that of Nigel Kneale's television play, *Murrain*, first shown on 27 July 1975. *Dead Woman* was in production at this time, so the shared elements of the stories is intriguingly coincidental. Something witchy was obviously abroad that summer.

CHRISTMAS NIGHT

Another story to reference 'Carringford', 'Christmas Night' mentions a number of actual and invented places around Hereford, notably Callow, a village about four miles south of the town.

Cwn Annwn: phantom dogs from the otherworld, whose nocturnal barking portends death. They pursue wrongdoers but also guide souls between worlds and are sometimes heard on Christmas Eve or Christmas Night.

Bibliography and Further Reading

Elizabeth Walter, *The More Deceived* (London: Jonathan Cape, 1960).
___. *The Nearest and Dearest* (London: Harvill, 1963).
___. *Snowfall and Other Chilling Events* (London: Harvill, 1965).
___. *The Sin-Eater and Other Scientific Impossibilities* (London: Harvill, 1967).
___. *Davy Jones's Tale and Other Supernatural Stories* (London: Harvill, 1971).
___. *Come and Get Me and Other Uncanny Invitations* (London: Harvill, 1973).
___. *Dead Woman and Other Haunting Experiences* (London: Harvill, 1975).
___. 'English Editing,' in *Murder Ink: The Mystery Reader's Companion*, ed. Dilys Winn (New York: Workman, 1977).
___. *In the Mist and Other Uncanny Encounters* (Sauk City, Wisconsin: Arkham House, 1979).
___. *A Christmas Scrapbook* (London: Collins, 1979).
___. *Season's Greetings* (London: Collins, 1980).
___. *Wedding Bouquet* (London: Collins, 1981).
___. *A Season of Goodwill* (London: Collins Harvill, 1986).
___. *Homeward Bound* (London: Hodder, 1990).
___. *The Spirit of the Pace and Other Strange Tales: The Complete Short Stories of Elizabeth Walter*, ed. Dave Brzeski (Birmingham: Shadow Publishing, 2017).

TRANSLATIONS

Janine Boissard, *A Matter of Feeling* (London: Hodder and Stoughton, 1979).
Bernard Clavel, *Lord of the River* (London: Collins, 1973).
Claire Gallois, *A Scent of Lilies* (London: Collins, 1971).
David Hamilton and Alain Robbe-Grillet, *Dreams of Young Girls* (London: Collins, 1971).
Leni Riefenstahl and Paul List, *Coral Gardens* (London: Collins, 1978).

The Author

Elizabeth Walter (1927-2006) was a British novelist, short story writer and editor of the Collins Crime Club for over thirty years. As an author she penned many stories in the field of supernatural and ghostly fiction as well as of 'quiet' horror. Walter's uncanny tales have appeared in famous anthologies such as *The Pan Books of Horror Stories* and *The Fontana Books of Great Ghost Stories*. She published five collections of short stories: *Snowfall & Other Chilling Events* (1965), *The Sin-Eater & Other Scientific Impossibilities* (1967), *Davy Jones's Tale & Other Supernatural Stories* (1971), *Come And Get Me & Other Uncanny Invitations* (1973), *Dead Woman & Other Haunting Experiences* (1975).